He looked at her, panic in his eyes.

"Sometimes I think I'm going insane." He reached his pack in three strides. "I've got to get out of Silverville. If someone's after me, next time I may not be lucky enough to escape with my life." He lifted the leather bag to the table and began stuffing it with the food on Bess's shelves. "I'll leave Bess some money to replace this. I am no thief, Lisa, but I have to go. Now."

As Lisa's shock wore off, her mind began to function at quick speed. "Why don't you take me to Juniper Junction? You can get a job on one of the ranches around there and lay low. No one around here will know where you are."

He paused to look at her. "The trip is a hard one for a man on horseback, much less a woman. That must be three hundred miles."

"I can make it."

"Have you ever ridden all day on a horse?"

"Once, while picnicking in the mountains." Her chin came up. "I can manage, John. I must get home to my mother. My father is out there somewhere—maybe dead—because of me."

ROSEY DOW resides with her husband and seven children in Grenada, West Indies. Their work in the country is as missionaries. Rosey manages to find time to write about one of her favorite places—Colorado—between sharing the gospel and home schooling.

Books by Rosey Dow

HEARTSONG PRESENTS
HP204—Megan's Choice
HP299—Em's Only Chance

Lisa's
Broken Arrow

Rosey Dow

Heartsong Presents

A note from the author:
I love to hear from my readers! You may correspond with me by writing:

Rosey Dow
Author Relations
PO Box 719
Uhrichsville, OH 44683

ISBN 1-57748-957-8

LISA'S BROKEN ARROW

All Scripture has been taken from the King James Version of the Bible.

All of the characters and events in this book are fictitious. Any resemblance to actual persons, living or dead, or to actual events is purely coincidental.

Cover illustration by Gary Maria.

PRINTED IN THE U.S.A.

one

When the final rays of twilight melted into night, Lisa Feiklin realized that Brent Cavenaugh had deserted her. She was stranded in Silverville.

Lisa stared out the diner's window at the shadowy silhouettes of horses and their riders as they ambled down the mining town's dusty main street. Sipping cold coffee from a blue enamel mug, she idly twisted a long lock of wavy black hair around a slender finger and pondered her predicament. What should she do now?

Her thoughts drifted back to the first time she had laid eyes on Brent—last summer at the Rocking H barbecue. If she had known then that her taunting looks and teasing glances might lead her to this place, she most certainly would have run the other way. Nevertheless, his dandified ways and angelic good looks had instantly captivated her. He'd looked so sleek in his sharply pressed cowboy garb, a black silk bandanna knotted exactly halfway between his Adam's apple and his ear; his strawberry-blond mustache twitching upward with his smile.

He had noticed her, too, and stood opposite her in the square dance. She could still feel the tingle that his touch produced when he had taken her hand to lead her in the promenade.

Later, in the line of people easing toward twin tables

loaded with bread and beans and beef, pies and tarts, Lisa whispered to her year-younger sister, Jessica, "Did you see Brent? He's the one in the red-checkered shirt."

"I saw him, sure enough," Jessica hissed back, her heart-shaped face showing disapproval. "You'd best stay away from him, Lisa. He's trouble."

Flipping fingers through her glossy black waves, Lisa chortled. "He's my kind of trouble, Jessica child. When you grow up you'll understand."

Just two weeks after their first meeting, Brent started spinning rosy dreams of marriage and a cabin in the mountains where they would always be together. He called on Lisa every Saturday night, squeezed her hand during long, moonlit walks, sent her love notes tied with red ribbon.

Never had one of Lisa's many other beaux been so romantic. Gazing into her mirror, she daydreamed of her new love by the hour.

At the end of Brent's fourth visit, Lisa's father, the stocky sheriff Rod Feiklin, pursed his lips and stared after the suitor's cantering palomino. "Lisa, I'm not so sure about that hombre. He's too polished. Something's mighty suspicious about him."

She slanted her eyes at him. "I like him, Daddy."

"He's turned your head with pretty talk, I'll bet." He shook his head in a warning. "Next time he comes around here, tell him to keep riding."

Turning her head away, Lisa did not answer him. After that, she met Brent by day in a copse of trees near the river. When he tried to kiss her, she'd laugh and push him away, exhilarated that he found her appealing, intoxicated with her own feminine powers.

ॐ

In late October, Brent touched the tiny mole at the corner of her lips and sweetly pleaded, "Come with me, Lisa." She watched his hazel eyes search her face before fixing upon her lips. "We'll go to South Dakota and find a preacher. I can't live without you any longer."

Mesmerized, she breathed, "Tonight. After midnight."

Like a knight rescuing a maiden from an evil baron, Brent waited under her window astride his palomino stallion. Instead of his usual Stetson and jeans, he wore a tailor-made black broadcloth suit and black bowler.

In Denver, the runaway couple boarded a stage heading north. Brent's arm stayed protectively around Lisa, and she felt secure and relaxed against his shoulder. However, when his grasp on her tightened and his hand found her waist, she began to squirm, wishing she could put some distance between them. After all, they weren't married yet. They would have a leisurely honeymoon in a plush hotel following the wedding. She would have time to warm up to him then. Sitting tight against him on a stage filled with strangers made her feel cheap. She glanced at his round cheek next to hers. Why couldn't he understand how she felt?

They had to wait a day for the next stage in Laramie. That evening, Brent stepped, uninvited, into her tiny hotel room. "Come here, Lisa girl." He smiled like a fox in a chicken yard.

She stepped away from his groping fingers, arching

her eyebrow in hopes of hiding her dismay. "Let's get some supper, honey. I'm worn out and hungry."

He dropped his hand, but the glint never left his eyes. Lisa, her heart pounding, swished past him and yanked open the door. Brent followed her with the air of a man biding his time.

❧

This was not the first time Lisa had attempted to elope with a man. She and Hank Penbrook had been boarding the stage when her father caught up with them and forcefully carried her home. Afterward, she had sobbed and blamed her father for interfering. Now, she yearned for him to appear again and rescue her. Brent made her feel hunted.

The cat-and-mouse game lasted for more than a week. As Brent's advances became more insistent, Lisa frantically searched her mind for ways to delay a showdown with him. A dozen times a day, she asked when they would stop to find a preacher. Brent remained vague, unresponsive.

For the first time in her life, Lisa regretted the haughty, flippant attitude that caused her to toss her head at her mother's warnings and her father's rules. More than anything in the world, she wished the scarlet Concord stage was headed toward Juniper Junction again.

In the Black Hills of South Dakota, Lisa's time ran out.

During a stagecoach stop, Brent escorted her into Silverville's solitary shack of a diner and they found seats at a rough plank table. The dining room's four other tables stood empty, except for the clutter of crusty, half-eaten dinner plates and half-drunk coffee cups. There was no waitress in sight. The smell of old grease hung heavy on the air.

Grabbing a chance to speak unheard by others, Lisa asked, "When are we going to stop traveling long enough to find a parson, Brent?"

He stiffened, then relaxed. He slowly brushed a forefinger over his strawberry-blond mustache as he studied her. When his hand glided down to the table, his slack mouth turned hard. "I'm tired of playing games, Lisa." He let out an exasperated breath. "After the way you led me on, I never dreamed you'd be such a Polly Prude." His head tilted forward. His hazel eyes bored into her. "If you play by my rules, I'll consider buying you a ring and calling on a preacher to do the honors someday. If you tilt your nose in the air, I'll dump you here without a penny."

Clenching her hands around her empty purse, Lisa swallowed and gulped for breath. "You promised to take care of me, remember, Brent?" Her pleading tone turned accusing. "You said we'd be together always, come rain or shine. What about your duty as a gentleman?" Lips tight, she gazed from his perfect hairstyle to his impeccable mustache, and a fresh realization dawned within her. "You can't act like a gentleman because you aren't one. You're nothing but a double-dyed fraud." Her chin came up. "I'm staying here."

"And do what?" He spoke low and intense. "You don't know a soul here, and you haven't any money. Where will you sleep? What will you eat?"

Black eyes flashing, she forced her jaws to relax enough to speak. "I wouldn't go another mile with you, Brent. Even if I have to sleep on a bare floor and eat sawdust."

A slim, graying waitress slapped a pencil-scribbled menu card down on the table between them. "Here's today's grub. I'll be back in a minute." She marched to the kitchen without waiting for an answer.

Brent patted at his coat pockets and stood, reaching into them. "I've dropped my wallet. I must have lost it on the stage." His longs legs stretched toward the door. He stood aside for an elderly couple to enter, then disappeared into the afternoon. The biting chill of late autumn reached Lisa from across the room as the door whooshed shut.

When the waitress returned, Lisa smiled nervously and tapped long, slender fingers on the wooden table. "My friend will be back in a moment. I'll wait for him, so we can order together."

"How about a cup of coffee meanwhile?"

"Thank you."

The coffee came soon afterwards, but Brent did not appear. Lisa fidgeted and stared out the smudged window. Her stomach rumbled. She smoothed down her lavender skirt, anxiety mounting every minute. More than an hour later, the last rays of an orange sun vanished from the rooftops across the street.

What shall I do now? The question echoed through Lisa's thoughts.

The waitress returned. "Looks like he got held up," she said with a small, cautious smile. As she spoke, she swept from her cheek a strand of gray hair mixed with blond, an unusual color. Yet, her hair was her best feature. She had a flat, long face with a straight nose. A curved scar circled her left cheekbone, giving her a harsh look, but her eyes were kind.

Lisa pulled the corners of her full lips into an upside-down smile. "I can't order until he comes back." She ran fingers along the strings of her empty purse. She ought to leave, but where could she go? With nothing to eat since breakfast, she was starving.

"It's okay, honey. We're not busy, so you can sit tight. I'll warm up your coffee." She brought the pot and poured. "My name's Bess."

"I'm Lisa. Thanks very much."

"Don't mention it." Bess hurried to serve the other table and didn't return for an hour. Lisa gnawed her lip and fought back tears. Resting her chin on her hand, she closed her eyes.

"You okay?" Firm fingers touched her shoulder.

Lisa jerked erect and stared at Bess. The older woman slid into the seat across from her. "You're in trouble, aren't you?"

Forcing her lips into a small curve, Lisa nodded. "My gentleman friend left me stranded. I don't know what to do. I don't have any money." She ran a thumb over the handle of her coffee cup. "Would the boss let me clean the kitchen in exchange for supper?"

Bess looked at the younger woman's ruffled cuffs

and embroidered bodice. "I reckon he might, but you wouldn't be much good in that getup."

"My suitcase is at the stage station. I have other clothes in it."

Bess watched her, considering. "I suppose he may give you a try. The girl who used to be our waitress and dishwasher moved to greener pastures last week. I've been doing triple duty for five straight days. I'm the cook here. . .for my sins." She stood. "I'll bring you a hot meal and send a boy to the station for your things. Now, let me go and mention you to the owner." She hustled back to the kitchen and returned five minutes later with a short, round man beside her. He was bald except for a fringe above his ears.

"This is Lisa, Mr. Brockwyn," Bess announced.

He let his eyes trail down Lisa from her crown to her fingertips. "This ain't no society parlor. She looks like she's never done a day's work in her life." Brockwyn was a full inch shorter than Bess, but he moved with a swagger and his fleshy lips held a cynical twist.

Lisa met his disdainful black eyes. She wanted to tell him what she thought of him, but desperation pinned her tongue.

"Please give her a chance, Mr. Brockwyn," Bess said. "I can't do everything myself for much longer. If she don't work out, you can always let her go."

Brockwyn spoke like a Gatling gun. "You will wait tables. Wash all the dishes and pots. After closing time, mop the floors. If Bess needs help, you do as she says. Report at six in the morning. Leave at eight at night.

Salary's five dollars a week."

When Lisa nodded, the manager trundled into the kitchen and let the door bump closed behind him.

Five dollars a week. Could she even afford a telegram to let her parents know she was safe?

"Thank you!" Lisa called after him.

"Save your thanks," Bess replied, shaking her head. "The job is no prize, believe me."

Lisa pulled in a sharp breath. "I forgot to ask him when I get my first pay. I'm starving."

Bess reached into her apron pocket and pulled out some change. "Here." Gold and silver coins clanked onto the rough table. "Consider this a loan until you get paid." She hurried away and returned carrying a heaping plate.

Beef and beans never tasted so good. Relief made Lisa almost giddy. With a job, she would be able to get a room somewhere nearby. A nagging voice asked her how soon she would get home, but she pushed the thought aside. One problem at a time.

In a chilly storage room, she changed into her drab brown work dress and forced the lavender frock into the suitcase. Twisting up her black tresses, she pinned her hair into a high bun, ignoring the wisps around her face.

Rolling up her sleeves, she summoned up enough grit to plunge her soft pink arms into an iron sink filled with cold, greasy water thick with stale food particles. She bit the inside of her cheek to hold back the disgust rising in her throat, then began to pull out stack after stack of plates and cups. Finally, she reached the bottom and yanked the drain plug. Water chugged into a bucket under the sink.

Bess called to her from the rusty stove three strides away. "Dump that waste bucket outside on the ground. I've got hot water in the stove reservoir for new wash water." Piquant wood smoke drifted upwards as Bess lifted a heavy iron circle from the top of the stove to add another small log.

A few minutes later, Lisa panted as she set down the pail of filthy water and tipped it over onto frozen earth. She paused, enjoying the frigid air on her burning cheeks. Already exhausted, she had yet to wash a single dish.

"Where are you from?" Bess asked half an hour later. The dining room had closed, and she poured leftover beef stew into a wide bowl.

Lisa looked up from the sudsy dishpan. "Juniper Junction, Colorado."

Bess replied over her shoulder. "Never heard of it."

"I never heard of Silverville either, until the stage drove in this afternoon."

"I've been in South Dakota for five years," Bess told her, setting the dented soup pot on the counter near Lisa's arm. "I used to work in Deadwood, but when I heard about the silver strike, I decided to come over here and get in on the excitement." She shrugged. "Didn't take me long to see that this place is just like the last one. You get up and go to work, you eat and you sleep, and you start all over again the next morning."

Lisa kept her eyes on the dishpan. Is that all she had to look forward to as well?

"You can bunk with me if you'd like. I have an extra bed. The waitress that left used to be my roommate."

"Thanks." Lisa straightened and drew in a slow breath. At least she wouldn't be sleeping in the icy storage room.

No thanks to Brent Cavenaugh. Now that her initial fears had calmed, hot anger rushed in. She scoured a pot with vengeance. Men were beasts! She'd had enough of them to last a lifetime.

two

By lantern light, Bess's cabin looked as dismal as the diner's kitchen. Nestled in a grove of cottonwoods one hundred feet from the kitchen's back door, the structure's half-peeled logs rose two feet taller than Lisa's head with a bark-shingle roof on top. Lisa studied the oiled-paper windows while Bess groped for the door latch. With a scrape and a groan, the door swung open and they stepped inside.

Across the room, the flame of a burning log in the stone fireplace had smoldered down to a dull orange gleam. Bess waved a hand at the only chair, a crooked, handmade affair that tilted slightly to one side. "Have a seat while I stir up the fire."

She set the lantern on a scarred table and bustled out the back door. In a moment she returned with three wedges of wood in her arms. "You can split logs before breakfast," she said, dropping her burden and lifting a poker to stir the coals. "I have to start work before dawn. You've got an extra hour before you have to be there."

Lisa nodded, her heart sinking. Did anyone ever sleep in this town?

The fire blazed higher, slowly warming the room. Nothing within the cabin's four walls looked appealing. The floor resembled a washboard, and the mantel shelf had one end broken off. Shivering inside her coat, Lisa noticed a ragged curtain on the west end of the room.

"That's our sleeping quarters," Bess offered, nodding toward the scrap of gray muslin hanging from two nails in the ceiling. "You can take the left cot."

Sick with exhaustion, Lisa pushed aside the curtain and lay down on the narrow rope-strung bed. A lump in the bare straw mattress gouged into the small of her back. A rotten smell pricked her nose. For the second time tonight, she swallowed back the revulsion tightening her throat and pulled the only blanket—a thin bit of stained wool—over her middle.

She closed her eyes and saw her mother's seamed face, haggard with worry over her rebellious daughter. How long until Lisa saw that dear face again? Tears of loneliness and despair seeped from the corners of her eyes. Utterly spent, she let them flow.

≈

From December to late March, Lisa worked from dawn until far past dark, six days out of seven. Her once-buxom figure grew slim and hard. Her hands developed calluses. Her hair lost its wavy sheen. She paid the milliner two bits for a scrap bag and used its contents to stitch a quilt. Stuffed with chipped corncobs, the cover wasn't exactly eiderdown, but at least it covered her from chin to toes. If she spread her coat on top of it and wore her shoes to bed, she felt almost warm.

After paying rent and buying her meals at the restaurant, she had only pennies left each week. The stage to Juniper cost twelve dollars.

Shortly after Christmas, she swallowed her pride and wrote to Father, asking him to come and get her. A month later, a letter arrived from him. Lisa's heart sank as she studied the familiar scrawl: *You have a job and a place to live. When you save enough money for the stage, you'll be welcome home.*

As the winter days hinted of spring, Lisa's desperation to return home became an almost living thing. A deep, wrenching despair coated her spirit like thick wax. She moved through her days as though sleepwalking. Speaking little. Thinking less. Her only goal—to survive another harrowing day, another frigid night.

During the coldest part of February, a tiny green bud of hope sprouted in her soul when a letter came from Mother. *Daddy will travel by stage to bring you home soon after the warm chinook winds.*

Smiling, Lisa folded the pages. Mama had finally worn down his resolve. Still, Daddy had gotten his way. Little Lisa had learned her lesson well this time.

❧

In the dead of the night on March 28, the drumming of horses' hooves on frozen earth jarred Lisa from her sleep. Her heart thumping, she stood and gathered the quilt around her shoulders. As she stumbled through the dark, she barked her shin on the end of the bed and let out a sharp gasp. Bess's cot squawked when she rolled over, but she did not waken.

Lisa hesitated in the living room, pausing near the fireplace. Although tempted to open the door, she balked at the thought of facing the bitter cold. Perhaps the stamping sounded only in her dreams and the horses ran only in her mind. Just outside the cabin a whinny set her pulses racing. For a full two minutes, she waited for a knock on the door, but the knock never came.

Scolding herself for her fear, she lit the rusty lantern with a flaming stick and pulled up the latch. An icy gust tore through her, but the sight outside her door drove all thoughts about the cold from her mind.

Two horses stood near the log cabin's front wall. The black carried a lumpy pack. A man slumped over the saddle of the bay.

Not wanting to spook the horses, Lisa set the lantern on the ground near the door and tiptoed forward. "Easy," she said, keeping her voice low and calm. "Easy, boy." She touched the bay's nose and ran her hand down his gaunt neck toward the man, murmuring softly all the while.

Was the rider dead?

"What's all the commotion?" Bess appeared in the doorway, swiping the sleep from her eyes with a leathery hand. Her hair fell loosely about her shoulders. Her coat tented over a ragged flannel nightgown.

"Someone's hurt." Lisa felt the man's icy hand. "Maybe he's dead. He's sure enough froze."

Bess stepped forward, slipping her arms into her coat sleeves and buttoning it around her as she moved. She grabbed the horses' reins and tied them to a nearby bush. Reaching for the man's dusty, jeans-covered knee, she said, "You'd be cold, too, if you were out here all night."

The man moaned softly.

"See here," Bess said. "Let's get his boots out of the stirrups so we can ease him down."

While Lisa pushed him upward on one side, Bess stood on the other to break his fall. He almost knocked her over. "He's been shot in the head," Bess panted. "It's a miracle he's still alive." She leaned over to grasp him under the arms. "Here, grab his boots. He's a heavy dude. I wish he'd laid off the grub a while before he did this."

With a good deal of huffing and tugging, the women dragged the two hundred pounds of dead weight over the threshold. After they had situated the unconscious man on Lisa's cot, which she'd hurriedly pulled in front of the fire, Bess forced frozen boots off frozen feet, coaxing all the while as though scuffed leather could her her.

Lisa draped her rustling coverlet around his chin, then tucked it under him and down both sides. Swinging an iron pot away from the fire, she poured steaming water into a basin and added cold water to cool it down. She found a cloth and began sponging the man's filthy, blood-streaked face. Fine dirt filled the tiny weblike lines around his eyes and the creases in his neck. Not grime acquired over a long time, but dust as though he had been digging or maybe plowing behind a horse for days.

Things didn't add up. He wore a bandanna, jeans, and narrow-toed boots. Cowboys despised farming.

"I wonder who's after him," Bess said in a few moments. "What if they trail him here?"

"We can't leave the man out in the cold to die."

As the crusty flecks of dried blood dissolved and the

dirt washed away, he looked painfully young—in his late twenties at the most. He had a Roman nose and a full, firm mouth. The left side of his short, dusty hair lay darkly matted to his skull.

"Look at this!" Bess said. His feet were swollen and raw around the toes and heels. The wounds had festered. "Looks like he hasn't had these boots off for a long time. Otherwise, he wouldn't have been able to put them back on."

"How did that happen, Bess?"

"You've got me. A cowboy would sooner saddle up to cross the street than use his shoe leather."

"He had two horses. Why would he walk far enough for his feet to look like that?"

"When he comes to, he'll probably tell us a good long tale."

"Should we do anything to his head?" Lisa asked, glancing at Bess as she gently eased a warm, wet cloth over his icy feet.

"Let's get him warmed up first," she replied shortly. "Throw some more wood on the fire. I wish Silverville had a doctor."

After several long minutes, his cold body turned warm, then feverish. The bullet had creased his scalp, leaving a wide gash in its path. Lisa cleaned the wound and bound his light brown hair with a few of the multicolored cloth strips from her ragbag.

Though he never opened his eyes, he sometimes moaned or moved his hand. For the next four days, Lisa ducked out of the diner up to ten times a day to check on him and try to force some broth through his clenched teeth.

The stranger's horses stood tethered in the lean-to where Bess stored her firewood. The same dusty earth that had caked the man also covered the hides of both horses. The outline of ribs shadowed the animals' skin. Pooling their funds, the women purchased three bales of hay and a quart of oats from the livery stable. Neither broached the subject of what they would do when that ran out.

Lisa spread a pallet on the floor, close to the warmth of the fire and near the cot so she could hear if he awakened during the night. She felt a keen understanding of his desperate circumstances and knew she must help him. Gazing at his still face in the flickering firelight, she wondered if he were an outlaw. He didn't look like one, but what did looks really show?

On the evening of the fourth day, Lisa jerked awake when a hand trailed along her arm. Eyes wide, she sat up and edged away from the sick man's cot.

The touch had been a glancing one, because the hand moved up to touch the green cloth binding the wound. His eyes squinted and blinked and turned toward her. Piercing blue, they seemed to look at Lisa from far away.

"W–w–what happened?" he muttered with a thick tongue.

"Someone shot you." Lisa knelt beside him.

He looked toward the ceiling, his eyes wide with fear. "He's coming after me. I've got to hide."

"You're safe here." She reached for the dipper hanging

over the edge of a tin bucket on the table. "Here, drink some water." Supporting his shoulders, she held the drink to his lips. "That's enough for now." She gently eased him back onto the cot.

"I've got to get out of here," he said, his eyelids lowering. "He's after m. . ." He was asleep before his lips formed the last word.

Lisa returned to her pallet and tried to sleep. In less than two hours, she must rise and face another back-breaking day. Finally, she rose to stoke the fire and put on coffee, her eyes constantly straying to the quiet form nearby. His relaxed posture told her that he was sleeping comfortably.

Her lips formed a half smile. Soon she would hear the answers to the dozens of questions now obsessing her.

If he wasn't an outlaw, why had someone shot him? Why was someone chasing him? She glanced at his pack propped in the corner, so heavy that Bess had to struggle to get it inside.

When Lisa left for work that morning, he was still asleep. She set the water pail near his hand, in case he awoke while she was out.

At lunchtime, Lisa saved some of her stew to carry to the cabin. When she crossed the clearing, a fresh warm breeze stroked her face and ruffled her hair. Pausing, she lifted her cheeks toward heaven and closed her eyes. The chinook. Daddy might be here within the week.

Wearing a wide smile, Lisa opened the door to the cabin and found her patient alert, one arm tucked under the back of his head.

"Well, you decided to wake up, did you?" she asked, a new light in her eyes as she closed the door firmly behind her. "I brought you some food."

"Thanks. I'm famished." His voice sounded raspy. "I've drunk almost all the water in the pail, and I'm still thirsty."

She smiled. "It's been four days since you had a proper drink."

"Four days?" He tried to sit up, blinked, and laid back down. "The room's spinning."

"You'd best take things easy for a while. The scrape on your head went pretty deep." She pulled the chair closer and sat near his shoulder. "Here. Try some." She lifted the spoon to his lips.

"My horses."

"They're out back, safe and well."

He opened his mouth for the spoon.

"Who is after you?" she asked when he finished chewing.

"I can't remember. Somebody was trying to kill me." His breathing quickened. "He was chasing me full tilt, blasting at me with a rifle." Beads of sweat formed on his brow. "I've got to get away."

Lisa reached for a damp cloth on the edge of a basin on the hearth to wipe his face. "You've been here four days and no one has come. Surely they would have found you by now if they could."

He relaxed a little, but his expression remained taut with anxiety. His hands clenched the sides of the cot.

She fed him the rest of the stew in silence, not wanting

to push him for more answers, afraid her questions would upset him again.

As she rose to leave, he said, "Say, what's your name?"

"Lisa. Lisa Feiklin." She touched her limp, knotted hair, suddenly aware of how frightful she looked.

"I'm John Bowers." He pulled the quilt higher and rolled onto his side as his blue eyes drifted closed.

Lisa shut the door behind her and paced down the path toward the restaurant, a troubled frown tightening her features. If John knew his name, he did not have amnesia. So why didn't he know who wanted him dead? Was he lying?

three

John sat on the edge of the cot when Lisa returned that evening with beef and beans for his supper. His lips formed a soft smile when she eased into the chair across from him and held out the plate.

"Thank you kindly." He centered his full attention on the food while Lisa focused on him. He had broad shoulders and moved with the grace of a strong man. A sandy brown lock fell over his forehead almost to his eyebrows.

When he handed her the empty plate he asked, "Who all lives here?"

"Bess Johnson and I. We work at the Silverville Restaurant just over there." She pointed toward the door and beyond.

"So, that's where you're getting the food?" he eyed the plate and looked into her face. "Must be costing you. I don't want to be a burden to you ladies." In a lithe motion he pulled a wide belt loose from his waist and turned it over.

Digging a finger into the folded black leather, he drew out a gold piece and pushed it into her hand. "Bring me back a steak with all the trimmings when you get off tonight. Get one for you and your friend, too." He lay down, and his eyes drifted closed. "Oh, and get some hay for the horses. Please don't mention to anyone that

I'm here. I'm a goner if that scoundrel gets wind that I'm here."

Tucking the coin deep into her coat pocket, Lisa closed the door softly behind her and trotted toward the kitchen. John wore old boots and scuffed jeans, so why did he have a loaded money belt around his middle?

Lisa moved in a daze the rest of the afternoon. When she confused three orders in a row, Bess said, "What-sa matter with you? You sick or something?"

"No. It's John," she replied, her hands moving through hot dishwater with practiced rhythm. "He gave me a gold eagle and ordered three steak dinners, one for each of us."

Bess's eyes widened as she smiled. "Well, I'd have never guessed it. Looks like we had a stroke of luck, him riding in like that."

"His horses were starving. Where did he get so much money?"

Bess lifted the lid off a pot of beans which had started bubbling over on the stove. "Maybe he's a miner."

"He's a cowboy. You know that."

"His boots were coated with dirt, as was the rest of him. That don't sound like a cowboy, no matter what kind of clothes he had on." Bess forked thick steaks onto two plates and added a scoop of beans to each. "But, you know the saying about looking a gift horse in the mouth. Let's just be glad he can help us." She laid wide slabs of corn bread beside the meat and turned toward Lisa. "Here's your order. Smile pretty and maybe they'll leave you a dime."

Lisa's lips tightened. "Those cheapskates never leave me anything. It's Ben Hardy and his brother, Al, from Sandusky Mine. They're filthy rich, too." She lifted the plates and headed toward the dining room.

"Howdy, Lisa, honey," Ben Hardy said. With his bristly hair and husky build and long, puffy face, he resembled a brown bear, right down to his slow expression.

His brother, Al, was slim and mean-looking with a missing front tooth and a blue-black shadow on his jaw. He kept his eyes on the food, never once looking at the pretty girl carrying it.

"How about walking out with me after you get off?" Ben said, giving her a wolfish grin. "I know a quiet spot down by the river where we could look at the stars."

"Sorry. I'm busy," Lisa said without a moment's hesitation. Ben asked her the same question every Wednesday and Friday. He never thought of a new place to go and never grew discouraged by her answer.

She offered a pasted smile as she served the meal, then hurried back to her dishpan, anxious to leave work early tonight. Maybe, if his head was clear and his stomach full, John would loosen up and tell her more about himself.

ᔥ

John pushed his empty plate away from him on the rugged table. "It's strange—how I can remember bits of my past, but not everything. I never heard of someone losing half his memory before."

"Where do you live?" Lisa asked from her seat on the hearth.

He pushed the lock of hair from his forehead and

stared into the blazing fireplace. The flames made dancing shadows on the planes of his face. He did not answer
for several minutes. "I'm not sure. All I know is that it's
in a grassy canyon with sheer rock cliffs on three sides.
She's a beautiful little spot in the spring, with a stream
rushing by and trees sprouting leaves." His blue eyes
turned toward her. "What about you? Where are you
from?"

"Juniper Junction, Colorado," she said softly.

From the other side of the hearth, Bess added, "It's a
hole-in-the-wall town somewhere north of Denver." She
stood and stacked her plate on top of Lisa's empty one.
"Thanks for the fine supper, John. I'm going to turn in."
She shoved aside the curtain and let it fall behind her.

"You miss your home, don't you?" John asked, moving to his cot and lying down.

"I'd give my eyeteeth to get back there."

"Why did you leave?"

She turned away. "Well, that's a long story." She has-
tened to change the subject away from herself. "Don't
you remember anything about who did this to you?"

His face tensed. "Whenever I think on it, my insides
turn to jelly." He pulled in two deep breaths. "I haven't
always been such a coward, Lisa. I've faced down gun-
toting four-flushers since I was knee-high to a pony. But
for some reason. . ." He paused then suddenly burst out,
anguished, "Maybe I've lost my nerve."

"That kind of a wound would take the fire out of anyone for a while," Lisa murmured, wishing she could say
something more to comfort him. She knew the same

anguish in her own heart, only her pain came from a different source.

"I'd have died without the help of you and Bess," he said.

"We only did what was right." She stood and gathered the dirty dishes. A part of her felt sorry for John, wounded and scared like he was. Yet, another part of her wondered if she could trust him. Would she ever trust a man again?

When she had dried the last plate, Lisa turned to look at John. He slept with one hand hanging down to the cold floor. Lisa picked it up and tucked it under the quilt, noticing a deep scar around the base of his callused thumb. The flesh wound looked rough, like a rope burn. Lying down near the fire with her coat pulled over her, she slept.

❧

"Lisa? Are you awake?"

Her eyes flashed open at John's voice. "What's wrong? Are you sick?"

"Why are you sleeping on the floor?"

Her face flushed. "We only have two beds."

He sat up and swung stockinged feet off the cot. "I'm not having you sleep on the floor because of me."

"You're sick. You need a bed."

"I'm not sick anymore." He eased down to the floor. "Get in the bed."

She sat up, blinking at him, her brain working at half speed. "You'll catch cold."

His face stayed calm, but his intense look told her that

he meant what he said. His voice stayed low. "Get in the bed, Lisa."

She pulled off her coat and handed it to him. Without a word, she lay on the straw mattress and pulled up the quilt. The cot felt wonderfully warm from his body heat. Her eyes drifted closed.

ॐ

When Lisa awoke, the cabin was silent and bright sunlight gleamed against the oiled paper. She sat up, whipping off the quilt. She was late.

Running a comb through her hair, she twisted and pinned the limp tresses up into a bun. Where was John? Raising the curtain, she saw him on Bess's cot, sleeping soundly. She watched his rhythmic breathing a moment longer, then rushed out the door and up the narrow path, bushes tugging at her skirt as she brushed past them. Bess would be at the end of her tether if she had to serve tables.

She burst into the restaurant kitchen as her housemate laid biscuits on six plates loaded with eggs, bacon, and fried potatoes. Bess jerked around. "There you are! I was beginning to wonder if I'd have to send Mr. Brockwyn after you."

Lisa grimaced and reached for three breakfast orders, balancing one of them on a bent elbow. "Sorry, Bess. I don't know why I slept so late." She hustled into the dining room and faced her workday at a breakneck speed. Yet no matter how hard she worked, she could not seem to make up for the first hour she'd lost.

That evening after work, Lisa carried two covered

plates out of the restaurant. Bess carried a third. When the weary women reached their clearing, they paused a few feet from the house, shocked to see glass panes winking at them instead of oiled paper. They glanced at one another, then hurried to the cabin.

When they burst through the door, John sat near the fire. Lisa's cot was no longer in the living room. He looked up, smiling widely at their surprised faces. "What's wrong? The restaurant on fire or something?"

"The windows," Lisa said.

"I got the boy from the livery stable to buy them for me after he delivered the hay. My way of saying thanks." He rubbed open palms on his knees. "When my head quits hurting, I'll tighten this place up to keep out the drafts."

"We didn't intend to make you work for your keep. You just need to get to feeling better," Bess told him. She took a plate from Lisa and handed it to John.

"I have to do something to fill my days. I may as well make myself useful." He reached for the fork Bess handed him. "This beef stew smells great!" He hesitated. "I've been too sick to think of this before, but would you ladies mind if I thanked the Lord for the food? Sayin' a grace has always been a custom at my house."

"Help yourself," Bess said. "Praying never hurt anybody."

From her place on the hearth next to John, Lisa bowed her head while he spoke in low tones.

"Father, thank You for protecting me against my enemies, just as You did for Your servant, David. Thank You for the hospitality of these two ladies. Bless them for helping me, Lord. Thank You for the food we are about to eat. Use it to give us strength to serve You. Amen."

When he finished, Lisa kept her head down and speared a fat potato wedge. His prayer had sounded so humble, so earnest. Yet doubt continued to tug at the back corner of her mind. Was he pretending so that they would lower their guard?

"I went outside to see Molasses and Ginger this afternoon," John said between bites.

"Molasses and Ginger?" Bess repeated, laughing. "Sounds like a gingerbread recipe."

John smiled. "That's the idea. Those horses were born within a week of each other. It was spring, and I'd just bought a cask of molasses and a sack of ginger. When one foal was black and one brown, I got the idea to name them after the fixings for my favorite cake."

"Is Ginger spicy?" Lisa asked, her sober mood forgotten.

"Actually, Molasses is the spirited one. I usually ride him and let Ginger carry the pack." A startled look came over his face. "Speaking of my pack, where is it?"

"Under that gunnysack," Lisa said, pointing to a back corner of the cabin. "Bess took it off the horse and put it there until you woke up."

Setting down his empty plate, John stood up. He blinked hard and touched his bandage. "I guess I moved too fast that time."

Lisa rushed to take his arm. "You'd best get back to bed."

"No." He gently brushed her away. "I'm all right now. I want to look in my pack."

Pacing forward, his expression showing his concentration, he knelt down and unfastened a buckle. Lisa sat and picked up her fork, still watching him. He reached inside the worn leather pouch, pulling out a handful of something before he stood. "I want you to have these." His open palm held a dozen dirt-crusted rocks.

Bess glanced at them, looked at Lisa, and turned to John, her face blank from shock. "Gold?" she gasped.

"Turn them in at the assayer's office and get yourself some decent furniture and some blankets." His hand began to waver as he held it out. "You saved my life. This is the least I can do."

Lisa's cheeks felt warm. "You don't need to pay us for helping you."

"You know we can use the money, Lisa." Reaching out, Bess took the nuggets from him and stood to drop them into the pocket of her faded green skirt.

John returned to his seat on the hearth and picked up his coffee cup. "Pretty soon I'll be able to split wood." He paused. "That is, if you don't mind my staying on for a few more days."

Bess smiled. "Stay as long as you like."

Lisa stabbed a morsel of meat and slowly raised it to her mouth. The more she learned about John, the more of a mystery he became.

❧

Two more weeks passed and Lisa's father still had not come. Lisa awoke each morning thinking, *Surely, this is the day he will come for me.* But each night she was disappointed. On Monday of the third week, she started to worry. Seven days later, she wondered whether he had met with an accident or had changed his mind and decided not to come, after all.

She nibbled at her food. Her face became gaunt and drawn. Finally, Bess gave her four bits to send a telegram asking if he had left Juniper Junction yet. Three days later the answer came: He had taken the northbound stage the day after Mother wrote her letter to Lisa announcing that he would come after the chinook.

Lisa wept into her pillow. If not for her rebellion, her father would be safe at home instead of lying in the wilds with a broken leg or worse. Someone had to do something to find him. But who? She'd never felt so alone in her life.

As his strength returned, John took over Lisa's job at the woodpile, and he built a new cot. His hair grew long—over his ears and onto his collar—until one night Lisa offered to cut it for him. Every few seconds, she would stand back to eye her work.

"I think I've cut it higher over your right ear than your left," she said with a giggle as she peered from one side to the other. "Let me trim the left side just a bit more." She snipped the scissors.

"Oh, no. Now that one's higher."

"Hold on," John said, laughing and raising one hand when she came at him again. "Let's just leave them uneven, okay? If you keep going, I'm liable to end up with a mohawk."

Her cheeks turned pink. "I'm awful sorry, John. Before we started, I told you I'm no hand at this."

He gently plucked the scissors from her hand. "I'm not worried about it in the least. As long as my hair's not swishing around my ears, then it's fine. I just can't abide feeling like I have a feather duster on my head." He grinned. "I'm much obliged for your help."

She reached for the broom, trying to ignore the tongue-tied, all-thumbs feeling she got when he looked at her with that laughing light in his eyes.

The next day, Bess purchased two ladder-back chairs and three eiderdown quilts at the mercantile. She filled her few shelves with canned goods and salted meat.

The cabin became snug under John's painstaking labor. Yet, even while enjoying these creature comforts, Lisa's misery continued to grow. What had happened to her father? Why had he not come for her?

Two weeks later, Lisa carried a dish of stew to the cabin for John's lunch and found him pacing in front of the fireplace. He lurched around, aiming a shiny Colt revolver at her head as she stepped through the door.

She screamed and dropped the bowl.

"Shut the door—quick!"

Her shaking hands fumbled with the latch. When it slid into place, she leaned her back against the door, watching him with wide eyes.

"Sorry, Lisa," he said, dropping the gun into its shiny leather holster. "I just got spooked in town, and now I'm kind of touchy." He swallowed and touched the gun at his side. His hand shook like a leaf in a strong breeze.

"What happened?"

"I went to the assayer's office to change in my nuggets

for cash. When I came out, I saw a fella across the street. He was wearing a black jacket and black flat-crowned hat with a yellow band around it."

"Who was he?"

"I don't know. I'm not sure I've ever seen him before." His brows drew together. His breath came fast and shallow through his open mouth.

"Why are you so scared, if you can't remember ever seeing him?"

He looked at her, panic in his eyes. "Sometimes I think I'm going insane." He reached his pack in three strides. "I've got to get out of Silverville. If someone's after me, next time I may not be lucky enough to escape with my life." He lifted the leather bag to the table and began stuffing it with the food on Bess's shelves. "I'll leave Bess some money to replace this. I am no thief, Lisa, but I have to go. Now."

As Lisa's shock wore off, her mind began to function at quick speed. "Why don't you take me to Juniper Junction? You can get a job on one of the ranches around there and lay low. No one around here will know where you are."

He paused to look at her. "The trip is a hard one for a man on horseback, much less a woman. That must be three hundred miles."

"I can make it."

"Have you ever ridden all day on a horse?"

"Once, while picnicking in the mountains." Her chin came up. "I can manage, John. I must get home to my mother. My father is out there somewhere—maybe dead—because of me."

"What do you mean?"

She blurted out the story of her elopement and the disaster that followed. Her voice grew shrill and intense. "Please take me with you. We saved your life. How can you turn away and leave me here when I'm so desperate to go?"

Jaw clenched, he drew in three long breaths as he looked into her pleading eyes. Finally, his shoulders relaxed. "Get your gear together," he said tersely.

"What about Bess?"

"Leave her a note, letting her know that we're leaving. But, don't mention where we're heading."

Lisa scrambled to her room and tugged her suitcase from beneath the cot. Dumping its contents onto the quilt, she pulled out a single change of clothes and a comb. The rest she left for Bess. Rolling her few belongings into her corncob quilt, she ran out the back door in time to see John tightening the cinch on his saddle.

"I've only got one saddle," he said. "We need another saddle and a third horse if we're going to make any kind of time."

"I'll ask Joe at the livery stable," Lisa said, dropping her blanket roll.

John said, "Stay here. I'll ask him."

"What if somebody sees you?"

"I'll go the back way." He ducked out from under the lean-to's low roof and jogged out of sight.

Lisa patted Ginger and counted her own breaths, willing John to reappear.

Twenty minutes later, he came around the corner leading a saddled bay mare. "Mount up while I tie on your blanket roll. No time to talk now."

Keeping the horses to a slow trot, they headed straight into the trees behind the cabin and circled wide around the town. Shivering with excitement, Lisa sucked in the sweet scent of pine mingled with the tingling aroma of freedom and home. She wanted to laugh, wanted to cry from sheer joy. When she reached Juniper Junction, she would never leave again.

four

Three days later, Lisa again felt like crying. But not from joy. She was raw from the saddle and weary beyond endurance. Aching for a sip of fresh, cool water, she gazed overhead at the stars and wondered how she had gotten herself into another unbearable situation. Juniper Junction seemed ten thousand miles away.

On the other side of their campfire, John snored softly. Lisa glared at him, irritated. The rocky terrain and incredible thirst didn't bother him. He listened to her complaints without responding—and without slackening their pace.

The night before, they had camped in the center of a thick aspen grove, safe from the eyes of anyone who might pass by. Utterly exhausted, Lisa fell asleep the moment she lay down. Her eyes flew open hours later, wide awake, her heart pounding. Over the constant chatter of crickets and night frogs, a moan, then a cry, came from the darkness. A man's deep voice turned shrill.

Had John's enemy found them? If she made a noise, she would be found out, too.

Straining her eyes, she tried to see through a darkness so thick she could almost feel it.

A tortured cry stopped her breath. "Mama, run! Don't let him get you!"

John was having a nightmare.

Lisa unwound the blankets from around her and, hands skimming the ground, crawled toward him, murmuring, "John, wake up." She found the edge of his blanket and followed it upward toward the sound of his voice. "John, you're dreaming. Wake up."

He gasped and lurched away from her hands. "Who's there?"

"You're okay. You were having a bad dream."

He lay back, his breathing quick. "Lisa? Are you all right?"

"Besides being scared half to death, I'm fine."

"Sorry."

"What were you dreaming?"

"Renegade Indians were after my mother. They were twelve feet tall with bear claws for hands."

"Did you have Indian trouble on your ranch?"

He grunted. "That's strange. No, we didn't. The Indians had already gone when we came."

Lisa sat on the corner of his blanket and wrapped her arms around her knees. "Tell me about your family, please."

He hesitated, then spoke slowly. "My father was a sharecropper in Georgia when I was born. He and Mama worked from sunup to sundown trying to scratch a living from the soil. When the cotton crop came in, they had to give half of their harvest to the landholder. Finally, Pa saved enough money to travel to St. Louis and join a wagon train. When he saw the green Wyoming hills, he decided to stay there instead of going on to Oregon."

"Where are your parents now?"

"Dead. They both died of cholera three years ago, shortly before I turned twenty-five. I've tended the ranch alone ever since." He shifted onto his side. "Say, that's more than I ever remembered before. I wish I knew where my ranch was. I'd light a shuck and go searching for it this moment."

"After you take me home, you mean." She shivered. "I'd best get back under my blanket. I hope I can find it again."

"Straight ahead about three paces."

Bent low, she kept reaching out until her hands touched the corncob quilt. "Found it." She arranged her skirts and pulled the cover around her. "Didn't you have a brother or a sister?"

"Nope. Only me."

Lisa's thoughts turned to her younger sister, Jessica. "You've not missed much by being an only child. My sister and I, well, we never did get along. All our lives, I was the one constantly getting into trouble, and she loved to brag about how she never did."

He chuckled softly. "I can believe that."

"What?" She sounded defensive.

"That you always got into trouble. Look where I found you."

"Thanks for the compliment."

"You're welcome. Now get some sleep." After a rustle of his blankets, he lay still.

Lisa pulled in her bottom lip, wanting to defend herself, but unable. Suddenly, she remembered that John was in trouble this minute. Was it of his own making?

Pulling the bumpy quilt over her head, she snuggled down and let sleep black out her thoughts.

On their fifth day out from Silverville, Lisa stayed in the saddle by sheer force of will. She hurt in places she had never thought about before. Her skin had fried in the sun and wind. She touched her peeling nose and wished again for a wide-brimmed hat. Would her face ever be the same?

After their short conversation in the darkness, John had returned to his usual silent self. Several times, Lisa tried, unsuccessfully, to draw him into conversation. When his headache returned, he tried to ease the pain by tying a damp bandanna around his forehead.

"Let's stop for few days," Lisa begged at noon when they paused just long enough to chew some hardtack for lunch. "You're in pain and so am I. The horses need a break, too."

He handed her his canteen. "If we can find a place with grass and water close by, we'll hole up and sit tight tomorrow."

Three hours later, they found the perfect spot—a meadow surrounded by firs. A swollen stream cut across one corner. Unsaddling the horses, John let them roll in the tall grass, then picketed them while Lisa gathered branches for a fire. In order to disperse their smoke and screen their fire, they set up camp among the trees.

"I'm going to make biscuits with the last of the flour," she told him when he returned.

"Fine. We'll stop in Laramie for supplies in a couple

of days." He took out his knife to shave off some wood slivers, added bark fibers, and then lit it with a flint. In minutes, they had a crackling flame.

Lisa formed biscuits between her hands and dropped them into a tiny iron skillet, watching John out of the corner of her eye. Of all the men she had known in her life, she had never met anyone like John Bowers. Not that her observations mattered. When they reached Juniper Junction, he would get a job, and she might never see him again.

Setting a tin plate over the skillet, she laid it on the fire and scooped coals on top of it using a long, wide stick. "When those are done, I'll fry some bacon."

He stretched out his legs and leaned on one elbow. "Too bad we can't milk a horse. I'm hankering for some pan gravy on those biscuits."

She grinned. "I believe there's a tin of peaches in the pack. Maybe that will do instead. I'll get it."

Sitting on opposite ends of a short log, they ate near the fire. The meal fell far short of Bess's cooking, but it eased the knot in Lisa's stomach and made her drowsy. Before the last rays of sun disappeared, she had rolled herself up in her blankets and nodded off into a deep sleep.

૨ə

When she opened her eyes the next morning, John was gone. The horses lazily cropped grass while a meadowlark chirped overhead. When Lisa moved, the bird flew up and away.

She stretched, enjoying the quiet, grateful that she did

not have to move.

The next moment, John stepped through the trees. "Here's breakfast." He held up two limp prairie chickens.

"I didn't hear a shot."

"I don't want to use my gun if I can help it. You never know who may be around to hear. I killed these by throwing a stick. It's not hard if you know how." He glanced toward the fire. "Before I left this morning, I put on a pot of water to boil. Now, I can scald and pluck these birds." Turning toward the fire, he plunged each one into boiling water and then laid it on the ground to rake off feathers. The smell made Lisa wonder if she was hungry after all.

She covered a yawn, then said, "You can fry them in the bacon grease from last night."

"Me?" He glanced at her, his left eyebrow raised as he pulled the last pinfeathers from the second hen.

"That's right, you." She slid deeper under the covers. "I'm on vacation today."

He watched her without blinking.

Lisa tried to ignore him.

Finally, she flung back the blanket. "Oh, all right! I'll cook them." She groaned as she rose to her feet, stifling the urge to massage the places that hurt the most.

"Say, are you okay?"

"I'm fine." She grabbed the chickens out of his hand, picked up his knife, and headed toward the nearby stream to finish cleaning the birds. Fresh, rippling water skipped from rock to rock and left a wake of white foam. Lisa paused to bask in the beauty around her. She would have a bath and fresh clothes today, even if she had to blindfold John and tie him into his bedroll.

The smell of bubbling coffee greeted her as she made her way back to camp. When she reached the fire, John handed her a steaming cup.

She took it from him, then set the brew aside to cool. No sense adding a scorched tongue to her woes.

While the chicken fried, she reached her hands toward the sky and bent over backwards. At last, her muscles were starting to loosen up a little, and the stretching felt so good. She suddenly wanted to move and have some fun.

John, his hat over his eyes, lay sprawled on the ground with his shoulders against the log.

On impulse, Lisa grabbed the hat and slapped it across his face. He yelped and reached to recover it, missing by a fraction. Laughing, she hiked her skirts and dashed into the meadow.

He clambered to his feet. "Are you crazy?"

"You're an old sobersides, John Bowers. You need to lighten up a little."

He followed her to the edge of the meadow, wearing an expression that was half amusement and half irritation.

"Well, what are you waiting for?" she taunted, twirling his hat on one finger. "Come and get this old thing if you want it."

He stooped to pluck a grass stem and stuck one end between his teeth. "Lisa, you're acting like a twelve-year-old."

Backing up, her left foot sank into a gopher hole and

she felt herself losing her balance. Her arms flew out and she sat down hard. . .right where it hurt.

Her face pinched into a grimace. "Ohhhh."

John dashed to her. "Are you all right? Did you hurt your ankle?"

Lifting her hand for a pull up, she let out a soft gasp as she got to her feet. "Not my ankle, no." She took a painful step. "That's what I get for trying to act like a kid when I'm pushing a hundred."

He chuckled and retrieved his hat from her hand.

Trying to pretend as though nothing had happened, she resumed her cooking, keeping her face turned away so he would not see her burning cheeks.

Unruffled as always, John sauntered back to his spot and sat down. He ate his fried chicken and rewarmed biscuits without speaking, then lay down on his bedroll to nap.

"John?"

"Ummm?"

"Stay put until I get back, okay? I'm going to wash up."

He reached for his Stetson to bury his face. "No problem. Just let me know when you get back."

Digging into her pack, Lisa found fresh clothes and headed upstream. The water, a few degrees cooler than lukewarm, felt wonderful. An hour later, she slid between her blankets and gladly forgot the world.

five

The next two days passed in agonizing monotony. After her initial soreness, Lisa's aches began to disappear. However, she still felt unspeakably tired. She day-dreamed of her four-poster bed at home, laden with down-filled tick and fluffy pillows.

When they rode into Laramie, they stayed only long enough to replenish their food supply. As they headed down the narrow main street, Lisa gazed longingly at three false-fronted hotels.

"Can't we stay just one night?" she asked, turning to the man beside her.

"Lisa, I can't take the chance." Beneath his hat brim, he scanned the boardwalks on either side. "If only I knew what he looked like. The way things are, any gun-totin' cowboy could be the fella who's after me."

Easing her gritty collar away from her neck, Lisa sighed and squirmed uncomfortably in her saddle.

❧

That night, she went to sleep without eating. Her head was simply too heavy to hold upright a moment longer.

Before dawn the next morning, she felt a rough glove on her shoulder. "Lisa. Wake up. It's time to hit the trail."

"Leave me alone!" She rolled away from him.

"We have to go."

"I want to stay here another day." Her eyes drifted closed. The next moment, she felt the blanket jerk away. Tepid water splashed her face. She screamed and sat up, hands raised to protect herself.

"How dare you!" She glared at him, fists clenched, wishing he were close enough to reach.

"We've got to go," he said mildly. "Now."

She stood to be at eye level with him. "I told you I'm not going. I need another day to rest." Staring him down, she took a step forward. "I'm not getting on that horse today; you hear me?"

Lips pursed, his blue eyes watched her. "I didn't want to scare you, but you leave me no choice. We are being followed. I've seen dust behind us since we left Laramie."

"Well, whoever it is surely can't be chasing you," she declared. "If he knew where you were, why didn't he come for you at the cabin?"

"Who says he followed us from Silverville? He may have spotted us in Laramie."

"Not likely."

He took a step backward, that haunted, wide-eyed look taking control of his face. "We've got to move. I can't risk finding out that it's him."

The fire of anger left Lisa's eyes as quickly as the blaze had erupted. She realized afresh the severity of John's predicament and his hidden terrors. Protective instincts overcame her desire for rest. Lowering her face, she turned away. "Give me a few minutes, and I'll be ready." She touched her hair. No time to comb the snarled mass again today. Did it really matter?

John poured her a cup of hot coffee and forked bacon onto the one tin plate they shared. Lisa ate hungrily, picturing in her mind scrambled eggs, fat sausages, and pancakes smothered with sorghum.

"Somewhere ahead is the Colorado state line," John said as he tied Lisa's bedroll behind Ginger's saddle.

Lisa grimaced. "That's been true since we left Silverville." Since the hat episode, she had baited John every chance she got.

"I meant," he said quietly, "we should reach the border today."

Who is the real person hiding beneath that shell? Each passing day this question grew more important to Lisa. She had made a personal game of learning the answer. Yet, it was a difficult game to master.

He moved to the campfire to gather up their few dishes while Lisa retired to the bushes to rub witch hazel on her healing wounds. Thank goodness she had remembered to bring the smelly stuff along.

"What was your mother's name?" Lisa called out an hour later as they cantered shoulder to shoulder across the plain.

"Martha."

"What was she like?"

He looked at her, irritated. "Why all the questions?"

"I'm trying to help you remember."

He pulled his horse away from her. "Don't trouble yourself."

She called across the widening gap between them. "If you remember who's chasing you, you won't have to run from every shadow!"

He urged his horse ahead of her without answering. They rode the next two hours in a silence that grated on Lisa's raw nerves. Riding with John Bowers was like keeping company with a stuffed owl.

At noon, they stopped under a wide rock overhang behind a copse of trees. Unsaddling the horses, John took his Winchester and set off in search of meat.

Lisa dug a frying pan and a packet of bacon from the saddlebag. Gathering twigs and small branches, she shaved off some wood slivers and tried to start a fire with the flint, as she'd often seen John do. She worked over it for the next hour. Gnats buzzed around her eyes. Mosquitoes swarmed every square inch of exposed flesh.

Finally, she'd had enough. Pent-up emotion from the past weeks and months swirled together until she felt she would smother under its weight. In a burst of red-hot fury, she slammed the flint to the ground, grabbed her head with both hands, and screamed out her frustration. Pausing long enough to draw in another full breath, she screeched again. Her shrieks ricocheted off the mountains.

Covering her face with her hands, she plopped down on a wide rock. Why had she done something so insane?

A few minutes later, John bounded into the clearing, his lips white. "What happened? Are you hurt?"

"No." Her face flamed. She tucked her chin onto her chest. "I lost my temper. I can't start the fire."

He stared at her, his eyes blue chips of light. "What are you doing trying to start a fire out here in the open with someone on our tail?" Toe-to-toe with her, he glared into Lisa's eyes. "I've put up with your bellyaching from morning to night. I've coddled you and lost time for you. Now this! You may as well run up a flag and ask that guy following us to come on over." He lifted his open palm, put it down, and raised it again.

Whirling, he stomped off into the brush. "I'll start the fire when I get back."

Lisa clapped her hand over her mouth. A giggle, then a chuckle came out. She leaned over, caught in a wave of helpless laughter. Stone-faced John finally got ruffled. He actually wanted to spank her. As if he could.

Wiping tears and chuckling, she scouted around for some bone-dry branches, then moved behind high, leafy brush that leaned over to touch the rock face about five feet up. She picked up the flint and started the fire on the third try. Adding wood carefully, keeping the flame low, she ran out of the tiny shelter to fetch the frying pan.

Bacon sizzled and popped when John returned with two skinned rabbits in his hand. Lisa hid a smile as he sat beside her.

"Got a blaze going after all, I see," he said, glancing at the bush above them. "Not a bad setup."

"I'll get the hang of things after a while." She held the fork and stared at the frying pan. "I'm sorry I scared you. I didn't mean to."

"I reckon I'm over the fright by now." He deftly carved

a rabbit into quarters and threw the fresh meat into the pan. "Just don't pitch such a fit again."

A giggle escaped, and he sent her a calculating look. "What's so funny?"

She tried to straighten her face. "I've never seen you so riled over anything before."

He grinned. "I reckon I'm just naturally easygoing. Always have been." He breathed in the aroma of frying meat. "That sure does smell good."

"Wish we had some potatoes to go with it."

"Lisa, you'd get along a lot better in life if you'd thank the good Lord for what He's given you without thinking about what He hasn't done yet." His hand stretched toward the fire, his scar a wide white streak on his palm. "We've got shelter, a beautiful sunny day, good food, and quiet. What more could we ask for?"

His soft words gentled her like a kind touch settles a nervous mare. She sat next to him while they ate, enveloped in a calmness she had never before experienced. When he stood, she reached out her hand for him to give her a pull up, then she stood before him.

"You're an unusual man, John Bowers," she murmured. "I've never met anyone like you before."

He grinned, but his eyes remained serious. "I could say the same about you."

She wanted to say more, but she forgot how. Her world centered on the deep pools in his eyes, his strong jaw, his quiet strength.

She did not want to travel any farther. But this time, her reluctance wasn't due to sore muscles and weary limbs. She wanted to stay here and bask in his comforting presence forever.

He took a step back and cleared his throat. Looking at the blue dome of sky overhead, he said, "We can make ten more miles before dark. We'd best mount up and ride."

Since they first left Silverville, they had ridden in tight formation, but now they seemed even closer somehow.

Two days later, Lisa felt a sense of loss when Juniper Junction appeared on the horizon.

❧

"Lisa, baby!" Sally Feiklin cried when she saw her daughter in the doorway of their home. She threw her pudgy arms around Lisa.

Blinking back tears, Lisa hugged her mother, so glad to be home.

"Where's your father?" Sally asked, peering past John, who stood just outside the door, to the tiny front yard where the white gate stood closed.

Lisa said, "Daddy never came." Fear formed a lump in her throat as she watched her mother's round face turn into a picture of worry.

"He took the stage a month ago to come for you," she gasped, panic in her eyes. "He said the stage would be easier on you, so he left his horse here."

Lisa heard John's boots on the plank floor. She felt his presence behind her as she replied, "We didn't hear about any accidents. I was hoping that he had returned home for some reason. What could have happened?" She looked over her shoulder at John. "Where is he?"

"He must be somewhere between here and there," he said, his dusty hat in his hands. "We didn't see him because we left the trail."

Lisa said, "Mama, this is John Bowers. He brought me home."

Sally glanced at John and nodded absently, her eyes reaching for the open door as though her husband would step through the gate at any moment. A dimpled hand pressed her cheek, and she cried, "What happened to Rod? He was on the stage."

Smaller and slimmer than her older sister, Jessica Feiklin stepped into the front room. Her dark hair had auburn highlights that matched the smattering of freckles across her nose. "What is the matter, Mama?" she asked anxiously, darting a short glance at Lisa.

"Daddy's lost," Sally sobbed, pulling a cotton handkerchief from her sleeve. "Lisa hasn't seen him."

John touched Lisa's arm as tears filled her eyes. She turned to face him. "What happened to him, John? He must be hurt or he would have come to me."

Jessica hurried to her mother. "Come and sit down, Mama." She put an arm around Sally and urged her to the green camelback sofa. Blinking tears, she glared at Lisa. "If it weren't for you, Daddy would still be here."

Lisa froze. She and Jessica had never been close, but this was more than she could bear.

Jessica hugged her mother, and both women sobbed.

Tears coursed down Lisa's face. She ran to her mother and knelt on the hooked rug to lay her head on the apron across her mother's wide waist. Sally reached down to cradle her wayward daughter.

The room filled with sobs and sniffles. A warm breeze lifted white lace curtains to brush twin Windsor chairs and the small table nestled between them. Sunlight reflected in two glass lamps on the mantel.

Some time later, Lisa remembered John, standing awkwardly near the door. Wiping her face, she slowly stood and moved toward him. "It is my fault," she sniffed.

"I'm going after him."

She peered at him through bleary eyes. "John, you're not well. You can't turn around and go back."

"I'm in no shape to fight about it now. I've got to find a place to sleep before I fall over."

She rubbed open palms over her burning cheeks. "You can stay here."

He glanced at the distraught women on the sofa. "I don't want to trouble your mother at a time like this. I'll get something; don't worry."

Her eyes lingered over his tousled, dust-colored hair, the dark stubble on his cheeks. She hated to see him go. "Take care of yourself," she murmured.

He touched her chin. "You do the same." He lifted his hat and settled it onto his head as he went out the door.

Lisa followed to close the latch behind him, her heart aching in a new way. What a pity she had given up on the male gender.

"Lisa, you must be starving." Sally's ragged voice broke into her daughter's thoughts.

She turned back into the room. "My stomach feels sick. I'm not sure I can eat anything."

"I've got some bean soup on the stove. Maybe that will make you feel better."

"I'll fetch some hot water first," Lisa said, heading toward the kitchen at the back of the house. "I can't sit down to eat until I've had a bath."

Lifting a pail to the top of the iron stove so she could dip water from the reservoir, Lisa held a pain-filled numbness inside. *Daddy,* she cried in her spirit, *where are you?*

&

John stalled his horses at the livery stable, then paced down the central street of Juniper Junction like a man walking in a deep sleep. He checked into the town's only hotel, a two-story building with a wide porch, to take a hot bath and sleep until suppertime. With a thick steak and a mountain of potatoes warming his middle, he returned to his creaky bed until breakfast.

Back in the dining room, he shoveled in a man-size stack of hotcakes without looking up. Standing to dig two bits from the pocket of his jeans, he glanced up and caught the eye of a lowbrowed man with curly black hair and a furtive crinkle about his eyes. The stranger instantly turned his attention to four fried eggs on his plate. John paid his bill and stepped into the morning light, his hat brim low over his brow.

Digging into his saddlebags, John took stock of the meager remains from their journey, then strode toward Harper's Emporium. He needed supplies before he hit the trail. Twenty strides later, he pushed open the shop's door and heard a tiny tinkling bell.

Small windows kept the interior of the store dim despite the brilliant sunlight outside. Harper's smelled of freshly ground coffee and new leather. Three barrels containing pickles, crackers, and coffee beans made a triangle at the left end of the counter near the coffee grinder. The back wall held shelves laden with canned goods, ammunition, and ready-made clothing for men and boys. A dozen bolts of dress goods lay stacked on the right end of the counter.

Edging between tables of shoes and woven baskets on his way to the back counter, John spoke to the slim, graying man standing under a sign marked Post Office. "A pound of beef jerky, a dozen potatoes, and five pounds of flour."

"Sure thing, mister." He picked up a scoop and lifted the lid on the flour barrel. "You passing through?"

"I reckon so. I'd thought about looking for a job, but now I'm not sure that I'll be around long enough to take it."

"The Circle C is looking for a cowhand who's not afraid to do a little farming on the side."

"Where is that?"

"Due west of town. About five miles."

"Add a pound of bacon and a hundred rounds of forty-fives to that, will you?"

Ten minutes later, John stepped out of the store with his saddlebags over his shoulder. He turned toward the livery stable, thinking that he would leave the bay here and fetch it when he returned.

Flipping a silver dollar at the livery man, he slapped

the saddlebags over Molasses and hit leather. On his way out of town, he stopped at the Feiklins's white-washed house, pretty as a painting with its white picket fence and tiny yard.

When Jessica answered the door, he lifted his Stetson. "May I see Lisa?"

She paused, sizing him up before answering. She had wide eyes, a serious mouth, and flat-planed cheeks. "Lisa's upstairs. I'll get her."

John stared after Jessica. He could imagine her at six years old, singsonging to Lisa, "I never have to stay after school and write sentences like you do."

Light steps sounded on the oak floor, and his jaw went slack. Before him stood a lovely lady with glossy dark waves held back by two tortoiseshell combs as it flowed down to her waist. She wore a powder-blue morning dress with tatted lace about the throat. She smiled, delighted.

"John, come in. I'm glad you came."

He swallowed. His thumb felt the grosgrain ribbon on his hat. He could not take his eyes off her. "Lisa. . .I hope I'm not disturbing you."

She laughed. "Of course not." She sat on the sofa and patted the seat next to her. "Where did you sleep?"

"I stayed in the hotel last night." He paused, trying to remember what he had come here to say. "I'm riding out to find your father."

"Today?" Worry creased her brow.

"Right away. When I get back, I'll look for a job."

"Mama sent word to the sheriff in Denver that Pa was

missing. The law will go after him. You don't need to go."

"I want to."

She put her hand on his sleeve. "Please don't put yourself in jeopardy, John. I couldn't live with myself if something happened to you because of me."

He covered her hand with his. "I'll stop here as soon as I get back." His eyes scanned her face, amazed that this was the same girl he had known for almost two months. Her nose was still shiny red from sunburn, but she was the prettiest thing he had ever seen. And she smiled at him like she meant it.

Gulping, he stood. "Good-bye, Lisa. I'll come back as soon as I can."

At the door she gave him her hand. "Stay safe. Please," she murmured, and stood, waving, as he rode away.

Turning west on Main, John caught sight of the dark stranger from the restaurant standing on the boardwalk. When John drew near, the man turned to look into the window of the milliner's shop and kept his back toward the road until John had passed him.

Glancing back a few yards later, he saw the dark stranger reach for the knob of the shop and push the door inward. Drawing in a shaky breath, John kicked Molasses into a canter.

A hundred emotions swept through John as he left Juniper Junction behind, most of them painful. He followed the trail heading west of town, intending to turn north when he found a likely spot. No sense making things easy for his pursuer. If such a man did exist. Again he glanced behind him, wondering if his imagination was playing tricks on him.

Suddenly, a gunshot split the quietness of the morning. John jerked as a searing pain cut into his shoulder. Gasping, he bent low over Molasses's neck and urged the mustang to a gallop. They veered off the trail and through a stand of pines, on and on until John lost track of his direction. The front of his shirt felt hot and sticky. His senses began to spin. A moment later, everything faded into darkness.

six

When John opened his eyes, a balding man with a broken nose was bending over him, creating a block of shadow from the blinding sun.

"Glad to see you're coming around, young man. I had to dig a bullet out of you, and you lost a lot of blood." The timbre of the stranger's voice sounded deep, throaty. His gentle hands bound a strip of white cloth about the injured shoulder.

John squeezed his eyes closed against searing pain. He groaned.

"I'll take him to the ranch," a rough voice said. "It's closer than going back to town. He may not make it that far."

The first man nodded toward the speaker then said to John, "You have family around here?"

Sick with pain, John shook his head. He tried to speak, but his tongue would not cooperate. Turning his head, he realized that he lay in the back of a wagon.

A grizzled old cowhand wearing a stained hat stood nearby with his forearms resting on the wagon's side. "Good thing we were passing at just the right time, Doc. This hombre would have been swapping howdys with St. Pete in another hour or two."

The doctor swung his legs over the buckboard and

slid down. The bouncing of the boards below John sent white-hot needles of pain through him. Tree branches overhead swayed into a crazy green blur, and blackness closed in.

ॐ

When John awoke, he lay on a narrow bed in a quiet room with a quilt pulled up to his chin. His eyes drifted to the long window across from him where puffy cloud shapes drifted across a cobalt sky.

Unfinished wood formed the walls and floor of the room, which was about half the size of Bess's cabin. John's clothes hung from two pegs near the door. Two straight-backed chairs stood close to the bed with a small table nearby. John's eyes drifted closed. Far away, he heard a baby's gentle cry and the barking of a dog.

Sometime later, the door eased open, and John awoke to see a slim black woman wearing a brown gingham dress covered by a long, white apron. She had graying cornrows straight back from her brow. She paused inside the door when she noticed him looking at her.

"Well, you decided to wake up, did you?" A soft smile warmed her seamed face. She had a kind light in her eyes and spoke with a thick Virginia accent.

His voice dry as crackling paper, John whispered, "Where am I?"

She stepped closer. "This is the Circle C. Banjo brought you here five days ago." She touched his forehead. "Praise to Jesus. It's cool. You was out of your head with fever, son. We's been a-nursing you day and night."

"We?"

"Me and Miss Megan, the lady of the house. I am Em Calahan. My husband, Chance, and I live on the other side of the meadow."

John watched her, trying to absorb her words. Suddenly he remembered something important. "I've got to go." He tried to sit up. "I've got to find Lisa's father."

Em gently pushed his good shoulder down. "You ain't a-going anyplace for a couple of weeks at least. You'll kill yourself if you try."

"But Lisa's father. . ."

She leaned closer, her tone like a mother to a stubborn child. "You'd best stay put. You'll not be any good to anybody passed out along some trail, will you, now?"

He closed his eyes. The ache in his shoulder made him want to grind his teeth.

"I'll fetch you some hot soup." Em bustled out, and John drifted into a pain-filled daze.

It seemed he had scarcely closed his eyes when a spoon nudged his lips. "Here you go. Open up now."

Warm chicken broth reminded his stomach that he had not eaten in days. He peered at Em. "That tastes good. You don't have to feed me. I can feed myself."

"Is you left-handed?"

John flexed his right arm under the bandage and felt a stab. Stifling a groan, he winced instead. He turned toward her and opened his mouth.

As the last drop of soup left the bowl, a slim cowhand with a weather-beaten face appeared in the doorway, the man who had stood beside the wagon. "Jem told me he's awake, Em. Mind if I come in?"

"The door's open," Em replied with a smile. She spoke to John. "This is Banjo. He and Doc Leatherwood found you on the trail with a bullet in you."

"I'm much obliged," John said weakly.

"Just being neighborly." His twinkling blue eyes sobered. "When I saw you laying there, it struck me that God had sent us along to find you." He pulled a chair close to the bed. "Who did this to you? Are you in trouble?"

John let out a tired sigh. "It's a long story. I don't have the strength to tell it all now."

"Let him rest, Banjo," Em scolded. "There'll be plenty of time for jawing later."

"What's your name?" Banjo asked.

"John Bowers."

"I'm Joe Calahan, but most folks call me Banjo because I'm always making music." He chuckled.

"You play the juice harp?"

"No. I sing."

Em laughed. "Croaks is more like it." She waved both hands at him in a shooing motion. "Out, Banjo. The boy needs some rest."

He grinned. "You win, you ol' drill sergeant." Standing, he said, "I'll come by tomorrow, John. Maybe you'll feel more like talkin' then." He strode out, boots loud, spurs jingling.

Em held a glass of clear liquid toward John. "This has laudanum in it to make you sleep."

He drained the glass, then grimaced. "I'm not sure which is worse, that or the pain."

Em picked up the soup bowl. "Sleep, Mr. John. I've

got to get myself home now. Megan will be in to check on you after a while."

"You don't live here?"

She chuckled. "This used to be my room before I got married. As I said before, Chance and I live in a cabin down the hill. Steve and Megan Chamberlin own this place."

"I thought I heard a baby cry."

Em beamed. "They have the cutest little girl you ever did see. Her name is Ruthie and she is six months old. I've been a-coming up days to help care for you, but now I've got to see to Chance's supper. He's been out plowing since before first light." She stepped toward the door and spoke over her shoulder. "Megan will be in after a while."

The medicine took effect, and John slept.

≈

Night had fallen when he next awoke. A coal oil lamp cast a yellow glow over his portion of the room and lit the way for a serene young woman with light brown hair drawn back in a bun. She carried a tray. Beside her, a fair-haired boy about twelve years old brought a pitcher. His eyes danced, alive with curiosity.

"Feel like some supper?" she asked. She had the same southern accent as Em, but more refined.

John tried to smile. "I could eat a steer all by myself."

"That's a good sign." She set down the tray and eased into the chair. "I'm Mrs. Chamberlin. You can call me Megan. And this is my brother Jeremy. His nickname's Jem. I'd introduce you to my husband, but he's in Denver taking care of some business. Won't be home till next week."

"I'm obliged to you for taking me in like this."

"We're glad to do it." She took the blue enamel pitcher from Jeremy and poured a glass of water. "Can you handle this?"

John reached for it with his left hand, sloshed a few drops, and brought it to his lips. The cool liquid made his parched mouth ache. "Say, this is cold."

Eager, Jeremy said, "It comes from a mountain spring behind the house."

Megan lifted a spoonful of chopped beef mixed with broth. "Jeremy will be your helper while you're recovering. Just call him when you need him. He'll stay nearby."

The boy hooked his thumbs under the straps of his washed-out overalls and grinned, his hair sticking out at odd angles like straw on a scarecrow. He had the unusual combination of blond hair and brown eyes.

"I'm obliged, Jeremy." John took another sip and handed the water glass to Megan. She fed him steak and potato stew until he held up his hand, palm out. "Thanks, ma'am, but I can't hold another bite."

For the next few days, John lay on the narrow bed, sleeping most of the time. In his waking moments, he worried about Lisa and her father, but he had no strength to hurry the healing process.

Jeremy never seemed to tire of sitting beside John, whittling at a fistful of wood and chattering about ranch life.

"We have a dog named Lobo," the boy said one afternoon. "He used to belong to the man who owned this ranch before we came along. He had gone wild and Megan tamed him. She named him Lobo because he looks like a wolf."

With his strong arm under his head, John gazed at a dark oval knot in the ceiling plank over him. "I used to have a dog named Shep," he said. "He got killed in a buffalo stampede when we were on the Oregon Trail. I was about six years old."

Jeremy's eyes widened. "You came over the Oregon Trail?"

"That's not so special. Thousands of folks did the same thing. We didn't go to Oregon, though. We stopped in Wyoming."

The boy's eyes narrowed. He leaned forward to study John's lean face. "Are you a brave man?"

Startled, John tried to decide how to answer. He did not want to lie to the boy, but could he bear to tell the truth? Waiting for a count of three, he said, "Why do you ask?"

"Em always says that a coward has a thousand lives but a brave man only one. So I was wondering if you have any lives left."

Despite his discomfort, John chuckled.

Jeremy lifted the piece of wood and gouged off a thick chunk. "Do you still live in Wyoming?"

"I guess so."

"You don't know?"

"I had an accident and hurt my head. I can't remember some things."

Jeremy stopped whittling to stare at him. "I heard of a man one time who forgot who he was. He couldn't remember his name or who his wife was or anything."

"I know who I am. I just can't remember some details like where I live." John's eyes felt heavy. "Would you mind going out for a while? I'm tired."

"Yes, sir." The barefoot boy scooted toward the door. He dropped his carving, stooped to pick it up, then let the door close behind him. Top-heavy and sagging on leather hinges, the wooden door always flopped open or closed.

That evening, Banjo came to sit with John. His gray hair had a crease where the hat clamped his head. He wore a faded flannel shirt and matching jeans. A barnyard smell came along with him. "Howdy, John," he said, clumping across the floor. "How's the shoulder?"

"Sore. Doc Leatherwood came out this morning. He says I cannot move it for another three days. He's afraid the wound will reopen."

Banjo turned the chair around and straddled it, his arms across the back. "Hey, enjoy the easy life while you've got it. Two nice ladies to fuss over you. Nothing to do but rest. What more could you ask?"

John grinned. "I guess it all depends on how you look at it. Last week I was half dead for want of sleep and wished I could stay in bed for two straight days. Now I'm taking it easy and wishing I could ride." He eased his forearm across his chest. "I never thanked you proper for helping me. You saved my life."

"That wasn't anything I did. The good Lord brought

me along at the right time and sent a doctor with me to see to you."

John peered at the old cowhand. "You're a Christian?"

"I reckon I am. What about you?"

"Yes, sir. That's one thing about myself I remember for sure."

"Jem tells me you've lost your memory."

"Only some parts of it. A bullet creased my skull about a month ago. It was past midnight when my horse stopped beside a cabin where two women lived. One of them woke up and found me before I froze to death."

Banjo leaned forward, his face concerned. "Are you in trouble, son?"

John sighed. "I wish I knew. That part is a big black hole in my mind."

"How did you come to Juniper?"

"I brought Lisa Feiklin home."

"Did you now?" Banjo sat up straighter. "She eloped with a hand from the Rocking H last—let's see—last October."

"He dumped her in Silverville, South Dakota," John told him. "She was one of the women living in the cabin."

"And she got you to bring her home?" When John nodded, Banjo said, satisfied, "I'm glad you did. She must have suffered a lot these past months. I wonder that her father didn't go and fetch her back."

"He tried to, but he never made it to Silverville. He's disappeared. That's why I've got to get out of this bed. I promised Lisa that I'd look for him."

Banjo rubbed his prickly jaw. "What was Sheriff Feiklin riding when he left town?"

"He took the stage."

"The stage?" His bushy eyebrows reached for his hairline. "What could have happened to him on the stage?"

"It's a puzzle. And that's not the only one. I don't know who wants me dead bad enough to follow me clear across the territory." John let out a long breath. "You may as well know the rest. I've lost my nerve. My insides turn yellow every time I think about that hombre who shot me." His eyes felt heavy, and he let them close.

Banjo stood and turned the chair back around. "I'll come again tomorrow evening. We'll talk some more then." He trudged out of the room and let the door fall closed, leaving the room in shadows.

John lay in a pool of cold misery, alone and afraid.

seven

The day after John told Lisa good-bye and rode away, she answered a knock on the door and found a tall stranger wearing an immaculate tan suit with a black string tie. He had on a white ten-gallon hat and the star of a U.S. marshal. When he saw her, he swept off his hat. His mouth widened into a gleaming smile.

"Yes?" she asked, her heart thumping. Did he have news about her father?

"Good morning. I'm Marshal Chandler Brinkman. Are you Mrs. Feiklin?" His mellow voice had a deep quality that made it easy to listen to.

"My mother is lying down. Can I help you?"

"Someone told me that the sheriff lives here. I was wondering if you may have a room I can rent for a week or so, as a friendly gesture to a fellow lawman." He took half a step forward. "I'm on an important secret mission and need to stay out of sight as much as possible. I can't stay at the hotel."

Wide-eyed, Lisa stepped back, holding the door open. "Please come in. I'll fetch Mama."

Shoulders back in military style, the marshal eased across the threshold, his eyes moving left then right over the modest furnishings.

"Please sit down," Lisa told him, waving a hand at the

sofa. "I'll be back in a moment." She paced sedately toward the side hall. Once out of the marshal's sight, she broke into a run, keeping to her toes so her shoes would stay silent, and burst into her parents' room at the back of the house.

Her mother lay under a wedding-ring quilt on a wide iron bed, her hair in tangles about her shoulders, her puffy eyes closed. She had not eaten anything solid since she had learned that her husband was missing.

"Mama! A marshal's here," Lisa said when she had shut the bedroom door.

Sally gasped and sat up. "A marshal? Has he come about Daddy?"

Lisa plopped down on the edge of the bed, making the springs groan. "No, it's not about Daddy. He said he's on a secret mission and needs a private home to stay in for about a week."

"A secret mission in Juniper?" Sally's mouth formed an oval. "What's the world coming to?"

Impatient, Lisa stood and tugged her mother's sleeve. "He wants to see you about a room."

Sally pulled away. "I can't go out there, child. It'd take half an hour to get myself dressed and fix my hair." She ran a pale hand over her fleshy, mottled face. "Go back out there and tell him he can have the loft room for two dollars a week. Ask him to give us an hour to get it ready for him."

Already at the door, Lisa said, "I'll get Jess to help me clean it up." She stepped into the hall. Closing her eyes, she drew in a deep, slow breath then exhaled with a long puff, trying to calm herself. Marshal Brinkman had a shining lock of black hair that fell across his forehead and a gleaming smile that took her breath away. The sight of those chiseled features, that broad build, revived old feelings that she thought Brent had killed forever.

Wetting her lips, she waltzed down the hall to the sitting room, mentally practicing her answer to him.

She reached the doorway in time to see Jessica hand their guest a tall glass of tea, then sit on the opposite end of the sofa and smile sweetly at him.

"Thank you kindly, ma'am," he said. "I've been riding since dawn this morning, and I'm bone weary." Lowering the glass after a long drink, he caught sight of Lisa. "Your sister was kind enough to get me a drink, Miss Feiklin."

Darting a glance at the glowing Jessica, Lisa paused, shocked at the change in her normally sullen sister.

"Can your mother see me?" Marshal Brinkman asked.

Lisa tried to pull her thoughts together. "She said you can have the loft room for two dollars a week. We'll need a couple of hours to get it ready for you."

"May I see the room?" He finished the last of his tea and handed the glass to Jessica as he stood. "A wonderful refreshment, Miss Feiklin. Thank you kindly."

Jessica stood. "I'll show him the room, Lisa," she said, staring squarely into Lisa's face.

"Mother asked me to," Lisa said lightly. "Step this way, sir."

Leading him toward the narrow stairs, Lisa said, "My father hasn't been seen for almost a month. My mother is taking his disappearance hard. She rarely comes out of her room these days."

"That's too bad," Brinkman said, close behind her. "Where was he when you lost him?"

"Somewhere in Wyoming, we think. We sent word to the sheriff in Denver about it, but we haven't heard anything yet."

"If I can be of service, please let me know."

At the head of the stairs she turned toward him. "That's kind of you."

He smiled. "Just doing my job, ma'am." He stepped up to her level. His eyes drew close.

Flustered, Lisa paced to the door at the far side of the short hall. "This is the room. The ceiling and wall are slanted on one side because of the eaves of the house. That's why we call it the loft room." She flung back the door and stepped aside so he could enter first. A faint dusty smell seeped into the hall.

Two dormers formed small openings in the slanted wall. A wide four-poster bed filled most of the room, with a narrow dresser and a single chair the only other furniture. A worn rag rug lay near the bed.

"Mighty nice," he said, turning around to take in every angle. "I'll take it."

"I'll tell Mama that you'll stay, Marshal Brinkman," Lisa said.

He moved toward her, still smiling. "Please call me Chandler."

"I'm Lisa." She felt her cheeks warming. "If you'd like to relax in the sitting room for a while, Jess and I will clear out the dust for you and change the linens."

"I need to tend to my horse first," he said, extending a spotless tan coat sleeve, indicating for her to precede him down the stairs.

Lisa kept her eyes on the stairs below her, attracted to the man who followed close behind her, caught by an impulse to hook him with her teasing eyes then carefully reel him in. She had done it so often, it would be easy. But this time she felt a strange uneasiness that held her in. Something inside her had changed—just what, she wasn't sure.

&

A few minutes later, Lisa carried a broom and a duster into the loft room with Jessica following, her arms full of linen.

"How old do you suppose the marshal is?" Lisa asked, propping the broom beside the door.

"Thirty at least," Jessica answered shortly. Her brown eyes had a watchful expression.

"He's mighty handsome," Lisa said, flicking the duster over a windowsill.

Jessica sniffed. "I knew you'd think that."

"You weren't exactly blind to the fact while you were serving him tea."

"I'm not man-crazy like you are, Lisa."

Lisa dropped the duster and stepped toward her sister, a hard light in her eyes. "Take that back."

"I won't." Jessica stood with hands on hips, leaning slightly forward, her lips tight. "If you hadn't gone chasing after that dandified cowboy, Daddy would still be here."

Hand raised to slap her sister, Lisa stopped in mid-motion. The truth of Jessica's words jolted her. With a sharp cry, she ran out of the loft room, across the hall, and into her own bedroom.

She slammed the door and leaned against it. Her anger turned inward toward herself. Much as she hated to admit it, Jessica was right.

&

That evening Jessica fried steaks and baked potatoes for supper. She put a fresh tablecloth on the table and pulled good china from the glass-fronted hutch in the dining room. When Lisa offered to help, she abruptly refused to let her.

Lisa shrugged and wandered to the sitting room where Chandler Brinkman sat smoking a pipe and peering through the gauzy curtain facing the street.

He looked up when she came in. "Good evening, Lisa. Would you like to help me?"

Arranging her navy skirt, she perched on the sofa. "If I can, I'll be glad to."

"I'm looking for a man in his midtwenties, about six-two, two hundred pounds. He rides a black horse."

"What's he done?"

"He stole a Wells Fargo shipment of gold nuggets about a month ago in South Dakota."

Her mouth turned dry. "What part of South Dakota?"

"A few miles west of Tombstone."

"Are you sure he's in Juniper?"

"I trailed him and a companion all the way from Wyoming." He looked closer at her pale face. "Do you know someone like that?"

"Not. . .not that I can think of." She touched the lace collar brushing her chin. "If you'll excuse me, I'll help my sister in the kitchen." She made a graceful exit, took a wide circle around Jessica at the stove, and stared out the glass in the back door.

Was John an outlaw? She could not believe that he was.

She glanced at Jessica. If Chandler mentioned his quarry to the younger Feiklin girl, would she tell him about John? Lisa chewed her lip, trying to think. *Asking Jessica not to mention John may cause her to do just that. Better not say anything and hope Jess hasn't noticed enough about John to connect the two.*

John Bowers was no thief. He couldn't be.

～

For the next three days, the marshal left the house before dawn and returned at dusk, his wide smile always intact. Lisa eyed his city-style clothing and wondered where he spent his time.

She figured that John should be in Wyoming by now. If Marshal Brinkman was indeed on his trail, he had lost the scent. The longer he stayed in Juniper, the colder that trail would become.

Smiling into the lawman's eyes on the evening of the third day, Lisa swept into the kitchen to fetch him a cool drink. She was playacting—a distasteful job—but if, by distracting the marshal, she bought John a few hours' time, it was worth the effort.

"I'll take that to Chandler," Jessica said when she saw

Lisa pouring tea into a tall glass. The younger girl's chin jutted forward; her eyes flashed fire then grew cold. "You always shove me aside when a handsome man comes around. Well, you're not doing it this time." She grabbed the glass from the porcelain tabletop and reached back to touch the French twist she had perfected that afternoon.

Drawing in a deep breath, she held herself erect and minced into the dining room.

A corner of her mouth quirked in, Lisa edged to the kitchen door to peek through the dining room and into the living room where Jessica perched on the sofa beside Brinkman.

What disgusted Lisa most was the realization that she saw herself in Jessica's movements, her practiced smiles, the provocative tilt of her head. What had happened to the prudish girl Lisa had left behind a few months ago?

Piling fried chicken, boiled potatoes, and peas on two plates, Lisa carried them through the back hall to eat supper with her mother. Since the marshal arrived, Jessica had made it plain that she wanted him to herself. Tonight Lisa could not face the overt snubs of her sister at the dinner table.

Lisa sighed. Jessica had turned a deaf ear to her advice. She would have to learn the hard way.

The next morning, Lisa strolled down Main Street's boardwalk to Harper's Emporium with the handle of a large basket over her arm. She put her hand out to open the door when a thin, wiry man with a prickly gray beard called her name.

Turning toward him, a question on her face, she waited.

"Howdy, Miss Lisa," Banjo said, removing his hat. "I was just about to call on you at home. Do you know a man by the name of John Bowers?"

Her heart took a dive. "Yes."

"He's at the Circle C with a bullet wound in his shoulder. He's asking for you."

"Is he. . . ?" She could not say the words.

"He's going to be all right, Miss Lisa," Banjo told her, grinning kindly. "He's worried about your father, and he wants to talk to you."

She touched the gingham-covered basket. "I've got to fetch some things for Jessica, then I can come with you."

"I brought the buckboard. I'll drive you over to your house."

She swallowed back the panic pressing her throat and forced her voice to calm. What if the marshal was watching their house? Would he follow her to John? "No, thank you, Banjo. I'll meet you in front of the hotel."

His shaggy brows drew down. He studied her a moment, then said, "That's fine, Miss Lisa. I'll meet you there."

Lisa rushed home and entered by the back door. She dropped the basket on the table and told Jessica at the sink, "I'm going out to the Circle C with Banjo Calahan."

Her sister spun around, shocked. "Just like that? What's happened?"

"I met Banjo in town, and he asked me to ride out. He'll bring me home by evening time."

Jessica's face creased into a teasing smile. "Isn't he a little old for you?"

Lisa picked up a damp dishcloth and flung it at her. "Very funny. Don't wait supper for me." She hurried to the door and glanced back to see a satisfied smile on her sister's face.

Banjo gave her a hand up to the buckboard seat and climbed aboard himself. "He'll be mighty glad to see you, Miss Lisa." He chuckled. "He's a fine young feller, John is. Fits into the family like he was born to it."

"What happened to him?" Lisa asked. "The last I heard from him, he was leaving to find my father."

"He got as far as the trail west of town. Somebody drygulched him. Doc Leatherwood and I heard the shot and found him a few minutes later. . .right about there." He pointed at a clump of trees fifty yards ahead. "He was unconscious and losing a lot of blood. If we hadn't happened along, I'm afraid to say what would have become of him."

"He was already weak from his head wound," Lisa said, shading her eyes to stare at the place where John had lain.

"How much do you know about him?" Banjo asked over the grating of the wagon's wheels on sandy soil.

She told him about waking up to find John wounded outside the cabin, about the gold nuggets, and the dirt covering him and his horses.

"Maybe he was mining," Banjo said, "and had a good strike."

"He was wearing cowboy clothes."

"Maybe he's a cowboy who decided to stake a claim and didn't want to spend money on a new outfit. I did some mining my ownself in my younger days. I didn't always dress the part."

"He had a money belt full of gold eagles, too." She sighed. "I believe he's honest, Banjo. He prays."

The old-timer adjusted his hat and squinted at her. "One thing I do know; he's bound and determined to find out what became of your father."

He flapped the reins, propped one boot on the front panel of the wagon, and bellowed out a verse of a hymn, "Would you be free from the burden of sin?"

Letting her shoulders sway with the jouncing of the buckboard, Lisa listened to him sing and wondered at her own answer to his musical question.

eight

When the buckboard broke through the last stand of pinion pine, Lisa saw the Circle C ranch house at the top of a rising meadow. The stone-fronted cabin had a wall of orange rock behind it and a wide expanse of sky to the east. A stable and chicken coop lined up along the rock face as well.

For fifteen minutes, the wagon rattled over a well-traveled trail toward a swollen stream.

"We just finished this bridge," Banjo said with a satisfied nod at the wide strip of planking before them. "We'll put up some rails soon's Chamberlin gets back."

Lisa gripped the edge of the seat as metal-strapped wheels rumbled over bare boards. She could see straight down into the water by her side, no planking in sight.

Banjo chuckled. "Don't worry, little lady. We used to just roll across the stream, water up to the axles, this time of year."

Lisa let out her breath and nodded. The trail rose before them in a wide circle around a field the color of misty green.

"We planted corn a week ago Saturday, and it's already sprouting. Good soil."

Lisa smiled. "You sound like you own the place."

He grinned. "I don't have a deed, if that's what you

mean, but I belong to the land." He glanced at her. "For years I rode the grub line or hopped from one mining camp to the next, no place to call my own. The Chamberlin family needed help when no one else would lend a hand, so I pitched my tent here, thinking that when their trouble was past, I'd move on."

He took off his hat, pressed a sleeve to his brow, and set it back on. "Then Jeremy came out from the East." He chuckled. "That little feller staked a claim around my heart the first minute I laid eyes on him."

"He's a bundle of energy," Lisa said, smiling. "I remember him running around at the corn harvest last fall. He never quit."

"Would you believe that a year ago he was stretched out in bed, his heart so weak the doctors wondered if he'd live?" His twinkling blue eyes darted toward the cabin as a blond boy burst out the door and into the yard, a wolf-faced dog at his heels. "Just look at him now. There's no way to explain that except'n that God did it."

Lisa nodded, but her mind had already reached into the house where a man lay on another sickbed.

&

Holding her spoon bonnet in one hand, Lisa appeared in the bedroom doorway with Em a few minutes later. John's head rose from the pillow. His face was chalk white, his mouth tense.

Em entered first. She lifted the blue enamel water pitcher and strode out as Lisa crossed the room and sat beside him. "John, what happened? Was it the same man? Did you see him?"

"The last I remember I was riding west of town, then I woke up here. I never knew what hit me."

Liquid pools formed in her eyes. "You've got to stay hid away. He'll kill you next time."

He tried to smile. "I'm not checking out of here before the good Lord allows. Soon's I'm fit, I'll be riding out to find your pa. Just like I said."

She pulled at the strings on her purse. "I've caused you nothing but trouble since we left Silverville."

"I wouldn't say that." He clasped her hand. "Please don't fret. I didn't ask you to come here to make you feel bad."

"If I. . ." She sniffed and pulled a handkerchief from her pocket. "If I hadn't run away, Pa wouldn't be out there hurt. . .or. . .or dead. And now you get yourself wounded again because of me." She shook her head and one comb slid lower over her ear. "Jessica's right, John. I'm no good."

She pulled her hand free and covered her eyes with the thin cotton cloth. John's quiet voice cut though her misery.

"No one's good, Lisa. Not me, not Jessica, no one."

She lowered the handkerchief, blinking salty, burning, swollen lids.

"Jesus forgave my wickedness when I was six years old. He can forgive yours anytime you care to ask Him."

"What if my daddy's dead?" she breathed. "How can I ever forgive myself?"

His mouth softened; his eyes looked deeply into hers. "Let's leave tomorrow in the Lord's hands. He's big enough to carry it until we get there. Don't you think so?"

Nodding, she dabbed the soggy cloth against her eyes and drew in a shaky breath. "Now that I'm here, how can I help you?"

"Your being here helps me," he murmured. "Until now, I haven't had the will to fight, to get back on my feet. I feel weak as a newborn calf."

She tucked the handkerchief into her pocket, her eyes on his navy-colored sling. "Let me stay here and take care of you."

His expression stiffened. "What about your mother? Isn't she ill?"

"Not physically. She took to her bed because she is worried about Pa. Besides, Jessica can see to her. Please let me stay." Her eyes darted about the sparsely furnished room. "I'll sleep on the floor if I have to."

The door scraped against leather hinges as Em stepped in carrying the pitcher. She paused, a puzzled look on her face. "Miss Lisa, why would a fine lady like you want to sleep on the floor?" Em asked, glancing from her to John.

Lisa's face felt as if it were on fire. "I was telling John that I'd like to stay and take care of him even if I have to sleep on the floor."

"Why, Miss Lisa, Miss Megan would never allow that. Besides, they's plenty of room. We could put Jeremy out in the stable quarters with Banjo so's you could have the loft. I know Miss Megan would be glad to have you."

"I'm not convinced that you ought to," John said. "Your family may not like it."

Lisa suddenly smiled, her spirit returning in a rush. "You're not in any shape to stop me, are you?"

His eyebrows lifted. "And here I thought you'd turned over a new leaf."

She stood and took off her wool shawl. "A new leaf, maybe, but the tree's still the same." Turning to Em, she said, "Would you mind showing me where to leave my things?"

Em's face wrinkled into a pearly white grin. "Sure thing, Miss Lisa."

Pausing long enough to send John a look that said, *Try to stop me,* Lisa left the room.

Outside John's door in the dining room, Em took Lisa's bonnet and shawl. "These can go on the shelf by the door." She turned to Megan, who sat in a wooden rocking chair before the living room fireplace. A flannel blanket covered her shoulder as she nursed the baby. "Miss Megan, Lisa would like to stay on to help care for John."

Megan's smooth features beamed a welcome. "Why, surely, Lisa. We will be delighted to have you. Please consider this your home."

"I'll tell Jeremy to move his things out with Banjo," Em said, her leather soles slapping against the stone floor. She stepped outside and called loudly, "Jeremy! Come to the house!"

"Sit down, Lisa," Megan said, reaching a hand toward the blue settee across from her. "I'm so glad you've come back to Juniper. Your mother was very worried about you."

"My father traveled north looking for me. He hasn't

come back," Lisa said, sinking to the soft seat. "I can't sleep for blaming myself. And now John's been hurt because of me."

"Because of you?" Megan reached under the blanket, lifted the tiny dark-haired girl to her shoulder, and patted the baby's back. The child immediately lifted her head and stared at Lisa, a thin stream of white drool trickling from her delicate mouth. Megan touched the baby's lips with a snowy white cloth. "Surely, John wasn't shot because of you."

"Someone's been chasing him for months. If he hadn't set out to look for Pa, they may not have found him again."

Megan nodded. "John told us about that." She smiled into her daughter's eyes then turned her attention to Lisa. "He's a nice young man."

"Why would someone want to hurt him?" Lisa said. "He can't remember anything about it. I know John wouldn't hurt a soul. Why would anyone be so determined to kill him?"

"You ought to get Banjo to help you. He's pretty good at following a trail."

"After two months? It would take a pretty good tracker to find a trail that old."

"Ruthie, would you like to say hello to Lisa?" Megan cooed. She turned the baby to sit on her knees, facing Lisa. Ruthie goo-gooed and waved her hands as her mother gently bounced her.

"She's adorable," Lisa murmured, smiling gently.

"The apple of her daddy's eye."

The door burst open, and Jeremy bounded in. He reached the loft ladder in three strides and scurried to the top. Em chuckled as she closed the door. "You would think that I just give that child a peppermint stick; he's so excited."

"Banjo's his favorite," Megan said. "They'll have some good talks out there in the quarters."

"I get the top bunk," Jeremy called from above.

Megan laughed. "I don't think Banjo will argue over that."

"Let me show you around, Miss Lisa," Em said, moving into the living area. The spacious main room of the cabin lay in an L shape. In front of the door was the living area with a dining room adjoining it. The back leg of the L was a narrow kitchen with cabinets on both sides and a large black stove ten feet from the dining room table. From the stone fireplace to the corner hutch behind the table, the marks of a craftsman were evident everywhere Lisa looked.

"There's a spring outside the house." Em led the way through the kitchen and toward a path out the back door. Lisa kept pace behind her.

Out back, between the cabin and the towering rock wall, lay a corridor fifteen feet wide and forty feet long. A high board fence stretched from the house to the stable. Across from the back door, a thin stream spurted out of a crack in the rock and into a stone-lined basin that overflowed into a narrow, man-made stream and under a springhouse. The water disappeared at the edge of a sharp drop-off on the east side of the house.

"Stay back from the edge," Em warned. "I's pulled Jeremy away from the lip of that cliff so many times, I's lost count." She chuckled. "He sure does keep me on my toes." Pointing to the left, she said, "That's the new stable down yonder. They had a fire here about a year ago that destroyed the old one. Now, in bad weather we can get to the stock through here—behind this fence and out of the wind."

She turned back inside. "They's a hot-water reservoir in back of our cookstove, if you need some. I tore up an old sheet for bandages. They're in here." She pulled out a drawer in the kitchen. "And there's alum powder in this little tin to sprinkle on the wound. I haven't changed his dressing yet today."

Lisa lifted a rolled strip of cloth from the drawer. "I need to get word to my mother that I'm staying here," she said. "She'll be worried if I'm not back by nightfall. I'll need a few clothes, too. Maybe I can send a list to my sister."

"I'll ask Banjo to ride into town," Em said. "He was planning on taking you back anyway." She pulled out a second drawer. "Here's a pair of scissors."

"Thanks, Em. You've all been so kind."

"You's welcome, Miss Lisa. I's sorry you're having so much trouble. If you need anything more, just give a holler."

Her hands full of supplies, Lisa returned to John's room. "Time for a bandage change," she said brightly.

He grimaced. "Not my favorite part of day, I'm afraid."

"I'll be gentle." She moved to the chair and lay the

supplies on her lap. "Now, let me see what you've got there. I'd just gotten used to bandaging your head, and you had to switch places on me."

"Sorry to trouble you. I should have had him shoot me in the head again."

She gasped then giggled. "I can tell you're feeling better already." Lifting the scissors, she said, "Tell me when it hurts, and I'll quit."

"Thanks a bundle."

28

Two days later, Dr. Leatherwood announced that John could get out of bed as long as he took it easy and made no sudden moves. "Great, Doc," John said, grinning. "I'll be riding again in no time."

The doctor, built like a boxer, shook his head, his face serious. "Not for another two weeks, you won't. You've had a big hole gouged into your shoulder. A gunshot won't heal over in a few days like a cut would." He snapped the clasp on his Gladstone bag and lifted his black hat. "I'll come around in another week and see how you're doing."

John held out his left hand. "I'm obliged, Doc."

Briefly grasping his hand, Leatherwood said wryly, "Next time you see a bullet coming at you, do me a favor and duck." He nodded to Lisa and stumped out of the room.

John swung his legs over the edge of the cot. Lisa stood close and gripped his strong arm. He looked up. "What do you think I am, an invalid or something? I can stand without help."

She turned loose of his arm. "Sorry."

He eased his weight onto his feet and straightened his knees, lifting himself erect. An instant later he swayed. "Whoa!" He blinked, and Lisa grabbed him. "I guess I'm weaker than I thought."

"I think you've had enough for one time." She held onto him until he sat down. "Rest a couple of hours and we'll try again."

His eyes drifted closed. "I think I'll sleep a while."

"Good. I'll go out back and do some washing. If you need anything, just call."

He didn't answer and she soft-footed out the door. Two hours later, she returned to check on him. He lay still, eyes closed, so she hesitated near the door.

Suddenly he looked at her and said, faintly accusing, "I've been waiting for you to come back."

"I've been scrubbing clothes—mine and yours. They're hanging out to dry." Stepping toward him, she said, "I have work to do, you know. Do you expect me to spend every second with you?"

He cocked his head on the pillow, his expression vaguely amused. "Lisa Feiklin, you're like a wild pony. You need taming."

She sat down and leaned toward him. She meant to speak with an arched tone, but her words came out breathy and soft. "You think you're man enough to do the job?"

His left hand flicked out and grasped behind her head. Before she realized what was happening, he pulled her down and kissed her.

nine

Lisa jerked back. "Why did you do that?" she demanded, her heart pounding.

John gave her a slow grin. "It seemed like the thing to do at the moment." When she didn't answer, his expression sobered. "Maybe I was mistaken."

He raised up on one elbow. "I'm sorry. I was out of line."

She leaned against the back of her chair and swallowed hard, staring at her hands tangled in her lap.

Her voice sounded husky. "You're a fine man, John. The best I've ever met." She paused. "I'm not good enough for someone like you."

He laid his hand over hers. "You're wrong there, Lisa. I know you've made some bad blunders, and you've been deeply hurt, but there is an answer for that."

She looked up. "You're talking about God, aren't you?"

"He's real, Lisa. He cares for you so much that He sent His Son to die for you."

That truth pierced to the marrow of her being. Unconditional love was something she had never experienced, yet longed for with all her soul.

"Just tell Him that you know you need Him," John murmured. "Ask Him to forgive you and make something new of your life."

Turning her hands to hold John's in both of hers, she

pressed her eyes closed and poured out her heart to the God she'd known only by name until now. She had always feared His holiness; now suddenly she felt His love, warm and full, flowing through her.

She blinked at John, who was peering at her with an intensity that she could feel. "He *is* real," she murmured.

He lay back, his face glowing. "You know what this means?"

She waited for him to go on.

"You've got a clean slate. No more kicking yourself over what happened last month or last year."

She raised his fingers to her lips, then her cheek, her heart too full to speak.

Jeremy burst through the partially open bedroom door. Lisa dropped John's hand and pressed the left comb more firmly into her hair.

"Mr. John, want to see my horse?" Jeremy held out an oblong lump with four sticks coming down from the corners. It looked like something Lobo had chewed.

"Let me see that," John said, smiling. He held the piece and turned it over. "Much better than your last try. You need to work on making the neck curve a little."

Jeremy took the carving out of his hand and dropped it into a massive front pocket of his overalls.

"Jeremy, since you're here," Lisa said, "will you help me get Mr. John out of bed. Last time he almost fainted."

"Fainted?" John demanded. "My head got a little dizzy, that's all. I didn't almost faint."

Lisa ignored him. "Jeremy, if you'll stand on his good side, I'll take the other one." She turned to her patient. "Ready?"

ও

Three days later, John and Lisa strolled around the front yard in the cool of the evening, enjoying playful breezes and the warmth of a late sun. The orange cliff glowed bronze behind the house, and two hawks played tag above its rocky summit. The cornfield below had turned a deep leafy green, its fledgling plants swaying gently.

Behind Lisa and John, Megan hung diapers on the clothesline, and Jeremy rolled a wheelbarrow out of the stable. Ears up and tail high, Lobo trailed his every step.

"Next week this time, I'll be able to ride out," John said, reaching up to brush back his hair from his forehead. It was getting shaggy again.

"Why do you always spoil a good time by talking about leaving?" Lisa asked, her hand resting on his arm. "The sheriff from Denver is looking for Pa. I don't want you to go, too. If you're hurt again, a guardian angel may not find you next time."

He laughed. "Banjo's a funny-looking angel. I'll have to tell him you said that."

She nudged him in the side with her elbow. "I was talking about myself. I found you first, remember?"

He touched her hand with his fingers that showed at the edge of his sling. "That's one thing I hope I never forget."

She smiled up into his blue eyes. "Speaking of forgetting, have you remembered anything more about who's chasing you?"

Gazing toward the east at silver-green prairie grass rippling in the distance, he drew in a deep breath. "I keep having a nightmare about a big man with a whip. I can see his white shirt and his hairy hands, but his face stays in the shadow of his Stetson." His jaw muscles worked in and out.

"You think that man is real?"

He glanced at her, his face showing pain. "I don't know. I always wake up shaking and cold, like I just came out of a fever. My insides turn to applesauce whenever I dream of him."

They roamed about the yard for another ten minutes, then slowly strolled toward the cabin. Once inside, John returned to his cot while Lisa helped Megan put supper on the table.

"I suppose I ought to be going home soon," Lisa said, holding a cloth-lined basket of rolls. "John won't need me much longer."

Brushing a strand of honey-colored hair back to her fat bun, Megan smiled softly. "You're welcome to stay as long as you like. It's been nice having another lady in the house again. I've been lonely since Em married and moved to the other side of the property."

"You've been awfully good to John and me. Especially after the scandal I caused last fall."

Megan set a wide bowl of chicken and dumplings on the table. "You've suffered enough over that episode, Lisa. It's not our place to add to your sorrows."

Ruthie's lusty cry in the bedroom cut off their conversation. Untying her apron on her way to her daughter, Megan said, "Call Jeremy and Banjo, won't you? I'll change the baby and be right there."

Lisa strode to the porch to shout, "Supper's ready!" then returned to the table to fill enamelware cups with water. Over the past week, John's appetite had returned twice over, and he could manage a fork with his weak hand. She stepped to his door and pushed it open.

From the doorway she asked, "Do you feel up to coming to the table tonight?"

He passed a hand over his forehead. "Sorry. I am feeling kind of tuckered after that walk. Would you mind bringing me a plate?"

"Coming right up." She let the door close and returned to the table. Filling a bowl with thick chicken soup, she pushed open the door with her shoulder. It gave against her pressure then banged shut after she passed through.

"Here's supper," she said with cheerfulness she did not feel. Just a few more days and he would saddle Molasses and canter away—maybe forever.

"I'm starved," he said, sitting up and reaching out for the bowl. He lifted the spoon and tasted. "Great soup. Just like my mother used to make."

Lisa paused beside him, wanting some space for her confused emotions. "Would you mind if I eat at the table tonight, rather than in here?"

He looked up, puzzled. "Is something wrong?"

She avoided his eyes. "I'd like to visit with the family. I've hardly spoken to them since I arrived almost a week ago."

"Go ahead. I don't mind." He swung his legs to the floor and plunged the spoon into a fat dumpling.

Lisa reached the table as Banjo slid into his seat. Megan came out of the bedroom with Ruthie on her hip. The baby wore a navy gown with white smocking on the bodice, her bare toes sticking out from under the hem. Jeremy darted in the back door, his slicked-down hair standing up at the crown.

"Banjo, look at my horse." He pulled his creation out of his pocket and thrust it at the cowhand.

Banjo took it and turned it over in his palm. "You've been working hard at it, Jem," he said, blue eyes twinkling. "What you have here is the rough shape. Now you need to work on the curves. You do that with tiny smooth cuts. I'll show you how after supper." He handed the wooden lump back to the boy.

Jeremy set it beside his plate next to Banjo and flung himself into the chair. "I want to make a figure of Lobo next."

Banjo chuckled. "That's the mark of an achiever, son. Always thinking ahead."

Megan sat at the head of the table, the baby in her lap. "Banjo, would you thank the Lord for the food?"

Lisa bowed her head while he prayed a short, simple prayer ending with "Bring Steve home safe to us, and heal that boy in the bedroom yonder so's he can go about the business You've given him to do. Amen." He lifted his head and reached for the serving bowl to hand it to Lisa.

"Thank you," she said, filling her bowl. She handed the food to Jeremy, her attention on Banjo. "What did you mean when you said, 'The business You've given him to do'? I hope you don't mind my asking."

"Not a bit. I was talking about John's trouble. Surely you know all about it."

She nodded. "I know as much as he does anyway."

Banjo leaned his forearm on the table, his voice

low. "He's got to go back and face his enemies, Lisa. Something has him scared spitless. He's got to go back and face his fear or give up his manhood."

Something squeezed in her middle. "I'm so scared. Every time he gets on the trail alone, someone shoots him. Next time they'll likely kill him."

"I know how you feel," Megan said, mashing a bit of potato with a fork while dodging Ruthie's chubby, grabbing hands. "Steve and I went through some trouble when we first came here. I thought I'd die when he rode out to face Victor Harrington." She shivered. "I still get the willies thinking about it."

Smiling, Banjo reached out to touch the baby's waving hand. Ruthie gave him a wide-lipped grin that showed a single tooth.

Lifting a tiny spoonful of potatoes, Megan found Ruthie's open mouth. "Steve will be home tomorrow. I can't wait."

"Maybe he'll bring me some peppermint," Jeremy said between mouthfuls of thick broth.

"Don't get your hopes up, buddy," Megan told her brother. "Steve may not have thought about satisfying your sweet tooth."

Jeremy's last dumpling disappeared in three bites. He scraped his plate clean and lunged to his feet. "I told Em I'd come over after supper." Dashing to the door, he pulled it open, calling, "Lobo! Here, boy!"

Her mind still on John's dilemma, Lisa said, "I don't think John's strong enough to go alone." Her eyes pleaded with Banjo. "Won't you please try to talk him into waiting a couple more weeks?"

Banjo's expression turned thoughtful. "What about your father? I'd think you'd want John to look for him."

"If John gets himself killed, he won't be able to help my father. Besides, the sheriff. . ." Her voice trailed away. She was beginning to wonder what had become of Denver's sheriff. All this time and no word had come. Would Jessica let her know if she heard something?

Confused and hurting, Lisa finished her meal without saying more. She knew Banjo well enough to know that he was trying to help her. But his kind of help didn't go down any easier than a helpful dose of cod-liver oil.

A few minutes later, a volley of horses' hooves in the yard drew everyone from the table and to the front door. Megan had a look on her face which spoke of her hope that the rider might be her husband.

Leading a bay mare that carried a side saddle, a slim young man slid from the back of a glossy blue roan, his legs reaching for the porch steps while his fingers pulled a slip of paper from the pocket of his blue flannel shirt. Lisa recognized her teenaged neighbor, Jimmy Bledsoe.

"Hi, Jimmy," she said, worry in her voice. "Did Mama send you?"

Flipping off his hat, he handed the paper to her. His voice sounded too deep for his small size. "Miss Jessica sent this to you."

Lisa's mouth felt dry. She unfolded the page and read, *The sheriff came back empty-handed. Mama's inconsolable. Please come home.*

ten

John spoke from the open door behind her. "What is it, Lisa?"

She turned and held the paper out, her brow puckered with worry. "I've got to go home."

Megan said, "We're still at the table, Jimmy. Would you like a bite of supper?"

"I'd be obliged." His stiff boots sounded on the porch steps.

Lisa pushed past John and, holding her skirts to one side, climbed the loft ladder. She stuffed clothes into her carpetbag without bothering to fold them. How could she face her mother? If she hadn't run off with Brent, this wouldn't have happened.

John was waiting at the bottom of the ladder when she came down. "I need to talk to you," he said.

She stared down at the bag in her hands, painfully aware of Megan handing Jimmy a plate, and Banjo drawing out a chair next to his own for the boy to sit down. Her feelings ran too deep to be hauled out and discussed in front of everyone.

John glanced toward the dining room. "Let's go out to the porch," he whispered.

Outside, he eased down to sit on the top step and reached for her hand, tenderly pulling her down beside him. She dropped the carpetbag and sat. The warmth of the sinking sun could not melt the icy knife of fear that pierced through Lisa.

John's voice made her turn toward him. "There's no one left to help your father. No one but me."

"If the sheriff didn't find Daddy, he's most likely. . ." She could not force herself to say the word. "He's not there to find."

She latched onto his arm. "Please don't go out there and get yourself killed."

He picked up her hand and held it like he would a wounded bird. Leaning close enough for her to see the gold flecks in his eyes, he murmured, "I hate to leave you." His glance wandered from her hair to her brow to her lips. "You've become very special to me, Lisa." Suddenly, his expression changed. He pulled away, dropping her hand. "I'm sorry. I shouldn't be saying such things to you."

Lisa found her breath and asked, "Why not?" a catch in her voice.

"I'm a broken arrow. Good for nothing." He looked down at his worn boots.

"Your wound will heal in time."

"I'm not talking about my shoulder." His voice became angry. "I'm yellow, Lisa. I never dreamed I would end up like this, but I have to face it. I'm yellow to the core."

She touched his cheek, and he looked at her. "If you're afraid, why do you insist on going?"

He gazed toward the eastern horizon, across miles of tall grass, swaying in the constant breeze. After a long moment, he said, "I guess I want to prove to myself that I can still be a man."

Without looking at her, he reached out and claimed her hand again. "After my folks died, a big rancher to the west of us thought he'd run me off. I wasn't much more than a kid, alone. . .scared to death. He brought four of his hands over to my place late one afternoon just as I was heading to the house to cook me some supper." The fingers in the sling curled together, forming a loose fist.

"They called me out and beat the fire out of me. Left me on the ground and rode away, laughing."

Lisa swallowed, the sound loud in the heavy silence between them.

"I crawled inside the house and doctored myself as best I could." He glanced at her. "It took me two weeks to get over that beating."

"What did you do then?"

A half grin formed on his lips. "I started sleeping and eating in a tight stand of aspen on the hillside above the ranch yard. I picketed my horses in a cave way off yonder. I knew those men'd be back. They wouldn't have such an easy mark the next time.

"Every day I changed my schedule, in case they'd started watching my place. I never took the same route to the barn or the well. They came about a week after I got better. This time they had torches and a keg of dynamite."

Lisa watched his jaw move as he talked. He had a shallow cleft on the side of his chin.

"One of 'em rolled the keg onto the porch while the

other lit a torch and headed for the barn."

"You just stood there and watched them?" Lisa breathed.

He glanced at her. "I was bellied down on the hillside with my Winchester.

"I nailed the one carrying the torch before he took three steps. He squalled and lit out for his horse. About that time, the man with the dynamite changed his mind, left the keg, and jumped into his saddle on the run. I took a shot at him, missed, and hit the keg instead. That hombre landed halfway up the hill with his back against a fir tree."

"Was he dead?"

"Naw. But I suspect he had a dislocated shoulder and a bear of a headache." He grinned. "And little green needles sticking in him from hoof to hindquarters." He turned serious. "That wasn't the last of 'em, but I kept my place. I finished 'proving up the place and got a deed."

His eyes found hers again. "It's not just finding your Pa that's driving me. Something happened to me somewhere around Silverville. I've got to find out what it was, and why I shiver in my boots whenever I think about that place. I'd be better off dead than the way I am. Can you understand that?"

She searched for her voice. "I've known a lot of men, John. They all turned out to be nothing but selfish beasts." Her voice wavered. "You're different from them. You're honest and caring and. . ." Biting her lips, she blinked hard. "What will I do if something happens to you?"

He dropped her hand and stretched his arm around

her. "You've given me a good reason to come back with a whole skin." There were those gold flecks again. "I love you, Lisa. And I will come back. That's a solemn promise." He gently kissed the corners of her glistening eyes, then reached down to her lips.

She clung to him, feeling completely protected for the first time in her life. He pulled her into a warm hug and said into her hair, "When I come back, will you marry me and come to the Lazy B?" He gasped. "I remember! My ranch."

Lips parted, Lisa looked up into his face; the wonder in his expression matched the joy cascading in her heart.

"It's about twenty miles west of Silverville, before you get to Sundance. I can see the fork in the trail where you cut off to go to the house." Almost nose to nose with her, his brilliant smile warmed Lisa. "After the explosion, I built a new cabin with three bedrooms and the biggest kitchen north of Laramie." He pulled her closer, her head nestled against his shoulder. "Will you go there with me when this is all settled?"

"I give you my solemn promise."

He kissed her again then turned her loose and grinned. "I'm going to hold you to that promise, Lisa. Don't even think of changing your mind."

The front door opened, and Jimmy Bledsoe stepped out. Lisa and John widened the gap between them, both turning to see who was there.

"Ready, Lisa?" the dark-haired youngster asked, glancing from her to John.

Lisa got to her feet and reached for her bag. "Send me

word when you can, will you?" she asked John.

"Will do." He stood and moved onto the porch so Jimmy could pass. "I won't be leaving for a few days."

She mounted the mare and waited for Jimmy to tie on her bag. The ride home seemed doubly long and ten times as lonely as the trip to the Circle C she had taken ten days before.

∾

From astride a trotting buckskin, Steve Chamberlin hailed the house as he arrived the next day after breakfast. From his window, John saw the tall, lean rancher hug his wife and lift Ruthie from her arms. Banjo came from the corral to slap his boss's back and swap howdys while Jeremy and Lobo did a happy dance around them all, the dog yapping and wagging his whole body.

Lying on his bed, his good arm under his head, John watched the happy family in the yard and felt a comfortable glow. One of these days he would have a home like the Chamberlins. He held the thought close, warming himself.

Half an hour later, Banjo knocked twice on his door and stepped through, bringing with him the mouth-tingling aroma of baking bread. His faded blue eyes seemed to laugh at some private joke. This was the first time John had seen him without his stained and weathered Stetson. "I've got a proposal for you, young man," he said, letting the door bump closed. "How would you like a riding partner?"

Head tilted, John watched him, waiting for him to explain.

"Yesterday, young Jimmy said that he don't have a job lined up for the summer yet, so I asked Chamberlin if Jimmy can stand in for me until we get back."

John sat up and eased the sling around his neck. "You're serious, aren't you?"

"Serious as the apoplexy." Banjo stumped farther into the room and rested his bones on the chair. "The question is, how soon will you be able to travel?"

Lifting his weak arm, John used his other hand to pull the sling's knot over his head and remove it. He flexed his elbow. "I reckon it's about time to do some finding out."

They left three days later, at the first light of dawn.

eleven

"Ever been up toward Silverville?" John asked Banjo when they stopped for a nooning near a sloshing, stone-filled stream. The men sat on either side of a tiny camp-fire where a coffeepot bubbled and four thick strips of bacon sizzled in a pan.

"Not for almost ten years," Banjo said, fork in hand. He eased the holster away from his jeans and stretched out one leg. "I did some mining in the Black Hills a while back, but never found much. If I'd only tried a few miles north, I might have made the strike that caused so much commotion in those parts last summer."

John worked his stiff right arm in and out. "You just said a miner's favorite words: 'If I'd only.' "

Banjo chuckled. "You've got 'em pegged all right. Mining is as close as I ever come to gamblin' in my life." He forked two pieces of meat onto a plate and held them out to John. "I've been meaning to ask your advice on a biblical question that came to me recently," Banjo said, filling his own plate.

Puzzled, John asked, "What is it?"

"You think there's anything wrong with me marrying my widow's sister?"

John paused, uncertain about what kind of answer Banjo expected of him. "I reckon not," he said finally.

The old-timer laughed deep in his belly. "Sorry, son, but I'm afraid I have to disagree. I could never marry my widow's sister because I'd be dead."

Looking skyward, John grunted and shook his head. "You got me fair and square." He chuckled and dug into his supper.

When he finished, he picked up his coffee cup. "Before I left Juniper I saw a man—just a glimpse of him—but I can't get him out of my mind. He was on the boardwalk in Juniper. A few minutes later, I was laid out on the ground with a bullet in my shoulder."

"You think he's the gent who drygulched you?" Banjo asked.

"I can't say for sure, but he sticks in my mind—a dark fellow with kind of a squashed-down face. His hair started growing just above his eyebrows." He took a bite and chewed slow. "I keep having a nightmare about a man with a big whip. He's standing over me while I'm on the ground. I never get a look at his face."

"You ever get bullwhipped?" Banjo lifted the coffee-pot and refilled the two tin cups.

John's cheeks billowed out as he exhaled, thinking hard. "I want to say no, but something won't let me." He looked at Banjo, fear in his eyes. "Sometimes I wonder if I'm going crazy."

"Simmer down, son. You're as sane as I am." The old-timer chuckled. "Some folks would say that ain't much comfort." Lifting his cup, he slurped coffee. "How long did the ride to Juniper with Lisa take you?"

"A week. We had to move slow there at the last and

ended up stopping a day for Lisa to rest. The trip was real hard on her."

Banjo stood and kicked dirt over the fire. "We'd best put some miles behind us. Chamberlin's waiting for me to get back."

Standing, John murmured to himself, "Chamberlin's not the only one waiting." He swallowed a grin and settled his hat.

Banjo mounted his lop-eared donkey, Kelsey, and sang, "Alas, and did my Savior bleed. . ."

When they cantered away from the clearing, John was humming along.

❧

When she reached home, Lisa found her mother lying on her bed, moaning. Exhausted tears streamed from her eyes and trickled toward her ears. Jessica sat beside her, sobbing into a handkerchief. When they heard the bedroom door open, both women turned to see who had come in.

"Lisa!" Sally wailed. "Your father is dead."

Lisa ran to her mother. "Don't say that, Mama!" She flung herself across Sally's prone form, hugging her and crying into her shoulder. "He can't be."

"He is," Jessica gasped. She gave a sobbing hiccup. "Indians got him, I bet."

Lisa raised up and glared at her sister. "You're not helping, Jessica. Keep your horrid guesses to yourself."

Jessica's heart-shaped face looked like a strawberry, puffy and red. She opened her mouth to reply, but Lisa cut her off. "If you say it's my fault, I'll whip you right here. You know I'll do it, too."

The younger girl covered her face with a damp hand-kerchief and wept in earnest.

Sally sat up, effectively putting Lisa aside, and reached for Jessica. "Now, now, dear. Don't take on so." She glanced at Lisa. "Make us some tea, will you, honey?"

Lisa stood frozen to the floor, her heart feeling as though it would explode. Remorse, sorrow, and fear swelled and swelled until her chest was a pain-filled mass. Pulling in a sharp breath, she rushed to the door and closed it behind her.

Her hands shook so badly that she could hardly fill the copper teapot. A fire still smoldered in the kitchen stove, so she added a small log through the round open-ing on top and replaced the cast-iron circle lid. While the pot heated, she reached into the cabinet for the square tin of black tea.

Her father was dead. She was slowly accepting the fact. If he was alive, he would have contacted them or come home by now. More than a month had passed since he left Juniper on that stage.

She ran stiff fingers across her scalp, dislodging her combs but paying them no mind. How could she live with herself?

Several minutes later, she remembered why she had come to the kitchen. Filling the metal teaspoon with dry leaves, she clipped the top shut. She moved the steam-ing pot from the hot circle to a cool one, opened the lid, and propped the spoon inside.

She opened three cabinet doors before she found the

wooden tray in its customary spot. Then she reached to the shelf above for three cups.

"Well, look who came home," a smooth voice said from the doorway.

Lisa whirled to see Marshal Brinkman grinning at her. He smelled strongly of sweet cologne.

"Mama sent for me," she told him. "The sheriff from Denver has given up searching for my father."

The marshal's chiseled features turned sympathetic. "I'm sorry to hear that. I'd offer to look for him myself if I weren't already on another case."

Reminded of her fears about John, Lisa turned back to the tray. "I need to get back to my mother. She's over-wrought." Quickly filling the cups, she lifted the tray. "Excuse me, please."

"Certainly. I'll rest my weary limbs in the living room." He stood aside for her to pass. She could feel his eyes on her until she turned the corner into the hall.

Her mother and Jessica seemed calmer when Lisa arrived. Sally reached for her tea and sipped it, her face so swollen that it looked painful. Jessica took her cup from the tray and held it in her hands. She didn't look at Lisa.

"Marshal Brinkman just came in," Lisa said, watching Jessica.

"Get him a drink, will you, Lisa?" Jessica said, patting her fiery cheek. "I can't let him see me like this."

Feeling like she was on the outside of their grief, Lisa carried her untouched cup back to the kitchen. She saw the back of the marshal's sleek black head from his spot on the sofa. He had his head angled back as though deep in thought.

She poured her cup of tea back into the pot, swirled the teaspoon to get more flavor from it, and poured the steaming liquid into a wide bowl so that it would cool. Adding some sugar, she carefully emptied the bowl to half-fill a tall glass then topped it off with cool spring-water and carried the drink to the living room.

"Would you like some tea, Marshal?" she asked when she reached the sofa.

He smiled up at her as he took the glass from her hand, his fingers brushing hers. "Why, thank you, Miss Lisa. And, please, call me Chandler, remember?" He touched the seat beside him. "Won't you join me for a few moments? I'd like to hear more about your father."

Her mind too numb to think up an excuse, Lisa sat. How could he be so callous as to want to talk to her at a time like this?

"There's nothing I can tell you about Daddy. He left here on the stage and disappeared somewhere in Wyoming. That's all anyone knows."

"Where have you been for so long?" he asked gently. "I've missed seeing you around."

Lisa swallowed and touched her mouth. "I was helping a sick friend."

"You're a lady of many talents, not only beautiful but compassionate as well."

Intensely uncomfortable, Lisa stood. "Please excuse me. I've got to see to my mother."

He tucked his chin down and leaned slightly forward.

"Certainly. Give my condolences to your mother and your sister."

When she reached the bedroom, Lisa found Sally alone with her eyes closed. Not wanting to disturb her sleep, Lisa trudged up the stairs to her own room. She locked the door behind her, lay across the faded quilt, and buried her face in her pillow.

Lisa walked through the next three days in a thick fog. She prepared small meals and worked hard at staying away from Jessica's reproachful eyes. Her mother and Jessica had not appeared in the main part of the house since Lisa's return. If not in her mother's room, Jessica stayed locked in her own. Lisa worried that they would break down, but she couldn't convince them to do otherwise.

Surprisingly, the marshal became more relaxed in his manner and suggested that he eat with Lisa in the kitchen. He dried dishes for her twice. Not wanting to offend their guest, Lisa reluctantly allowed him to help, but she feared that Jessica would suddenly decide to come out and stumble into what appeared to be a cozy tête-à-tête. Worse, the younger girl would never believe Lisa's explanations.

While Lisa and Chandler lingered over a second cup of coffee on Friday evening, a knock at the back door made Lisa start. She hurried to open it while Chandler watched from his seat at the table.

The Bledsoe boy stood outside, his face flushed with exertion.

"Jimmy, what's wrong?"

He pushed a slip of paper toward her. "I just rode in. John asked me to give this to you."

"Thanks. Would you like a cup of coffee?"

"Can't," he said, stuffing hands into the pockets of his jeans. "Mama will want me to come home right away." He stepped off the back stoop and Lisa closed the door.

She opened the page and read, *Banjo and I are going north. Won't be back for a while. Don't worry. John.*

"Bad news?" Chandler asked.

"Uh. . .no." She shoved the note into her skirt pocket. "It's nothing, really." Returning to the table, she asked, "Would you like more coffee?"

"I've had plenty, thanks." He stood and gathered plates. "I'll help you with these dishes, then maybe we can play some checkers. What do you say?"

"I suppose so." She picked up her plate and glass and turned toward the counter. Chandler moved in the same direction, his coffee cup in his left hand. They collided. The coffee cup skimmed off the saucer and shattered on the floor.

"I'm terribly sorry," he said, kneeling to pick up the pieces.

"It was my fault as much as yours." She set down her dishes and hurried for the broom.

"I'm not usually so clumsy," he said when she returned. "I'll replace the cup, of course, if you'll tell me where your mother purchased it."

"It came off Harper's back shelf. It's nothing special, believe me. Don't trouble yourself."

Three minutes later, she left the kitchen to fetch her

mother's dirty dishes. Jessica had refused to eat tonight.

When she returned, Chandler had his white sleeves rolled to the elbow and was pouring hot water into the dishpan.

"I'll wash," she said, unbuttoning her cuffs.

Throwing a dishtowel over his shoulder, he made a small bow. "Whatever m'lady desires." His gentle laugh should have warmed the atmosphere. Instead, it sent a surge of distaste through Lisa. She wished that Jessica did not find him attractive either.

Arms deep in sudsy water, Lisa rubbed a cloth over plates and cups while Chandler rambled about his case.

"The man I'm after seems like a nice fellow to those who don't know him. He's got an innocent face and likes to talk religion." He shook his head, deeply regretful. "It's a shame he's got such a black heart."

He glanced at Lisa's tight face. "I apologize. I'm boring you." Reaching toward the pan of clear water beside her, he seemed to lose his balance and knocked against her.

She lurched back, indignant.

He lay down his towel. "I don't know what's wrong with me tonight, Lisa. I think I'd best sit down for a while."

"Are you sick?" she asked, watching his face. His mouth drooped at the corners and his eyes seemed a little unfocused.

"I don't think so," he passed a hand over his forehead. "I'll sit down a while, though. I feel a little weak." He ambled out of the room, reaching out to touch the corner of the door and the back of a dining room chair as he passed them.

Lisa finished scrubbing the last pot and set it to drain on a towel. She stopped in the kitchen doorway, shocked to see Jessica on the sofa beside the marshal.

"Forgive me for neglecting you," Jessica was saying to him. "My father and I were very close."

Chandler leaned toward her. "I've been worried about you, Jess. You don't know how badly I feel about your father. I wish there were something I could do to help."

She sighed. "Your being here is a comfort, Chandler. I just had to come out and see you for a while."

Lisa edged around the dining room table toward the hall and solitude. Relieved that Jessica would take the marshal off her hands for the evening, she was also troubled at the relationship that seemed to be developing between them.

She reached her room and pressed fingertips to her throbbing temples, trying vainly to put two thoughts together in her grief-muddled brain. She had to break Jessica away from that man.

She reached into her pocket and drew out John's letter. Holding it to her lips, she sat on the bed to read it through again and kiss the signature. *Please, God, protect him and bring him back to me.* The page still tight in her hand, she lay down and stared at the ceiling.

twelve

The next morning, Chandler Brinkman appeared while Lisa was frying eggs. Brilliant sunshine and the aromas of baking biscuits and bubbling coffee made the kitchen an inviting place.

"Good morning, Lisa," he said, pulling out a chair at the enamel table.

A metal spatula in her hand, she looked up, surprised. "Good morning. What keeps you in today?"

He smiled. "Would you like to take a buggy ride with me later?"

She turned her attention to the eggs bubbling in the pan.

"How about a picnic?" he went on. "I found a small lake just north of town. We could ride out in time for lunch."

Lisa turned her back toward him, trying to think. She did not want to go, but maybe this was a chance to divert his attentions from Jessica.

Lifting four sunny-side-up eggs from the pan, she slid two on each plate and cracked four more into the skillet.

"I'll pack a basket," she told him, her voice casual. She had planned to scrub some clothes this morning. Maybe she could still do the washing if she hurried.

A nagging voice told her she should not be going out

while her family was in mourning. She considered the thought, then pushed it away. It was more important to protect Jessica from that man than to follow a tradition that might not apply to them. They could not even hold a funeral until they were sure Daddy was really gone.

Lisa was puffing from exertion but ready when Chandler drew his horses to a halt in front of the house shortly after eleven o'clock. She breezed into her mother's room, where Jessica sat in the rocking chair and read aloud from *Harper's Weekly* to her mother on the bed.

"I'm going out for a couple of hours," Lisa said, pulling on her white gloves. "I've left fried chicken and boiled potatoes on the back of the stove whenever you're ready to eat."

"Where are you going?" Sally asked. Sitting up, she let the counterpane fall away from her cotton nightgown.

"Is it Chandler?" Jessica demanded. "You've been spending a lot of time with him lately, haven't you?"

"Why not? You've been hiding in the back of the house."

Jessica took a step forward, her finger marking her place in the magazine. "Keep your claws out of him, Lisa. He's mine."

"He's no good for you, Jess. I know he is handsome as a Greek god and he knows how to make a girl feel special, but he's trouble. Believe me."

Her sister's eyes sparked fire. "You're trying to put me off so you can have him to yourself, aren't you?" She stood.

Unwilling to get into a scene with Jessica, Lisa drew

back. "I'll be home by midafternoon." She pulled the door shut and hustled to the living room where Chandler waited with the loaded picnic basket over his arm.

"All set?" he asked, looking her over from crown to flowing skirts.

She lifted her yellow calico bonnet from the shelf by the door. "Ready," she said and swished past him. She had worn an extra crinoline today, making her pink skirts billow. Laying the bonnet over the braided double crown on top of her head, she tied the ribbons.

Outside, she paused when she saw the black surrey, a bobbing fringe around its flat roof, the sides open to catch the breeze.

"How lovely! Where ever did you find it?"

Chandler chuckled. "I rented it from Mr. Harper at the Emporium." He held out his arm. "May I?"

"Thank you," she said, suddenly glad she had come. Chandler may not be her first choice for a companion, but the fresh smell of timothy and sage wafting down from the hills made her want to spread her wings.

With practiced ease, Chandler handed her up to the carriage seat. Pulling her skirts inside the half door, she glanced toward the house. Was that Jessica's face in the window?

Before she could tell for certain, Chandler sat close to her on the leather seat and shook the reins, leaving the house far behind.

"What a beautiful day!" Lisa exclaimed when the buggy left the last of Juniper's buildings behind. Ahead lay rolling hills with spruce and pine clumped between rocky boulders. A chipmunk darted up a scrub oak as they passed. It paused on the trunk to look back and flick its stubby tail before scampering to the safety of the top.

"I know how to pick them," Chandler said. "A day and a girl."

She chose to ignore his meaning. "How far is the lake?" she asked.

"Just over that hill." He pointed far up the trail. "I found it last week and spent a solid hour just sitting there and feeling the quiet. It's a perfect spot for a relaxing afternoon."

"It sounds wonderful."

They drove for several minutes in silence. At the crest of the hill, Chandler tugged the reins and the horses turned off the trail onto a rutted lane.

Lisa tried to lean and sway with the surrey, but several times she had to hold onto the side to keep from slipping off the seat. The wheel on her side slid into a hole and she felt the jarring thump all the way up her backbone. "How much farther?"

"The place is just behind those trees," he said, an unusual suppressed excitement in his voice. Screened from the road by a long line of spruce trees, the horses slowed their pace and stopped, the harness creaking.

Tall grass dipped and swayed around them. On the other side of the carriage stretched a broad expanse of bare earth dotted with scrub brush.

"There's no lake here," Lisa said sharply. "Why did you stop?"

The marshal reached under his jacket and pulled out a

Colt revolver. His voice sounded flat. "This is where we get out." He aimed the gun at her middle and looked her full in the face, his handsome features slanted into something cruel. "You heard me. Get out."

She felt for the latch on the door, still watching the black bore in the gun. "You hurt me, and this country won't be big enough to hide you."

His lips formed a wicked grin. "Don't worry. You're only the bait to catch a bigger fish. If you're the praying kind like your milksop boyfriend, pray he'll come and rescue you."

Her jaw dropped until her mouth came open. "How do you know about him?"

"I followed you here from Laramie. This marshal badge was just to get your confidence. I knew if I waited long enough, you'd lead me to him. And you did."

Aghast, she cried, "I did not."

"I picked your pocket last night, my dear. Uncle Gil knows all."

"Who's Gil?"

His smile had a mean curve. "Yours truly." He waved the pistol. "Now get down."

Wishing she were dressed to run, Lisa jumped to the ground. Wearing button-up shoes and four crinolines, she would not get three yards before he caught her.

He followed her down and pulled two strips of rawhide from his pocket.

"My folks will miss me come nightfall," she said, her eyes darting left to right, desperate for a way out. "They'll send someone after you."

He chuckled. "You took care of that for me." Moving toward her, he wrapped the strip of leather around one wrist and reached for the other. "I left a note saying that we'd eloped. From what Jessica told me, that's nothing new for you."

She wrenched away from him and beat his chest with her fists. "How dare you!"

Laughing aloud, he caught her and threw her to the ground. Like a rodeo contestant working over a calf, he tied her wrists and ankles in less than twenty seconds, using his knee to hold down her kicking legs. "No sense screaming, Lisa," he said when she stopped to catch her breath. "Nobody can hear you."

She cried furious tears while Chandler unhitched the horses and pulled two saddles from the back of the buggy. Sitting up, she tried to wipe her sticky face on her skirt but had little success. She could feel bits of grass and twigs in her loosening braids.

Pausing before her, he smiled broadly, pleased with himself. "On the trail from Laramie, John always managed to stay far enough ahead of me so I couldn't get a shot at him. Then when I did get a chance, that meddling cowhand came along before I could finish him off.

"I spent days watching that cabin to see if I could catch him alone outside, but he never moved out of the house without someone around."

He leaned close to her face. "But with you as my hole card, I'll get him all right. He'll beg me to take him and let you go."

After saddling the horses, Brinkman opened the picnic

basket and filled his saddlebags with cold chicken, biscuits, and a tin of molasses cookies.

"Harper won't miss his surrey until late tonight," he said. "It'll take him a while to find it here. We'll have plenty of time to get away." He closed the leather flap and flipped the bags across his shoulder. "Okay, mount up," he said abruptly.

"Where are you taking me?" Her voice was ragged.

"Don't you know?" he mocked. "Back where you came from—Silverville. You're going to catch John Bowers for us."

"No!" She lunged at him again, straining her bonds until she tore her flesh.

Brinkman stepped back. He laughed when she landed facedown at his feet. "If I weren't such a gentleman, I'd give you a swift kick to teach you some manners. Now get up, you wildcat. We've got to ride."

Moaning out her frustrated rage, Lisa moved to the strawberry roan he had tied to a tree. Untying her ankles, he gave her a leg up to the stirrup. Her skirts lay around her in a jumble when she found a seat in the saddle, and she could not do anything to fix them. "I'm not exactly dressed for an afternoon ride," she called angrily as he mounted the bay.

He did not bother to answer. Looping the reins of her horse to his saddle, he set off at a canter.

ঝ

Less than a day's ride ahead of Lisa and her captor, John and Banjo rode into Laramie shortly before sundown of their second day on the trail. A booming metropolis compared to Juniper Junction, Laramie was a hub for soldiers, pioneers, and merchants. It had several wide streets and two private schools—one Baptist and one Catholic. A blacksmith's rhythmic hammering and tinny saloon music sounded above the rumble of wagons and clopping of horses in the street.

The men tied their horses in front of the stage station, a squat building with tiny windows and a bench leaning against the outside wall. Above the door a tiny sign said simply, Stage.

Seated at a low table with a long cash box on one side, the attendant—an obese man with a greasy face and red stubble on his three chins—looked up when they walked in. "Howdy, gentlemen," he wheezed. "Have a seat."

Hats in hand, Banjo and John sat in wooden chairs in front of the table, the only furniture in the room. The stench of an unwashed body was stifling. Banjo spoke first. "We're looking for a man who came through here about six weeks ago, a sheriff named Rod Feiklin."

The fat man pressed an arm against the table and stretched out a leg so he could lean forward. "Never heard of him. Lots of men come through here. I can't remember all of them."

"Feiklin stands about five feet eight, weighs over two hundred pounds."

The attendant chuckled deep in his chest. "A little guy, huh?"

"He's about fifty years old and has a big red nose," Banjo went on. "He would have been wearing his tin star."

Impatient to get back into the fresh air, John tapped his fingers against his knee while the big man considered.

"Come to think of it, maybe he did come through here." His eyes folded into half-moons as he squinted at the ceiling. "He bought a ticket for Silverville, I think it was. Impatient as all get out, he was. He acted like I could make the northbound stage leave the following day instead of at its usual time on Wednesday."

"Thanks for your help," Banjo said, standing to shake hands.

"Anytime," he replied, shaking hands with John next. "Pardon me if I don't stand up. Bad knees."

John and Banjo paused outside the door, settled their hats above their ears, and paced down the dusty street, nearly deserted this late in the day. Across from the bank, a three-story house had the roof and sides on but the empty windows and doors showed an unfinished shell.

"I wonder whose mansion that is," John said, pausing for a closer look. "It's got to be the biggest house in Laramie. Going up fast, too. I didn't notice it the last time I was here." He walked on. "There's no sense leaving right at dark. We may as well take advantage of being in town." He stopped beside the street and looked both ways. Pointing to a restaurant, a bathhouse, and a hotel, he said, "I only want three things—a six-inch steak, a hot bath, and a soft bed."

Banjo chuckled. "You and I'll get along just fine. Lead the way."

Five minutes later, they ducked through the low doorway of Sal's Kitchen to trade their money for what their empty stomachs were crying for.

꿍

The next morning when he awakened, John's head had a pounding pain so fierce that he could not eat breakfast.

"We'll stay here a day," Banjo said, staring down at his friend on the narrow bed. There was a decisive note in Banjo's voice.

"I can ride," John insisted weakly, his eyes closed.

Banjo chuckled. "You can't hardly lift your head." He drew a chair near the window. "Lie still and catch about eighty winks. Then we'll talk about riding."

The next thing John knew the sun was setting on the horizon. His head felt some better, but the hour was too late to head out. After another steak-and-potato meal, he took a long soak in a galvanized tub of steaming water and fell into bed for six more hours of oblivion.

Well before dawn, the two men were already five miles out of Laramie and heading due north. A chill wind blew down on them from the mountain peaks, causing them to turn up their collars and hunch their backs. The horses felt it, too, and eagerly picked up the pace.

By midmorning, the temperature rose until John took off his coat and laid it across the saddle in front of him. He spotted a ten-point buck in the distance, a majestic shape against the darkness of a stand of fir trees.

"Looky there," he breathed to Banjo, pointing.

The old-timer nodded. "Nice rack," he said. "I haven't seen one that big since sixty-eight down near San Antone. I was riding point for a cattle drive at the time and couldn't take off after that one either."

John grunted as the buck bounded into the trees. "There's more to life than having a big rack on your cabin wall."

"Yeah, like having a beautiful girl in your kitchen." He sent John a meaningful look and urged his donkey ahead.

Red around the ears, John grinned and fell in behind him.

The closer they drew to Silverville, the more tense John became. Fifty miles north of Laramie, he suddenly drew up, his face covered with sweat. "Hold on, Banjo," he called. "I need a breather."

Kelsey's head reached toward the sky as Banjo turned him back and rode close to John's mount. "What's wrong? You sick?"

John lifted his blue bandanna to wipe his face. "I don't think so. All of a sudden I felt like someone dumped a cold bucket of water over me." He took off his hat and ran shaky fingers through his hair.

Banjo scanned the area. "That rock face over yonder looks like a likely spot for a cave. Let's take a look. It's late enough; we may as well camp." He urged the donkey forward.

John slowly followed. A cave was exactly what he did not want to find. The thought of sleeping in a black hole made his face tingle and his stomach feel tight.

Unaware of John's agitation, Banjo moved along the side of the flat-topped orange boulder. "Nothing here," he said in a moment. "Maybe on the other side."

"Forget it," John croaked.

"What?"

"I'm not sleeping in a cave. I'll sleep in the open first."

Banjo cocked his head, studying the younger man's ashen face. "What's gotten into you, boy?"

"I don't know. But I'm not sleeping anywhere closed in like that."

Without further comment, Banjo found four beech saplings close together and tied a corner of his massive poncho to each, forming a makeshift roof to cover their bedrolls. "If it rains hard, we'll still get soaked to the hide," he said, "but it's better than nothing, I guess."

Moving slow, John took the saddle off Molasses and let him roll in the grass. He dropped his gear under the poncho and sat down to lean against his saddle and hold his head in both hands. He felt like the sky was a top, spinning round and round above him.

Banjo knelt next to him. "Say, you are sick. I hope we didn't jump the gun and leave the ranch before you were ready."

"No," he shook his head like a drunken man. "It's not that. It's my mind. All of a sudden, everything went out of kilter." He looked across the meadow beside them, intent, watchful. "Something happened here. Something bad."

"This is the middle of nowhere. What could have happened?"

John's face turned red. He shouted, "If I knew that, I wouldn't be in this shape, would I?"

Banjo drew his face back and squinted at John. "Where did that come from?"

"Just leave me alone for a while, will you?" he said gruffly. He slid down until his head rested against the saddle. Turning on his side, he drew his knees toward his chin and closed his eyes.

thirteen

When John awoke, darkness had fallen. A tiny glow to the right showed him the source of a wonderful smell: camp stew. Pulling his feet under him, he stood and shambled to the fire where Banjo sat with his back against a log, whittling at a stick.

The old man looked up when John reached the light. "Well, howdy. Feeling any better?"

John sank to the ground and rubbed his face. "To tell the truth, I'm not sure how I feel. It's sort of a cross between getting back on a horse after you've been throwed and working up the nerve to ask a girl to a church social. Kind of excited and terrified at the same time." He glanced at Banjo. "I'm sorry I got so rough with you a while ago. I don't know what came over me."

"Don't fret yourself, son. You've been under a lot of strain." Handing him a bowl of beef and potatoes in thick broth, he said, "I scouted around some while you were asleep. It looks like there's been quite a bit of traffic over yonder on the other side of that big rock. Not a trail exactly, but a lot of riders coming and going." He picked up his own bowl and lifted his spoon. "Come morning, I'll branch further out."

The stew tasted salty. John savored each bite. "We're

at least twenty miles south of Silverville."

Banjo nodded. "The stage comes along here, if I'm not mistaken."

"That's right. The only trail from Laramie to Deadwood is just across that rise. That's the same stage the sheriff was riding on his way to fetch Lisa."

"Is that a coincidence or a clue?" Banjo asked. He poured himself a second cup of coffee and held out the pot to refill John's cup. "I wonder when the next stage is due."

"That's one question I can't answer." John turned his attention to the food and finished the stew. "Did you find any water close by?" he asked when his plate was scraped clean.

"About fifty feet over yonder." Banjo pointed with his chin. "It's too dark to see to the dishes now. We'll catch them in the morning."

John handed the plate to Banjo and aimed through the brush toward the stream, finding his way by moonlight and sheer instinct. When his toes sank into damp earth, he sank to his haunches and felt ahead of him until his hand splashed into cool water. Leaning forward, he washed his face then cupped his hands and drank deeply.

An owl hooted and John looked upward. A crescent of bright moon shone behind the dark web formation of cottonwood branches intertwined with pine. In a moment, he bent and drank again.

Back at the campfire, he told Banjo, "I'm tuckered. See you in the morning." He untied his bedroll from the cantle, lay down, and immediately sank into deep sleep.

❧

"I think we should change our tactics from here on," Banjo told John the next morning while they ate the last of Megan's cold biscuits for breakfast. "We've got to start playing like Injuns. I'm not a spooky man, but something about this situation gives me the by-jimminies. I couldn't sleep last night. I kept waiting for a bogey man to jump out'n the bushes."

John didn't know whether to laugh or not. "Are you joshing me?"

"I'm dead serious, son. Something evil's around here."

John swallowed hard. "I sure am glad you came along. If I were alone, I'd probably be hiding with my tail curled up between my ears." He shook his head, disgusted.

"You've got just as much grit as the next man," Banjo said gruffly. "Whatever's got you buffaloed, it's more than just a little nick on the skull." His bushy eyebrows twitched. "If you're too stubborn to believe that, you've got your head in the sand and the wrong part of you is sticking up."

Grinning, John reached up to adjust his hat. "I'm not sure if that makes me feel better or worse." He cleared his throat. "What makes you so sure you know what's going on inside my brain?"

"If I was a woman," he said, chuckling, "I'd call it intuition. Since I'm not, you can choose whatever name you want."

Swallowing the last crumb of his breakfast, Banjo reached for his saddle. John did likewise. Keeping their mounts single file, they stayed close to the flat-topped boulder.

"Here's the spot I was talking about," Banjo said, kicking his boots from the stirrups and swinging down. "Lots of traffic, but no real trail. Does anything about this place ring a bell with you?"

John paused in the saddle to take in his surroundings. They stood in the middle of a dusty stretch behind some trees with hills rolling away to the east, the boulder south of them now. Below them, a rutted trail wound away to disappear in the distance. Dropping to the ground, he squatted next to Banjo to study horseshoe prints scuffling the dirt.

"These are two, maybe three days old," Banjo said. "See how the edges are blown away? None of them are sharp anymore."

Circling slowly, scanning the area, John froze for an instant, then leaned forward until his face was a foot from the ground. "Look at this one," he said, pointing to a horseshoe print with a *V* notched on one end. "I know that horse."

"Who owns it?"

He looked at Banjo, shocked. "I do."

The old-timer knocked his hat to the back of his head. "You don't say."

"I had three horses when I came to town that day—Molasses, Ginger, and. . .Sally." He spoke slowly as though pulling the words from deep inside a barrel, leaning over to grasp each one. "Sally's a black with a white chest and one stocking. I bought her for thirty dollars from a stranger in Sundance. He wanted the money to stay in a poker game."

He reached over to touch the print. It crumbled.

His gaze sweeping the ground, Banjo swung north looking for more prints. "There's another one, heading northeast. Let's see where they lead."

Stopping often, they inched along until noon. At one o'clock the trail died.

"Wouldn't you know it?" John said, his voice showing frustration. "We're finally getting somewhere and—*poof*—they disappear like someone in a sideshow act."

Banjo rubbed his jaw. "They must have taken the main trail for a ways. We can take it, too, and see where they turned off."

John massaged his sinking stomach. "How about some grub first?"

The old-timer grinned and reached for his saddlebag. "Today's menu is beef jerky with jerky for dessert." He threw a strip to John, bit off a chunk of his own piece, and stuck the rest in his pocket.

Keeping an eye out for other riders, they rode north on the trail for almost a mile. Finally, John said, "I hate to admit it, but my head feels like a blacksmith's anvil on horseshoein' day. Can we find some shade and rest for a while?"

Banjo squinted at the sky. "I'd say we're about an hour away from suppertime. I'll stir us up some flap-jacks and fry some more bacon."

"Sold," John said. He pointed toward a stand of pinion pine to the northeast. "How about there?"

Trotting easy, they entered the trees and soon found a narrow stream just deep enough to fill a coffeepot without letting in sand with the water. Banjo led Kelsey across the stream and staked him where he could drink and find grass.

Knowing how Molasses loved an open space to stretch, John let the horse drink then unsaddled him and let him roll in the grassy meadow for a while. He would stake him later.

John gathered sticks and built a fire while Banjo dug the makings of supper from his saddle. The cowhand ambled to the stream with a cup and his cooking pot turned mixing bowl.

Two minutes later, John heard a boot snap a twig behind him. He whirled, gun in hand, and found himself between three men—one tall and fleshy, one scrawny, and one short. Each held a Winchester, his face hard, his eyes flat.

The blood rushed to John's temples. For an instant he thought he would pass out.

"Stand up, partner," the smallest man said in a shrill, harsh voice. Shorter than the others by at least five inches, he seemed to be the leader. "Drop your hogleg, and we won't put a bullet in you."

"Yet," the slim man on the left muttered, his face tilted back, his expression taunting.

"Wh–what do you want?" John stammered.

"We want you," Shorty said. "Come along peaceful like and you won't get hurt."

"Where's your saddle?" the third man asked. He had

bristly brown hair and a long, puffy face with a bearlike body to match.

"Yonder by that pine tree." John kept his eyes away from the area where he had last seen Banjo, hoping the men had not spotted him.

Hairy arms big as ham hocks lifted the saddle while the slim man caught Molasses and brought him in.

John stood like a statue, praying that Banjo would not stumble into the hornet's nest that had suddenly swarmed around him.

"Tie him up, Ben," the leader shrilled. The big man pulled a piggin' string from John's saddle and lumbered toward him, a mean smile showing the wide gap between his front teeth.

"Welcome to the Sandusky operation, mister."

Those words sparked across John's brain in a flash of white light. He saw the rawhide tightening around his wrist, smelled the foul odor of the man binding him. Suddenly, a rush of violent emotions and soul-crushing memories took away his breath. The next instant, the world spun, and everything went dark.

≈

Unaware of his friend's predicament, Banjo knelt by the stream and stirred his flapjack batter. A moment later he dipped up more water to add to his pot, moving in practiced silence. He never made noise in the woods. Long years of living by his wits, in a land filled with renegades and outlaws, had made the habit a vital part of his life.

Moving his spoon through the pale yellow mass, he added a few more drops of liquid and suddenly stiffened.

Men's voices drifted toward him, the words unintelligible. Who had come into camp? Setting down the pot, he crouched lower into the bushes, setting down his feet with special care.

He eased back down the trail toward camp and dropped to his belly when he heard a shrill voice say, "Tie him up." The camp came into view as John collapsed on the ground.

"Put the bag on his head," the short fellow said, "in case he wakes up before we get there."

"This guy looks familiar, Andy," the slim man said, glancing at the leader.

"Al's right," the bruiser panted, raising John's limp body to his shoulder like he was a sack of grain. "This guy looks like the man we're hunting. Some luck, huh? Finding him like this?"

The small man holstered his gun. "Tie him to his saddle, Ben. We'll deliver him to Hogan before we put him on a team. He may have sent Gil on a wild-goose chase."

Al hooted. "Hogan never makes mistakes. You know that." They all laughed, a harsh, mocking sound.

"In his dreams," Ben added.

Banjo eased back to the stream. Out of sight, he crossed the water and grabbed Kelsey's reins. The donkey made a rasping noise. Banjo clamped a hand over his nose and waited.

When he heard the sound of pounding hooves, he leapt into the saddle with surprising agility for his years, urged Kelsey across the stony stream, and held him to a slow walk on the trail.

He reached the clearing in time to see four horses disappear into the trees on the other side of the meadow. A big man held Molasses's reins and did not seem to notice that John's head sagged hard to one side of his saddle.

Banjo circled the clearing at a trot and followed them a few yards to the right of their trail, keeping track of them using his ears instead of his eyes.

When they reached another clearing, he again veered right to stay within the trees. He didn't intend to catch up to three armed men for a showdown. He would wait until they stopped and watch for a chance to split them up or catch them by surprise.

After three miles, Banjo ran out of good cover. He drew up under a wide cottonwood and watched his quarry ride into a small settlement. A long narrow building that looked like a bunkhouse stood on the east of the yard; a wide stable and corral on the south and a tiny clapboard house on the west all appeared gray in the late afternoon sun. He blinked and took a second look. The windows of the bunkhouse were all boarded over, as were a few on the house, as well. What was this? A deserted ranch? An outlaw hideout?

Leaving Kelsey under the tree, the old cowhand pulled his Sharps .56 from its scabbard and walked close enough to see sunlight reflecting in the remaining windowpanes of the house. He dropped to a belly crawl until he reached the last bit of scrub brush before the yard. There he froze.

Ten yards ahead of him a potbellied sentry wearing

filthy mining garb and carrying a Henry rifle ambled from the bunkhouse to the main house and about-faced.

Moisture sprang up on the Banjo's brow. This was a heap more than he had bargained for.

About that time, a troop of at least twenty men marched in single file from the north. Each man had a long rope around his left elbow, joining them together. Shoulders slumped, covered with grime, they kept their eyes on the ground in front of them as they trudged ahead.

Banjo squinted. What were they? Convicts? There was not a jail of any size from here to Laramie.

John Bowers was nowhere to be seen. Two of the four horses Banjo had trailed here had also disappeared. Easing his Colt from its holster, Banjo settled down for a long wait.

fourteen

Still a day's ride behind John, Lisa gritted her teeth against the pain that had become her constant companion. Her wrists had deep abrasions from the rawhide's constant friction against her soft skin. Old wounds from her initial ride over this rugged trail had reopened with searing vengeance so that contact with the saddle meant sheer anguish. This time she had neither witch hazel along to relieve her distress nor a sympathetic companion to give her time to rest.

Her pink dress lay in ragged tatters around her ankles, her crinolines torn beyond repair. She had not washed her face or combed her hair since the day she left her mother's house for that bogus picnic by the lake.

"We'll camp here," Chandler said, swinging down from his horse. He let Lisa stay in the saddle while he scouted around for sticks to build a fire. Chin resting on her chest, she stared straight ahead, her mind a muddle of agonizing sensations, her prayers mainly for the safety of a tall, sandy-haired man with calm blue eyes and a gentle touch.

A gruff voice broke through her stupor. "Okay, missy. Time to light and set." The deep mellow tones he had used in Juniper had disappeared altogether. The real Chandler Brinkman—known to his friends as Gil

141

Harris—was no gentleman.

He tugged at her elbow, and she slumped to the ground. Her legs were nothing but twin pillars of pain. Pulling her up by the shoulders, he half-carried her to a nearby pine and set her down beside it. "No sense tying you up anymore," he mumbled. "You can't run no way."

Lisa leaned against the rough bark and let her eyes drift closed. If only she was just pretending that her legs wouldn't work. If only she could run like the wind and lose herself in the woods, where the breezes flowed cool and soft and there was plenty of water rushing down from the mountains.

Gil pulled a greasy paper filled with salted meat from his pack and sliced off a couple of thick slabs with a dirty pocketknife. The evening after they had left Juniper, he had carefully packed away his tan suit and changed into greasy overalls and a flannel shirt with a hole in the elbow. His white hat he slipped into a cloth bag and tied behind his saddle, exchanging it for a flat-crowned hat the color of mud. The transformation was miraculous. Gil had missed his calling. He could have starred in a traveling drama troupe.

The smell of frying meat brought Lisa to full awareness. Her mouth tingled at the aroma rising from that dented skillet. Her last full meal had been breakfast the morning before her capture.

Gil pulled her tin of cookies from his pack and popped off the lid. He glanced at Lisa. "Here, have some supper," he said, tossing two of them onto her soiled dress.

Pulling her legs around, she winced and swallowed

hard. "Could I have some water?" Her voice was raspy and weak. She felt almost surprised at the sound of it.

Gil nodded absently and lifted his canteen by its canvas strap. He stood briefly to swing it over beside her and resumed his cooking.

Licking her lips, Lisa stretched her bound hands toward the canteen and lifted it, unscrewed the metal cap, and raised it, shaking, to her mouth. The tepid liquid trickled across her tongue and down her dry throat. She gulped greedily.

"Hey!" Gil jerked the canteen away from her, jarring her teeth. "You'll get yourself sick drinking that way." He picked up the cap where it dangled from a tiny chain around the canteen's neck and screwed it on.

Revived somewhat by the water, Lisa held the cookies and stared into the fire. She had been on the trail for four days. It seemed an eternity. In the saddle before sunup, riding until dusk with no midday break. How much more could she stand?

"How long until we get there?" she asked suddenly, her voice cutting through the noise of crickets and cicadas stirring in the night.

Gil waited to finish chewing his bacon before he said, "We'll be there tomorrow night. Probably after dark." He grinned, his teeth gleaming in the firelight. "Just think, you may be able to sleep on a real bed." He chuckled as though he had just told some kind of private joke.

Ignoring him, Lisa ate the first molasses cookie with the haste of dire hunger. The second she consumed in small bites as though savoring it would unwind the knot in her stomach. She had no hopes that Gil would share his meat with her. He hadn't thus far. Why would he change now?

The pins holding up her hair had fallen out two days ago, leaving two prickly braids that brushed her neck and caused constant irritation. When one of them caught on the tree bark, she reached back and pulled it forward, snapping the thread at the bottom and combing it out with her fingers. Soon the second braid also lay loose about her shoulders.

She raked her hands across her scalp, pulling out leaves and twigs and longing for a hot tub of water and a cake of Octagon soap. Her first chance, she would get some of the expensive, scented soap that Harper kept under the counter for his special customers.

Gil unrolled his blanket near the fire. As talkative as he had been at the Feiklin house, he wasted few words on his captive. Picking up a strip of leather from his pack, he came toward Lisa and knelt before her, his hands nimbly working the strap around her ankles. "Just in case you recover your strength after that hearty supper." He paused long enough for a mocking smile. "Sleep well, little princess."

Lisa clenched her hands, fighting the urge to strike at his grinning face. The last time she hit him, he hadn't given her a drink for half a day.

Sensing her desire to lash at him, he chuckled as he stood and walked away.

Pulling her hair over her shoulder to keep it out of the

dirt, Lisa lay on her side on the hard earth. Her eyes closed and weary tears sprang from their corners. *John,* she cried in her heart, *where are you?*

John woke up to find himself strapped to a wooden chair in the middle of a bare room with the windows boarded over. A glimmer of light came under the door, and some men argued in the next room.

"I say we kill him!" Andy said.

A calm, well-modulated voice replied, "Why didn't you do it when you found him then?"

"We wanted to see what you thought first, boss," Al replied.

Andy added, "He's already escaped once. Why should we give him another chance?"

"Because we're short of men. We lost three more this morning." The head man paused. "I agree that he must be disposed of, but we can put him to use while we do it. Give him half rations and put him on the digging crew."

Squinting, John stared into a black corner, memories washing over him. He had come to town with twenty beeves to sell in order to buy spring supplies. At Silverville, he had made the sale, filled his pack saddles, and gone on his way. Ten miles south of town, the same three men had kidnapped him and brought him here.

Over several weeks, he had taken gold nuggets from his digging and dropped them down his shirt. With the help of several other prisoners, he had escaped during the weekly camp cleanup. Through sheer brass and dumb luck, he had retrieved two of his horses and his pack before he fled.

Twenty minutes out of camp, someone had come galloping after him on a palomino with plenty of bottom. There had been a mad chase covering five miles with several shots fired at him. John headed for Silverville, hoping to get some help. That is when he must have been wounded, because the next thing he remembered was waking up at Lisa's cabin.

The door to the dark room flung back, and a bulky figure appeared shadowed in the light from the next room. "Okay, Bowers. We're taking you to the bunkhouse. You're lucky. You can have your old cot back. The guy who got it after you just kicked the bucket."

From behind him, Ben tugged at the straps that bound John's arms to the chair, then pulled his hands toward his back and tied them together. "On your feet now."

Feeling dizzy, John hesitated and got a slap on the side of his head.

"I said, on your feet!"

Blinking, John staggered after his tormentor to a door at the back of the room and found himself outside in the moonlight. He stumbled once, then ducked to avoid a second blow.

In the yard, the fat sentry paused to watch them cross. Rattling a key in the lock, Ben flung back the door of the bunkhouse, shoved his prisoner inside, and slammed it shut again.

Squinting to see through the dull glow of a single lantern hanging from the ceiling, John leaned back against the rough-hewn door. Swallowing, he fought back a rush of despair. After all he had been through, to end up where he had started. How could he bear it and keep his sanity?

Someone pulled at the rope on his hands, and they came loose. John rubbed his wrists. Before him stood two rows of bunks with a center aisle the width of a broom handle. Hollow-eyed faces covered with whiskers and a thick coating of dust stared at him, waiting for him to move or speak.

"Hey, John!" A dull voice came from his left, about halfway down the row. "Over here. It's me, Charlie. You can have the bunk next to mine again."

"Charlie Randolph?" Like a man in a nightmare, John lurched down the center aisle, touching each bunk for support as he passed. He licked his thick lips. "Charlie, I need a drink."

"Get him a drink," someone called from the end of the line. A gray-whiskered man with skeletal cheekbones came toward him with a tin cup clenched in a wavering hand.

John emptied the cup in three gulps and handed it back. "Thanks." He met Charlie at the next bed.

"Welcome home," his friend said with a poor attempt at a smile. "We've been lonesome around here without you."

John placed his palms on the top bunk beside Charlie but was still too shaky to heave himself up. Hands reached out to help him.

When he lay back on the bare mattress, Charlie's

gaunt face came toward him, his nose like an eagle's beak. "John? What happened to you, boy? I thought you were going to get us some help."

"They followed me out of here and put a bullet in my head. It only creased me, but I lost my memory. I couldn't remember where I'd come from or why." He scanned the anxious faces surrounding him. "I'm sorry, men. I let you down."

"How's your head?" Charlie asked.

John touched his temple, suddenly aware that he had lost his hat. "It's a mite touchy. I still get powerful headaches sometimes, but I'll live, I reckon."

"Not if you stay here too long," a slow voice drawled from somewhere in the back of the crowd.

"How'd you get caught?" someone asked from the darkness.

"I met a girl."

Somebody whistled. Another man gave a low hoot.

When the noise died down, he said, "Her father's missing. I came to look for him."

Charlie asked, "What's his name?"

"Rod Feiklin. He's a sheriff."

"Hey, Feiklin," Charlie hollered. "John here's been a-lookin' for ya."

John rose on one elbow and tried to focus his eyes to see through the faint light. In a moment, he saw a wide shadow that slowly formed into a man who had once been husky. He had a bulbous nose and thin, wispy hair. His jowls shook when he spoke.

"You've seen Lisa?" His voice had a firm resonance

that came from somewhere around his knees.

"She's at home with your wife, Sheriff. I found her in Silverville and took her home to Juniper Junction."

"How's Sally?"

John hesitated. "She's taking it hard, your being gone and all. The girls are a mite worried, too."

Feiklin thumped a shaky hand against the wooden bunk. "We've got to bust out of here!" He glanced around. "Look at us, a bunch of tough men acting like kids afraid of a mean schoolmaster." He ran a trembling hand over his face. "God help us. We've got to get out."

John sat up. His head felt clearer than it had since he woke up. "Listen," he whispered, waving them closer. The men gathered near until he could feel their breath and smell their desperation. "I've got a friend on the outside, an ol' codger named Banjo."

"Hot diggety," Feiklin said, glancing around. "I know him. He's a salty old cowhand. He packs a Sharps fifty-six, and always hits his target."

Muted excitement swept through the twenty men huddled close.

"We'll help all we can," Charlie said, "but we don't have much strength left. After another escape attempt last week, they cut our rations again." He ran a trembling hand over his spiky hair. "That Gil knows a dozen different ways to kill a man."

John grunted. "So do I. After the first time." His voice grew stronger. "We'll need some kind of weapons."

"Let's break apart one set of bunks to use for clubs," Feiklin said. "If Banjo doesn't make his move tonight, a couple of us can double up, small guys like Peterson and Smithy, until he does. This place is like a fortress. Banjo may need to size up the territory before he makes his move. He can't see much in the dark."

Several of the bigger men began tugging at the last bunk near the back wall. Five minutes later, the splintering of wood told of their progress.

Lying on his back, John closed his eyes. Banjo had better be out there. If not, they were sunk.

fifteen

After the initial excitement died down, the men returned to their bunks wide-eyed and waiting until, one by one, they fell into troubled sleep. John lay awake until dawn. Now that he knew what he was afraid of, his fear had turned from sheer, numbing terror into a galvanizing dread that would give him the strength to fight back. He clenched and relaxed his right hand. It felt good. Almost the same as before he was injured.

He must have dozed. When the front door slammed, he sat up, blinking and dazed. Harsh sunlight streamed in for an instant before a big man stepped through.

"All right, on your feet! File out for the grub line!" It was Ben with a wicked gleam in his slow-moving eyes.

Charlie nudged John. "Better move quick. Ben's looking for trouble this morning."

John slid his feet to the floor and stayed close behind his friend. When they reached the doorway, Ben stared at John. "Thought you'd run, did you? Well, look at you now. You ain't so all-fired smart."

Forcing his eyes to look straight ahead, John kept a lid on his temper. To lash out now would only make matters worse.

Standing at the steps to the main house, Al had a long-handled ladle in his hands beside a tall pot. The men filed toward him and waited while he slopped some kind of brown porridge into wooden bowls and handed them out.

When John reached him, he tipped the ladle and dumped most of its contents back into the pot. What landed in John's bowl would not fill three good-sized spoons. "Eat hearty," Al said, his lips pushed out, his eyes mocking.

Following the others across the yard to lean against the outer wall of the bunkhouse, John glanced furtively around, wondering if Banjo were there or not, wishing he knew a way to communicate with him.

Tipping up the bowl and raking porridge out with his fingers, Charlie eyed John's portion. He licked his fingers and said, "Here, take some of mine. You won't last two days on that kind of feed, you just wounded and all."

John covered his bowl with his hand. "Thanks, Charlie, but you need it more than I do."

A few minutes later, Al came along with the empty pot in his hands and each man dropped his bowl into it. When Al shambled back to the big house, they turned as one man to face the yard, each holding out his left arm. A hank of rope over his shoulder, Ben progressed down the line, binding elbows with the smooth, quick movements born of long practice, and the group moved toward the northern rise.

John glanced back and saw Ben bringing up the rear, a long bullwhip in his hand.

At the top of the hill, he saw a small shanty three hundred yards ahead, near the base of a mountain. A few yards away, a black, timber-outlined hole told why they were here. The Sandusky Mine, the richest strike since the Comstock Lode, lay just ahead.

A lanky man with a Winchester leaning on his shoulder unlocked the shanty and began throwing shovels and picks to the men. Grimly, without speaking, they trudged ahead into the gaping mouth of a living death—no light and no breeze to cool their sweaty faces and brighten their weary minds.

At the entrance to the cave, John stiffened. The old, nameless terror came at him with a rush. His feet froze in his boots. He could not move.

"You there!" Ben bawled. "Get on in there." He cracked the whip.

"John!" Charlie said, shaking his arm. "Snap out of it."

White and shaking, John drew in two deep breaths and rolled his head from side to side, like an angry bear. Finally, he lifted his right foot and stepped inside. When he felt the darkness swallow him whole, he broke into a sweat. "I can't go on," he murmured. "I can't."

Feiklin stepped back two paces and paused beside him. "What's the trouble?"

"I can't stand closed-in places," John said. "Never could. I've got to get out. I can't breathe."

Feiklin jerked him around. "Get a grip on yourself, boy! You've got to go ahead. If you go back outside, they'll kill you, sure."

John swallowed. "It was bad when I was here before, but this time I can't make it. I feel like my chest's caving in."

"What about us?" Charlie demanded. "You're the only one strong enough to attempt another escape." He grabbed and shook John's wounded shoulder.

The pain shocked John out of his panic. Drawing in a loose-lipped breath, he knocked Charlie's hand away. "Okay. I'm all right. Let's go." Letting his mind go blank, he found his place in the row of men digging at the end of the tunnel. Moving in rhythm, he worked the stiffness out of his shoulder until he hardly felt any pain at all.

෴

The sun's final rays flickered above the horizon as Banjo watched Ben hustle John across the yard and lock him into the bunkhouse.

When the last light of day disappeared, so did Banjo's hope of getting John out before tomorrow. Moving in darkness was difficult when a body knew where he was headed. Trying such a feat on new ground was nothing short of foolhardy.

Edging back to Kelsey, he turned the donkey away and rode for half a mile to a thick forest, which sloped down into a lush valley. Within the safety of dense darkness among the pines and junipers, Banjo spread out his blankets and slept for six hours.

Morning light found him back at the camp with his shirtfront dug into the dirt, watching for signs of life. He kept his position when the men filed out for breakfast and when they headed off for parts unknown in the north.

Still on foot, he circled wide, out of sight of the camp. He came closer on the north side until he stopped, his target in view—a mine with men swarming over it like so many ants and armed guards out front, one of them with a bullwhip.

Lying flat in the dust until noon, he pulled some jerky from his pocket and sipped water from his warm canteen, ignoring the soft rumble of his neglected stomach. The workers before him did not slacken their pace for the noon hour or the supper hour either. As twilight approached, they plodded back to camp. Banjo stayed behind them long enough to see the guard click a large padlock on the shanty and turn his duties over to another man.

Banjo reached the shelter of his lookout post near the yard just in time to see the last few prisoners drop their empty bowls into Al's pot. They then proceeded wearily into their bunkhouse prison. Now that he knew the routine and the lay of the land, a plan took shape in his mind—fairly simple, but with the Lord's help, it just might work.

While Banjo watched, a husky guard paced from the clapboard house to the makeshift jail, his Henry rifle aimed at the ground. He turned and retraced his steps, taking his time as twilight turned to dusk. A full moon, already high in the sky, gave an eerie cast to the landscape, where shadows covered the hollows and moonbeams made white stones glow.

While the guard's back was to him, Banjo left the security of his bush and, bent over at the waist, ran for a depression near the bunkhouse. Holding his Sharps away from his body, he flung himself down, pulled off his hat, and raised his head enough to get a look at the guard.

In the center of the yard, the sentry suddenly stopped. He turned full circle, peering through the moonlight as though he could feel Banjo's stare from the shadows. Finally, he stretched his arms wide, arched his back, and loudly yawned. He shifted the Henry to his shoulder and continued his rounds.

Easing his legs to a more comfortable position in the shallow ditch, Banjo hunkered down, watching for a chance to overcome the guard.

Two men stepped out of the house, one wide and tall, the other slim. They paused to speak to the sentry, then mounted and rode out, passing ten yards from where Banjo lay.

Time was running out. That guard would need a replacement soon.

Tense as a bowstring, Banjo felt around on the ground for a fist-sized stone and waited, his breath keeping pace with the guard's footsteps. At the bunkhouse door, the man turned. He was humming "Old Susanna."

Three paces later, Banjo sprang like a cougar after a rabbit. The guard collapsed. Pulling him close to the back side of the bunkhouse, Banjo dug a couple of rawhide strings from his pocket and tied him, hand and foot. He stuffed a dusty bandanna into his mouth for good measure.

Returning to the ditch for his rifle and hat, Banjo circled wide to the north.

Across the rise, he squatted behind a cedar tree and

saw the dim form of the small tin-roofed shanty near the mouth of the mine. He hesitated, his ears alert for a human sound. There it was. The soft grating of boots on earth.

When the lanky guard reached the back of the shanty, Banjo hoofed it to the next patch of brush. He played the game until he was close enough to hear the man's gentle cough and make out the outline of his Montana Slope Stetson against the sky.

Inching forward another three feet, he crouched behind a boulder that reached to his chest, waiting for just the right moment to spring.

"Say, Tom!" a shrill voice shouted from the darkness.

Banjo jerked like he had been struck. He huddled close to the rock, his face peeking around the side of its cool surface.

A short, slim man's form strode over the rise. "Got any rolled cigarettes with you?"

"Yeah." Tom propped his rifle against the shanty while he held the bottom of the pocket and pulled a package out with his other hand. He dug a forefinger into it. "Here's one." He held it out. "That makes four you owe me. Ask Roger next time."

Grabbing the cigarette from the guard's hand, the man headed back without saying so much as a thank-you.

Banjo closed his eyes and prayed. On his way back to the main house, would the borrower notice the absence of the other guard? A moment later, the door to the house slammed, and Banjo let himself breathe a little.

Tom shook his head at his friend's rudeness, then

hunched over with his hands cupped around a flaming match to light a smoke for himself. He stood about six feet from Banjo, facing away.

The old man came to his feet and reversed his hold on his Sharps rifle. Swinging it by the barrel, he caught the man on the side of the head with a thunk that sounded like a melon falling off a wagon.

The guard tumbled sideways and lay still, the match flung harmlessly away. Banjo picked up the man's Winchester and propped it against the rock beside his Sharps. He took the revolvers from both of Tom's holsters and stuffed them behind his own waistband.

Taking hold under Tom's arms, Banjo dragged him about two wagon lengths to the left and into the mine entrance, his boots making twin trails in the earth.

Banjo pulled off the man's belt and boots, looping the belt around the guard's knees and pulling it tight. Then, he folded back the strap of leather and tucked under the end—not hard to loosen once the man came around, but he wouldn't be doing any running with his legs asleep.

Returning to the shanty, Banjo used a large stone to hit the padlock and knock it loose. He scraped a match on the corner of his boot sole, and raised it high to see what the storage room held.

Against the back wall stood six crates marked "Dynamite." Three tall cans of kerosene were nearby. Against the left wall hung several tools: hammers, a wide crosscut saw, a small handsaw, crowbars, and a length of rope. Below them lay two dozen shovels and several pickaxes. Two stacks of dented, galvanized buckets almost reached the ceiling on the right.

The match went out and Banjo stood in the dark, his mind cataloguing the items he had just seen. This was the hand he had been dealt. Now, how was he going to play it?

Pulling out his knife, he cut off a length of rope and returned to the mine to tie the hands of the unconscious guard.

Fifteen minutes later, he made another wide circle around the compound. This time, the bunkhouse was his objective. Besides the two rifles, he carried a coil of rope and three pickaxes, which made quiet movement a challenge.

The moon shone too brightly for Banjo's comfort. A gentle breeze felt damp against his face. Now that both hands were occupied, his nose began itching like mad. He raised one shoulder and bent his face toward it. Not very satisfactory, but that would have to do for now.

The sound of two horses approaching from the south sent Banjo down on his belly. He lay in a shallow depression in the darkness, his Sharps tight in his right hand, the other weapons close by on the ground. One of the Colts in his waistband gouged into his stomach. He reached under his shirt to adjust it.

The horses halted across the yard near the main house where the light splashed from a window. One of the riders dismounted. He walked around his horse, out of sight. A few minutes later he reappeared, his arm around the shoulder of a smaller companion who seemed to have trouble walking.

The door opened, flooding them with light as they moved inside. Banjo blinked. He would know that long wavy hair anywhere. The small rider was Lisa Feiklin.

Banjo lay there for a full five minutes without moving. He had known the same sensation as a boy when he fell off a tree limb and landed flat on his back. Like then, he had to take a few minutes to catch his breath.

What was Lisa doing here of all places?

Loud angry voices came from an open window in the main house. "Why did you bring her here? We've already got Bowers. You know what they do to a man who hurts a woman? Gil, your head is like a gourd, full of nothing but air."

"How was I to know you had him?"

"Whether we had him or not, you shouldn't have brought her here. We can't just turn her loose now, can we? Ever think of that?" A door slammed and the conversation cut off.

His face grim, Banjo rose to a crouching walk and approached the bunkhouse. He tapped lightly on the back door and prayed there was no guard posted inside. The Sharps held ready, his mild eyes continually scanned the grounds around him.

"Yeah?" a weak voice called.

Banjo backed up to the door and angled his mouth close to the splintery wood. "It's Banjo. I need to talk to John." He swallowed. Each second seemed like hours.

"Banjo?" John's low voice vibrated with hope. "Can you get us out?"

The old-timer spoke into a crack around the door frame.

"I've got some weapons for you. The third window down from here has a crack in the boards big enough to pass a revolver through. I've got three here. I'm leaving a rifle and some picks by the back door, too."

He moved down and handed the weapons inside. Invisible fingers caught them. "John?" he whispered.

"I'm here."

"The minute you hear a big explosion, blast away at the lock to the back door, and everybody pile out. We'll meet south of here in the woods. I left Kelsey over there."

"What about horses?"

"When you pass the corral, take them with you. Tell the men to ride out like their tails are on fire. Then you meet me behind the house."

"What do you have in mind?"

"I just saw Lisa ride in with a big hombre. They've got her in the house."

"What!"

"Simmer down, boy. You'll be no good to me with your brain in a stew."

"Sheriff Feiklin's in here."

"Well, what do you know?" Banjo passed a hand over his leathery face. "I'd best be going. Get yourselves ready in there."

Familiar with the ground now, Banjo bent low and crab-walked through the darkness. The journey back to the supply shanty took less than fifteen minutes. Easing the door open, he lifted a can of kerosene and unscrewed the top.

A heady smell filled his nose and throat as he backed out of the door and off to the left thirty paces, letting the liquid slosh out of the can in an unbroken line. When he figured that he'd gone far enough, he hustled back to the doorway and lay the can on its side, in line with the damp streak at the door. Kerosene glug-glugged out.

Banjo scampered back toward the end of the line. Halfway there, the moon went behind a cloud, and he could not see the trail. He dropped to a crouch, his eyes squinting toward the heavens. In a moment, the billowing mass of gray moved on and a beam of light shone down upon him.

The damp trail looked like a giant black snake. Banjo lit a match and dropped it on the reptile's head. With a whoosh and a flash, the fire zipped along the ground. Banjo raced to dive behind the boulder, his hands over his ears, his eyes squeezed tight.

Ka-boom!

Through his closed eyelids, he could see surging brilliance. He smelled the inferno, felt the heat. A few seconds later, bits of metal and wood fell around him.

sixteen

Inside the bunkhouse, John blasted the lock on the back door the moment he heard the explosion. Three shots and the door swung free. Instantly, a wall of club-wielding men pressed forward, shoving John aside in their haste. When the last one passed him, John looked over to see Sheriff Feiklin beside him, a pistol in his hand.

"Let's go. Lisa's in trouble."

They stepped into the night, their eyes already accustomed to the gloom. Instead of heading for the corral, the mob in front of them ran toward the main house, shouting and waving their sticks.

"What are they doing?" John cried. "They're going to get killed. All of them."

"Let's go around back of the house," Feiklin said, stepping forward.

John caught his sleeve. The door to the house opened, and a tall man shoved Lisa outside ahead of him, a black ropelike noose looped around her neck. Behind him came two men with rifles aimed at the crowd.

"Come any closer and this little girl pays," the big man shouted.

John felt a physical stab in his middle. He stared at Lisa's form outlined in the door and recognized the object around her throat. A bullwhip.

That voice pulled up every nightmare that John had agonized through these past months. The man with the whip had Lisa.

Hidden by deep darkness beside the bunkhouse, John waited for his insides to quiver and melt. Instead they pulled together into an iron knot. He cocked his pistol. "I'm going after him," he told the sheriff.

"She's my daughter," Feiklin wheezed. "You'll have to shoot me to keep me from coming along."

Turning, John ran on his toes until he reached the back of the bunkhouse. He found the empty ditch and dropped into it. Grunting, the sheriff landed beside him.

John whispered, "We'll crawl on our bellies until we get past those guys' line of sight, then we'll bust into the house the back way and surprise them."

"Just get me close to that man who has Lisa." Feiklin's voice was hard. "I'll take him with my bare hands."

John licked his lips and moved down the ditch. *Not if I get to him first.*

On the steps, the two men with guns pressed forward. Andy shouted, "Throw down your weapons or somebody's going to die. Do it before I count five or I'll shoot the closest man to me."

A few men threw down their clubs. The mob lost its heart and became a milling, confused crowd.

"Now get back into the bunkhouse. All of you." Andy started down the stairs as John rounded the corner of the house, heading toward the rear. With the sheriff breathing down his neck, he cocked his revolver and tried the back door. It was open.

The room inside was dark, but light from another area came through the doorway. Taking wide steps, John stepped across the bare pine floor and peeked around the doorjamb. The next room, a kitchen, stood empty as well.

Keeping close to the wall, John headed toward the front of the house. At the door to the sitting room, he stopped and stared at the back of a wide pair of overalls and a flat-crowned hat. He knew that man. It was Gil Harris, the most cruel of the gang.

In an instant, he stood behind Lisa's tormentor with his gun pointed at the man's neck. "Turn her loose."

Harris stiffened.

In one movement, he flung Lisa away from him and dropped into a squat. Moving like a frog, he bounced up, his shoulder knocking John sideways.

Clawing for a hold and finding none, John fell off the step, his gun flying out of his hand. The big man moved to the side of the step where the light spread out the door and onto the ground. The end of the long bullwhip flipped at the ground by the big man's ankles.

On his back, John looked up at the man in his nightmares—Gil's face hidden by the shadow of his hat.

"Whatsa matter, Bowers?" Gil asked. "You look a little down in the mouth." He chuckled and popped the whip. "It's about time you learned a lesson."

Using his heels, John scooted away and tried to roll out of his reach. Before he'd moved far, the whip caught him around the waist and spun him back.

From the place she had fallen, twenty feet away from

him, Lisa screamed, "John!"

Gil let out a harsh laugh and pulled back for another lash.

Chest heaving, John watched the lithe movements of his opponent. *Get ahold of yourself, Bowers. Use your brain instead of your brawn.*

The second lash caught him across the chest, making him cough. Only two blows and he felt like his torso was on fire.

Bracing himself, John stayed still, his mind focusing on the movements of the other man. When Gil drew back for a third strike, John watched for the moment his arm began the arc downward.

The same instant, he raised his left arm high across his body. The whip caught him just below the elbow and wrapped three times around. When it was tight, John jerked with strength born of desperation. The whip flew from Gil's hand.

John flung the weapon away.

Though it seemed like a century since Gil had released Lisa, mere seconds had passed. Sheriff Feiklin and Banjo leapt from the shadows and got the drop on the two men pointing guns at the crowd.

John saw them, but Gil didn't notice. He jumped from the steps, intent on his prey.

"John!" Lisa called again, struggling to get up. "Watch out. He's the man who kidnapped me. He's brutal."

Lisa's words lit a fire in John's brain. He got to his feet.

"Whoa, there!" Banjo called. "We've got everything

under control. There's no need to fight him, John."

"Let him come, Banjo," John said. "We've got something to settle here." Elbows bent, hands loosely clenched, he moved lightly on his feet, waiting for his chance.

"What do you think you're doing, Bowers?" Gil taunted, his fists high in front of his face, bearing down on John like a train engine. "You're yellow as a canary. You know you are."

John's senses tensed to an agonizing pitch—screaming for action. He lunged in as his fist came up and caught Gil just below the breastbone, a pile driver with every ounce of his strength in it.

The big man crumpled to his knees, his hands covering his belly, then fell on his side in the dirt.

"Don't count your canaries before they're hatched, Gil," he said, stepping back. He waited for his shoulder to ache, but the pain never came.

Turning toward the crowd, he searched for only one face. He saw her hair instead—a massive tangle with bits of twigs in it. She lay tight in her father's arms, her head pressed to his chest. She seemed to be sagging against him.

As John reached her, she said to her father, "I'm sorry I've caused so much trouble, Daddy. If anything had happened to you, I'd never forgive myself."

His voice unusually husky, he said, "When I was a youngster I had to learn my lessons the hard way. I reckon you're like your old dad." Bending down, he kissed her cheek.

John came near.

"Lisa, honey, I think someone wants to see you," Feiklin said.

She lifted a tear-blotched face and saw John. Sobbing, she held out her arms to him. He pulled her to him and realized that she was dead weight in his arms.

"What's wrong, Lisa?" he cried, swinging her up into his arms as though she were a small child. "What did he do to you?"

"He made me ride until my legs were raw and bleeding. He only had one bedroll, so I had to sleep on the ground. And he wouldn't give me hardly anything to eat." Bright tears glimmered in the light of the lantern. She tightened her arms around his neck. "I thought he was going to kill you."

Holding her close, John laid his cheek against hers, and she dampened them both with fresh tears.

The sheriff touched his daughter's hair. "I take it you kind of like this fellow."

Turning toward him, she nodded, a new glow on her face.

Sheriff Feiklin's slow grin made his jowls quiver. "I'm glad you finally learned what a real man looks like." He said to John, "Let's get these varmints to the closest jail and head home. I'm hankering for some of Sally's dried-apple pie."

They looked up to see Banjo stride out of the house with his Sharps pointed at a spectacled man wearing a black suit. "Hey, Feiklin," Banjo shouted. "Recognize this hombre? It's Patrick Hogan, from the assayer's office in Laramie. He weighed out my diggings many a time. He's the brains behind this two-bit outfit."

"Then those slimy brothers, Ben and Al Hardy, must have been the brawn." Lisa nodded toward the two as several of their previous captives shoved them into the center of the yard. A shiver of revulsion raced down Lisa's back as she recalled Ben Hardy's frequent invitations for an evening stroll during her weeks at the Silverville Diner.

Feiklin threw a length of rope to Charlie, hovering nearby. "Hog-tie 'em till we can deliver these rogues to the marshal in Silverville."

Charlie pulled the hemp tight between his fists and approached the unhappy outlaws. "It'll be a pleasure."

While the freed workers headed to the corral to find their horses, John pulled Lisa into the shadows beside the house and held her close. "I thought my heart would stop when I saw you here," he murmured. "I wanted to charge across the yard and knock Gil flat for daring to lay his filthy paws on you."

His lips met hers for a long moment. Then he spoke into her hair. "You haven't changed your mind about marrying me, have you?"

"Not a chance." Snuggled in his arms, she reached over for another velvet kiss. For the first time in her life, she knew exactly where she was meant to be.

"John?" Banjo called a few minutes later. "Where are you?"

Loosening his hold on his intended, John stepped into the light from the still-open door. "Here we are."

The old-timer strode toward them. "We're going to ride into Silverville to turn those hombres over to the law. Then we'll head south. Some of the men have already cut out for home." He glanced at Lisa and grinned. "For someone in such a misery, you sure do look happy." To John, he said, "I take it congratulations are proper?"

"Yes, sir." John's expression matched Lisa's.

Banjo chuckled. "I'd shake your hand but both of them seem to be occupied." He turned back the way he had come. "It's time to mount up."

"How will I get back?" Lisa asked. "I can't ride anymore."

"You can sit sideways in front of my saddle. Silverville is only a few miles from here. Don't worry; I'll hold on to you." He gave her a little squeeze.

Lisa leaned her head closer to his ear. "While we're on the subject, there *is* one thing you've got to agree to before I'll stand before a preacher. Cross your heart."

He smiled into her eyes. "Anything your heart desires."

"Buy me a carriage. Once we get to Silverville, I'm not sitting on another horse for as long as I live."

A Letter To Our Readers

Dear Reader:

In order that we might better contribute to your reading enjoyment, we would appreciate your taking a few minutes to respond to the following questions. We welcome your comments and read each form and letter we receive. When completed, please return to the following:

Rebecca Germany, Fiction Editor
Heartsong Presents
PO Box 719
Uhrichsville, Ohio 44683

1. Did you enjoy reading *Lisa's Broken Arrow*?
    ❑ Very much. I would like to see more books
       by this author!
    ❑ Moderately
       I would have enjoyed it more if _____
       _____
       _____

2. Are you a member of **Heartsong Presents**? Yes ❑ No ❑
    If no, where did you purchase this book? _____
    _____

3. How would you rate, on a scale from 1 (poor) to 5 (superior), the cover design? _____

4. On a scale from 1 (poor) to 10 (superior), please rate the following elements.

    _____ Heroine   _____ Plot

    _____ Hero   _____ Inspirational theme

    _____ Setting   _____ Secondary characters

5. These characters were special because _____

_____

_____

6. How has this book inspired your life? _____

_____

_____

7. What settings would you like to see covered in future
    Heartsong Presents books? _____

_____

_____

8. What are some inspirational themes you would like to see
    treated in future books? _____

_____

_____

9. Would you be interested in reading other **Heartsong
    Presents** titles?   Yes ❏   No ❏

10. Please check your age range:
    ❏ Under 18   ❏ 18-24   ❏ 25-34
    ❏ 35-45   ❏ 46-55   ❏ Over 55

11. How many hours per week do you read? _____

Name _____

Occupation _____

Address _____

City _____ State _____ Zip _____

·····Hearts♥ng·····

·······Presents·······

Great Inspirational Romance at a Great Price!

Heartsong Presents books are inspirational romances in contemporary and historical settings, designed to give you an enjoyable, spirit-lifting reading experience. You can choose wonderfully written titles from some of today's best authors like Peggy Darty, Sally Laity, Tracie Peterson, Colleen L. Reece, Lauraine Snelling, and many others.

When ordering quantities less than twelve, above titles are $2.95 each.
Not all titles may be available at time of order.

SEND TO: Heartsong Presents Reader's Service
P.O. Box 719, Uhrichsville, Ohio 44683

Please send me the items checked above. I am enclosing $_____.
(please add $1.00 to cover postage per order. OH add 6.25% tax. NJ add 6%). Send check or money order, no cash or C.O.D.s, please.
To place a credit card order, call 1-800-847-8270.

NAME _____

ADDRESS _____

CITY/STATE_____ ZIP _____

HPS 6-00

Hearts♥ng Presents
Love Stories
Are Rated G!

That's for godly, gratifying, and of course, great! If you love a thrilling love story, but don't appreciate the sordidness of some popular paperback romances, **Heartsong Presents** is for you. In fact, **Heartsong Presents** is the *only inspirational romance book club* featuring love stories where Christian faith is the primary ingredient in a marriage relationship.

Sign up today to receive your first set of four, never before published Christian romances. Send no money now; you will receive a bill with the first shipment. You may cancel at any time without obligation, and if you aren't completely satisfied with any selection, you may return the books for an immediate refund!

Imagine. . .four new romances every four weeks—two historical, two contemporary—with men and women like you who long to meet the one God has chosen as the love of their lives. . . all for the low price of $9.97 postpaid.

To join, simply complete the coupon below and mail to the address provided. **Heartsong Presents** romances are rated G for another reason: They'll arrive *Godspeed!*

"Come in?" he asked Ashley as they parked in his driveway.

She didn't hesitate, which relieved him. "Sure," she said and climbed out.

His own exit took a little longer, and Ashley was waiting for him on the porch by the time he rolled up the ramp.

Nell took a quick dash in the yard, then followed eagerly into the house. The dog was good at fitting in her business when she had the chance.

"Stay for a while," he asked Ashley. "I can offer you a soft drink if you'd like."

She held up her latte cup. "Still plenty here."

He rolled into the kitchen and up to the table, where he placed the box holding his extra meal. He didn't go into the living room much. Getting on and off the sofa was a pain, hardly worth the effort most of the time. He supposed he could hang a bar in there like he had over his bed so he could pull himself up and over, but he hadn't felt particularly motivated yet.

But then, almost before he knew what he was doing, he tugged on Ashley's hand until she slid onto his lap.

"If I'm outta line, tell me," he said gruffly. "No social skills, like I said."

He watched one corner of her mouth curve upward. "I don't usually like to be manhandled. However, this time I think I'll make an exception."

* * *

CONARD COUNTY: THE NEXT GENERATION

Dear Reader,

Those of you who have been with me for a while in Conard County have probably noticed my concern with our returning vets and their problems, especially PTSD. That has been a cause of mine for a long, long time.

Since it has finally been accepted that PTSD is a real syndrome, efforts have been ongoing to find better ways to treat it and better ways to help people deal with it. Advances have been made in terms of medication and therapy, but there's not one magic solution that works for everyone. Many times it can only be eased.

Service dogs have recently come into the picture. They are able to sense the PTSD victim's beginning distress and give a warning to get the sufferer to a safer place. Sometimes the dogs themselves are enough to provide stability when the world goes crazy, and can pull the victim back from the edge and keep them calm and anchored in the present.

In this story our hero, Zane, not only suffers from PTSD, he is also a paraplegic in a wheelchair. Like many of the people I have known who are paralyzed, he deals well with his physical disability, choosing to accept it as a challenge. But Zane also has PTSD, and his service dog, Nell, does more than pick up his socks or open doors. She calls him back.

She also brings Ashley into his life, a schoolteacher with a huge heart. Nell is apparently determined that Zane not remain alone.

Rachel Lee

A Conard County
Homecoming

——

Rachel Lee

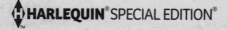

Recycling programs
for this product may
not exist in your area.

ISBN-13: 978-0-373-62351-8

A Conard County Homecoming

HARLEQUIN®
www.Harlequin.com

Printed in U.S.A.

Rachel Lee was hooked on writing by the age of twelve and practiced her craft as she moved from place to place all over the United States. This *New York Times* bestselling author now resides in Florida and has the joy of writing full-time.

Books by Rachel Lee

Harlequin Special Edition

Conard County: The Next Generation

The Lawman Lassoes a Family
A Conard County Baby
Reuniting with the Rancher
Thanksgiving Daddy
The Widow of Conard County

Montana Mavericks: 20 Years in the Saddle!

A Very Maverick Christmas

Harlequin Romantic Suspense

Conard County: The Next Generation

Guardian in Disguise
The Widow's Protector
Rancher's Deadly Risk
What She Saw
Rocky Mountain Lawman
Killer's Prey
Deadly Hunter
Snowstorm Confessions
Undercover Hunter
Playing with Fire
Conard County Witness
A Secret in Conard County

Visit the Author Profile page
at Harlequin.com for more titles.

To Ashley R. Granger, a very sweet lady
who offered to let me use her name for a character.
Thanks, Ashley!

Chapter One

Zane McLaren pulled into the driveway after dark. Operating the hand controls of his van with the ease of familiarity, he parked so that the newly constructed ramp would be near the sliding door in the side of the van.

It was ready. His old family home had been prepped for his wheelchair existence, and only the service dog on the front seat beside him seemed happy to realize the journey had ended. Nell, a golden Lab, woofed her approval as he turned the engine off.

Arriving after dark had been a choice. By now everyone in Conard County, Wyoming, who cared to hear about it knew that Zane McLaren was coming home for the first time since his parents' funerals nearly fifteen years ago, and the ramps he'd had constructed before his arrival let them know his condition if they hadn't already heard from workmen or his housekeeper.

The fat had probably already been chewed over by those who remembered: great high school athlete in a wheelchair nearly twenty years later as a result of his military service. Heads had shaken, and curiosity had awakened.

The thought of that curiosity had brought him home in the darkness. He wasn't ready to face a parade of well-wishers, many of whom would be mostly interested in discovering how bad off he was.

He'd lost the use of his legs two years before. Rehab had followed, then adaptation to his new life. Now he just wanted to be left alone. He'd have been more anonymous in a city, but the wars had left him with other scars, too. He couldn't handle the noise, the traffic, the constant crush of people. He needed quiet and solitude, and he figured this was the best place to get it. Once everyone understood he just wanted to be left alone, they'd leave him alone. As he seemed to remember, people in this town were mostly respectful.

If it didn't work out, he'd sell the house and move on. There was nothing holding him anywhere now.

He pivoted the driver's seat and used his arms to lift himself into the wheelchair behind. Ready to go. Nell jumped off her seat and came to stand beside him, her tail swishing happily.

She was probably desperate to hit the grass, he thought with mild amusement. After locking himself in place, he pressed a button. The van door pulled open. The pneumatic lift extended itself, carrying him outside. Then another button lowered him to the ground. When he'd rolled off, Nell jumped to do her part. She nosed yet another button, the lift rose and retracted, and the door eased closed. He scratched her ears, letting him know he was pleased with her. She grinned back at him, happy.

"Go do your stuff," he told her.

She didn't need a second suggestion. She dashed immediately to the grass and began sniffing around. Apparently, the choice of where to relieve herself required some investigation.

Smiling faintly, he reached for the wheels of his chair and pushed himself toward the ramp. It felt sturdy beneath him; the slope was gentle enough, with a surface that had been roughened with outdoor carpeting to prevent slipping. Safe in the rain. Heating wires below for the snow. Perfect for his needs.

He reached the porch and pivoted, waiting for Nell. For the first time, it occurred to him that he might need to hire someone to clean up after her. He could do it unless the ground became soggy enough to bog down on, or the snow too deep. Little things. It was most often the little things that caused him problems now and often took him by surprise. He already had a handle on most of the big things.

Sitting still, waiting for his dog, he allowed the autumn chill to start reaching him. A lot of warmth came from movement, as he'd learned, and he wasn't moving much at the moment. Still, he waited patiently. Nell was on new ground and probably needed to check it all out. He didn't have the heart to interrupt her.

At last Nell finished up and came racing to his side. He unlocked the front door with a key that was as old as he was, and together he and his dog entered his old home, flicking on lights as he went. He ignored the stairway to the two upstairs bedrooms. That part of the house was unavailable to him—not that he needed it.

The house smelled different, but it had been thoroughly cleaned, and work had been done inside to ready things for him, like a new shower and a sturdy framework over his bed. Eventually, if he decided to stay, he'd have to change the kitchen as well, but that was going to be an expensive proposition. Right now he could manage well enough with standard counter heights and sinks. He'd had to learn.

The dog bowls were waiting, and he quickly filled one with water and bent to place it in Nell's new feeding stand. Most things he'd been able to ship ahead, but some had had to be replaced. This was one of them. While she lapped water eagerly, he went to the pantry and found that the housekeeper he'd hired had filled it as directed. Everything was on the lower shelves or floors, nothing too high for him to reach. The bag of dog food in one corner was the first thing he grabbed. Nell had been awfully patient today, and she danced eagerly as he filled her bowl. Instead of putting the bag away, he set it to one side for the moment.

Opening the refrigerator wasn't exactly easy, as it was a tight space for him in his chair. He knew Nell could do it for him if he just tied a towel to the handle, but he was jealous of every bit of independence he could protect.

Opening it, he found everything he'd requested. For now he just grabbed a beer.

Home. He wondered if he'd ever feel he was home again.

Then he heard the knock on his front door and almost decided not to answer it. He'd come here to be by himself and didn't want a tide of well-meaning or curious neighbors sweeping through. *Ignore it*, he thought.

* * *

Ashley Granger knocked on Zane's front door, a little nervous but determined. His housekeeper, Carol Cathcart, had worked with her for years as an aide at her school before taking this job with Zane, and the two had become friends of sorts. Carol had been the one to mention Zane was arriving today.

In her hand, Ashley held a warm Dutch apple pie she'd made after school as a welcoming gift for Zane. Ashley had thought a pie would be a nice gesture. Especially her famous Dutch apple.

She remembered Zane from school, sort of. She'd been five years behind him, which had precluded a friendship of any kind, but it was hard not to be aware of him. A great athlete, popular, good-looking…everyone knew Zane, if only at a distance. Then he'd left to join the military, and the last time she'd seen him had been at his father's funeral years ago. His mother had died a year earlier.

Which meant he had few ties with this town, nearly twenty years later. She was kind of surprised he'd choose to come back here, but he had, and it seemed to her that an apple pie was the least she could do.

She rapped again, but there was no answer. He might need time to get to the front door—she really had no idea how mobile he was now—or maybe he was already in bed. He must have had a long drive. Glancing at her watch yet again, she thought that nine o'clock didn't seem so late, but this was probably a different time zone for him.

Well, the pie would hold until tomorrow.

She had just started turning away when the door opened and a rough voice said, "What do you want?"

Okay, that was a pleasant opening. She had a bit of a temper, and it flared now. She faced him. "Nothing. I was just going to give you a pie."

But in an instant her mind took a snapshot of a broad-shouldered man, still wearing a jacket, sitting in a wheelchair. Beside him, a golden Lab stood watch. God, was it possible the years had made Zane more attractive? The boy had become a man, even more appealing.

Dark eyes, dark hair a little on the shaggy side, the same strong jaw, but older. Much older. The years had taken a toll, leaving his face weathered and a bit lined. Harsh suns and winds, and maybe losing the use of his legs.

"Of course," she continued stiffly, "if you don't want it…"

But then he pushed his chair back from the door. "Come in," he said gruffly.

On legs that felt rigid for some reason, she entered a house that was a clone of her own, except for the decorating. There was little decorating here except that left behind by his parents.

She started to reach for the door to close it against the growing chill, but the dog beat her to it, nosing it shut until she heard the latch click.

"What a beautiful dog," she said after clearing her throat.

"Nell. My service dog."

"Then I guess I shouldn't pet her."

"Only with my permission." Then he pivoted his chair with amazing ease and led the way to the kitchen. "No coffee," he said over his shoulder. "I didn't make any."

She hesitated. "I didn't come to stay. I just wanted to give you this pie. You don't have to entertain me."

"Good."

Well, that was blunt, she thought as her initial irritation began to give way to an unexpected, inexplicable amusement. So he was a hard case. Well, if that's how he wanted it, fine.

"I'm Ashley Granger, by the way," she said as they entered the kitchen. "You probably don't remember me."

"No."

Ah, monosyllables. When he waved at the kitchen table and its ancient Formica, she placed the pie on it. There was only one chair, and she wondered if she should even sit. But then he pointed to it, so she pulled it out and sat.

He wheeled himself closer to the table and picked up the beer that was sitting there. Then, as if suddenly remembering himself, he asked, "Want one?"

"No, thank you. Anyway, I live next door and Carol mentioned that you were arriving tonight, so I made a pie. No big deal. And I promised I wasn't here to visit. You must be tired after your trip."

She felt a poke on her denim-clad thigh and looked down. Nell was looking up at her with great interest. "Um…"

"Does she frighten you?"

"No," Ashley said. "But I'm not allowed to pet her, and I think that's what she wants."

"Sit, Nell," he said. "It's okay." Then those dark, strangely unrevealing eyes settled on Ashley again. "Go ahead and pet her, but just briefly. She's not supposed to get spoiled."

So Ashley forked her fingers into amazingly silky

fur, and she could have sworn the dog grinned at her. All too soon Zane called her to heel and she went to lie beside his chair.

"So Carol mentioned me," he said after taking a sip from his longneck. "How much has she said?"

"Has she been gossiping, you mean? She's no gossip. She said she'd taken a job as your housekeeper. The only other thing she said was that you were arriving tonight. Otherwise, not a word."

He nodded slowly. "Thank you for the pie. But I may as well be honest. I came home because I need my space and my quiet."

"A hermitage."

"Pretty much."

She nodded but felt a twinge of disappointment. She'd like to get to know him, and she didn't feel isolation was the best way to deal with his problems. Surely, he needed a community, people to spend time with, to give him a sense of belonging.

But it was not her decision. Having lived her entire life here, except during college, she was used to being surrounded by good friends and people she knew. She couldn't imagine wanting to be as alone as Zane wanted.

She had promised she wasn't here to visit, but it felt oddly wrong to just leave quickly. Maybe that was her own social upbringing, not the situation. Then he startled her, just as she was deciding to depart.

"Maybe I do remember you," he said quietly. "Your hair. It's almost exactly the color of a new-minted penny. I don't think I've seen that before."

"Strawberry blonde," she said, with a little shrug of her shoulder.

"No, it's almost unique. That's why I noticed it once. You were just a kid, but the hair was eye-catching."

"Well, thank you." Surprised by the tack he had taken, and feeling just a smidge uncomfortable over the attention to her hair, she didn't know what else to say.

"What do you do?"

"I teach fourth grade."

He nodded. "Do you like it?"

"Most of the time. It has its moments, like anything else, I suppose."

He pushed his wheelchair closer, so that it fit under the table, and rested his folded arms on it. "I'm not really good company these days," he said flatly. "I need you and everyone else to understand that. Right now I've got a bag full of stuff I need to work through, and sometimes I can flip out a little. Noise and crowding bother me. So I'm better just left alone, because I don't want to be rude and I don't want to scare anyone."

She blinked. Well, that was food for thought. "You want me to tell everyone to just stay away?"

"As many as you can. Just call me antisocial, because that's what I am."

What a change from the popular high school athlete. She couldn't even imagine what he'd been through or the ways it must have affected him. All she knew was that he evoked a very deep sadness in her heart with those words. "The detritus of war," she murmured before she realized she was speaking aloud.

"Exactly. That's me. And while I appreciate the pie, I really don't want a stream of people at my door."

"Okay." She frowned. "Except that I didn't mean *you* were the detritus. That's what you're dealing with."

"How the hell would you know?"

Her legs started to gather under her. This would be a good time to leave, she thought, but then she saw his hand gripping Nell's ruff. Clinging. This man needed more than himself, and he didn't even know it.

But it was pointless to argue. She had no background she could use to claim that she understood what he faced. What did she know, after all, about being paraplegic, or suffering from PTSD, which was what she guessed he meant about frightening people. Only what she'd read, and that simply wasn't enough.

Did he really think he could handle this all by himself? Or did he want solitude for something darker? She certainly couldn't imagine healing in a vacuum.

"I have a boy in my class who's quadriplegic," she remarked, trying to ease the tension he'd brought into the room with his confession.

"So?"

"I think he'd love to have a dog like Nell. I bet she can do almost anything."

He looked almost sideswiped by the change in direction. Maybe he'd hoped she'd get mad and walk out. But something in Ashley had stiffened. This man could be as rude as he wanted, but she wasn't just going to walk away and forget him. That seemed wrong even though he was asking for it.

"Anyway, Mikey's family can't afford a service dog. We've got a K-9 officer in the county now who trains police dogs, and he's doing a little work with service animals for people who can't afford them. Maybe, if you can crawl out of your shell long enough, you could tell him what a dog for Mikey would need to be able to do."

She was a bit startled to hear the acid in her tone, because she hadn't intended it. But there it was, clear as the words she had spoken. That did it, she thought. He'd never want to set eyes on her again. Who was she to imply criticism of a wounded vet?

She pushed her chair back, ready to leave now, but Zane stopped her. "What's his name, this K-9 officer?"

"Cadell Marcus."

"Maybe I'll call him. I dunno." He rubbed his hand over his face.

"Sorry," she said. "You've only just arrived—you must be exhausted from your trip. I shouldn't have pressed you about anything. I only meant to say welcome home and leave the pie."

But as he dropped his hand from his face, she saw him staring beyond her. Far beyond her, as if he were seeing another place and another time. She froze, wondering if she had triggered a problem for him somehow. Maybe her being here was enough. She waited, not sure if he'd want her to just leave, not sure he'd even hear her if she bade him farewell.

God, she wished she knew what to do.

Then she learned something very important—Nell knew what to do. She rose onto her haunches, put her forepaws on the arm of his chair and stretched her head up until she could lick his cheek. Over and over again.

At first Zane didn't react. Not even a twitching muscle. His gaze remained black, almost empty. Nell continued to lick his cheek with occasional pauses to nudge him gently.

It seemed to go on forever, although it could only have been a minute or two. Then Nell barked and Zane blinked, his eyes focusing once again. He reached out to wrap his arm around the dog, giving her a squeeze before letting her go. At once she dropped to a sitting position beside him, but she never took her attention from him.

Ashley added it all up and realized that the least of Nell's service was performing physical tasks for Zane. She was an emotional lifeline, drawing him back when he neared the precipice. Providing comfort more than physical care.

God, it was terrible to think of what had brought Zane to this point. Even her worst imaginings probably failed completely.

"I'm sorry," he said finally, his voice sounding rusty.

"No need," she answered promptly. And really, she didn't think he needed to apologize for being haunted by the demons of war. Almost nobody could escape that unscathed. At least she assumed that had been what just happened. She hoped she hadn't triggered it.

Deciding he must be uncomfortable now, considering what she had witnessed, and considering he'd already expressed his desire to be left alone, she again gathered herself to rise, opening her mouth to say good-night.

He forestalled her. "Sorry you had to see that. Did it last long?"

She settled back into the chair. "A minute or two. Don't apologize. I just hope I didn't cause it."

"There isn't always a cause. It just happens. It happens less when I'm away from known triggers, but it still happens. And I guess you've figured out that Nell does more for me than open doors and grab my socks."

"She seems wonderful," Ashley answered sincerely.

"She is. She responds immediately when I start to... slip, and she helps call me back quickly. Before Nell I could fall into flashbacks that lasted hours. Once it was even days." He grimaced. "My neighbors didn't much appreciate that last one."

She hesitated then asked because she wanted to know. "The flashbacks...they don't help you at all?"

"No."

Well, that was pretty grim. Dissociative episodes with no purpose except to make him miserable. A mind so overwhelmed that it kept trying to absorb what had happened and was totally unable to do so. Reliving horror.

"Thank God for Nell," she said finally. It seemed like such a weak response to what he had revealed.

He patted his lap, and she watched with amazement and amusement as Nell jumped up and did her best to curl up on him. The dog licked his chin, and for the first time she saw Zane laugh. Such a nice laugh. The dog apparently liked it, too, wagging her tail rapidly.

"She barely fits," Ashley remarked.

"She has to work at it," he agreed. His hands ran down Nell's furry back. "She's a lifesaver."

Somehow she didn't believe he was exaggerating.

"Anyway, I was lucky. Some of my friends got together and gave her to me. I guess the little boy in your class could use the same kind of luck. So this Cadell guy is also trying to provide service dogs?"

"He's trying. He mainly trains police dogs, search-and-rescue dogs, but he's aware of the need. He consults with people who can help him figure out how to do it. Your advice might be very helpful."

He nodded. "Thing is, I don't know how she was trained. When I got Nell, she was on top of it all. I guess I could email one of my friends to see if they know who the trainer was. The trainer would be more helpful than I could ever be."

It was probably true, but Ashley suspected this was another way of keeping his isolation intact. Who was she to question his methods of dealing with his problems?

"Thanks," she said. "Mikey could sure use something to brighten his days. He hasn't been paralyzed long, only the last year, and he still has trouble dealing with it. The idea that kids can just bounce right back from anything… Well, it's not always true."

"How was he hurt?"

"Thrown from a horse. His mom told me his back was broken in several places and he became quadriplegic. They're grateful he's still alive, but I'm not sure Mikey always is."

"Why should he be?" Zane asked roughly. "God spare me the Pollyannas. Pardon me, but it doesn't always help to hear how lucky you are."

Ashley drew a breath. She wasn't shocked—she knew he was right, but few people said such things so baldly.

"Count your blessings," he said. "Sure. That works. On a good day. On a bad day you just wish you'd never survived."

The stark truth rendered her speechless. Every single word that sprang to mind in answer struck her as a useless aphorism. This man was dealing with very real and very ugly memories and impulses. No words could offer any kind of succor.

"Now you know," he said. "That's why I don't want to fill my life with people. I've rattled you badly several times since you walked through my door. Who the hell needs to be around that?"

"I'm fine," she protested. Then, seeking safer ground

immediately because she wanted to change the direction of his thinking as quickly as possible, "Don't you need some modifications in this kitchen?"

Startled, his head jerked back a bit. Nell jumped down from his lap and took up her watchful position. "My kitchen?" he repeated.

"Well, what else can I talk about?"

He frowned faintly. "The weather?"

"Cold and getting colder. I love autumn. What about the kitchen?"

To her amazement, a slow smile made it halfway across his face. "The kitchen has to wait. Expensive, and there's no point in doing it unless I decide to stay here."

"Ah." So he wasn't sure he was settled.

Deciding once again it was time to make her departure, she rose. "I hope you enjoy the pie. It was a pleasure to see you again, Zane. Sorry I intruded for so long."

She zipped her jacket, knowing it would be even colder outside now. "I'll see myself out. And, by the way, if you should need anything, I'm next door." She pointed. "I'm home most afternoons and evenings, because a teacher's day doesn't end when school lets out and I always have paperwork. Good night."

Then she marched out of that house with enough to think about that she'd probably be up late into the night.

She had no idea what she'd expected when she knocked on his door, but now she was deeply disturbed. Whoever Zane had become, he didn't at all resemble the young athlete she remembered.

He probably remembered that kid, though, and it couldn't make his life one bit easier now.

* * *

Zane sat in his kitchen, not moving, for a long time. The smell of the apple pie filled the room, and he clung to it as he kneaded Nell's neck.

Simple things. Good things. The schoolteacher had reminded him. Neighbors and apple pies. Running next door for a cup of sugar. Friendly faces on the streets. A world he hadn't known for a long time.

She was cute, that one. Beautiful, even, but there was no room in his hell for a woman. He'd only drag her down. Adapting to a wheelchair hadn't been as difficult as dealing with himself and the wars.

Would he like to have the use of his legs back? Sure. Would he like to erase his memory? Absolutely. He'd trade his legs for a clean slate.

But he wasn't going to get either, so he had to find a way to make peace with himself. That was proving difficult indeed.

He'd tried group counseling with other vets. It had helped to know he wasn't alone in his reactions, feelings and nightmares, but that didn't get rid of any of them. He'd tried medications that were supposed to improve his PTSD, but he'd tossed them all because of Nell. She did more good for him than any pill. Anyway, until they invented a pill for selective memory loss, he was bound to live with himself.

It wasn't that he hated himself. But he'd been a sailor and done a SEAL's job, and inevitably horror had been etched on his memory.

Sighing, he rolled out of the kitchen, away from the enticing aroma of the pie and to his bedroom where one carved wooden box, a gift from a friend, waited on his aged dresser, set there by Carol when she unpacked the boxes he'd sent ahead. Opening it, he took out the medal presentation cases within and looked at the wages of his war.

A Purple Heart with a cluster pinned to the ribbon, the cluster for his second wounding, the injury that had paralyzed him. A Bronze Star with multiple clusters. A Silver Star with clusters. A Navy Cross. Campaign and other ribbons, but they didn't hold his attention. Those stars and the Navy Cross in particular said he was a hero.

Why didn't he feel like one? He snapped the cases closed and put them back in the box. Once he'd mentioned that he was thinking of ditching them, but an aging Vietnam vet had told him not to. "Someday," he'd said, "you'll want them. Or someone else who loves you will. Put them away and save them. They're the only reward you'll get."

The only reward. Yup.

He closed his eyes, remembering the kid who had signed up nearly twenty years ago, wanting the GI Bill, liking the promises the navy gave him of an education. Not much later he'd found himself getting an education of a very different kind. To this day he couldn't begin to explain to himself why he'd volunteered for the SEALs. Maybe because he was eighteen and full of hubris or too much testosterone. He honestly didn't know.

But he'd done it, had passed all the arduous training, and had become a very different man in the process. He had been molded into a weapon.

Funny thing was, he didn't regret that choice. Never once felt he'd made the wrong one. But now he paid the price in memories that never left him.

One hell of an education, indeed.

Shaking his head a little, he wheeled back to the kitchen, deciding to have a piece of the apple pie Ashley had left. The aroma was making his mouth water.

Nell sat hopefully beside him as he cut into the pie. *Treat.* She had very speaking eyes, he often thought. Hard not to read that she wanted her biscuit or a rawhide bone.

The pantry was still open, so he said, "Nell, get a bone."

Her tail wagging, Nell trotted into the pantry, found the plastic bag of bones and brought them out, dropping them onto his lap. He ripped off the paper label across the top and pulled the bag open. In the process, he loosened the staples holding it shut, and he made sure to gather them into a pile on the table. He'd hate for Nell to get into trouble with one while picking up the bag.

She accepted her rawhide bone with a woof and a wag then settled on the floor to gnaw happily.

And now he could taste the pie. It was every bit as scrumptious as it smelled. Closing his eyes, he savored the first mouthful, tasting its every nuance with pleasure before he swallowed. It had been a long time since he'd had a good pie, but this one was spectacular. Whether he wanted further contact or not, he was going to have to compliment the chef on this one.

Which meant making a connection he really didn't want to make. Ashley Granger was a beautiful young woman, and he didn't want to put any shadows on her face or in her heart.

While he didn't wallow in self-pity, he always tried to be straight with himself. His ultimate conclusion was that he was poison. Until he found a stable place inside himself, a way to reenter normal life, he didn't want to poison anyone else.

He looked down at Nell, his companion and aide, and once again saw his life with stark clarity. All these years, with one mission coming after another, with the time he wasn't in the field mostly used for training and planning, he'd never felt like a fish out of water. The member of a tightly knit fellowship, surrounded by comrades with the same job, the same worldview—he'd belonged.

Now he was a man who couldn't walk and who depended on a dog to keep him from sliding into a past that he no longer lived.

Yeah, he had no business bringing anyone else into this mess, even peripherally, until he got his head sorted out.

But Ashley sure had tempted him.

Chapter Two

Ashley went to school in the morning with nearly a bushel basket full of apples for her students. She'd swiped some for the pie yesterday, but the basket was still brimming. A great time of year for apples, and she'd made a tradition of ordering a bushel each fall for her students.

They all loved apples, and while she limited them to one a day, they still disappeared fast. With a class size of nineteen, four to five days would nearly empty the basket. When they got down to the last few, a spelling bee would determine who got the last of them.

Her students usually loved the treat, and she felt good about being able to give it to them. Special orders were no problem at the grocery, and she'd been doing it for so many years that the produce manager always had a list of prices and quality for her. This year he'd recommended the Jonathans, a type of apple she loved herself.

The students began arriving, and when they saw the apples, excitement began to grow. They'd heard of her tradition. "Not until after lunch," she reminded them.

Then Mikey's mother rolled him in and pushed him up to the table the school had provided specially so he could get his wheelchair under it comfortably. It was also wider than usual so his mother could sit beside him throughout the day and help with his assignments. She turned the pages in the books for him to read, and when worksheets had to be filled out, she asked him which answers he chose.

Today Mikey appeared to be in a fairly good mood. Ashley had the greatest admiration for his mother, Marian Landau, whose patience never seemed to flag. It couldn't be easy for her to drive him in every day and then sit beside him throughout the school day. She could have chosen homeschooling, but she had told Ashley that she wanted him to have social interactions.

"They might not all be good ones," Marian had said. "I know how cruel kids can be. But I also know how nice they can be, and I don't want him raised in isolation. Sooner or later he'll have to deal with the rest of the world."

So far this year, not a single student had been cruel to Mikey. Some hung back, as if uncomfortable, but a few routinely made an effort to speak to him, or to ask him to join their groups when they split into them.

A fund-raiser was being planned to get Mikey a better wheelchair, an electric one he'd be able to control with puffs on a straw. Dang, those things were expensive, Ashley thought as she called her excited and slightly rowdy group to order. But then so were service dogs, and Cadell Marcus was already trying to solve that problem. She spent a moment's hope that Zane would actually call Cadell and offer some advice.

"Okay," she said when everyone was settled and looking at her, "there's an apple rule. The rule is simple. If we get all of our morning's work done before lunch, everyone gets an apple. If you guys cut up and waste time…uh-oh."

Giggles ran through the room. She smiled and plunged into the morning's math lesson. The introduction to fractions always caused some confusion, but today she had apples and a small paring knife to help her. Given the times, she'd had to get permission to bring that knife, small as it was. She couldn't help remembering her own childhood, when every boy had carried a pocketknife. No more. The zero-tolerance policy that had begun sweeping the nation a couple of decades ago had finally reached this little town. Considering how many of her students lived on ranches, at home they very likely carried their pocketknives and used much more dangerous implements.

An awful lot of her students, girls and boys alike, would be going hunting this fall with their parents. In fact, one of her lessons at this time of year was about hunting safety and laws. Sometimes she was able to get the game warden, Desi Jenks, to come in and give a talk.

But fractions required her whole attention, even with slicing an apple into halves, quarters and thirds. It was difficult for kids, for some reason, to see it for real and then transfer it to symbols on paper. That always took a while.

Eventually she had the pleasure of seeing understanding begin to dawn.

By the end of the day, however, despite recesses to let them run off energy, her kids were getting antsy. Their response to weariness was not to fall asleep, but to need something new to do. When she dismissed them, they tore out of the room like a stampeding herd.

But Mikey and his mom remained. They always did, to avoid the crush. Ashley pulled her chair over to chat with them a bit.

"How's it going, Mikey?" she asked. "Do you hate fractions, too?"

He smiled shyly. "They're easy."

"Well, glory be," Ashley said, clapping her hands together. "*Someone* gets it."

Mikey laughed.

Marian spoke. "Cadell is trying to get us a service dog. I think I mentioned that. Well, he's trying to train one for us."

"I can hardly wait," Mikey piped up.

"But…" Marian hesitated. "The dog *can* come to school with him?"

"Of course. Just let me know before you bring him so I can lay the ground rules." She looked at Mikey. "You are going to make so many kids jealous, being able to bring your dog to school."

As soon as she said it, she wished she could take the words back. She was sure Marian didn't find anything about Mikey's situation enviable. She was relieved that Mikey didn't take it wrong. He laughed. "Yup. I'm special."

"You sure are." Ashley looked at Marian and saw the shadows in the woman's eyes, the unguarded moment when her entire face sagged. Their eyes met, understanding passed, then Marian put on her cheerful face again.

"Time to go, Mikey."

Ashley walked them to the front door and waved them goodbye before returning to her classroom to gather up her own items. Lesson planner, papers to grade and some books she used for planning.

A teacher's day was never done, but she didn't mind it in the least. Nothing could compare with watching a child conquer a difficult subject or idea. Nothing could compare with the child's moment of triumph when understanding dawned.

The fractions, however, were going to take a little longer. She laughed to herself and headed out with her jacket and backpack.

As she was leaving, she ran into the seriously pregnant Julie Archer, the kindergarten teacher. "Coffee this weekend?" Julie asked. "Connie and Marisa have already said yes."

"You sure we won't be meeting in the waiting room at the hospital?"

"I wish!" Julie smiled. "Nobody told me the last month would be the longest. Nobody."

"Why scare you?" Ashley asked. "Besides, since I've never been pregnant, I couldn't possibly have told you."

"The other girls could have," Julie retorted. "Lucky Marisa, she was early. So, Saturday. Around two?"

"Unless something comes up, absolutely."

By the time she arrived home, Ashley was beginning to feel her own fatigue from the day. Those fourth graders kept her on her toes. They were bright and inquisitive, and heaven help her if she ever misspoke or inadvertently contradicted herself. Which, she reminded herself, meant they were paying attention.

But it wasn't a job that gave her a chance to let her guard down and relax, and today she'd had lunchroom duty as well.

She glanced toward Zane's house. His van was still in the driveway, but otherwise the place looked unoccupied. Well, he wanted to be left alone, and she guessed he was getting what he wanted.

Inside she started a small pot of coffee for herself, hoping to find a little energy for the work ahead. Her students had done a lot of math problems for homework last night, plus today's worksheets, and she needed to grade them all. The quicker the response, the better the students learned.

Then there was dinner. She looked in her pantry, then in her fridge and nearly groaned. There was food, but not one thing looked appealing to her. Besides, for some reason she didn't feel like cooking. What she wanted to do was pull a box or can off the shelf, or a dinner tray from the freezer, and be done with it.

Her fault for not following her program of cooking on weekends and freezing meals for herself. She'd let it slide, and now she was going to pay. Even a search to the very back of her freezer didn't yield a container of stew or lasagna.

She finally poured a cup of coffee for herself and sat at her kitchen table, drumming her fingers on the wood, thinking. She was more efficient than this. Usually. But lately she seemed to have been letting things slide, like her meals.

And when you let things slide, as she told her students, you got yourself into the last-minute woes. Now, tired or not, she needed to cook.

Mentally throwing her hands up, wondering what had been getting into her lately, she went back to the pantry and started rooting for ingredients. She prided herself on efficiency, so what was going on?

She found some yellow rice and remembered the thick slices of ham she'd bought to cook for breakfast. Some of that cut into the rice would make a meal along with veggies. Saved.

She was just pulling her rice cooker out from under the counter when she heard a knock at her door. It didn't sound like the usual *tap-tap*. The raps were spaced farther apart. Curious, she went to open the door.

Nell, Zane's golden retriever, was standing there, wagging her tail with a rawhide bone in her mouth. She must have used that to knock on the door. Wow.

Then she looked past Nell and saw Zane in his wheelchair at the end of her sidewalk.

"Check her saddlebag," Zane said. "Your pie plate is in there."

"Oh, thank you! You could have just called me to come and get it." But she looked down at the dog and smiled. "However, I do like your errand girl." Bending, she dared to give Nell a quick pat before lifting the flap on the saddlebag and pulling out the glass dish.

She straightened. "So she knocks on doors, too?"

"Yup. The pie is great. I still have nearly half of it in my fridge, but I'm not sure it will survive until morning. Thank you."

"Glad you enjoyed it." Then awkwardness hit her. Ordinarily she would have invited him in for a cup of coffee. But there was no way he could get up the three steps to her porch. Her house was as inaccessible to him as a fortress. Discomfort commingled with sadness washed through her. This was awful.

He gave a whistle, and Nell turned and trotted back to him.

Ashley decided to just be frank about her awkwardness. "I'm sorry I can't invite you in for coffee, but I don't know how you could get up here."

He smiled faintly. "That's what I have arms for. Anyway, I only wanted to bring back the pie plate. My mother guarded hers like a dragon with a hoard of gold. If a neighbor didn't bring one back soon enough, she'd go over to hunt for it."

Ashley had to laugh. "I'm not quite that attached." He started to wheel away when impulse took her by surprise and she said, "I was just about to start making my dinner. Yellow rice with ham, broccoli on the side. Would you like some?"

He froze. She watched it happen. He didn't even look at her, but he was no longer moving. Oh, God, he'd warned her he wanted to be alone, and now she'd ignored him. After this, he might never want to talk to her again, and she would have only herself to blame for that.

Or he could just bite her head off right now and leave her in a quivering mess. God, what was wrong with her? He'd been perfectly clear, and she'd just been perfectly stupid.

Then he astonished her. He turned his head and looked at her. She braced for the scolding. Instead, he said, "I'd like that, if you don't mind."

Then he rolled away along the sidewalk and up his ramp.

She didn't move for a minute or so while he entered

his house, with Nell's assistance for the door, and disappeared.

She *had* heard that right, hadn't she? He'd *like* her to bring over dinner?

Back inside, she changed out of her wool skirt and sweater into jeans and a blue flannel shirt. Okay, then. If she was going to cook for two, she was going to do it over there. If that was too big a trespass, she wanted to know it now.

She had never been into playing mind games. While she felt bad for all Zane had been through, that didn't mean she was going to let him run hot and cold like a kitchen tap. Either he wanted *real* company, or he didn't. If he expected her to just bring over a plate of food, she wasn't about to do that. She was part of the package.

She jammed most of what she needed into her rice maker and a paper bag to carry the rest of it next door, then looked at the fresh pot of coffee she'd just made. Dang, she wanted another cup of coffee. There'd been none since this morning.

Well, she seemed to remember he had a coffeemaker on his counter. If not, she'd come back for hers. For now, she switched it off.

She had the odd feeling she was about to enter a boxing ring. Well, time would tell.

Zane wondered what had possessed him. Asking her to bring dinner over? The next thing he knew, she'd probably be delivering food to him and trying to help him in ways he didn't want to be helped.

Independence mattered to him. Yeah, he needed some assistance, like the bar over the bed that helped him transfer to and from his wheelchair. The shower seat and security bars. The dog, his wonderful Nell.

But most of that meant he could still look after himself in ways that mattered. He could cook on a counter that was at chest height, although it wasn't the easiest thing. He could do most everything one way or another with a little adaptation.

But he really *did* have a problem with PTSD. Why it had all blown up on him after he lost the use of his legs, he didn't know. He'd survived a lot of years going in and out of danger and war with few apparent problems. Then, *wham!* It was almost like once the focus was broken *he* became broken.

Unfortunately, when the shift had occurred in him, he'd found triggers everywhere, things that could throw him back in time. Sounds, smells, even some voices. And sometimes he couldn't figure out any reason for it to hit him. Those instances were the worst of all, because he had no idea what to avoid. Sometimes he didn't even have a flashback, just a surging, almost uncontrollable rage.

So he'd come here to wrestle with it by himself. He knew there was a group here he could join, but he wasn't yet ready to do that again. It would be good for him, but the move had disturbed him in strange ways and he felt a need to settle in first.

Wondering at himself, he wheeled to the kitchen and began the complicated process of making coffee. He had to lock his chair in place and pull himself up on his elbows to fill the pot and put the grounds in the basket. Practice had made it easier, but it was a crazy dance all the same. Still, he'd have had to live without coffee and a lot of other things if he hadn't learned to pull himself up.

Once the pot was turned on, he settled back into his chair. Then came the knock at the door. He unlocked his chair and rolled out to greet Ashley, thinking that he needed to get new knobs for the door. Nell could operate the lever kind, but the round knobs just picked up a lot of tooth marks.

But for now, he turned the knob himself and allowed Nell to do the rest of the work as he backed away to make space for Ashley to enter. She had her arms full.

"What's that?" he asked.

"Dinner," she said cheerfully. "I'm cooking it here, because I am not running back and forth with plates of food. I mean, really."

Nell closed the door, then the two of them followed Ashley into the kitchen.

"Oh, good, coffee," Ashley said. "I've been jonesing for a cup all day. Can I pour you one when it's ready?"

He could do it for himself, but for once he bit the irritable retort back. "Sure. Thanks. I didn't mean for you to go to all this trouble, Ashley."

"Maybe not," she answered as she unpacked her bag and the rice maker. "I seem to remember asking you. My idea. Not a problem."

She hunted around to find what was available. Kitchen utensils had been left there since his parents' time, and he was reasonably certain that Carol had included them in her cleaning.

Out came a wood cutting board, a chef's knife, some small bowls, a measuring cup and a microwave dish.

"I am so grateful for microwaves," she said as she bustled about. "I'd starve to death if I couldn't thaw and cook in one. That'll do for the broccoli. But first the yellow rice." She lifted a yellow bag. "Personal recipe."

He had to chuckle a little in spite of himself. "I think I've had that recipe before."

"Probably. Someone stole it from me and put it on supermarket shelves everywhere."

She dumped the contents into the round rice cooker, then began to dice a thick slab of ham. "Meals in minutes, that's me," she remarked.

Soon she swept the ham into the cooker with the edge of the knife, added the water, plugged it in and pushed a button. "Maybe twenty minutes on that," she announced.

Then she headed for his refrigerator. "I hope you have butter."

"I do."

"Good, I like it on my broccoli."

After putting the frozen broccoli in the microwave dish and dotting it with butter, she pulled a spice container out of her brown bag and sprinkled it on the veggies.

"What's that?" he asked.

"Mustard powder. It makes the taste milder, and anyway, it's good."

He backed away until he was beside the table, watching her whirl around his kitchen with practiced ease. It had been a long while since he'd enjoyed the sight of a woman cooking, and she seemed to like it. She shortly proved him right.

"It's always better to cook for someone else," she said. "Cooking for one is so boring. I make a lasagna, put most of it in my freezer in meal-size containers and then eat it forever. I also do that with other foods that

freeze as well to try to give myself some variety. But…
I slipped up the last few weeks, so tonight I cook. Nothing fancy, but if I'm going to do it, it's nicer to share."

He was sitting there like a lump, he realized. At least
he could try to make conversation. "So you don't like
to cook?"

"Not for just me. Sometimes I cook for my friends,
which is fun. A bunch of us gals get together regularly
and take turns. Not doing that this weekend, though. I
guess we're meeting for coffee."

It almost sounded like an alien world to him. Meeting friends for coffee. How many times had making
coffee meant freeze-dried crystals and water warmed
over canned heat? When he had the crystals and dared
to make even a small flame.

Finally she brought two mugs of coffee to the table.
"Black?" she asked.

"Nothing else." After all these years, he wouldn't
know what to make of any other kind.

She handed him a mug then took the seat across from
him. "I'll clean up after."

"I can do that," he said quickly.

"Sure, if you want. It means I get to hang around
longer waiting for my rice cooker."

His eyes popped to her face, and he realized she
was teasing him. *Teasing* him. The fact that he hadn't
recognized it immediately, the fact that it had been so
long since anyone had teased him when it had been a
routine part of his life in uniform…well, he really *had*
put himself in a long, dark tunnel. And maybe not all
of it was necessary.

But until he could trust his reactions, be sure some

little thing wouldn't just cause him to blow, he felt it was safest to protect others.

But who was he protecting, really?

Shaking his head a little, he remained silent while Ashley served dinner, giving him a plate heaped with yellow rice and a good-size portion of broccoli.

"Thank you," he managed to say. Did one ever get tired of always having to thank others? He sure did. He was used to taking care of everything himself, and his new status in life often irritated him.

Yet, he reminded himself, this woman was guilty of nothing except kindness. He could have turned down her offer of dinner. He could have kept his fortress walls in place. But he hadn't, so the least he owed her this evening was courtesy.

The problem was finding something to talk about. God, he'd been so self-absorbed for so long he had only one subject—his own problems. Disgraceful.

"How was your day?" he asked. That seemed ordinary and safe.

"Pretty good," she answered. "I used apples to teach fractions, which are always a pain to kids, but hey, they got to eat the results of the work."

He drew up one corner of his mouth. "How many kids in your class?"

"I'm lucky. Nineteen. A pretty good size at that age. Not so many that we can't do class projects. And Mikey seemed to be in a great mood today."

He nodded, eating some more rice. "This is great."

"I love it, too," she agreed.

"So, Mikey. How does that work when he's quadriplegic?"

She sighed, and her face shadowed. "His mom has

to come with him every day. Bless her, she never seems to mind. But someone has to be able to turn pages for him and write his answers on worksheets. There are a whole lot of people working on a fund-raiser to get him a motorized chair he can control with puffs of air, and someone's looking into mounting an ebook reader on one for him. I mean…well, you'd know. Independence isn't easy to find. This world is not designed for the disabled."

"No, it's not," he agreed. Although he was pretty sure it was getting easier in some ways. But still. He thought of a fourth grader consigned to a future of quadriplegia and it pained him. Talk about the unfairness of life. At least what had happened to him had been a known risk of his job. All that kid had been doing was going for a fun horseback ride.

"Anyway," Ashley continued, "he's adapting remarkably well. Very resilient. He impresses me."

Unlike him, Zane thought sourly. Although paraplegia wasn't his biggest problem; his mind was. If he ever managed to whip that into shape, life would probably be better.

However, a sudden change in perspective gave him a view of himself as others might see him, and he didn't like it. Oh, well. He knew the rages that could bubble up unexpectedly inside him. He never wanted anyone else to suffer from that. Who cared what anyone on the outside thought? All they'd ever see was the guy in a wheelchair.

"Do you know anyone around here?" Ashley asked.

"After all these years? I doubt it. Doesn't matter, anyway."

"No, I guess not."

Well, he had told her he wanted to be left alone. Then the first asinine thing he did was let her bring him dinner. "I told you I'm antisocial."

She nodded, then studied him with those startling blue eyes. "It can't have always been that way. In the military you were part of a team, right?"

"I'm not in the military anymore."

"No kidding," she said a bit tartly. "However, we have a few guys in this county who might get where you're coming from. They've walked in your shoes, and some of them have had to struggle with being home."

"So?"

He guessed that was it for her. She rose, leaving the remains of her dinner on the table. She grabbed her jacket and slipped it on, then picked up the rice cooker and the bottle of mustard powder. "You said you could clean up. Have at it."

Then, without another word, she walked out. He heard the front door close behind her.

A whimper drew his attention to Nell, who was sitting beside him.

"Damn it, dog, I don't need your opinion, too."

She gave a little moan then settled beside him with her head on the floor between her paws.

Yeah, he was a jackass. He knew it. He nurtured it. Better to be alone with his demons than inflicting them on innocent people. That had become his mantra.

At that moment he wondered if it wasn't also his excuse.

Ashley sighed as she stood in her kitchen cleaning the rice cooker at her sink and wondering where that burst of temper had come from. That man seemed to bring out the worst in her. Yesterday she'd gotten acidic with him, and today she'd walked out on him—rather rudely, if she were to be honest about it.

And why the heck had he accepted her offer of dinner? He'd obviously been uncomfortable, and finally he'd felt it necessary to make it clear yet again that he wanted to be left alone. He didn't even want to talk with other vets.

When she summed up the total of conversation that had passed between them, she figured it wouldn't fill one typed page.

God, she didn't want to be a snippy, sarcastic person. A good reason to grant his wish for solitude. It would be easy enough to pretend he wasn't even there.

Her life was full enough anyway, what with school and helping with the project to get Mikey a better wheelchair. In fact, there was the fund-raiser at the church on Saturday evening that she still needed to do a few things for.

But she couldn't help feeling bad for a man so alone, even if it was by choice. She spent a lot of time as a teacher making sure that no child was left out or ostracized, because a sense of belonging was so important to human beings.

Well, Zane was a grown man. None of her business, no matter how she felt about it. Plus, he'd kind of warned her that he was still a bit unstable mentally. PTSD. Awful. Certainly not something she could help him with.

She dried her hands, then pulled out her folio to start correcting papers. Except for taking dinner over to Zane, she'd have started a while ago. Time to catch up.

Immediate feedback was important to learning. Nothing the kids had done today would matter to them in a week.

The phone rang just as she was spreading her work on the table. She picked up the cordless handset to hear her friend Julie on the line.

"Hey, word has it you were seen visiting Zane McLaren. How is he?"

"Very much antisocial and very much wanting to be left alone. Straight from his lips."

"Oh." Julie sighed. "That's sad. Any number of people have mentioned him to me, wondering how he's doing."

"And he said he'd very much appreciate not having a parade of well-wishers at his door, so pass it along."

"Well, dang. I thought we'd have something new to talk about."

Ashley laughed. "Hurry up and have your baby. Then you'll be too busy for gossip."

Julie's answering laugh poured through the phone. "I'm sure Trace would agree with you. I can't figure out if he shares my impatience or if he just wishes I'd settle down."

"Maybe a bit of both. Listen, I've got a bunch of papers to correct. Saturday, right?"

"Oh, that's why I called. The weather's going to be beautiful Saturday. A couple of the girls suggested we meet at your place and have our coffee on the porch. You have a big enough porch and enough chairs."

And she lived next door to the mystery man, Ashley thought wryly. "Sure, that's fine. Who's bringing the coffee cake?"

"Marisa said she would. She's looking forward to turning the youngster over to Ryker for a few hours."

"I can imagine. Okay, Saturday. Here."

"Done."

Ashley hung up, shaking her head. She wondered if she ought to give Zane a warning, then decided she was being ridiculous. He didn't have to poke his head outside. He could just tough it out indoors.

Chapter Three

Saturday afternoon turned into the last taste of summer. Autumn leaves still blew gently around on the breeze, but the weather was warm enough that light clothing allowed the women to sit outside on Ashley's porch.

Julie Archer had been Ashley's friend forever, and now that they taught at the same school, the friendship had only deepened. They could discuss various student problems with a deep understanding. Julie's auburn hair and green eyes had always made her a striking woman. She also rarely withheld her thoughts.

Connie Parish was older than the rest by a little over a decade, but she had fit seamlessly with them. The mother of three as well as a sheriff's deputy, she had her hands full and she swore the Saturday get-togethers were a lifeline.

Marisa Tremaine had been widowed a few years ago, and now was married to her late husband's best friend, who also happened to be a good friend of Julie's husband.

Ashley sat as the lone spinster among them and she was quite happy with her lot, thank you very much. She honestly couldn't imagine how she would handle the addition of a family to her already busy life.

"So Nora and Hope couldn't make it?" Ashley asked about two of their other kaffeeklatsch regulars.

"Getting ready for the fund-raiser tonight. Hope must be out of her mind. She promised ten dozen cookies. And Nora is bringing five pies."

"Wow." Ashley blinked. She felt like a skinflint with her offering of a few dozen rum balls.

"We're getting there," Julie said. "With the bake sale tonight and the donations, I bet we come close to our mark for that wheelchair."

"I hope so," Connie remarked. "I was blown away by the price of those things. It's not like you're buying some toy for your amusement. It's essential."

Ashley answered, "And it has to be able to do more, like change his position so he doesn't get sores and lift him so his mother can help him get into bed. It's not your basic model."

The women sat silent for a moment, and Ashley guessed those with children were imagining themselves in the shoes of Mikey's mom.

Then Julie visibly shook herself. "We're close. And Trace's friend Ken is working on a tablet to attach so Mikey can do a lot of things simply by using his chin on a push plate. I have half a mind to wrap that chair in aluminum foil and put NASA stickers down its side. It's going to be halfway to a spaceship."

That leavened the moment. Soon laughter returned and stories about everyone's kids began to be shared. Ashley never ceased to be amazed by the inventive hijinks kids could get up to. She didn't see a lot of that in the classroom, where they were usually on their best behavior...or what passed for it.

She went inside to get a fresh pot of coffee and warm up her friends' mugs. When she stepped outside, Nell was standing there, wearing her saddlebag.

"So you have a secret admirer," Julie joked. "Whose dog?"

"Zane's. I guess he sent something over. Nell is a service dog."

"Oh, wow, wouldn't Mikey like that," said Connie.

"I'm trying to persuade Zane to work with Cadell on the kinds of things Mikey might need. Or at least I mentioned it."

Curious, she passed the coffeepot to Marisa and let her pour for everyone. Opening the saddlebag was easy enough; it wasn't snapped closed. Inside she found an envelope addressed to her.

A message from Zane? Surprised, she dropped onto her chair and opened the flap of the envelope. Inside a brief note was wrapped around a check: "For the wheelchair."

Not even signed, but when she looked at the check, she gasped and her heart slammed. "Good heavens!"

"What?" the other women demanded.

She looked up. "Zane just sent a check for five hundred dollars for Mikey's chair."

A chorus of exclamations greeted that news. In a moment everyone was talking at once. This brought them a long way toward their goal and doubled what they had expected to make from the bake sale at the church.

The check was made out to Ashley, probably because Zane didn't know the name for the fund-raising group, but as she held it, her resistance to Zane and his attitude melted away. It was a generous act, very generous, and a trusting one. He clearly had no doubt she would put the money where it was intended to go.

Wow.

But Nell still sat in front of her, looking up as if her mission wasn't complete. Ashley jumped up, saying, "Stay, Nell," and went inside. She tucked the check in her wallet, then pulled open the drawer where she kept writing materials for rare occasions when a handwritten note was needed.

On a notecard that said *Thank You* on the front, she wrote, "We are all so very grateful for your generosity, Zane. This will go a huge way to getting Mikey his chair. We can't thank you enough."

She signed her name and the name of the group, then stuffed it in an envelope with his name on the front.

Outside, Nell still waited patiently. Ashley lifted the flap of the saddlebag and tucked the note into it. She gave Nell a scratch behind her ears, then said, "Take it to Zane, Nell."

Tail wagging, the dog was off like a flash.

All heads turned to follow the dog as she dashed across the yard, leaped onto the ramp and disappeared inside.

"Wow," said Julie.

"Wow," agreed Connie.

"We've got to get Mikey a dog like that," Marisa said.

"Next step," said Connie. "I think trained service dogs are nearly as expensive as the wheelchair."

"It doesn't matter," Ashley said. "I was talking to Dory and Cadell last week. He's working on training a dog already, and Dory said she'd meet any expenses on that."

Marisa nodded. "And she made a large contribution to the wheelchair fund. She's serious about helping."

Marisa stood up. "This has been fun, gals, but Ryker is probably desperate for some relief. Jonni's going through a difficult stage. I think *no* is the only word she doesn't understand."

"And I need to get my daily walk in," said Julie.

Soon everyone had said their goodbyes and left, and the porch was empty of everyone except Ashley. The afternoon was beginning to cool a bit, and she thought idly about getting her jacket or just going inside. She had time before the bake sale tonight.

She closed her eyes, enjoying the fresh air, full now of the scents of autumn. Then something bumped her knee.

Her eyes flew open, and she saw Nell sitting in front of her. No saddlebag this time.

"What are you doing here?" she asked the dog.

Her answer was a doggie grin and a tail wag.

Then she heard Zane call, "Dang it, Nell, what are you doing?"

She looked over to the house next door and saw Zane sitting on his porch. "You didn't send her?"

"I absolutely did not, and she's never supposed to leave me unless I tell her to go. Now look at her."

"Are you blaming me?" Because that's what it sounded like.

"Hell, no. But that dog thinks for herself, and I can't imagine what she's thinking now. Nell, come."

Nell started to rise then sat down again.

"Nell," Ashley tried, "you need to go to Zane."

Nell looked over at Zane.

"Go on," Ashley urged.

"Nell, come," Zane repeated.

With something that sounded very much like a sigh, Nell rose and trotted back over to Zane.

"That was weird," he said. "She's never done that before."

"Well, I swear I'm not encouraging it. I didn't even give her a treat of any kind."

"I'm sure you did nothing wrong," he answered. "She just took a notion. If this happens again, she may need a training refresher."

"Maybe curiosity overcame her. Or maybe since you sent her once, she thought it would be okay to come again."

"I wonder." Then he astonished her with a laugh. "She's far from an automaton. That's why I said she thinks for herself. And she's bright. Maybe she's getting bored over here. As soon as I get my trike together, I'll get her some more exercise."

"Trike?"

"An extra wheel attached so the front of my wheelchair so if I hit an obstacle while moving fast my chair can't tip and throw me into a face-plant."

She nodded, picturing it. "Need any help putting it together?"

A long silence greeted her offer. She had just about decided to go inside when he answered. "If you can spare an hour or so sometime, it would be helpful."

Ah, a crack in the armor. Well, every step was a good one. And after that donation he'd made, she'd have gladly done a whole lot to help him out. "Tomorrow afternoon?" she asked. "About two, maybe?"

"That would be great." Then he turned and disappeared inside with his dog.

Well, well, well, she thought, deciding to head indoors as the chill began to get to her. Time to get ready for the bake sale tonight, anyway. She had a shift from seven to nine. Anything left over would be sold tomorrow after services, but she hadn't signed up for that. There were plenty of willing hands when it came to Mikey.

And very few when it came to Zane, but he wanted that way. At least he could accept help when it was offered. She supposed that was a big step for a professed hermit.

The next day when she came home from church, Ashley was practically walking on air. Not only had the bake sale gone well, but upon seeing how close they were getting to the goal for the wheelchair, quite a few checkbooks had come out to add larger amounts.

Then, this morning, the pastor had announced that they'd received the grant they'd applied for. They could now order Mikey's wheelchair, "with racing stripes if he wants them," the pastor had joked, causing the entire congregation to rise and applaud.

The standard coffee and doughnuts afterward had been a happier-than-usual affair, with a lot of smiles and laughter. Everyone was feeling pretty good, and the pastor was going to make the trip out to the Landau ranch to tell Mikey and his parents the good news.

For her part, Ashley was looking forward to sharing the news with Zane. His check had been a huge help in putting them over the top, as had the grant. Now they had a little elbow room to get the child exactly what he needed.

She was still surprised that Zane had sent so much money, though. After announcing he was a practicing curmudgeon, apparently Mikey's plight had touched him.

She knew so little about being paralyzed. She supposed she ought to frankly ask Zane what other things they might be able to help Mikey with. So much that the family had had come from disability aid, the bare minimum, and she couldn't even begin to imagine the lacks the family might still be experiencing. Right now either parent could lift Mikey into bed or onto a couch to sit, but what would happen as he grew? How many other needs must be met?

Zane would probably have a good idea, if he was willing to share.

Zane cussed himself for being a stubborn mule. At some point, he was going to have to admit that he couldn't always be completely independent, and he was looking at a case of it right now.

The toolbox had a handle. He'd been able to lean over the side of his chair, heft it and carry it into the kitchen. The box of parts for his extra wheel was a different matter. It sat on the floor in the small extra downstairs room defying him, and he had no way to reach it or move it.

Nell watched him, tilting her head quizzically from side to side, unable to do a damn thing about it. He was glad he'd swallowed his pride enough to ask for Ashley's help, even though it galled him, because otherwise...well, he'd have had to hire someone, he guessed. Not impossible, but he didn't know where to begin in this town, and anyway, he didn't feel comfortable about it. Maybe it was some leftover machismo, but for some reason he didn't want to hire someone to put his wheel on. He wanted to do as much of it himself as he could.

Stubborn cuss, that was him. Unfortunately, stubbornness could lead to stupidity, and he was coming dangerously close. Instead of just hiring help, now he was imposing on a neighbor. Didn't that make a lot of sense, he asked himself with a snort of disgust.

Nell apparently heard Ashley's arrival before he did. She dashed away to the front door and waited for the knock or the bell. Trusting Nell's instincts, Zane wasn't far behind.

He opened the door to see that beautiful strawberry blonde dressed for work in jeans and a flannel shirt. She'd even caught her hair into a ponytail, which was cute. And she was smiling.

"Ready to start?" she asked.

He hesitated even as he began to roll back from the door to give her entry. "I should have just hired someone. I can't keep imposing on you."

"I didn't have to say yes, and I don't feel imposed upon." She looked down at Nell. "Okay to pet her?"

"You might as well. She seems determined to become part of your life, too."

Ashley laughed, then squatted, giving Nell a good rub and scratch around her neck. Then she rose and stepped past, allowing the dog to close the door. "So what do we need to do?"

"Assemble the parts to attach the wheel to this chair.

Once it's all together, I can put it on or take it off with some locks. Naturally, because it wouldn't work indoors, but..." He shrugged. "Thing is, I like to get a good speed going when I'm out with Nell. She wants to run, and the workout feels good to me, too. So...this is all about stability."

As he spoke, he was wheeling his way back to the spare room. Nell's steps followed him.

"Will Mikey need something like this?"

"I doubt a motorized chair will allow him to go fast enough to worry about it. How's the fund-raising, by the way?"

"Fantastic," she answered enthusiastically. "Between your check—which was awfully generous—the bake sale last night and a small grant we finally received, Mikey's new wheelchair will be ordered soon."

He summoned a smile. "I'm glad to hear that."

She touched the box on the floor with her toe. "Parts in here?"

"All of them."

She nodded, as if grasping why he couldn't get to it himself. "Do you want to assemble it here?"

"In the kitchen. I'm going to need a place to sit while we do it, because I need to get out of this chair."

"Got it." She squatted and began to pull packing tape away. "Anyhow, if you have any suggestions for things Mikey might need, let me know. We've got a small list of things, but who knows what we overlooked."

"He lives on a ranch?"

"Yeah."

"Well, if he wants to get outside, he's going to need good, wide wheels. Like these," he said, patting his own. "Like you'd find on a mountain bike."

She peered up at him. "I'm quite certain none of us thought of that. Any other ideas, let me know. As the pastor said this morning, we now have enough to give him racing stripes if he wants them."

Once again Zane felt an unusual smile on his face. "Flames. I suggest flames."

Ashley laughed. "Yeah, he'd probably love that."

As she pulled out parts, she carried one piece after another into the kitchen.

"I can carry some of that," he protested. "I just couldn't reach the floor."

Her head snapped up. "Oh. Yeah. Sorry."

He felt like a jerk, but he wasn't going to let her do all the lifting and carrying. He wouldn't ask that of anyone.

She piled some of the stuff on his lap and he wheeled himself out to the kitchen, where he was able to place the smaller stuff on the table. Of course, some of it had to go on the floor again, which was kind of like moving his problem from one room to the next. He could have rolled his eyes at himself.

But the light was better in the kitchen, and they were going to need it for an assortment of screws, which naturally weren't all the same size and were all black.

Once everything had been moved, he levered himself with practiced ease from his wheelchair to a kitchen chair. It bothered him to have her see him move his legs with his hands, but there was no way to avoid it if he didn't want them draped every which way.

At least she didn't appear bothered.

"I really should have just found someone to hire," he said again.

She eyed him. "Yeah? Well, if I can't help you get

this together, you can do that. I'm not sure who deals with this stuff, though. A bike shop?"

He hadn't really thought about that himself. Back in Virginia, he'd gotten everything he needed provided by the VA and some of his old buddies. And once his chair was all put together, occasional tightening with a wrench kept it that way.

"I never thought about a wheelchair tipping," she remarked as she handed him a piece he asked for from the floor. "I've seen those extra wheels, but I never knew what they were for."

"Well, this is what *I* need it for. I can't speak for everyone else. Anyway, you see those small wheels on the back of the chair? Everyone has them because the likeliest way for us to tip is backward. My front rig is more for speed. I want to go fast. It helps prevents a disaster from a crack in the sidewalk."

"I bet Nell loves racing."

"The faster, the better."

The next hour went smoothly enough. They paused once to make some coffee, but otherwise Ashley was kind of quiet and focused on following directions when she needed to. And as usual, he managed to do most of it himself and then, too late, wondered if he was making her feel useless.

"I couldn't have done this without you," he said as he tested the fittings.

"Sure." She smiled faintly.

He turned to look straight at her and wondered if he'd managed to offend her somehow. It was entirely possible. His social skills had gone to hell some time ago. Well, if he had, maybe it was all to the good. She was entirely too attractive to have around much, especially since he didn't want to drag any woman into his world.

"Wanna take it out for a spin?" she asked.

One way to get through what now felt like an awkward moment. His fault, as usual. "Sure. Nell would love that."

He shifted from the kitchen chair back to the wheelchair.

"You amaze me by how easy you make that look," she remarked. "I bet it took some practice."

"Everything takes practice." He lifted his feet onto the footrests, then backed the chair up enough to turn it and head for the foyer.

Ashley opened the door for him, since the extra wheel put it beyond his reach. "I've got to get some lever door handles," he remarked. "I keep thinking about it and forgetting it. Nell could manage those."

"Good idea."

She was withdrawing from him. He could feel it. Good. The more distance, the better—for both of them. Nell pranced alongside him. She recognized the signs of an impending run.

Before he started down the ramp, he paused to look at Ashley. "Thanks so much for your help. Nell thanks you, too. She's needed a good outing for some time."

"Sure." She smiled, a smile that would have dazzled him if it had reached her eyes. He left with Nell, wondering what the hell he'd done wrong. And doubting that he'd ever know.

Ashley went home after watching man and dog depart at a pretty good clip down the sidewalk. She really hadn't been all that much help, except for picking up things from a floor he couldn't easily reach. She probably couldn't imagine half the challenges he must routinely face.

But she shouldn't really care. He'd warned her off at the very beginning, and she was still surprised he'd asked for her help. She suspected he hadn't liked having to do it. There was something about his determination to put the whole contraption together himself.

She could understand his desire to be as independent as possible. Things she and most other people took for granted were denied to him now. He'd probably piled up a whole lot of dings to his ego since he became paralyzed. Self-sufficiency was his goal, and she was quite sure that ordinarily he managed it.

But then there'd been his remarks that had led her to believe he suffered from PTSD. Maybe for him that was an even bigger problem than being able to get around. The psychic wound could be far worse than the physical, and probably was. Worse yet if he couldn't predict what would set it off or when it approached.

Yeah, if she suffered from something like that, she might want to hide out, too.

Sighing, she pulled out her schoolwork and made herself a cup of cocoa, deciding to finish her grading at the kitchen table rather than in the office she'd made for herself in the spare room. It was a nice, cozy office, but she preferred it on cold, gray winter days when it felt warm and snuggly. On a day like today with brilliant light pouring through the kitchen windows, the office would have felt more like a cave.

Today she had a lot of chicken-scratch problems with fractions. Number-two pencils didn't always erase well, and while the darker lead was easier on her eyes, black smudges covered everything. She had to smile. Most of these kids tried so hard, and judging by the smeared erasures they'd tried extra hard with this.

She wouldn't be surprised if they needed to spend a few more days with fractions. These assignments would certainly tell her.

But her thoughts kept wandering to Zane. A complicated man—surely an understatement. His gift to the fund-raiser for Mikey had been more than generous. His desire to be left alone had been belied by his acceptance of dinner with her and then his request for help.

But after he'd asked for that help, he'd made her feel all but useless. He hadn't been rude or anything. It was almost like he needed to prove something. Yes, she'd been able to help, but only a little, mostly with picking up things he couldn't reach.

She supposed that was help. What had she expected when she went over there? That he needed her to assemble the whole piece?

Not likely. She'd done what he needed and no more, and now she should examine her own reasons for being disturbed by that. After all, she routinely told her students to complete tasks on their own, giving help only when their efforts seemed doomed.

Was Zane so different? He was following the advice she would have given to her students. Do it yourself... if you possibly can.

So what was eating her? The absence of a lengthy, in-depth conversation?

She closed her eyes and leaned back a bit, thinking about him. Dang, he was attractive, especially when he managed a smile. Those rare smiles leavened his whole face and drew her to him. But he didn't want her to be drawn, and maybe that was her entire problem.

All her life men had been interested in her. While she wasn't one to stare into a mirror, she knew she'd been blessed with reasonably attractive looks and hair that caught men's eyes. She'd never gone begging for a date unless she didn't want one. Usually she didn't. The attraction wasn't often a two-way street, and less so as she grew older. Most of the time when she dated, she got turned off to the guy relatively quickly. One longer relationship had left her feeling as if he were trying to shoehorn her into a Donna Reed–style box. That was not for her.

Now she was on the other end of that equation for the first time—a guy who wasn't interested. Maybe that was all that bothered her.

She laughed out loud at that and decided she'd gone round the bend when it came to Zane. She was happy with her life, felt nothing was lacking. Was she going to let the hermit next door throw her off balance?

Nope, she decided. She had her work and her friends, and she really didn't need a romance to muck it up.

Which brought to mind her first boyfriend, all the way back in high school. When they had broken up after a month or so, she'd been giddy with relief. With him out of the picture, she could get back to her *real* life, with her friends, pursuing her own interests.

She should have learned from that, but she hadn't. No, she'd tried a few times more…and felt every bit as giddy when it was over.

Then a thought struck her, causing her cheeks to flame. What if Zane couldn't have sex? That seemed highly likely given his injury.

Which meant being attracted to him, if he recognized it, might only make him feel worse.

She stared straight at the probability, work forgotten, and realized she needed to tread very carefully with him. Keep it friendly or stay away.

Because the last thing she wanted to do was make him feel worse.

Chapter Four

The following Friday when Ashley pulled into her driveway after school, she glanced toward Zane's house. All week it had looked as if nothing over there had moved or changed. She hadn't even seen Nell out in the yard.

Oh, well, none of her business. She'd been working, and since her class was prepping for tests next week, she'd had a lot to do after school and at home. She held regular tutoring sessions after classes were over for the day, and attendance increased right before tests.

No kaffeeklatsch this weekend. Everyone was busy. She'd miss it, but it happened from time to time. Halloween was right around the corner, and as soon as the tests were over, she was going to have a whole bunch of kids making paper pumpkins with weird faces. She also needed to dig out some of her decorations from the attic to add to the festivities.

The kids were already getting excited, barely restraining themselves in their eagerness, but the tests put a layer of sobriety over them. Fun would have to wait.

In the meantime, it gave her a kick to drape fake spiderwebs around her shrubs and hang a ghost and a skeleton from the limbs of her trees. She hadn't quite gotten to the point of going for orange outdoor lights, but the best part for her was seeing all the little kids in their costumes.

Once inside, her grocery bags and backpack on her table, she thought again of Zane. No sight or sound of him? No evidence he'd been out? Not even the sight of Nell running around the front yard to do her business?

It may have been coincidental, but it niggled at her, anyway. What if something had happened?

She finally decided to head over and find out if he was okay. She could withstand getting chewed out, but she'd never forgive herself if he were in trouble and she'd ignored him.

She rushed to put her cold and frozen items away. The rest could wait. Jacket zipped against the deepening October chill, she hurried out her front door and next door to Zane's. The autumn evening was starting to darken, and she supposed it was a good thing that she could see lights inside the house.

When she reached the front door and knocked, she heard nothing for a minute, then the sound of scratching, as if Nell were on the other side trying to open the door.

Then with a click, the knob turned, and Nell pulled the door open for her.

All was quiet. No sign of Zane. Her heart sped up,

and she stepped inside. Nell closed the door behind her then headed toward the kitchen. Ashley followed.

Zane sat with his head on the table and six or seven beer bottles in front of him. He didn't stir even when Nell nosed him. The place smelled like a brewery.

She could tell he was breathing, however, so she guessed he was sleeping it off. She just wondered if he might need some medical attention. Alcohol could be so toxic.

Tentatively, she called his name. "Zane? Zane, wake up."

He groaned faintly but stirred, which she guessed was a good sign. Then he pushed himself upright and looked at her from half-closed eyes.

"What are you doing here?"

"Nell let me in. I'm being a nosy neighbor. I was worried about you."

"No need." His speech didn't sound slurred, and gradually his eyes grew clearer. "I've been having trouble sleeping," he said when he saw her glance at the beer bottles. "They helped. I'm fine."

"Okay." Much as she hated to leave him like this, he wasn't asking her to do anything else. "Surely you can find something better than alcohol to knock you out. It's lousy for sleep and it's a depressant." With that she turned to leave.

"Hey," he said, his voice challenging, "who made you the expert?"

She faced him. "My aunt. She died of cirrhosis when she was forty-seven. You'd left by then."

Now he was fully awake, his gaze sharp. "I'm sorry," he said. "I'm so very sorry."

"Nobody made her drink herself to death," she replied frankly. "Certainly a lot of people, me included, tried to prevent it, but…" She shrugged. "Anyway, it's a lousy sleeping pill."

"I know," he said quietly. "And I didn't drink that all today. I've been feeling so tired I've let things go."

It was an apology of sorts. Without asking for permission, she grabbed the bottles and carried them to the sink, where she rinsed them. Then she opened the window over the sink to let in some fresh air.

"Recycling?" she asked.

"Don't have any yet."

She supposed it might be a problem for him to get all his bottles, cans and whatever to the transfer station. She imagined him trying to carry large bags to his van. Even if he could manage that, would the guys at the station be willing to unload them? "Want me to take it for you? That is, if you're not opposed to recycling."

For a second it looked like a dark cloud was lowering on his face, but then it blew away and he simply looked weary. "Or Carol could do it."

Ashley let it go for now. Carol was his hired housekeeper. Maybe it made him feel better to pay for a service than to accept a favor. She set the rinsed bottles on the counter.

"I can clean up after myself," he groused.

Lovely mood, she thought as she dried her hands on a kitchen towel. "I'm sure you can. I'll be on my way." Turning, she closed the window, because there was absolutely no way he could reach it, then started toward the door. Nothing required her to put up with his lousy moods or even intervene in any way if she happened to wonder if he was still alive. Zane could go dig himself a hole and stay there as far as she was concerned.

But as she stepped toward the door, Nell moved in front of her. She eased to the side, and Nell blocked her again.

"Come on, Nell," she said.

Zane snorted behind her. "I guess she doesn't think I should be alone."

Ashley pivoted. "Do *you*?"

For a few seconds, he didn't move. It was as if everything had stilled in the room, in the air. Then slowly, almost jerkily, he shook his head.

Was that an invitation? Well, she'd dealt with enough kids in bad moods and with problems to decide that it was, however reluctant.

Instead of just sitting, she started a pot of coffee, figuring it might help him with the last of the beer coursing through his system. He didn't say a word even when she placed a mug in front of him and sat with him at the table.

After downing half the mug of coffee, his gaze focused on her again. "You don't have to feel responsible for me."

"I don't," she answered, a half-truth. She'd feel some responsibility for any neighbor having a rough time.

"I told you I'm not fit to be around people yet."

"So it's been a rough week?"

"They happen. Trouble sleeping, more than anything. Nightmares. Agitation."

She drummed her fingertips against the side of her own coffee mug, then stopped. "Nothing can be done for it?"

"Yeah, there are pills. I hate the way they make me feel. Not myself."

"So beer is better?"

Amazement struck her as he suddenly half smiled. "Yeah, I make a lot of sense."

She smiled back helplessly.

"There was a time I could run off this kind of feeling," he remarked. "It's harder in a wheelchair. Oh, I can do it, but with all the stops at corners and so on, I'd probably have to spend most of the day working up a sweat."

"Maybe you need a gym. The hospital installed one a few years ago. Anyone can use it."

"I guess I should look into it." He shook his head a little, closed his eyes briefly, then drew a deep breath. "I remember being a pleasant person, once upon a time."

"You don't think you're pleasant now?"

"Hell, no."

A very sad self-evaluation. Ashley smothered a sigh and sought a way to make a real connection that had nothing to do with this man's troubles. The kind of connection she figured he needed a whole lot. The thought of him having no one to distract him in his life…well, she didn't know much about what he was going through, but she suspected being left alone to brood about it wasn't helping anything.

"You need to meet some people who get it," she finally said. "We've got any number around here who've come back from war. We *do* have an active veterans' group. Sitting here all alone… I know it's none of my business, but it doesn't seem like the best way to handle this. Too much time inside your own head."

"Which isn't a very pretty place," he remarked. "I

don't know. Clearly the hermit thing isn't going to make it. A gym might help. And poor Nell gets so worried about me. Dang, I don't even know if I walked her since this morning."

"She opened the door for me," Ashley said a little wryly. "I think if she were desperate..."

"When I'm not myself, she knows she's not supposed to leave me." With that he called Nell and began rolling to the front of the house. The dog trotted happily beside him, tail high. "I've been neglecting you, girl," she heard Zane say.

Well, he didn't sound inebriated, Ashley decided. Maybe it was time for her to leave. She'd done enough of the nosy neighbor routine for one night. She followed them to the door. Zane rolled out onto the porch, and Nell took off like a flash, sniffing around the scrubby front yard as if it were full of wonderful secrets.

The dog's exuberance was beautiful to behold, and Ashley couldn't help pausing to watch Nell with a smile. "She sure loves life," she remarked, then froze as she wondered if she'd said exactly the wrong thing.

"Yeah," he answered. Then he surprised her. "Take a seat on the porch swing if you want."

She glanced at the swing on the far side of the porch, then at him. "You'll get cold if you stay out here."

"Nell can bring me my sweater or jacket if I ask her. Stay."

It didn't sound like a command but almost like a request, so, hesitantly, she crossed to the swing and sat on it. It creaked a bit and moved. She doubted there was any way he could get on it himself. At least not without help. He rolled his chair over to sit beside her.

"It's a quiet evening," he remarked.

"It won't be for long. Once Halloween hits, the kids are officially on the countdown toward Christmas. The excitement winds them up so they're running all over the place, and of course, their families will be shopping."

"The calm before the storm, huh?"

She laughed quietly. "Tests next week for most of the students. Once those are over, little reins in the excitement."

"Did you get excited when you were a kid?"

"Of course. Didn't you?"

"Always. Seems like a long time ago, in a land far away."

She twisted to see him a little better and pushed the swing with one foot to sway gently. "Sometimes life hits us so hard that things that happened only recently seem like they were years ago."

She heard him draw a deep breath. "Yeah." Then he surprised her yet again. "Do you decorate for Halloween?"

"Just a bit. Some phony spiderwebs, a skeleton or two hanging from my tree. Why?"

"Just thinking about it. It's better than thinking about anything else at the moment." He turned his chair a bit so that he was looking right at her. Nell dashed up, apparently done with the yard, and settled right beside him.

She chewed her lip, a bad habit she'd picked up from her friend Julie, then asked, "You want to do something?"

"Maybe I should dress up like Frankenstein. Come on, Ashley, what kid is going to want to come up here to take candy from a stranger in a wheelchair?"

Bitterness laced his words. Her heart winced, but she kept the feeling from her face. "A lot, I'd think. Nell would help, too. She could probably hand out the candy."

To her relief he started to laugh. "She probably could." Leaning to one side, he reached down to pat the dog and stroke her ears. "Gotta do something about that doorknob, though."

"She *was* sure chewing on it."

"It's probably all scratched and covered with tooth marks then." Again he laughed. "Like I care. I don't know what I'd do without her."

"She's remarkable." Ashley decided to plunge in again. "Do you think you could talk to Cadell about what Mikey would need?"

His face shuttered for an instant, and she had the feeling he was holding some kind of internal conversation. "I'd need to meet Mikey," he said. "I'd need to know what he can still do and what he wants. And by the way, I'm no expert. I don't know how the dogs are trained."

"Do you know who trained Nell? Maybe Cadell could call him. He's said several times that he'd like help with training service dogs. His bailiwick is police dogs, search-and-rescue dogs, bomb-sniffing dogs…"

He interrupted her. "We need bomb-sniffing dogs *here*?"

She had to laugh. "No. Not really. But we did have a scare a couple of years ago, and the sheriff started pining for a dog. Which made me think… Have you met Jess McGregor?"

"I haven't really met anyone," he reminded her drily. "Who's this McGregor?"

"Jess is the guy who had the bomb scare. He's a physician's assistant at the hospital clinic. An amputee. He'd probably be the perfect guy to set you up at the gym. And from what his wife has mentioned, he's still struggling a bit, too, from the war."

Again that stony face returned. Ashley nearly kicked herself. They had been doing all right with casual conversation about Halloween, but she had been the one to bring it back around. The guy had enough to deal with. He absolutely didn't need additional pressure from her.

"I'm sorry," she said. "I shouldn't press you. If you need anything, send Nell over."

But before she could rise, his hand snapped out and gently gripped her forearm. "Stay. Please. I've lost my social skills. I fall silent at all the wrong times." He let go of her immediately.

"But I've been pushing things on you that you don't want. I shouldn't do that." Really, she shouldn't. She decided she spent too much time being a teacher. Did she want to order the lives of everyone around her? Oddly, though, she missed his touch on her arm.

"You're trying to give me stuff to do instead of brooding. You're transparent, Ashley."

She felt her cheeks color and was grateful that it was dark.

"It's okay. I need some pushing, I guess. This whole hermitage idea isn't helping me sleep, it's not getting rid of the anxiety and it doesn't prevent me from slipping in time."

"I'm sorry." She stared out into the night for a few minutes, then asked, "Do you ever regret your choices? Most people regret at least some."

"No." The single word was uncompromising. After a minute or so he continued speaking. "I don't regret volunteering, either for the navy or the SEALs. I still believe we were doing important work. I just hadn't counted on how it could mess up my head. That was an unexpected…dividend, I guess."

"Lousy dividend." God, this was sad. She remembered so vividly when he'd been the star athlete who seemed to have the world on a string. Now he was a haunted, tortured man who couldn't even go out for a real run. Life could be so cruel sometimes, like with Mikey. What had that kid ever done except mount a horse to go for a ride as he had many times before?

"What exactly happened with Mikey?" Zane asked. "I think you told me but I'm forgetful sometimes." He tapped his head.

"Thrown from a horse. Like most ranch kids, he was pretty experienced, did a lot of riding. But a snake scared the horse, the horse bucked Mikey off, and I guess we should be glad that both horse and Mikey survived."

"That sucks," Zane said flatly. "Stinking bad luck. In my case I was in a war zone. I was choosing to take the risks. But that kid…" He shook his head.

She had the worst urge to reach out and take his hand. To find some way to offer comfort even though she couldn't think of anything that would actually work. "So your paralysis isn't your biggest problem?"

"My paralysis is a challenge, that's all. No, it's the other stuff."

She thought about that for a few minutes. A challenge? The thing she thought might cast anyone into a hellish depression was just a challenge? "That's a re-markable attitude."

"I got bigger problems." He shrugged. "Lots of peo-ple have bigger problems. I'd like to meet this Mikey kid. Think it's possible?"

Ashley didn't hesitate. A man who felt his paralysis was simply a challenge would probably be very good medicine. "I'm sure he'd like to meet you," she an-swered. "Want me to set it up?"

"Yeah. With some leeway in case I have a bad day and I'm taking cover behind the furniture."

He said it lightly, but Ashley understood there was nothing light about it. This man inescapably relived things most people would never know. "You'd like Jess," she said. "We've got some other former SEALs and special-ops types around here, too. If you ever want to see a face other than mine, let me know."

"Your face is nice to look at."

The compliment amazed her. She looked quickly at him and saw he was smiling. "Okay," he said. "Meet Jess. Check. Bring him over some time."

She rose reluctantly. "I have a lot of schoolwork to do yet. I'm sorry, I have to go."

"I hope you mean that. You'd be the first person in a long time." But he nodded, gave her again that half smile that didn't quite reach his eyes.

Ashley walked away, feeling as if she had interrupted something by going over there. One of his episodes of PTSD? Maybe. She just hoped it didn't pick up where it had left off.

Zane watched her walk away before he realized he was getting chilled. Once inside with Nell, he helped

himself to some of the remaining coffee while she settled nearby with her bone. The rinsed beer bottles sat
on the counter like accusing fingers.

"Couldn't wake me up, huh, Nell?" He received her
quizzical look. He must have gotten too drunk to respond and she'd given up, even when he'd started to
sober up. Not that it was part of her job description to
wake him up from an alcoholic stupor.

The alcohol had silenced the screams in his head, but
Ashley had been right—that wasn't a good way to go.

Sitting alone in his kitchen as the night continued
to deepen, and with a background sound track that
wouldn't quit—the noises of war kept playing—he
faced himself.

The SEALs had demanded more of him mentally,
physically and emotionally than he ever would have
believed possible. He'd met every challenge, passed
every test and performed every mission and duty they
had given him.

So what had happened to that guy? Lack of legs? A
challenge, as he'd said. No, something had pried his
brain open and let stuff out of the can that he'd never
expected to see again.

But why? That was the thing no one could explain
to him. Why? It was a natural reaction to trauma, last-
ing longer when the trauma had endured longer. But
why? Because the brain couldn't absorb it all in one big
chunk? Or was there something else going on?

He wished he knew, because it would be another tool
to use. Damn it, he needed some tools. Drugs took the
edge off, but they didn't get rid of it. Nell did a lot for
him, pulling him back from the edge repeatedly.

But time and again, sometimes for reasons he couldn't

begin to detect, he headed back to that edge. Vets and counselors both had told him it usually eased up with time. It might never go away totally, but it would ease.

He just sometimes wondered if he could hang on long enough.

But his thoughts soon drifted back to Ashley. The woman had kind of barged into his life, but he didn't mind it. Not at all. Very much the teacher, though, pushing him to meet other people. He wasn't sure about meeting the amputee, Jess McGregor. It sounded as if he'd found the keys to the kingdom already.

But that Mikey kid. That one grabbed him. Bad enough to be paraplegic and approaching forty. Quadriplegic at nine or ten? Unthinkable. Rolling out of the kitchen, he went to get his laptop computer and bring it back to set on the table. Nell kept happily gnawing away, apparently not sensing that she was needed just now.

At least he'd managed to get Wi-Fi in this town. The new thing, the installer had told him. He could plug into the router if he wanted to, but the capacity to go wireless everywhere in the house was good. Made his life easier, although he didn't spend a whole lot of time doing it.

It didn't take him long to find Cadell Marcus and his rather sketchy page about dog obedience training, with a brief mention of his work with police dogs. The guy didn't seem into tooting his own horn. Or maybe around here, he didn't need to. Zane hadn't been gone so long that he didn't remember that everyone knew everyone else around here. They must be telling some interesting stories about him now.

He picked up his phone and dialed Marcus. He expected to get voice mail, given the guy's webpage said he was also a sheriff's deputy, so he was surprised when the man himself answered.

"Hi, Deputy, this is Zane McLaren. Do you know Ashley Granger?"

"Sure thing. A friend of my wife's. At least so far as any woman who keeps her head buried in a computer can have friends, which is the story of life with my wife. And I know who you are. What's up?"

"Ashley said you were looking for help to train a service dog for Mikey… I'm sorry, I don't know his last name."

"There's only one Mikey I'd be thinking about. Mikey Landau. Yeah, I'd like to help him with a dog, but I'm kinda limited in my knowledge. I mean, I can practically train a dog to stand on his head and whistle 'Dixie,' but I need to know what's useful. You have a service dog?"

"Definitely."

"Well, I'd love to see it in action. Do you want to come out here? Ashley can show you the way and it would give me more of an idea right now than watching your dog in the house."

"I can do that," Zane answered. "I'm hoping to meet Mikey soon, too, because it would be good to talk to him about what he wants and needs."

"Tell you what," Cadell Marcus said. "Get Ashley to set it up and we can all meet with Mikey and you and your dog. Seeing your dog in action might help Mikey make his wish list."

Well, that sounded like a real freaking party, Zane

thought as he hung up. Hadn't he vowed not to do this again?

But then he thought of that little boy and told himself to man up. He might be able to help a kid.

Chapter Five

Early on Sunday morning, with Zane at the wheel of his van, Ashley guided him toward Cadell Marcus's ranch. Other than a few brief words in passing, they hadn't spoken since Friday except when Ashley finally managed to pull everything together with Mikey Landau and his mother, Marian.

Ashley was a little disturbed by how often she thought of Zane, by how often she felt an urge to run next door. Well, maybe today would satisfy the urge and it would leave her alone. He certainly hadn't reached out to her in any way.

"I hope I can talk to this kid," he said as they turned onto a rough county road. "I told you my social skills aren't what they used to be. You've experienced it."

She looked toward him. "I think you'll find Mikey easy to talk to. You have a little bit in common to begin with, and he's just a kid. He'll probably bubble with questions and all you'll have to do is answer them."

"So he can still breathe on his own?"

"Yes, thank God."

"That's good."

Silence fell again. Nell had ceded her front bucket seat to Ashley without any hesitation. Now she stuck her head forward and sniffed. Instinctively, Ashley started to reach up to pet her, then caught herself. Not without permission.

But almost at once, Zane pulled over onto the dirt shoulder and turned off the car. "Sorry," he said.

Nell had pushed forward between the seats, and Zane gripped her fur while she sniffed him then licked his face.

Ashley wondered if she should get out of the car to give Nell more room to do whatever it was she did for Zane, but the dog didn't seem needlessly worried. She licked Zane's face several times, and then a shuddering sigh escaped him.

"It's okay," he said.

All of sudden, Ashley was very glad she hadn't tried to get out of the van. She would have hated for Zane to think she was afraid. "Stress?" she finally asked.

"Maybe. I think I told you, I don't always know the triggers. But this wasn't bad. It barely started before it was over." He rubbed Nell a few more times then started the van again. "It's all gotten a lot better because of Nell. She catches me as soon as it starts. I don't know what this kid is experiencing, but it would be great if he could have a dog like Nell."

Ashley had no doubt of that. Her hands knotted a bit in her lap. Zane was getting to her. His loneliness, the problems he had to live with. She wished with all her might that she knew how to make life better for him. A man with just a dog didn't seem like a whole lot for anyone.

"You know," he said suddenly, "this was exactly the kind of thing I intended to avoid when I came here."

Her stomach fluttered uncomfortably. "Meaning?" She hoped he wasn't referring to her.

"Getting involved. I'm not good for people."

"I wish you wouldn't say that." Anger sparked in her. "You need to give other people a chance to decide that for themselves. Anyway, it's kind of you to agree to help Mikey if you can, and after that you can go home and pull the door in after you."

He didn't respond immediately, but finally he gave a quiet laugh. "Firebrand."

Well, she *had* been a little out of line, but she wasn't prepared to take it back. The man clearly had some very generous impulses, to judge first by his check for the wheelchair and now by this. Yeah, he was having a rough time, but that didn't mean he was *bad* in any way.

"Think I'm drowning in self-pity?" he asked abruptly.

"I don't know. I don't see enough of you to know. I gather you're dealing with some heavy emotional baggage—hardly surprising given your past—but you're also the same guy who dismissed his paralysis as a challenge. That doesn't sound like self-pity. But really, I don't know what made you think you couldn't have a friend or two."

Another silence ensued. They were nearing the turn onto Cadell's drive when he spoke again.

"My neighbors."

"What about your neighbors?"

"They got me evicted. I was crazy. I had rages. I annoyed them and frightened them when I wasn't quiet. I scared them when I emerged from a bad spell and went out to the store looking like a mountain man. And that was just part of the list. They were scared I could get violent. Harm them."

"Did you ever?"

"No."

"Never threatened?"

He glanced at her. "No. Not until I realized I had a week to get out unless I wanted police help to do it. Then I was tempted to say something. Instead I spent most of the week packing while being yanked back from the edge by Nell."

Shock filled her, followed by an anger so strong she barely recognized it as her own emotion. She'd been angry about a lot of things in her life, but few things made her this mad: child abuse when she caught it was the only thing that sent her over the top. Then she felt her heart start to break.

Now this. "What did you do after?" she asked quietly, pointing him to the left turn. The sign by the road made it pretty clear they had arrived. He braked and turned carefully onto the gravel.

"Got a motel room by the week and decided to move back here as soon as I could get the place ready enough. If I upset folks around here, they might be able to get me committed, but they can't evict me."

"No one here is going to do that to you."

"How can you guarantee it?"

"Because I know a lot of vets who'd come racing to your side."

He shook his head a little. "Where I was before? I

was near the VA hospital. My support group. By the time they showed up, it was too late."

It was her turn to shake her head as they bumped down the drive toward the house. God, this was almost too awful to think about. "I bet you didn't call any of them, either."

He surprised her with a dry response. "Now what could have given you that idea?"

She might have laughed at his self-deprecating humor, except she was still too mad. She couldn't believe his neighbors had treated him that way. Surely, they must have known his situation? Everything inside her roiled as she thought of that ugliness, all of it directed at a man who had suffered in the service of his country.

"They had kids," he said as he parked next to Cadell's official vehicle. "Of course they didn't want me there."

He'd said sad things to her before, but this one made her chest tighten and her eyes burn. It was amazing that after that he'd even be willing to meet Mikey. That he cared enough to try to help someone else's kid.

She shot him a sidelong look as he began to unbuckle himself and decided that Zane McLaren was one heck of a stand-up guy. Better than he even knew himself.

She wished there was some way she could get him to see that.

All of a sudden he froze. "Are those *ostriches*?"

All the tension fled from the van, and at last Ashley felt it was safe to laugh. "Yes. For real. Cadell inherited them. He was thinking about getting rid of them, but his new bride won't let him. They love her."

"Someday I want to hear that story."

"Well, he kind of had a love-hate relationship with them at first. They can be nasty, I guess."

Then she saw Cadell come around the side of the house from his backyard kennels. "There's Cadell," she said and climbed out to give Zane enough room to pivot his seat and get into his wheelchair.

Cadell greeted her warmly with a one-armed hug, then turned his attention to Zane, who was by now lowering himself to the ground with his lift. Nell hopped out beside him, and when he'd rolled onto the ground, she hit a switch and everything folded and closed back up.

"Now that's a well-trained dog," Cadell remarked, watching Nell trot alongside Zane as he wheeled toward them.

"Very," Zane said, extending his hand. "Zane McLaren."

"Cadell Marcus. Is the ground too rough for you to come around back?"

"No problem. I'll enjoy the workout."

Cadell smiled. "I want to hear all about this dog of yours."

"Nell."

"Hi, Nell," Cadell said. The dog's tail wagged in acknowledgment. "Mikey and his mom should be here in half an hour. That'll give me some time to pick your brain."

"Just so long as you understand I didn't train her. I'm enjoying the fruits of it, but it owes to other people."

Cadell nodded. "That's okay. Once I see what she can do, I can get another smart dog to do it. And maybe add on some things that Mikey will need."

The two men were making their way around the side

of the house now. Ashley followed, listening, sensing the birth of a bond between them.

"He'll need more and different things than me," Zane said. "I've still got useful arms."

"Yeah," Cadell answered. "I get it. And I'll tell you a secret."

Zane tipped his head upward as they reached the edge of the kennels and a fenced and wired corral. "What's that?"

"Today, if you'll let me, I'm going to ask Nell to teach a few things to another dog."

Zane stopped wheeling. "Nell? Teach?"

"Trust me, she can. And she'll be proud of it. Plus, Mikey will enjoy seeing it. If you'd ever worked on a ranch with a bunch of herding dogs, you'd know how well they can teach each other."

"I'm looking forward to seeing this," Zane replied. "I know how smart Nell is, but I never thought of her as a teacher. Or maybe she's been teaching *me*." He glanced around to Ashley. "No offense to you, Teach."

Ashley laughed. "None taken."

Cadell guided them to a bench beside the corral where Ashley could sit. Nell perched immediately between her and Zane.

Cadell spoke. "In my work with police dogs, we tend to stick to German shepherds and Belgian Malinois, but in my readings it seems Labs often make the best service dogs. You know anything about that?"

"Not exactly. Most of the ones I've seen have been retrievers or Labs like Nell here, but I've seen a few other kinds, smaller dogs. I guess it depends on what they're needed for. Big dogs are good for doing a lot of tasks that a short dog couldn't manage. For example, I met a woman whose dog warns her she's about to have a seizure. She had a small dog, a mixed breed, but he was perfect for her. That's all he had to do. Alert her."

"But Nell does a lot more, obviously."

Zane stroked her head. "A lot more. When I drop something, she picks it up for me. She can bring me items from the cupboards or pantry, at least from the lower levels. She lets people in the house and closes the door after them. I've had her bring me the phone a few times. The list goes on. The thing is, Cadell, I try to do as much as I can for myself. It would be awfully easy to become lazy and let the dog do it all, but it wouldn't be fair to either of us. Mikey's going to need a lot more than I do."

"Obviously." Cadell was looking thoughtful.

"If I wanted," Zane continued, "she could bring me clothes from my dresser. She's brought me beverages from the fridge. Cleaned up after me. But most of all I need her to help me keep stable."

Cadell nodded. "Well, we'll just have to see what Mikey needs when he gets here. I'm sure his mom will have some ideas. Is it all right if I take Nell into the corral with another dog?"

"Sure. Nell, go with the man."

Ashley watched in amazement as Nell glanced at Zane then walked away with Cadell. Soon she was in the corral, and another dog was joining her. A short-coated golden Lab ran around playfully while Nell sat and watched as if indulging a young child.

"Nell runs around, doesn't she?" Cadell called.

"When I tell her it's okay."

"All right then. Let's see if I can get her to make Joey here sit."

To Ashley that looked like an almost impossible thing at the moment. Joey was on a personal romp.

But then Cadell spoke. "Nell, sit. Joey, sit."

Nell sat; Joey kept running. "Joey, sit," Cadell said.

There had to be a better way, Ashley thought. Didn't most trainers use treats? She thought she remembered watching someone teach their dog to sit by repeating the word and raising a treat before the dog's nose so that the dog sat down automatically to get it.

But not Cadell. Once again, "Joey, sit."

Apparently that sent some kind of message to Nell. She took off after the miscreant. Bit by bit she rounded him up until he was in the middle of the corral and looking a bit confused. Then Nell sat and woofed.

Joey looked at her and started to move away. Nell lowered her head and woofed again. Then, to Ashley's absolute amazement, Joey imitated Nell and sat.

"And there it is," called Cadell.

"What just happened?" Ashley asked. "I don't get it."

"Dogs have their own language," Cadell said. "Nell let Joey know she was the boss when she chased him, then she cemented it. Joey will now, within reason, do what Nell shows him how to do."

With that Cadell approached the fence and looked at Zane. "Can you come out here from time to time to help?"

Zane visibly hesitated. "Just with Joey?"

"Man, I've got a dozen people who need service dogs. But if that's all you got time for, I'd be happy with it. Nell can teach the basics fast, then I take over and the dog will start accepting the commands from me. Dogs train quickly, but they learn faster from each other. So, whenever you can."

"I'll help," Zane said. "Some, anyway."

"Great. I'll give Nell back to you now." He opened the gate, and when Zane called, Nell came dashing to his side, leaving a slightly confused Joey behind.

When Joey stood up, Cadell said, "Joey, sit." Amazingly, the dog did. Cadell grinned. "Way to go." Then he walked over and patted the dog. "Okay, guy, you can run now."

Joey looked up quizzically, but with a little push from Cadell, he started bounding around again, working off puppyish energy.

Cadell closed the gate and rejoined them. "Now, maybe we've got a little something to show Mikey when he gets here."

Which seemed to be now, Ashley thought, hearing what sounded like a car door slamming.

"You guys wait here," Cadell said, trotting out to the front.

Zane looked at Ashley. "I wouldn't have believed that if I hadn't seen it."

"I wouldn't, either," Ashley admitted.

Zane surprised her, reaching across Nell to take her hand. "Thanks for talking me into this." This time the smile reached his eyes.

"I didn't talk all that hard. This was *your* decision." But his hand holding hers felt so good. His touch was warm and strong without being uncomfortable. She turned her hand over and tightened her grip on him, just a little, to let him know his touch was welcome, but she was nearly overcome by the worst urge to just lean into him and find out what he smelled like, what he felt like, how his arms around her would make her feel.

How awful it would be to do that to him. That man

was paraplegic. It would be the worst tease of all time to let him know about her steadily growing sexual interest in him. She dismayed herself. But she didn't let go of his hand.

Soon she heard Mikey's excited voice. "Ostriches! Real live ostriches! I heard about them but I didn't believe in them!"

A smile stretched Ashley's cheeks, and when she glanced at Zane she saw he was smiling, too. The boy's excitement was contagious.

"I want to see more," he said.

"After the dogs," Cadell answered. "But you still can't get close. They might peck you."

Twisting on the bench, Ashley saw Cadell pushing Mikey's wheelchair over the rugged ground while Marian walked beside them. She looked delighted at the outing, almost as delighted as her son.

"I have to admit," she said, "I never imagined they'd be so big."

"Dinosaurs," Cadell said lightly. Then he pushed Mikey's wheelchair to a position near Zane. Mikey's smile faded into a serious expression as he looked at the man.

"You can use your arms?" Mikey asked.

"Yeah," Zane answered. "That makes me lucky. And my dog, Nell, helps a lot. Nell, say hello." He pointed to Mikey.

Nell rose and walked over to the boy in the wheelchair. First she sat and looked at him. Then, as if realizing he couldn't reach out to touch her, she inched forward and rested her head in his lap.

Ashley glanced at Marian and saw the sheen of tears

in her eyes as Joey murmured, "Wow." Then the boy's head popped up. "I want one, too," he told Cadell.

"That's what we're here for. See Joey out in the corral? We're going to train him for you. It'll take a little time and you're going to have to talk to me a lot along the way so I know what you want and need. You okay with that?"

Mikey's entire face brightened. "Oh, yeah!"

Before long, Mikey was out in the corral with both Nell and Joey, Nell helping Cadell make some basic points.

As much fun as it was to watch, a half hour later Ashley heard Zane sigh faintly. She immediately turned her attention to him. "Are you okay?"

"Yeah. Tired. Stress."

She hadn't thought about that. He'd come here to be a hermit, and now he'd spent a great deal of time with a bunch of strangers. He wasn't used to that, and it must be exhausting. At once she stood up. "Cadell? We need Nell back. Zane's getting tired."

"Mikey probably is, too," said Marian, speaking for the first time. She'd obviously been enthralled watching her son feel excited about a new world opening up.

She came to stand in front of Zane. "I can't thank you enough." She offered her hand.

He shook it briefly. "Thank Cadell and my dog. I'll see you and Mikey again, I'm sure."

"I hope so. Mikey's been feeling like the odd man out. I think you helped with that whether you know it or not."

Zane seemed lost in his own thoughts as he rolled himself back to his van, Nell at his side. Ashley didn't say anything, figuring he'd pushed himself about as far as he wanted to go for one day. It had been amazingly generous of him.

The silence continued on the drive back to town. Ashley wanted to tell him what a kind thing he'd done today, but somehow she didn't feel he'd appreciate it. He struck her as a man who did what he chose for his own reasons, and complimenting his generosity would probably feel like a patronizing pat on the head.

Anyway, the hermit had probably already had as much human interaction as he wanted for one day. When they got home, she was going to thank him and go back to her place.

Then she remembered his story of how his neighbors had treated him, and the ache returned. She got that people could be difficult to live with, but surely they must have known he was a vet. For crying out loud, he was a man in a wheelchair! But he'd made excuses for them, saying they had children to worry about.

She sighed quietly, wondering about the whole story. Maybe when he went over the edge it could be loud and frightening. Maybe he yelled things that people didn't want their kids to hear. About war. About death. She could grasp that, but to evict him?

Not the kind of neighbors she wanted.

As they neared town, he broke the silence. "Is Maude's still as good as it used to be?" He referred to the City Diner, which everyone called by its owner's name. Maude was an unforgettable gorgon, and she remained in business only because of her fabulous cooking and scrumptious pies.

"Yes, it is."

"Wanna stop and get something?"

Her brows lifted. Once again he was taking her by

surprise. "I thought you'd had enough of people for one day."

"I can also recover, you know. I don't want my own cooking today. So…should I stop? I'd like your company."

Maybe that would make it easier for him? Because he'd never really expressed a desire to spend time with her before. But Maude's was often loud, and those plates and cups banging on the table could sound like gunshots.

"You remember she slams down the cups and plates?"

He nodded. "I appreciate you wanting to spare me, but there are some things I need to get past. Going into the diner is at the top of my list. I've thought about those steak sandwiches of hers for years. And the pecan pie."

"Okay, then." She was game if he was. And Nell would be there if he started to have a problem.

There was a van-accessible handicapped parking place not too far down from the diner. He slid into it and turned off the ignition before facing Ashley. "I can't make any guarantees," he said. "I could go off the edge."

"I didn't ask for a guarantee. If you want to try, I'm game."

One hell of a woman, Zane thought as he went through all the steps of getting himself out of the van and his wheelchair onto the sidewalk. Nell, still wearing her vest, realized something unusual was about to happen. He didn't put it on her for hanging around the house.

He looked at Ashley and once again thought how beautiful and appealing she was. His groin gave a throb of desire, and he gave a moment of thanks that his injury hadn't deprived him of his sexual abilities. Partial spinal cord injury. One advantage in that, not that he'd taken much advantage of it.

But it made him feel almost like a whole man, being able to look at a stunning woman and feel his body respond. It made him feel so good that he didn't mind that he couldn't do a damn thing about it. At least not now. It *did* put a smile on his face.

The diner didn't have a ramp, but the lintel wasn't too high for him to manage. He sensed Ashley's desire to help—she had this way of fluttering quietly, something she probably did often as a teacher—so he reassured her. "I can do this. I'll ask you to open the door, though. Nell might damage the knob."

"All right." Smiling, apparently glad to be able to do *something*, she pulled the door open. With practiced expertise, Zane tipped his chair back a little, got his front wheels over the lintel, and entered the diner.

It didn't surprise him when the place quickly quieted down and every eye fixed on him. He'd known it would happen. He just hoped he didn't have a lot of people who wanted to come over and recall his high school exploits. He wasn't that kid any longer. Not in the least.

Ashley quickly pulled a chair out of the way so he could roll up to the table. Nell parked right beside him, at the ready. Ashley sat across from him.

Then, bit by bit, the diner's normal noises resumed. And little by little he allowed himself to relax. Nell thrust her head under his hand, asking for a pat now that she could relax as well.

Maude, looking as if she hadn't changed one bit in

all the intervening years, stomped over with two menus. "Good to see you back, Zane. Coffee?"

"Yes, thanks. Ashley?"

"Ashley likes them latte things I make."

"Indeed, I do." Ashley smiled. "Thanks, Maude."

"I guess some things do change," Zane remarked as Maude went to get the coffee. "Lattes here? Never would have dreamed."

"I'm still wishing for a Mexican restaurant. And a Chinese one, too. We *did* get a chain pizza place on the edge of town, though. Popular hangout."

"Mostly with young folks," he guessed. "Man, what I'd have given for that when I was..." He stopped. He didn't want anyone else taking him down that particular avenue of memory, so why do it himself?

"It came too late for me, too," Ashley remarked, easing a moment in which tension had started to grow in him again.

Nell poked his arm with her nose and he looked down. "I'm okay, girl."

High school was so far in the past, and so much had happened to him since, that it felt almost like someone else's memory, or like a book he'd once read. He couldn't even connect with that young man who'd had such a sunny future and had been blessed with so much athletic talent and so many friends. That guy had used his gifts in the SEALs, forever putting a wall up between him and his youth.

He looked across the table at Ashley, who was studying her menu as if she didn't already have it memorized. When he looked at his own, he saw that it hadn't changed a whole lot. Maude's famous steak sandwich was still there, and his mouth watered a bit in anticipation. Ashley chose a chef's salad for herself. Women and their salads, he thought with amusement. Men and their steaks… He almost laughed.

While they waited for Maude to serve them, a tall, powerfully built man with streaks of gray in his dark hair came over. Zane felt tension creep along his nerves. He recognized the expression in the guy's eyes.

"Hey, Ashley," he said pleasantly. "Introduce me?"

Ashley bit her lip for a second before looking at Zane. Not knowing what else to do, Zane offered his hand. "Zane McLaren."

"Seth Hardin. I must be one of the few guys who didn't grow up around here, so I never met you before. I'm the old sheriff's son. Nate Tate's kid."

Well, that explained the resemblance, but not the expression in the eyes. Seth pulled out the chair beside Ashley. "I won't interrupt your dinner. I just wanted to introduce myself to a fellow traveler."

Tension began to wind in Zane again. "SEALs?"

"Yeah. Retired a few years ago. Team 2."

"Team 3."

Seth nodded. "There are a few of us around, spec-ops types. Ashley knows my number if you ever want to hang out with any of us. We usually get together on Thursdays once a month to chew the fat together. There's my wife, too. Former combat search-and-rescue pilot." Then Seth stood. "Nice meeting you." With a smile and a nod, he walked out.

Zane's lunch plate clattered onto the table in front of him. Ashley's followed. For a brief while Zane didn't even smell the delightful aromas.

Then Nell nudged him back to awareness, and he saw Ashley eyeing him with concern.

"I'm fine," he said. "Fine. Let's eat."

"That was nice of Seth," Ashley offered as she speared some of her salad.

Was it? Zane supposed it was. After all, he'd exposed himself by coming in here, and if the worst that happened was meeting a fellow SEAL, he'd be doing well. He knew he'd taken a risk facing the noise and Maude's famous slamming of plates and cups on the tables, but he'd only had the slightest slip, almost undetectable to him but picked up by Nell, who had yanked him right back.

"I wonder if Maude would kill me if I gave Nell some steak."

"I don't know." Ashley grinned and looked around until her gaze landed on Maude. The large woman, frowning as usual, stomped over to them.

"Something wrong?" she demanded.

Ashley spoke before Zane could. "Zane wants to give his service dog a little of his steak. Do you mind?"

Because Maude's feelings had to be treated more carefully than she treated her customers. Zane had been amused by that in the past. He decided to be amused now.

"Don't give that dog none of your supper," Maude groused. "You need to eat."

She walked away, leaving Zane and Ashley to look at each other.

"Guess not," Ashley said, her lips quivering.

"Guess not," Zane agreed. Not that Nell was supposed to eat when she was on duty. Nell knew that, but he could almost feel her salivating. It wasn't like she had a chance at steak every day. But she remained calmly beside him, attentive to him, not to his plate.

He was on his second mouthful of that piece of heaven known as a steak sandwich when Maude slammed yet another plate on the table, one that held a decent-size steak all cut up. "Give the animal that. Just make sure you put the plate on the floor. Don't need no health inspectors on my back."

Before Zane could thank her, she had moved away, talking to other customers in her gruff way.

"Um, wow?" Ashley said.

"Yeah. Wow."

"Need help getting the plate to the floor?"

"Thanks, but I think I can do it. If I can't, I'll let you know." Twisting, he managed to bend far enough to get the plate to the floor without dropping it. Nell eyed him. "Eat, girl. It's okay."

Nell didn't need a second invitation. It also didn't take her very long to empty the plate, but as she licked her chops, she looked completely content.

He bit into his own sandwich while Ashley said, "Dogs eat so fast. I always wonder how they can enjoy it."

"I think they're wired differently when it comes to food. Imagine a wolf pack lazing around sharing an elk."

She laughed. "Good point, Zane."

The sandwich was every bit as good as memory had claimed, and before he left with Ashley, he ordered a second to take home with him. Ashley had finished only half her salad and scooped it into a takeout box while he waited.

Little by little, now that he was done eating, departing diners and newcomers passed his table. Many said quietly, "Welcome home, Zane." They didn't pause, didn't stop to try to converse, just made those quiet statements.

The wheelchair, he figured. It made people uncomfortable. They probably didn't *want* to have a conversation, because they just didn't know what they could say.

Great conversation killer, he thought as he pushed himself back from the table. "I got it," he said to Ashley as she started to pull out her wallet. "Please."

She nodded, smiling faintly. With his boxed dinner on his lap, he wheeled up to the cash register and pulled his wallet out of his breast pocket.

Maude came around and stared at him over the counter. "No charge."

"But…"

"I said no charge. Don't be arguing with me. Trust me, it won't happen again, and I better be seeing a lot of you around here."

Zane hardly knew how to react. On the one hand, she was being generous, which he didn't need and which kind of embarrassed him, and on the other, it sounded as if she were scolding him. Well, he remembered there was no arguing with Maude. "Thank you," he said. Funny how hard it was to say those words sometimes.

"Thank *you*," she answered. "Now get outta here. Weather's turning bitter and that jacket ain't enough. Hope you got a better one."

Chapter Six

Maude was right about the weather. The drop in temperature just during the time they'd been inside was startling. When he was securely buttoned into the driver's seat, he looked over at Ashley. "I didn't expect any of that."

"If you want friends in this town, you seldom have to look hard."

He leaned forward, turning on the ignition, pulling them back onto the street. "I don't remember the old sheriff having a son."

"I'm not surprised. He didn't know about it, either. Apparently his wife, to whom he wasn't married at the time, got pregnant with Seth while Nate was in Vietnam. Her dad made her give the baby up, and what with her father's interference, I guess, Nate never heard about Seth until Seth showed up on his doorstep, a grown man in his late twenties. The whole county buzzed about that one."

"I can just imagine," Zane answered drily. "Gossip enough for months."

"Almost ended the Tate marriage, too, from what I remember. Anyway, everything's all patched up and fine for years now."

"And his wife? A CSAR pilot?"

"She was. Afghanistan, mostly. Anyway, she's piloting our medical and rescue helicopters now."

Things had certainly changed around here, he thought as he drove back to his house. Even Maude, who had once seemed as unchangeable as the mountains, had softened up a bit.

A veterans' group meeting. He didn't remember if there'd been one when he was in high school, but he supposed he wouldn't have been interested. His thoughts turned back to those years, and he realized he had some assessing to do.

"Come in?" he asked Ashley as they parked in his driveway.

She didn't hesitate, which relieved him, which meant he hadn't done something to disturb her today. Yet. "Sure," she said and climbed out.

His own exit took a little longer, and Ashley was waiting for him on the porch by the time he rolled up the ramp.

Nell took a quick dash in the yard, then followed eagerly into the house. The dog was good at fitting in her business when she had the chance.

"Stay for a while," he asked Ashley. "I can offer you a soft drink if you'd like."

She held up her latte cup. "Still plenty here."

He rolled into the kitchen and up to the table, where he placed the box holding his extra meal. He didn't go into the living room much. Getting on and off the sofa was a pain, hardly worth the effort most of the time. He supposed he could hang a bar in there like he had over his bed so he could pull himself up and over, but he hadn't felt particularly motivated yet.

But then, almost before he knew what he was doing, he tugged on Ashley's hand until she slid into his lap.

"If I'm outta line, tell me," he said gruffly. "No social skills, like I said."

He watched one corner of her mouth curve upward. "I don't usually like to be manhandled. However, this time I think I'll make an exception. What brought this on?"

"You have any idea how long it's been since I had an attractive woman in my lap?" With those words he felt almost as if he had stripped his psyche bare. Had he gone over some new kind of cliff?

Ashley didn't know what to make of this. His words had been an apology of sorts, but he'd still pulled her onto his lap. She twisted her head, trying to read his face, knowing he'd been honest in his way, but seeing doubt begin to creep into his eyes.

It was true she didn't like being manhandled, even in small ways, but this felt different to her. As if actions had needed for once to replace words, even with her. But the doubt troubled her. She didn't want him to think he'd offended her or done something wrong. It had taken a long time to get this close to him, to get him to go out to Cadell's place, to see him willing to enter the diner and share a meal with her in front of other people. The last thing she wanted was for him to crawl back into his hole.

Taking a huge risk, she lifted her hand and pressed his cheek until his head turned toward her. Then she stole a kiss right from his lips. She couldn't be any clearer. She just hoped he wouldn't think she was a tease, given his paralysis.

Instead he wound his other arm around her and pulled her in for another kiss, his mouth warm and firm on hers, his tongue entering her mouth as if he hoped to find her soul within.

Glorious desire ran through her like a hot river. She'd thought a lot about Zane, but she had never allowed herself to think very much about how sexually attractive he was. He was in a wheelchair. She didn't want to make him feel bad in any way. But now…now…

He tore his mouth from hers and pressed her ear so close to his chest she could hear his heartbeat. It seemed to be racing as fast as hers. She just wished she could melt into him.

He cleared his throat. "I'm going to let go of you."

Of course he was, she thought as disappointment caused her stomach to drop and her mood to sink. What else could he do?

Without a word, she slid off his lap. She thought about leaving but decided that might be a bad thing to do so soon. Hard to believe that late-afternoon sunlight still poured into the kitchen, that everything slammed back into place as if an earthquake hadn't just happened.

She struggled to find her voice. "I think I'd like a beer." *Go for the normal, as if nothing had happened. Don't make him feel worse.*

"In a sec," he answered, his voice still rough. "You need to know something."

"What?"

"That being in this wheelchair doesn't make me harmless."

She blinked, not sure what he meant. Not harmless? She'd never thought of him as being harmless, legs or no legs. He looked as if he could be a threat with just his upper body. "I never thought—"

"That's not what I mean. I don't mean I might hurt you, although I guess I could. No, damn it. I meant... I can still have sex. I didn't lose that. So... I—I shouldn't be pulling you into my lap. I have no right, and I don't want to upset you."

"Upset me?" Her head was whirling now. He'd just given her some wonderful news—for him, at least— and he was worried about upsetting her? "I think that's great, Zane. Really great. It makes me so happy to hear."

"Yeah." He looked away. "Thanks. But I got a whole bunch of problems you don't want to deal with, so..."

He was confusing her more by the minute, bouncing around, trying to say something he couldn't quite get to, she guessed. Was he trying to say that nobody would want a paralyzed guy? Hardly. That no one would be willing to deal with the emotional toll war had taken on him? Some might not be, but she knew some spouses who did and never complained.

His isolation struck her anew, and she wished she knew how to ease it. "That beer?" she said again. Give him time to figure out what he wanted to say. Give her time to try to figure out why he'd said it.

Without a word, he rolled to the fridge, maneuvered the door open and brought two beers to the table.

"Thanks," he said as he popped the caps off the long-necks.

"For what?"

"For pushing me to help Mikey. Kid's a real pistol. I think he had a good time."

"I'm sure he did. Did you?"

"Yeah, actually. Even enjoyed myself at Maude's."

She smiled, holding the icy beer. "So I guess you don't have to be a hermit all day, every day."

"Maybe not." He took a pull on his beer. "Being in Maude's, though…"

She waited, trying to get a handle on her own roiling feelings. She wasn't sure what had just happened or what might happen next. Or if anything was going to happen. But her stomach felt full of butterflies, her entire body still ached with need from being in his arms and she had a strong suspicion he'd probably find a way to keep away from her. Maybe that was best. She still didn't know him that well. She'd seen plenty in him that she liked, and plenty that ought to be worrisome.

"Something about being at Maude's," he said, starting again. "I don't think much about my days before the navy. Especially now. That person seems like such a stranger."

"You said something about that, didn't you? Like a book you'd read?"

"Did I say that out loud?" He arched his brow. "Anyway, yeah. A character out of a movie. Doesn't feel real to me anymore. But I was thinking back to it and realized I was a bit of a knucklehead."

She hadn't heard that expression in forever. "How so?"

"I told myself I was joining the navy so I could go to

college. Considering how fast I leaped on the chance to become a SEAL, I don't think so anymore."

Again she was hesitant to speak for fear of saying the wrong thing. This man had warned her he could be a minefield with his PTSD, and she sure didn't have any idea what might trigger it.

A sound drew her attention, and she saw Nell contentedly chewing on a bone nearby. Apparently, the dog thought everything was okay.

"So, I've been kind of wondering at what really happened. What I was really thinking. Was it that I couldn't give up being an athlete, a big fish in that little pond? That I still had something to prove to myself? God, I can hardly remember that kid. All I know is I volunteered for the toughest, dirtiest job in the service."

She nodded silently.

"Something made me take a sharp turn within a few months of enlisting. But maybe it wasn't a sharp turn at all."

"Maybe not," she said cautiously. "If you don't regret it…"

"I don't, which probably sounds fairly crazy coming from a guy in a wheelchair who sometimes loses his marbles and needs a dog to keep him in the here and now, but I don't regret it. I don't like some of the memories. Hell, no. But I did an essential job. Nothing will take that awareness from me. Wait a sec."

He pulled back from the table and left the kitchen. She heard his chair rolling down the hall, then a little while later rolling back again. Nell never left her bone, and Ashley considered the dog to be the best barometer around.

When he pulled up to the table again, he put a

wooden box on it. "My medals." He opened the lid and pulled out the presentation cases, opening them and laying them out before her. The only one she recognized was the Purple Heart, and it had a cluster. Did that mean he'd been wounded more than once? She'd ask later, not now. Let him get through all this.

He pointed. "Silver Stars, Bronze Stars, the Navy Cross...all those say I was a hero. But you know what? I don't feel like a hero. I did a job. An important job. And there wasn't one of my comrades who didn't deserve those medals at least as much."

He sighed and stared at the cases. "No hero. But I don't regret it."

"But you're troubled?" she asked tentatively.

"Only by wondering why I jumped into it when that wasn't my conscious plan. It's like something knocking on the door in my head and I can't let it in."

She stared at the medals, thinking they were poor symbols at best of what he'd been through. Impressive, but nowhere near like the doing of all that.

"I used to talk about throwing these away," he said, closing the cases and putting them back in the box one by one.

"You didn't think you deserved them?"

"I didn't think I deserved them any more than anyone else. Plus, they were like a reminder, which at times I didn't want."

"But you kept them."

"Yeah, a Vietnam vet talked me into it. Told me that someday someone who knew me would want them. Or that I'd get around to wanting them, because they were the only damn reward I was ever going to get."

Ashley drew a sharp breath as her heart squeezed. The only reward he would get? A pile of medals?

But in her heart she knew he was right. People thanking him for his service didn't begin to touch on all he'd done for his country. How could it? They didn't know; they hadn't been through it. Maybe it was a nice but nearly meaningless gesture from his point of view.

"So," she said, "you ever get annoyed by people thanking you for your service?"

He surprised her by laughing. "Sometimes. The first few times it feels good. Then it begins to sound rote. When I ditched the uniform, I was glad not to hear it anymore."

"I can imagine. Then you get treated like crap by your neighbors."

He shrugged, his laughter vanishing. "We all had our problems. They had theirs. Mine were adding to them."

"Are you really that forgiving?"

"Who am I to judge?"

Good Lord, what an amazing man. He might be gruff and sometimes prickly, and want little to do with people, but he'd just said he couldn't judge the neighbors who'd kicked him to the curb like so much trash.

She suspected he judged himself a whole lot and far more harshly. "Zane?"

He looked up from the beer he was turning slowly in his hands. "Yeah?"

"Apply a little of that forgiveness to yourself."

His brow lowered, and she wouldn't be able to blame him if he grew angry with her. She had no right to tell him anything, and certainly nothing so personal.

Then his brow smoothed. "You got it in one, Teach. I'm my own judge, jury and executioner."

"Executioner?" The word made her heart stop. Was he suicidal?

"Figure of speech. I'm not going to do anything that crazy. Too much karma to work out." Then he smiled faintly. "Sometimes you see right through me. When I got some therapy, they told me the same thing. Quit blaming myself. I did my job. I'd have something to apologize for if I'd deserted. Give myself the same breaks I'd give the next guy. Good advice, hard to do."

"Advice is usually hard to act on," she said drily. "If I'd followed all the good advice I'd been given, I'd be a nominee for sainthood."

That drew another laugh out of him, and almost helplessly, she joined it. He was a bit mercurial, but she was so glad he could still find laughter in himself. Not only glad, but relieved.

But the laughter faded, the quiet settled in again, and he seemed lost in thought. Nell was still content, apparently unconcerned, so he must be all right.

Taking a chance, she asked, "Didn't you have Nell when you were in your apartment? Before those people…well, they were horrid. What could you possibly have done?"

"No Nell then. As for what I did, I don't remember most of it. You see, when it hits, I'm somewhere else. Back over there. On a mission. Being shot at, seeing my buddies get hit… I'm really not aware of what I'm doing here sometimes. So I guess I was noisy, angry and did a lot of cussing in front of children, and I scared some people. At least that's what they told me. About a week after I moved into that motel, my buddies brought me Nell. It's because of her I didn't get evicted again, I'm sure."

She just shook her head, hurting for him.

"It's better now, obviously," he continued. "Nell. It's been a year. Mostly I've learned to avoid triggers. She's good at sensing when something is disturbing me, and she distracts me. And she never lets me get too far away mentally. I gather that's a big improvement. Well, I know it is. I'm here more often than not now. A year ago I wouldn't have dared to go out to Cadell's ranch for fear something would happen. I wouldn't have wanted to meet a kid, because I might lose touch and say things no kid should ever hear."

Impulsively, she reached out and took his hand. He didn't pull away, but he glanced at her before returning his gaze to the wooden box in front of him and the beer bottle beside it.

"You have a really bad case," she said.

"I did, I guess. Not unheard of. Better now. So I'm grateful. Especially grateful for Nell."

"I'm sure." She squeezed his hand gently, then let go. "We don't do enough to care for our vets. One of our high school teachers was widowed by the war. A year or so later, his best buddy came to visit her, to keep a promise. He'd suffered brain trauma and was kind of wandering, wondering what he could do. It turned out he was pretty good at helping around her farm, and they married eventually."

"Meaning?"

"Meaning I don't think he got very good care, at least not until he met my friend. They discharged him with all kinds of problems, and except for the way things fell out, he'd probably be living under a bridge." She tried to tamp down her anger, but it had already sparked. "No, we don't take good care of our vets. Not in some ways."

"There's no cure for PTSD," he pointed out.

"Well, maybe they need to get to work on it. It's not just vets who have it. All kinds of people who've been traumatized have it. Some can talk it out. Sometimes it never goes away. For some it just eases eventually. I have a college friend who became a journalist. She has PTSD from covering the scenes of accidents, fires, murders, plane crashes... She had to quit finally. A decade later it doesn't bother her as much. And talk therapy didn't help her deal with those pictures burned into her brain."

"It wouldn't," he agreed. "It can't. But with time... I hear they're not as strong and don't pop up as often. Nell's helped to give me some time." He paused. "Does Mikey have a problem?"

"Not that anyone's aware of. Not yet, anyway. He doesn't remember his accident at all. He woke up four days later in a hospital bed with no memory of it."

"Maybe that's a blessing."

"He sure has enough to deal with as it is. I just hope the memory doesn't come back. The darn kid still wants to ride a horse."

"Really?" Zane smile faintly. "Guts and gumption."

"Maybe. Somebody's talking about building him a special saddle, but his mom won't hear of it. Not yet, anyway."

"I can kinda understand her viewpoint."

"So can I." Ashley leaned back in her chair. "Listen, am I overstaying my welcome? You're an avowed hermit, remember?"

Again she drew a laugh from him. Something about today had made him feel very good. Getting out? Meeting people?

"I may be getting over being a hermit little by little. But in all seriousness, don't be surprised if I pull back into my shell occasionally. Sometimes it's best just to leave me alone."

"I can deal, as long as you understand that if I start to worry about you, I'm going to be knocking on your front door. And unless you lock it, I suspect Nell will let me in."

He chuckled. "Yeah, she probably will. Walk in any time, Ashley. You give me hope."

Hope? Her heart slammed. "Me?" She almost squeaked.

"Here I am hanging out with you. You've put up with me for hours now. I never thought that would happen again."

Wow. Just wow. She was complimented and stunned all at once. "I don't feel like I'm putting up with anything," she said truthfully. "You're okay to be with."

"Just okay?" The words sounded as if he were teasing, then he said, "Want to join me and Nell on a walk around the block? I need to get a bit of a workout, and I'm sure she needs to stretch her legs."

Nell's ears had perked the instant she heard "walk," and now she was looking hopefully at Zane. Ashley smiled. "I'd like that, but I need to run next door to get a warmer jacket. It was getting cold out there. Be right back."

"I'll meet you out front."

The air had turned bitterly cold, making the autumn sunlight feel warmer by comparison. The early twilight was setting in as the sun sank behind the mountains, especially with the days shortening. Very soon it would be dark. Definitely time for a winter jacket.

Hers was hanging in her small hall closet, and her gloves were still tucked in the pockets. All ready to go. Her ears felt nipped just from the brief time outdoors, so she pulled up her hood before stepping outside.

Zane and Nell were waiting for her. Nell was dancing a bit at the end of her leash. Zane wore what appeared to be a down-filled black jacket, which added to his bulk. He'd turned his head over to a stocking cap that sheltered his ears, and he gripped the push rims with hands clad in leather gloves.

"Nell's certainly ready," he said as she skipped down her steps to the sidewalk.

"This has got to be cold even for her," Ashley remarked. "Holding still is probably painful."

"Do you jog at all?"

"When I can. Why?"

"I like to keep up a good clip. It won't be an easy walking pace, so let me know if I'm getting ahead of you or wearing you out. I mean it."

"No problem." She really didn't expect one. She did jog several times a week unless something intervened, and she couldn't imagine that he could go *that* fast in his chair.

She was shortly proved wrong. He wasn't kidding about keeping up a good pace. He pushed those rims over and over as hard as he could. Nell was trotting quickly at his side. She was probably the only one of the three of them who could have gone any faster, and not for long.

"Not fair," she said a bit breathlessly to Zane as they hurried down the sidewalk. "That dog has *four* legs."

He laughed. "I'll slow down soon, unless you want me to right now."

"Full steam ahead. I'm doing fine."

The air wasn't quite cold enough to make her chest ache, but it wasn't far from it. She loved cross-country skiing as a hobby, but rarely did she go fast enough to cause her bronchioles to want to spasm. Today was no threat, and it felt good to be stretching her body this way.

He was right, though, about having to stop at every corner to check for traffic.

"You know, there's a track at the junior college you could probably use if you want to keep a steady, fast pace."

"Maybe I'll check it out sometime," he said. "What kind of surface does it have?"

"I don't know exactly." She hadn't thought about what he might need for his wheels. "The high school is a cinder track. You probably couldn't use that, but the college has a fairly new track with a different surface."

"That might work."

Dang, he didn't sound the least breathless. She was beginning to feel out of shape.

But then he slowed down. "Close to a mile," he announced.

She thought about it. "I've never measured distances in town. How do you know?"

"Practice. It was actually 1.6 klicks. Over a kilometer and a half. Everywhere I've been in the world, the metric system has been more useful."

She strolled beside him at his more sedate pace. The twilight was arriving, the streetlights popping on. Nell occasionally wanted to sniff something, so he paused and let her.

Ashley watched, amused. "Did you tell her she's off-duty?"

"I always give her a chance to be a dog when I slow down like this. She needs it. I enjoy it. And trust me, she never loses her awareness of me."

They passed a few people, but given the time of day and the chilling weather, Ashley supposed most were inside preparing dinner and keeping warm. Those they did pass simply waved and called out a hello. No one tried to stop them for a conversation.

Her cell phone rang, and she struggled to get beneath her jacket and pull it out. It was Connie.

Connie's voice filled her ear. "Julie's gone to the hospital in labor. Trace is quietly freaking. You coming?"

"I will shortly. Thanks for letting me know, Connie."

She stuffed her phone into her jacket pocket. "After we get home, I need to go to the hospital. My friend Julie is in labor. I gather her husband could use some moral support."

"Don't wait on me. Go ahead."

She looked down at him in the dimming light, then noticed that Nell had lost all interest in trees and grass but was poised beside him. Focused intently on him. Something was happening.

"After we get you home," she said firmly. "Right, Nell?"

Nell gave a small whimper and nudged at Zane's arm.

Zane muttered, "Oh, for the love of…"

Nell rose and laid both her front legs on his arm.

"Listen to your dog, Zane," Ashley said firmly. "If you don't she'll lick your cheek and you'll grow icicles."

The humor didn't work. Nell's touch didn't work.

Just like that, Zane had gone away.

Ashley looked at Nell. "Let's get him home." She moved to the back of the wheelchair and Nell dropped to all fours, understanding. Something inside Ashley had quieted until all feeling fled. A self-protective emotional crouch. All she could think of was the fact that as big a man as Zane was, the wheelchair was surprisingly easy to push.

A most excellent wheelchair.

For a man who seemingly had just dropped off a ledge into the pit of hell.

Zane was astonished when he realized Ashley was pushing him toward the ramp to his house. "What the heck?"

"You zoned out. Nell was worried. I wasn't going to leave you sitting in the middle of a sidewalk. You don't remember?"

"Not a thing," he admitted. Well, not exactly true. He'd been remembering another place and time. Not for the life of him could he imagine what had cast him back there. A quiet street, his dog, his new friend, streetlights coming on…he'd never had an assignment that included streetlights. But something had kicked him over.

"I can get up the ramp," he said somewhat forcefully. He grabbed the push rims, taking over. He knew the instant Ashley let go.

"You had somewhere to go," he said.

"It can wait."

"It doesn't have to. I'll be fine."

"Zane…"

"I need to think about what just happened. I don't know why I cut out. Go worry about your friend and her husband. You'll be more useful."

"Fine." Her tone took on an edge.

He started pushing himself up the ramp, but he paused once to watch her walk away and into her house. Bad enough he'd zoned out, but did he have to talk to her that way? She hadn't done anything wrong.

But it was best for her if she stayed away. Best for him. Never mind that he'd been enjoying her company. No one deserved having to deal with him.

"Come on, Nell," he said unnecessarily as he reached the porch and leaned forward to fling to the door open.

Just him and the dog. It was safest. No one got hurt. Because he seemed to have a built-in capacity for doling out pain.

Chapter Seven

Ashley battled irritation as she entered her house and began to strip for a shower. What the heck had she done? She'd brought him home when he zoned out. Was that a crime?

Standing under the hot shower spray, washing her hair, she decided that she might be overreacting. The guy had evidently had an episode. He didn't seem to have any idea of why, and he'd been surprised to find himself back at home. That must be hell to deal with. Plus, he probably hadn't come back entirely from wherever he'd gone. So, yes, he'd been short, had wanted to get away from everyone. For all she knew he was both worried and exhausted. He might have been battling demons while he went away. Bad memories. They would hardly put him in a good mood.

By the time she'd finished blow-drying her hair

enough that she wouldn't freeze by the time she got to the hospital, she was feeling a whole lot more charitable toward Zane. He couldn't help it. She knew that. What did she expect? That he'd come back from a bad episode and be all cheerful and sunny?

Of course not.

She pulled on a warm blue jogging suit and her other pair of running shoes, grabbed her wallet so she'd have money to ferry coffee and food to Trace if he needed it, then bundled up and headed for the hospital.

A glance at Zane's place showed that lights were on, so he wasn't sitting in the dark. That much was good, she supposed.

But what an odd day. First the visit to Cadell's ranch, where Zane had seemed to unwind and make a connection with Mikey. Then the utterly unexpected invitation to join him for lunch at Maude's, followed by asking her to walk with him.

Maybe he'd overloaded. He probably wasn't used to that much company anymore. It was as if he'd been reaching out for the first time in what must have been a very long time for him, given what he had told her, and then something had snapped inside him, isolating him once more.

She guessed she could understand that. She could certainly forgive it. Whether she'd expose herself to more of it remained to be seen. Attractive as he was, he might be more of a complication than she was truly willing to deal with.

At the hospital she went to the maternity waiting room and found Connie there with Trace Archer, Julie's husband. A tall, lean man, he couldn't be a stranger to tough times. As she understood it, he'd been shot in his right hand and to this day suffered an awful lot of pain from it. Julie had once confided his only relief from it would be amputation. So far he hadn't wanted to use that escape hatch.

She gave Trace a quick hug. "So where are we?"

"Likely going to be an all-nighter," Connie answered. "Marisa wanted to come, but Jonni's down with some kind of stomach bug and while she could have left him with Ryker, she didn't think the bug would be welcome here."

Ashley shook her head, smiling. "I'm sure it wouldn't be. Can I get anyone coffee or something to eat from the cafeteria?" She knew Trace swallowed coffee as if it were the staff of life.

"I'd love some coffee," he said. "But please, not from the machine in the hall."

Ashley grinned. "I read you. Connie?"

"Nothing for me unless you see a reasonably fresh-looking turkey sandwich. I haven't eaten since breakfast."

As Ashley walked through the halls toward the cafeteria, she remembered the half a salad she'd left behind. Oh, well. Besides, she wanted something a little more substantial now, anyway. Hunger had started gnawing at her stomach during the walk with Zane.

Nearly everyone she passed recognized her and knew that Julie was in labor. It was the kind of good news no one felt the need to keep a secret. She paused briefly a few times for short, general conversations, then entered the cafeteria. They were still serving dinner, and there were some good sandwiches to choose from. She got Connie her turkey and also picked up a roast beef for Trace. He might not feel like eating, but if this went on all night, he'd need the energy. Nerves probably had his candle burning at both ends. It wasn't as if he'd been through this before.

When she got back to the waiting room with her tray, Trace had begun pacing and Connie was skimming a magazine. Connie must be a calming influence, Ashley thought. She'd done this more than once. Yet Trace was pacing.

"Here's your coffee," she said to Trace. "And a roast beef sandwich. You'd better eat. You need to keep your energy up."

"Maybe in a bit," he answered, taking the large coffee. "Thanks."

Connie looked up, a smile dancing in her eyes. "Men suffer more than we do, I sometimes think."

"Well," said Trace, "I was supposed to be with her. How calm can I be when I'm stuck out here?"

Ashley exchanged looks with Connie, then asked, "Trace, you're supposed to be her coach?"

"We took classes together."

Connie rose, tossing the magazine aside. "Ashley, you stay with Trace. I'll find out what's going on."

"Absolutely." She bit her lip in worry as she wondered what had gone wrong. If Trace was supposed to be his wife's coach, shouldn't he be with her?

Trace perched on a chair, coffee in his good hand, his banged-up one in a leather glove and cradled close to his body as if he didn't want it to bump anything.

"Connie will find out," Ashley said as reassuringly good. "All that practice as a cop? She gets answers."

He offered her a mirthless smile. "I just want to know what's going on. Is something bad happening? God, Ashley, I love that woman."

"I know you do." She wished she had comforting words, but she seemed to be out of them. In fact, when she thought about it, she'd been unable to offer any real comfort to anyone in a while. None for Zane, certainly, and now none for Trace. When had life gone so cockeyed?

But now she, too, was worried about Julie. They'd grown up together. She didn't want anything bad to happen to her friend. Nothing. She desperately wanted Julie to come through this with a healthy baby.

Impulsively, she reached out and laid her hand on Trace's thigh. "It'll be okay."

Empty words, but he nodded. He gave her the faintest, palest of smiles.

It had better be okay. If something went wrong, she wasn't sure she'd be able to handle it any better than Trace.

Then Connie popped into the room. "I just spoke to her, Trace. She's fine. Somewhere something glitched, and they didn't have a record that you were to be her coach. So you can go in now. You, too, Ashley, but briefly. Julie asked for you."

As Ashley walked down the corridor with Trace, she said, "I can't believe they'd keep the husband out, paper or no paper."

Trace had begun to feel better. He smiled. "Maybe we have a tendency to faint."

That drew a relieved laugh from Ashley. "Somehow I don't think you will."

"Sure. Like I've ever heard my wife scream before. That could be very different."

Ashley hadn't thought about that. "Julie doesn't strike me as a screamer," she answered. "She strikes me as a cusser. If it gets rough, she may divorce you before morning."

Trace laughed, his whole demeanor changing. "Yeah, she could do that. You never have to wonder what that woman thinks about anything."

When they entered the labor room, it was surprisingly quiet. A fetal monitor beeped, but Julie was sitting with the head of her bed up, her knees a bit bent and a smile on her face, quickly banished by a grimace as a contraction came.

Her brow looked a little damp with perspiration. She reached out the hand that wasn't attached to the IV to Trace, and he took it. "Everything's fine," she said. "Everything. I kept asking where you were, and nobody seemed to get it. I decided you must not have arrived yet."

"I've been sitting in the waiting room wondering why they wouldn't let me see you."

"That's what Connie said. Somebody fell asleep at the wheel. It doesn't matter now. Hey, Ash, how you doing?"

"I'm doing fine. It's you we're all thinking about."

"Considering billions of women before me have done this, I wouldn't waste a whole lot of concern." She winced and began panting. At once training kicked in and Trace started coaching her.

Looking around, Ashley found a chair and pushed it over so Trace could sit beside his wife. When Julie relaxed again, Ashley said, "I got Trace a roast beef sandwich." She held it up. "Think you can get him to eat?"

"Put it on the table," Julie said. "It's going to be a long night. I'll get him to eat it. But he probably wants more coffee."

"She got me some," Trace objected.

"Ha. I've never seen anyone drink coffee the way you do."

"I'll get some more," Ashley said quickly. Whether Trace wanted the coffee or not, she felt these were moments he'd like to share privately with his wife. He was certainly entitled to them.

A nurse buzzed in to check on things just as she was leaving. She apologized to Trace for not bringing him in sooner. "Honestly, we don't try to lock out fathers. I really can't imagine how this happened."

Ashley slipped out and trekked toward the cafeteria again. She wondered if she ought to stay the night to shuttle coffee back and forth.

Connie caught up with her near the cafeteria. "I'm thinking about going home. Julie said the nurses are predicting she won't deliver before morning. First babies take a while."

"Until they don't," Ashley remarked, causing Connie to grin. "Listen, I can sleep in tomorrow. Are you on duty?"

As a sheriff's deputy, Connie's hours could be irregular. "Nope, I'm off, and I'm honestly glad Ethan can babysit. Sometimes I need a break from that, too."

"Three little kids? I'm not surprised. The oldest is probably more help, though."

"She helps when her life doesn't get in the way. But you spend all day with youngsters."

Ashley laughed. "And I get to send them home at the end of the school day."

"I forgot that lucky part."

A couple of hours later, however, Julie didn't seem to want much company other than Trace's, so Connie and Ashley both left, promising to return early in the morning.

"Big event," Connie said as she climbed into her cruiser. "The first one is the best."

"Maybe someday I'll know." Not that she'd ever been in a rush. Content with her life as it was, she wasn't looking to change it drastically anytime soon.

Trace called with the news, waking Ashley at seven in the morning. "Healthy baby boy, Julie's resting, and no, we haven't decided on a name yet, because I don't want my son to be called Trace." There was tired humor in his voice, though, and happiness. "Julie wants to see you, Connie and Marisa, but not until much later. No offense, Ashley, but she's pooped."

"None taken. I'm just thrilled for both of you." Happiness for Julie suffused her morning. She'd watched her friends go through this and had some idea of the magic of bringing a child into the world. She also had some idea of the work and fatigue involved. Time to go grocery shopping and start cooking a lot of refrigerator and freezer meals so Julie and Trace could focus on their new baby. She almost whistled a tune in delight.

A quick check of the weather warned her that the day had remained as chilly as the night. She dressed in a fresh green fleece top and pants, stuffed her feet into boots rather than running shoes, and was just pulling on her jacket when she heard a scratching at the door.

Startled, she held still and listened to be sure she'd heard something. The scratching came again, quiet, as if whatever was doing it didn't want to create damage.

She opened the door and looked down into Nell's

brown eyes. The dog didn't look happy and whimpered a bit, shifting from leg to leg.

Ashley didn't need any more invitation than that. Quickly zipping her jacket, she stepped out into the cold morning and watched her breath create clouds. Nell hurried her across the yard to the ramp. The front door of Zane's house was open a crack.

Even though the dog pushed the door wide-open, she hesitated on the threshold. "Zane?"

She was answered by a heartfelt curse.

Nell whimpered and took a few steps toward the living room, then looked back.

Ashley took the hint, closed the door against the cold and hurried into the living room. Dismay and concern immediately filled her as she saw Zane lying on his side on the floor, the tipped wheelchair not far away.

"What happened?" she asked, hurrying to him.

He cussed again, and using his arms, pulled himself a few inches toward the old sofa.

"For Pete's sake, Zane, what happened? And let me help. Stop cussing."

He didn't exactly follow that last order. "I'm too heavy," he growled. "You can't help. No legs. Just deadweight."

A pang speared Ashley, but she refused to let sympathy for him get in the way of doing something practical. "Cut it out. Either let me figure out how to help or I'm calling the EMTs."

"Hell, no."

She didn't ask him what he was objecting to and didn't give him a chance to explain it. She had a bit of temper, too, and it was rising again. Stubborn cuss, she thought. How long did he plan on lying there? Nell obviously couldn't lift him.

Thoughts of making sure he had a way to call for help ran through her head as she squatted beside him. "Okay," she said. "Listen to me. I can see how strong your arms are. I doubt you need me to pull on you to get you to the sofa. What about if I help lift you at waist level? Or just your legs?"

Mercifully he fell silent and motionless, reflecting on the problem. "Deadweight," he said. "I can pull it, but I'm dragging on the rug. I need to get rid of this damn rug. Too much friction."

"Rug, later. You, now. Where should I lift, Zane?" Never mind the question of what he had planned to do about the tipped wheelchair once he reached the couch. They could discuss his planning later. And they were going to, she decided. Absolutely.

"Let me try lifting your legs. Would you be better on your back or on your front?"

Again he was silent for a few seconds. "On my back," he decided. "For now at least." As he spoke, he used one arm to turn himself over.

Now he would no longer be dragging himself, but using his arms to lift and walk backward. She could see the advantages in that immediately.

Kneeling, she got between his legs, slipped one arm under each of his thighs and said, "Tell me when to lift."

He nodded, his expression steely. "Now."

He was no lightweight, and whatever he was doing in physical therapy had clearly kept his legs strong. She could feel the heft, feel the muscles even though they were flaccid. Still, lifting them was not impossible.

He pushed up with his arms and walked back on

them while she held his legs. The couch was coming closer. He stopped once, not seeming to be out of breath, so she suspected he was halting for her sake. Since her arms had begun to ache a little, she wasn't about to object.

They didn't talk at all during that break. She wondered if he was feeling awful about needing her help. Well, probably. He was over here trying to be self-sufficient, a self-proclaimed hermit, and now this.

They crabbed their way closer to the sofa until he was sitting upright against it. Ashley shook out her cramping arms. "You know, Zane, you shouldn't be afraid to call for help sometimes."

"Why? Because Nell came for you?"

She sparked. "You ought to be damn glad she did. I have no idea how to get you off the floor, so you better start thinking. As for Nell, except for her you wouldn't be relaxing now."

Nell, who had lain down to watch the process, perked her ears at the sound of her name.

Zane sighed. "You're right. She wasn't supposed to leave me, but I guess she had a better plan."

"Well, since she can't dial the phone..." Ashley crossed her legs, still sitting on the floor, and spread her hands. "Don't you keep your cell with you all the time?"

"I left it on the table. Even I get forgetful at times. Besides, I didn't need to call anyone."

"Of course not. You could have just cussed your way to the couch over the next several hours."

To her surprise he smiled faintly. "Guess so. Thanks, Ashley. You were a great help."

"Was? You still aren't back in your chair, and I have no idea how we're going to manage that from here."

"I can do it. It's not easy. Of course, it helps if the chair is upright and locked."

She looked at it doubtfully. Or maybe amazed. "Really, you can get from the floor into it?"

"Sure. If I couldn't I doubt I'd be able to live alone. I have a seat in my shower. I have a bed with a rod over it to lift myself. I have lots of useful things around here. But some things I still gotta do by sheer strength."

She nodded slowly, wondering at the dimensions of the problems he faced. She suspected she didn't know the tenth of them.

"If you wouldn't mind, turn the chair upright and bring it over here. I'll show you."

So she turned the chair over, brought it to him and watched as he set the locks. "Hang on to the push bars, if you don't mind. Just for some extra stability, but I've done this when I'm all alone, so don't get uneasy."

Then, with a strength and ease she could scarcely believe, he lifted himself on to the couch and turned himself partially over while holding onto the wheelchair seat and pressing on the couch seat. Then, with a great thrust of his arms, he lifted himself from the couch until he was sitting sideways in the chair. Another twist and he was seated properly.

"I can't believe you just did that!"

"There was a time I wouldn't have believed I could do it, either. It's one of the reasons it's so important to keep my upper body in shape." Leaning forward, he lifted his legs and settled his feet on the footrests. "All done."

She was impressed. Totally impressed. She bet he could have done it without the couch if the chair hadn't tipped. He probably wanted to get to the couch just to get off the floor and decide what he needed to do next.

"So what exactly happened?" she asked, studying the rug. "How did you tip?"

"Honestly? I don't remember. I came back to myself cussing a blue streak with Nell licking my face, and I was on the floor. I must have zoned again. I don't think it lasted very long, though, because my face wasn't totally covered in dog slobber."

"What a description!" Since he was making light of it, she decided to do the same. To a point.

He rolled toward the kitchen, and because he hadn't indicated in any way that she should leave, she followed to make sure there weren't any aftereffects. And to discuss some important arrangements, whether he liked it or not.

She watched him stretch and reach to make coffee and remarked, "I bet the shop class at the high school would love a project of making your kitchen more useful to you. And I happen to know the shop teacher."

He glanced over his shoulder. "I'm managing."

"I can see that. Of course you are. But wouldn't it be nice to have things at a comfortable level? You could do even more then if you wanted to."

He switched on the coffeepot and turned his chair so he was facing her. "Have a seat, Teach. How much are you going to press me about this?"

"I don't know. I just don't see why your life should have to be harder because you're more stubborn than an army mule."

For an instant she feared she had gone too far. His face reflected no expression. Then a loud laugh burst out of him. "Touché, Teach. Touché."

Relieved, she pulled out the one chair at the table and sat. "We need to talk about some other things. Like you being able to call for help when you need it. I get that you're an independent person. I think you're absolutely amazing. But if something bad happens you have to be able to reach out. So carry your cell with you all the time. Please. Nell knows to come get me, but what if I'm not home?"

His smile faded. She suspected he didn't like to be faced with his limitations, but that was too bad. Now she had to worry about him because he'd refused to let her call for the EMTs for help... She hesitated. "Do you know how often the fire department gets calls for a lift assist? Very often. And they don't mind doing it. If you want, I'll introduce you to the chief and let him explain that they don't mind. You're not the only person in this county who has a problem getting up once they've fallen. Every year someone from the department comes to talk to my class, and every year they talk about how much they like being able to help people."

"I thought they'd prefer a fire."

She couldn't stifle a laugh. "I'm sure they do. Smoke eaters, every one."

But the tension she'd felt growing in him eased. After a few seconds he nodded. "You're right. I'm too stubborn. But I need to be stubborn. There are a lot of things I can do now only because I didn't give up."

She nodded, believing he was right but also hurting for him. He'd once been a SEAL. A powerful man. Someone capable of feats that no amount of training could make possible for just anyone. He'd lost more than his legs. He'd lost his purpose, his identity. He'd had to carve out a huge chunk of himself.

She couldn't imagine what it must be like for him. And she desperately wished there was some way to make it better. So often in life, she wished she could make things better for someone, usually when there wasn't a damn thing she could do.

"I'm sorry," she said finally. "I have no business lecturing you. I'm just worried about you."

"Why in the hell should you worry about me?"

"Because I like you a whole lot."

At that instant, every bit of air in the room seemed to vanish. Their eyes locked, and she wondered if she'd ever breathe again. Her insides turned to hot syrup.

"How much do you like me?" he asked baldly.

She swallowed and managed to drag in some air. Why the heck had she said that? It wasn't necessary, and it opened the door to all kinds of complications she was sure they both wanted to avoid. "Let's not go there," she said, her voice sounding rusty. "You don't want it. You've made that clear. And I'm happy with my life the way it is. Just leave it."

She looked away a moment, deciding to change the topic *fast*. "Julie had her baby, a boy. Trace called to tell me this morning. No name yet. He says that's because he doesn't want his son to be called Trace."

Several seconds of silence followed, then Zane chuckled. "I guess that means Julie does. Most dads would leap at that."

"Would they?" Feeling calmer internally, she was able to look at him again. Why had she danced so close to a possible flame? She decided she'd better think about that later. "So how did you tip your chair?"

"I was probably diving for cover."

That bald statement painted an image so clear in her

that it was inescapable. No more intellectual acknowledgment that this guy's psyche had been wounded. No
more vague thinking about the PTSD he was dealing
with. Somehow those words, when combined with finding him on the floor, made it vivid, extremely vivid.
Real. Something she finally had to face head-on. She
closed her eyes, absorbing the blow, truly anguished
for him.

Where did people ever get the idea that they could
send soldiers off to war and get them back completely
unchanged, completely unscarred? That they should
be able to live that kind of horror and then just forget
about it? Because it made the people at home so uncomfortable?

At every catastrophe, counselors were brought in to
help people deal with death, destruction and loss. And
those were usually instantaneous, or relatively short-
term. There was nothing short-term about going back
to war time and again. To go on the kinds of missions
she suspected SEALs went on. Seth Hardin had mentioned something about six months on and six months
off. Like that could erase the six months on mission?

"What are you thinking?" Zane asked. "You're not
looking very happy."

"I don't look happy all the time." Then she relented.
For once he was reaching out to her, and she didn't
want to shove him away. "I just suddenly got hit by reality. The reality you're experiencing. It's one thing to
think about in the abstract—it's another to get punched
with it."

He frowned and his hands clenched. "You feel
punched?"

"By what you're enduring. No intellectual exercise."

"Sorry. I didn't want to do that to you."

"I know. You didn't try. It was just when you said you'd probably been diving for cover...well, I guess some little protective shell I've been wearing just went away. It's okay. I think I needed to lose it."

But he swore, anyway. The next thing she knew, he'd wheeled up next to her and reached out, lifting her right out of her chair and onto his lap.

"Don't wiggle," he muttered. "I don't want to tip again."

She held perfectly still until he held her firmly on his lap, and wondered what she was doing there. She certainly hadn't said anything to make him feel like he needed to hug her, but that's what he was doing. Or maybe he needed the hug.

She felt as if part of her had just been run through a shredder and the results weren't pretty. Just like him, now she was going to have to put herself back together in a new configuration.

She leaned into him, sensing his strength—and not only his obvious physical strength. This man had fought in wars, and now he'd come home with the war on his back and was still fighting. She began to truly comprehend the huge suicide rates among veterans.

"Ashley?"

"Yeah?" Breathing wasn't getting much easier. He could probably hear it in her voice.

"I want you."

Well, that did it. She couldn't breathe at all now, her eyes closed and she softened throughout her entire body as a heavy beating began at her center. "And?" she whispered.

"I shouldn't. I can't be good for anyone right now. You saw why. But I still feel it…"

She was still wearing her jacket, but he pulled down the zipper and slipped his hand inside, cupping her breast through fleece. His thumb stroked over her engorging nipple, somehow extremely sensitive even through fabric. "God, you feel good. Tell me to stop. Please. I don't know how to handle this…"

Something in his tone called her back from the precipice. He wanted her, but he was worried about it. Either he feared the coupling for some reason or he feared the outcome. She managed to pull in a long, shaky breath.

She opened her eyes, reached for his cheek and turned his head toward her until she could brush a kiss on his lips. Hoping her legs would hold her, she slid carefully off his lap.

She looked at him, sitting there with his face tight, his hands clenched.

"Sorry," he said. "I should have more self-control."

"Don't expect the impossible," she said as she gathered herself and recentered. "I want you, too. But promise me something?"

"If I can."

"Don't tease me like that again until you're ready to go through with it." She zipped up her jacket and settled her knit hat more firmly on her head. "I was going to the store. I want to cook some food to put in Trace and Julie's freezer so they can concentrate on their new son. I'll see you later."

Then she turned and walked out of the house, feeling as if she was leaving part of herself behind. A connection had just been made. She felt as if some cord stretched between them now, and she had no idea whether that was good or bad.

She'd find out, though. She was sure of that.

Chapter Eight

Julie came home with the baby a day later. The girls had all gotten together, and the freezer on Julie and Trace's mud porch was full of easy-to-reheat meals. The layette had been taken care of weeks ago, so there was little to do.

Knowing that Julie would be tired and just want some quiet with her family, Ashley didn't hang around for long. Just long enough to add some more oohs and ahs to the ones they'd provided late yesterday and to remind Julie and Trace that they were there if the new parents needed any help at all.

But Trace would be there, Ashley thought with a smile as she headed back to school, her lunch hour over. He'd apparently had some kind of dangerous hush-hush job before but had retired on disability because of his hand. He was looking around for ways to occupy himself, and Ashley thought one had just landed in his lap. Julie wanted to continue teaching kindergarten. House husband, anyone?

Mikey had bubbled during the morning, telling everyone about the service dog Deputy Marcus was going to train for him, and about Zane's Nell. By the time she got back from lunch, the kids had decided to beg her to get Zane to bring Nell to the classroom.

Oh, Lord, how was she supposed to manage that? She could just imagine Zane's reaction. She quieted the excitement as best she could, promising to ask but reminding them that Mr. McLaren wasn't perfectly well yet and might not feel up to it.

Some disappointment tempered their eagerness, and they settled down. Ashley continued with her lesson plan, preceding tomorrow's testing. Then Halloween would take over. Dang, she hoped they forgot their desire for Zane to visit them. She'd been surprised that he'd been willing to meet Mikey, self-professed hermit and all, but he'd done well with the boy, maybe because they had something in common with their disabilities. But a whole classroom of nineteen kids? She wasn't seeing it. Let the approach of Halloween drive everything else from their minds, please. Well, except their schoolwork.

On the way home she bought a large pumpkin to put on her porch, although she wouldn't carve it until the day before. She vividly remembered the year she'd been early and the fruit flies had found her pumpkin. Ugh. Never again.

For the classroom, she had some plastic pumpkins that lit up and a simple skeleton to hang in one corner. After the tests. She also stopped at the bakery to order a couple dozen decorated cupcakes for her students. Bad, she knew, but she compromised by having them made with pumpkin bread and skipping the icing in favor of some plastic pumpkin faces to be pressed into them. After all, part of her job was supposed to be teaching nutrition. Kids would eat cupcakes and candy regardless, but she could err a little on the side of "not too bad."

She used the side door of the house after her shopping, entering from her driveway through the mudroom. Nice that these older homes still had them. She couldn't imagine how difficult it would be without one. Even as just one person, she tracked in plenty when it was rainy or snowy. Nice to confine it to one place and leave her boots there. Easy to clean when it dried.

She unloaded groceries and the pumpkin, checked her messages, and then decided to give Julie and Trace a quick call just to see if they needed anything. Trace answered, sounding a bit tired. "Not much sleep. All's quiet now, Julie is snoozing and I'm next in line. I thought babies slept a lot."

Ashley suppressed a laugh. "They do. Usually. Sometimes, though…"

"Yeah, Julie thinks the baby's aware of the big change from the hospital to here. Maybe it's draftier or colder. I don't know. Are babies that aware?"

"Probably more than we want to think. No cussing, Trace."

It was his turn to chuckle quietly as he hung up.

Then Ashley realized she had surprisingly little to do. Review sheets had been the work in class today, and they'd all been corrected on the spot, to help prepare for tests.

She could evade herself no longer. Plopping down in her living room, she thought of Zane again. Of being on his lap, of his bold move that had left her weak with desire, followed by his declaration that she should stop him because he was no good for anyone.

It bothered her that he felt that way, but he might be right to the extent that he wouldn't be good for *her*. She was also aware of her own tendency to develop a strong emotional attachment with any man she had sex with. She'd figured that one out a long time ago and reordered her priorities accordingly. Relationship before sex.

So what was happening to her now? She didn't need all the problems with this spelled out for her. Definitely not. He wasn't well because of his PTSD. His paralysis…well, she felt that wouldn't necessarily be a problem for her. It hadn't bothered her yet except for what it meant to him.

But falling out of his wheelchair because he was diving for cover? A whole different ball of wax. That would be part of any relationship with him. Before she took a single step toward that, she had to check herself, to be sure she wouldn't hurt him by being unable to live with his disability.

That was hard to know. At best right now it would be a guess, but the only way to be sure would be to live with him. Ha! Talk about a recipe for disaster.

Anyway, he'd said he wanted her, not that he wanted a relationship with her. Big difference. If he wanted a one-night stand, he was going to have to look elsewhere, because it wasn't going to be her. Some women might be built that way, but she knew for sure she wasn't.

Sighing, she got up, changed into more casual clothes for cooking and decided to make herself a small casserole out of smoked turkey, boxed stuffing, green beans and leftover mashed potatoes. Thanksgiving in a bowl. With some turkey gravy from a jar, it was scrumptious and easy.

Which got her to wondering what she was doing for Thanksgiving this year. One of the gals always invited her to join their families, and usually she accepted, bringing all the pies and a relish tray. Connie had three kids, so the spread was always big, especially if the rest of the Parish family was eating at her place. But sometimes they went to Micah Parish's ranch for the dinner, and then she wasn't invited. Nothing was meant by that. It was a huge family gathering, and there were so many members of the Parish family she often felt out of place even at Connie's house.

Maybe she should think about making the dinner herself. Marisa and Ryker had no one else except their baby. Julie wouldn't have time or energy even to think about it. Yeah, she could do it here. She started thinking about how many of her friends to invite and how many she could fit in her snug little house. Man, they'd be shoulder to shoulder. It might be fun.

She'd just finished layering her casserole and sprinkling some fried onion rings on the top when she heard a familiar noise at her front door. Nell.

Wiping her hands on a towel, she hurried toward it, grabbing her jacket along the way.

Yup, it was Nell, looking impatient yet strangely happy. Almost grinning. Surely she was misreading the dog.

"What happened now, girl?"

But there was only one way to find out. She followed the dog at a trot and entered the open door of Zane's house.

"Zane?" she called out.

"In the kitchen."

She headed in there and found him to be perfectly all right. In fact, he looked about ready to start cooking. "You're okay?"

"I'm fine. Why?" Then he looked at Nell. "You didn't," he said to the dog.

"She did," Ashley confirmed.

"She's not supposed to do that, dang it. She's never supposed to leave me unless I need medical help. What's gotten into her?"

"Beats me." Ashley had a suspicion, though. Not that she'd say it out loud. She looked down at the dog, who was now sitting, grinning and swishing her tail hopefully. "Have you made dinner yet?" she asked.

"Just starting."

"Well, stop. I made a casserole big enough for four, and I was about to pop it in the oven. Let me just bring it over and bake it here. Meanwhile, you can try to figure out why Nell is interfering with your life."

"Humph," he grumped. "Maybe she thinks I need to change it."

"Don't ask me," Ashley said lightly. "Be right back." And there she went, forgetting all her good resolutions about involvement and relationships. Sheesh. Maybe she needed a head doctor.

Zane stared in perplexity at Nell. She'd never gone off like this before. He guessed she liked Ashley, which made the dog a great judge of character, but he didn't want her messing up Ashley's life by running over to get her every time she felt bored.

"Are you bored?" he asked the dog. As if she would answer. Well, he couldn't blame Nell if she occasionally wanted a different face in this house. He wasn't the greatest company. Or maybe he just needed to get her out for more walks. It would probably do both of them some good. He'd been confining his walks to the dark hours so he wouldn't run into a lot of people. It was safer than facing the questions or concern and sympathy. Safer than listening to people recall the athlete he'd been so long ago.

Considering he still hadn't figured out all his triggers, the less he had to do with people, the better. He didn't know if they still rode people out of town on a rail, but he'd sure as hell been evicted from his apartment.

He didn't want to make a scene in the street, upset people, maybe scare kids. He also didn't want to become the dangerous hermit that kids crossed the street to avoid and eventually built horror stories around.

He sighed, thinking he was going to have to parse things out before too much longer. And maybe that's all Nell was trying to tell him. *Figure it out, jerk. There are answers.* Maybe he'd just given up looking for them. That eviction had hit him in the gut in ways that still surprised him.

Ashley returned, bearing a medium-size glass casserole dish, covered in aluminum foil. "Nell," she said. "Close the door."

Nell took the order like the champ she was. Ashley turned on his oven to preheat it. "I call this Thanksgiving in a bowl," she said. "Some of my favorite holiday foods in it, including smoked turkey."

"Sounds great." He hesitated, aware that he needed to be sociable. It got even harder when he was beginning to crave the woman with all of his body that was still capable of feeling anything. "You know, Ashley, I never heard about your parents. Did they move away?"

She sat facing him and shook her head. "The weirdest thing. They went to the Texas coast for a vacation. Mom got caught in a riptide and Dad went to rescue her and… The riptide had just started, they were beginning to put up the warning flags, but too late for my folks."

She looked away, and he hated himself for asking. "I'm sorry. Truly sorry. And sorry that I stirred it up."

"You didn't. It's been hard, I still miss them, but it was eight years ago, Zane. I've learned to live with it."

"It's hard when it's so unexpected like that."

"Maybe not as hard as watching your parents suffer from terminal illness," she answered, thinking of his parents, both of whom had been claimed by different kinds of cancer just a year apart. "I don't know," she added. "I can't compare. Maybe there is no comparison."

The oven beeped that it had preheated, and she went to put the casserole in. "Timer?"

"On the counter, probably in the vicinity of the wine bottles. I haven't used either of them."

She found and set the timer, then said, "Why so much wine? Especially if you don't drink it?"

"Mom loved to cook with it." He smiled. "There was one period when I was young that I got awfully sick of every meal tasting like burgundy. I don't know what got her started on that kick, but apparently she stuck with it after I left, because there are a few unopened bottles there."

"The others could be vinegar by now," she remarked as she returned to the table.

"It's possible. I haven't felt an urge to find out." He shook his head a bit. "When did you buy the house next door? You decided not to keep the ranch?"

"Wasn't much of a ranch anymore," she said. "Mom and Dad sold it maybe ten or so years ago to a neighbor. No son to leave it to—I wanted to teach—not ranch, and they started wanting to do a bit of traveling. So they bought that house."

He nodded slowly. "I hope they got more trips in than the one to Texas."

She smiled and he was relieved to see it. "Yeah, they did. Europe for three weeks, a cruise that Mom swore was the most relaxing experience of her entire life, Mexico…they stuffed in quite a bit once they were free to do it and had some extra money."

He smiled back at her. She actually sounded happy that her parents had done those things, even if the last trip had resulted in their deaths.

"I suppose," she said slowly, "that you've seen a lot of the world."

"Not the kinds of places you'd take a vacation." Far from it. There were pockets of hell on earth. Places he'd never wish any human being to be caught in. Unfortunately, people were there. He yanked himself back from the edge. He didn't want to flip out again, not in front of Ashley. She'd seen the results once, and he knew he'd disturbed her.

He needed to stop thinking about her, anyway. Yeah, he wanted her. But he had nothing to offer anyone except a broken body and a broken mind. He should keep reminding himself of that before he hurt someone. However, there was no escaping the fact that being a hermit was going to be a little difficult.

Nell had brought Ashley over here on purpose. Zane had absolutely no doubt of that. Then there was the Mikey kid, and his need for a service dog. Meeting that boy had pierced him. Imagine being that young and facing life with quadriplegia. He reckoned he was damn lucky himself.

"Zane?"

"Hmm?"

"You were frowning. Is something wrong? Do you want me to leave?"

"God, no!" His reply was vehement.

Her brows had knit. "Did I do something wrong when I mentioned that you must have seen a lot of the world?"

He shook his head. "Not you. It's okay. I just started thinking about things I shouldn't think about, so I put it away, thought a little about you, then about Mikey. I'm fine."

She smiled, evidently willing to move on. "Mikey's something else, isn't he?"

"I know he's awfully positive, or at least he was at Cadell's place. And he made me feel that I was truly lucky."

Her face shadowed a bit as she nodded. "I can see that. Every time I try to have a pity party over some ridiculous thing, it doesn't take long for some thought to pop into my mind to remind me how lucky I really am." She smiled at him. "I have a Pollyanna brain."

He laughed at her description, and the laughter felt

good, easing the windup he'd felt growing and had been stepping down on. *As long as you can laugh...* He couldn't remember where he'd first heard that, but he suspected it was true. And he'd seen people laugh in the most god-awful circumstances imaginable. "So what do you have pity parties about?" he asked.

To his surprise, she blushed faintly. "Well, that's the thing. When I get that way from time to time, it's usually because a lot of small stuff has gone wrong and I feel like the universe is piling up on me. Now you take each item individually, and it feels really stupid. But if Murphy's been hanging around for a few weeks, making every blessed thing go wrong..." She shrugged. "I especially love the periods where I seem to be all thumbs and keep dropping things. Or the ones where I mess up every recipe I try to cook. I know I'm just distracted and not paying attention..."

"Why do you get distracted?"

She tilted her head to one side, just a bit. "I have students. Some of them don't always do well. Some of them struggle. Some of them are living with abuse. Now that last one, the instant I get proof, I can do something. But the others? I worry."

"You have a gentle heart." It was true, he thought. She had a bit of temper, which he'd seen on a couple of occasions, but mostly she was good-hearted. Gentle.

He remembered her gorgeous hair from when they were in school ages ago, but the years between them had made it impossible to know her. Besides, he'd been busy with his own life, full of sports and a girlfriend, and she lived on a ranch, which kept her away from many school activities. Not that he'd have been much interested in someone so much younger. Years were a great separator at that age.

But those years no longer mattered, and as far as he could tell she had grown up to be an exemplary woman.

As he sat there with her, however, her presence kind of pushed him back in time to high school, to his life before.

"You know, I've mentioned this before," he said abruptly, "but I can hardly remember the kid I was before I left."

"I'm not surprised. That was a while ago. I don't remember much of high school, either."

"I'm not thinking so much in terms of things that happened. Some events stand out in my mind, of course, but it's more who I thought I was. What was going on inside my head."

"And how it took you to the SEALs?"

"Bingo." He shook his head a little. "That wasn't my conscious intent, as I told you. Nope. I was offered a slick scholarship after I completed my training. Looking back, I sometimes wonder if that promise would have panned out regardless. Anyway, I guess it's impossible to reenter my head all those years ago."

His change in course had been troubling him lately, mostly since coming back to Conard City. He remembered that when he'd passed all the testing and had been admitted to training—which had been an extreme test itself—he'd written home about it. The answer from his mother had said more than words. She'd congratulated him then added, "I hope you made the right choice." That could have meant a lot of things, so he'd just assured her he had and then had lost himself in one of the world's toughest training programs.

By the time he emerged, he'd been cemented to his comrades and the SEALs as if they had been welded into one. Which they had been. The bonding had run deep. Being invalided out had left him feeling as if his skin had been ripped off.

All those years, all those faces, all those voices—a brotherhood. Which was not to say some of the guys couldn't be jackasses, but...they were still welded together. It had felt unbreakable. Then, *bam*! It had been broken.

"I think," he announced suddenly, "that I may never figure out why I changed my mind about what I was going to do in the navy, but I know what it cost me to have to leave."

"I can't imagine."

He looked at her sweet face surrounded by those copper curls and said, "What if you couldn't teach anymore? Suddenly. Without warning. No adjustment time."

He watched her face change, suffusing with horror or loss, he couldn't tell which.

"You *do* understand," he said quietly. "It would just about kill you, wouldn't it? Well, I'm dealing with that, too. It's gotten a lot easier, but I'm still dealing with it. I guess that's why I keep trying to figure out why I did it in the first place. Like that will answer anything."

Then she said something that reached his walled-off heart. "You know, I don't think it would hurt me as much to have to give up teaching as it hurt you to leave the SEALs."

An ache he usually suppressed blossomed in him. "Why?"

"Because I'd still have all my friends and other activities. You lost it all, Zane. All of it. That's worse than I can imagine."

Mercifully, the oven timer dinged and Ashley rose, turned it off and hunted for hot pads or oven mitts. She found the mitts, a very pretty pair, in a drawer near the oven.

Where was this conversation going, she wondered. She was beginning to get uneasy. He was looking for an answer she wasn't sure he'd ever find, but at the same time he was reaching out to her in a way that almost hurt. As if in some way his loss was becoming hers.

She decided to change the subject quickly. "Halloween this coming week. Do you want to hand out candy?"

"I think the kids would be scared to come to my porch. I'm a stranger in a wheelchair."

"With a dog," she reminded him, then remembered her class. "Oh, God."

"What?"

His expression was curious, no darkness there. Well, what if her question totally changed that? She almost didn't ask, then realized she'd just about promised her kids she would.

"You can say no," she began. "But my class listened to Mikey this morning and they were begging me to ask you to come talk to them and tell them about Nell. Actually, to bring Nell to school."

To her amazement, his face didn't turn to stone. In fact, he didn't even frown. "So I have Mikey to thank for Nell's sudden popularity with the fourth grade?"

Ashley laughed as she pulled the casserole out of the oven. "I guess so. But like I said, you can say no."

"Well, I can hardly send Nell alone. We're joined at the hip."

She placed the casserole on the counter. "It needs to set for a few minutes. Are you volunteering to come meet nineteen rambunctious nine- and ten-year-olds?"

"Not yet, but I'll think about it. I enjoyed meeting Mikey." His eyes settled on her. "Kids are different, Ashley."

"How so?"

"So innocent. So blunt. So curious. Even though I was deemed a problem for kids at the apartment house, I never held anything against the kids. Never."

"They probably weren't behind the attempt to evict you," she said forthrightly. "I know people just a bit. Adults create more serious problems than most kids ever will."

She started hunting for a serving spoon and plates. She could have asked him, but she needed a moment to collect herself. He'd shared some very personal stuff with her, and now he was actually thinking about coming to visit her class? The avowed hermit?

Nah, he wouldn't do it. He wanted to be left alone, and the stimulation of a classroom full of kids might not be good for him. She hated to think how he might feel if he had an episode at the school. Heck, she'd feel awful herself if something triggered him because of her request.

Well, she'd kept her promise to her kids. She'd wait a few days and then ask him what he'd decided.

She put the plates on the table, moved the casserole to the center and began scooping some onto his plate. "Say when. Turkey, green beans, gravy, mashed potatoes, stuffing."

"Sounds fabulous and I'm starved."

So she gave him several large scoops before giving herself a much smaller portion. For a beverage, she gave them each a glass of ice water. "Don't burn your mouth."

He laughed a little. "Do you know how long I went wishing I had something hot enough to eat that it could burn my mouth?"

Then he surprised her by reaching for her hand. "I think I need to be thankful. Can you say grace, please?"

Bowing her head, trying to ignore a totally inappropriate response to his touch, she complied with a prayer she had learned in childhood. When she looked up, his eyes were still closed.

"Thank you," he said. "I keep forgetting I have blessings to count."

Tears burned in her eyes, but she refused to let them fall. She didn't want to make him uncomfortable, but he was reaching deep inside her, touching her in ways she realized she had never been touched before. He was winning a place in her heart. Well, her friends and her students had a place there—why shouldn't Zane?

Turning her attention to her meal, she assured herself it would be all right. Just friends. He'd let her know he wanted her, but both times he'd backed away, so he could be trusted not to try to take it further.

In the meantime, better to think of other things. "So, Halloween?"

"I need to get some candy."

She smiled, glad he was going to meet the area kids. "Just don't wear a scary costume."

"What?" He widened his eyes humorously. "You don't think I'm scary enough just as I am?"

She had to laugh. "Actually, you're not scary at all. I imagine you could be if you wanted to, but you're not scaring me."

"Good," he said and let it drop.

"Then there's Thanksgiving," she continued. "I've pretty much decided I'm going to have a few friends at my place, rather than wait for them to invite me, which they usually do. Connie will be tied up with her big family, but there's Marisa and Julie and their husbands and babies. Amber and Wyatt probably can't come, because he's a judge and he always has a big bash at his place..." She realized she was rattling on and looked up. Zane was smiling faintly at her. "Sorry."

"No need. The casserole is fabulous. It's like most of a Thanksgiving meal."

"That's the idea. Anyway, Zane, you're on the invitation list if you decide you want to come. Up to you. I don't think it's going to be a whole lot of people, but I'll keep you posted so you can decide if you'd feel... uncomfortable."

"Thank you." Then he laughed again. "You and Nell. You're trying to change my life."

"Sorry."

He shook his head. "No need to be sorry. Since I got here, I've been feeling a whole lot less like I just need to lick my wounds."

Her heart leaped. "You're feeling better?"

"I don't know. I just know for a long time, especially after the eviction, I felt caved in on myself. Maybe I'm past it." He looked to the side. "What do you think, Nell?"

The dog woofed.

"I thought so, since you keep running over to bring Ashley here."

"Or maybe she could smell what I was cooking," Ashley joked. "Is she allowed people food?"

"Not usually. Okay, I cheat once in a while," he admitted.

"I think that's part of having a dog. I'll give her just a bit of this, if that's okay?"

"Let's skip it. Onions and garlic, in sufficient quantity, could make her sick."

She bit her lip, thinking. "I don't want to trespass with Nell. She's already doing something she shouldn't, like coming to get me when you didn't need help. I guess I shouldn't even feed her a dog biscuit."

Only then did it occur to her what she'd done. She'd invited Zane to Thanksgiving at her house, a friendly gesture but poorly thought out. He hadn't answered, and while she hadn't expected an immediate answer, for the first time she realized what he was probably thinking about: How the heck was he going to get into her house? No ramp. Which would mean asking for help, and she'd already seen how little he liked to do that.

"Oh, man," she said quietly, forgetting her meal.

"What?"

"I just thought... My house isn't very accessible. I didn't mean to put you on the spot, Zane." She lifted her gaze to him and found him still smiling faintly, almost gently.

"You are the most thoughtful person," he said.

"Clearly not. I put my foot in it."

He just shook his head. "Nope. Let me think about it, okay?"

"Absolutely." But now she felt miserable. She'd practically thrown his disability in his face with an invitation she shouldn't have made impulsively. Dealing with her kids, she had to be more forward thinking than this.

He surprised her by reaching for her hand again. "Stop it."

"Stop what?"

"Feeling bad for inviting me. You know what you just did?"

"Yeah." With no way to take it back. No way to truly apologize for reminding him he could no longer just go anywhere he wanted, that he sometimes needed help. She ought to staple her lips together.

"No, not what you're thinking," he said quietly. "You just treated me as if I didn't have any disability at all. Like you were sitting with a normal friend at this table."

Mild shock rippled through her. What a remarkable way to respond to her ham-handedness. She turned her hand over to clasp his fingers. "You're amazing."

"Hardly that. But thanks for letting me know you don't constantly see that I'm crippled." He squeezed her hand and let go, picking up his fork again.

Ashley sighed, feeling relieved and hoping he wasn't just being nice. "I hate that word. *Crippled.*"

"Well, it's true."

"I still don't like it."

He arched a brow at her. "Why dance around it?"

"I'm not dancing around anything. I just don't like that word. It always strikes me as somehow cruel. You can use it if you want. I don't like it."

"I've been living in a very different world these last eighteen years. Very little nicety."

"Then I must sound like a prude." That also didn't

make her feel very good. Was she becoming the stereo-typical schoolmarm?

"Not at all. I was just explaining. I told you I'm rough around the edges. Most of my social skills were prac-ticed among a group of men. Gotta tell you, it's a dif-ferent world."

She believed him. At last she let go of her concerns and decided to just enjoy the meal. For a guy who hadn't wanted to be bothered at first, he was being extraordi-narily friendly to her. Just enjoy it.

"Did you ever marry?" he asked her as he contin-ued eating.

"Nope."

"Surprising."

"Why? I swore off men a long time ago. Not worth the effort. Relationships break up and it's painful. Then there was the time I learned I was the other woman just a bit too late."

"Man," he said. "That stinks."

"It sure did." She managed a laugh. "Best to avoid those complications. So what about you?"

"A few casual relationships. I wasn't the type to rush into anything, and I was seldom home long enough to take it slow. By the time I shipped home, whoever she was had usually found someone else. Can't say I blamed them."

"Why not?"

"Because waiting for me was like waiting for bad news."

Chapter Nine

Waiting for me was like waiting for bad news.

Zane's words followed Ashley through the next few days. Through the tests, through the grading, through the building Halloween excitement as her class helped her decorate the room and special arrangements were made for Mikey to supervise some of it because he couldn't physically help.

In the streets outside, Halloween erupted into the world on nearly every front porch and front yard. While no one yet went all-out on the holiday—nothing like Christmas—nearly everyone found at least a small way to make the already special day more special for the trick-or-treaters.

In the early twilight, electric pumpkins leered their crazy smiles at passersby. Ghosts made of sheets with straw heads stuffed inside hung from tree limbs. An occasional house sported orange lights. One house in particular had a yard full of cutout black cats in all sizes made by the home owner.

And keeping the lid on her kids was getting more difficult. Their excitement was contagious. Her spirits lifted with theirs.

Then there was Zane. She hadn't seen him or heard from him since the night she'd brought the casserole over. Now it was the weekend again, with Halloween on Monday evening. Like every other teacher, she warned her kids not to stay out too late. The next day was a school day.

Some of the stores downtown set up to hand out candy as well. The hospital would x-ray the candy and apples for free.

So everything was right in the world. Except she hadn't heard from Zane. Nell hadn't come over, so she had to assume he was okay. She still wanted to set eyes on him.

She carried a bag of groceries and another bag full of candy for the kids into the house and decided she needed to carve her pumpkin at last.

But even as she put everything away and brought the pumpkin inside for carving, she couldn't get her mind off Zane.

She scolded herself for her foolishness. She had no claim on him and no business worrying unless there was a reason. As she put the pumpkin on her kitchen counter, however, she realized what was really bothering her. They'd had a very frank discussion over that casserole, and part of it had been about her making a mistake by inviting him to Thanksgiving and him calling himself a cripple.

While she didn't ordinarily obsess about things, she was obsessing now. No amount of telling herself to think about something else was really helping. Zane danced around in the back of her mind all the time. If she had half a brain, she'd just stay away until the fascination passed.

The weekend coffee with her friends evaporated. Connie was on duty all weekend. Julie was preoccupied with her new son—who had apparently been named after his father, over Trace's objections—and Marisa said she and Jonni had a cold and Ryker was taking care of them.

It was one of the few times Ashley regretted being single. The feeling didn't last long, however. All she had to do was remember her past mistakes. They stood in her mind like large yellow warning signs on a road.

All things considered, she'd gotten off easy. No divorce, no kids from a broken home. Yeah, it was okay.

But as she looked at the pumpkin and thought about hanging out the decorations she'd pulled down from the attic and placed in the living room, she decided she didn't like the faint anxiety that was nagging at her because of Zane. She was worried. What if something had happened and Nell hadn't come to get her? Or she'd been at school and...

"Oh, cut it out," she said to her empty house. She grabbed her jacket, picked up the pumpkin and went next door. She'd say hi, ask if he wanted to carve this pumpkin because she could get another one, and then maybe she could settle down.

She spared only a moment to recognize that she might be getting herself into some heavy emotional ground here but assured herself she'd get past it. She'd gotten past stronger emotions than this strange, unfulfilled attraction.

It would certainly help to learn he was doing just fine without her company. Yeah. That was what she needed to discover.

Zane opened the door to her, Nell at his side and wagging her tail.

"I came to visit the dog," she said, "and I wondered if you might like to carve a pumpkin. If you don't already have one."

Zane looked down at Nell. "You have a fan club," he told her, then smiled at Ashley. "Come on in. Isn't that the pumpkin I saw on your porch?"

"Yeah, but I can always get another one. How have you been?"

He let Nell close the door behind her, and she stole a moment to fill her eyes with him. Every time she saw him, he seemed to have grown more attractive and the pull she felt toward him was even stronger. Maybe this visit hadn't been such a great idea.

"I was just making some coffee, if you'd like some."

"I'd love some." She let him lead the way to his kitchen.

"Just put the pumpkin on the table. I was going out to get candy and maybe a pumpkin this evening."

So he was doing fine and hadn't needed anyone. She almost blushed in private embarrassment, glad that he couldn't guess she'd been obsessing about him all week.

"I've been okay," he said. "I accepted an invitation to the vets' group. I'll go next week."

And he was putting his life back together. What did he need her for now?

"Your friend Seth is pretty persuasive," he continued

as he ferried cups of coffee to the table. "Other than that I've been doing a lot of thinking."

"Good thinking?"

"Necessary thinking. It's been a week since I had an episode. That's made it easier. Time to try to find a way to make a life, I guess."

Her heart leaped with furtive hope. Maybe he was finding something good in himself. She took the chair and watched him roll over to the table. "So...what's changed?"

"Since I got shipped home, it's been like...well, I don't know how to explain it. It was tough, sure. A lot to deal with. The PTSD especially unnerved me. Even when I was okay, I was worrying about the next bout. So I guess I hunkered down. Tried to build a bunker, not that it could keep anything out. Then the eviction. I decided I was through. Finished. Done."

She nodded, understanding what he was saying. "Very hard."

"Ah, it was just cowardice."

She gasped. It pained her to hear him talk about himself that way. "No, not really. Not after all you'd gone through."

"Cowardice," he repeated. "Hiding from the world? Hiding from my problems? If there's one thing I should have learned as a SEAL, it's that life isn't fair, that turning your back on the mission is desertion and..." He shrugged. "Not to say I won't backslide, but I've got a new mission. Take this mess and make something useful out of it."

The smile that filled her face also filled her heart. "Oh, Zane, that's wonderful!"

"Remains to be seen," he said gruffly. "But I'm beginning to believe I had my head screwed on backward for a long time."

He'd had an awful lot to deal with, she thought. Of course he'd had trouble sorting himself out. She remembered how impressed she had been when he'd said he saw his paralysis as a challenge. Apparently, he'd decided to take on everything else the same way.

"Unfortunately," he said, "I can't batter my PTSD into submission. But I think if I find a way to keep busy doing something productive, away from obvious triggers, I might have less trouble with it."

"I don't know enough about it to judge, but it sounds good to me." When he offered his hand, she took it and tried not to think about how badly she wanted to settle herself on his lap and feel his arms around her again. His hand on her breast. His mouth on hers.

Whoa! This guy was living next door to her. No getting away. She'd better be careful.

But deep inside she'd begun to have feelings she hadn't had in many years. Excitement. Anticipation. Unspoken hope that something would happen. Like a teen in the throes of a crush.

It had better wear off, she warned herself. Zane had his mission to work on, and she didn't want any problems for either of them.

"So your kids want me to bring Nell to school?"

Surprised, she felt her jaw drop a little. Really? But what if he changed his mind? He could in an instant if he started to have problems. But that was true in any case. Pleased that he'd offered, cautious that he might not be able to do it, she expressed appreciation but was careful not to nail him down. "Would you? They'd love it. But there'll be a lot of racket…"

"I think I told you I like kids." His smile was crooked. "Just no fireworks."

She got his meaning. "No fireworks," she promised, trying to sound casual.

Then he leaned forward in his chair, bringing their faces closer together. "Do you have any idea how easy it is to talk to you? It's been a long time since I shared so much with anyone. Somehow with you it seems natural."

Warmth suffused her. "What a compliment." But she wasn't thinking about that. She was *feeling* his nearness, something very different indeed.

"With you," he said slowly, "things just spill out of me. And it's good, because when I hear myself saying them, it's as if stuff falls into line."

"Well, I've often found that saying something out loud makes me realize how stupid it is."

He cracked a surprised laugh. "That, too. But you're special, Ashley."

Now she blushed, something she hadn't done in a long time. "Not me," she said.

He shrugged. "You don't have to believe me, but it's not like I haven't met women since this happened. Do many women want to indulge in noble self-sacrifice?"

She drew a sharp breath, horror stealing through her. Could he really believe…? She felt as if he had just stabbed her. Wounded her. Her stomach turned over, but then anger arrived. "That's not me," she said sharply, pushing back from the table. "Sacrifice yourself!" Which was a terrible thing to say when she considered how much he had sacrificed for his country, but damned if she was going to wither. If he felt that way…

"Not you," he nearly snapped. "Sit down, damn it. And I guess you're not always easy to talk to after all."

Ouch. She winced and tried to let go of the anger as she slowly settled into her seat again, reluctantly willing to give him a chance to explain.

"Are you always so defensive?"

Oh, man, she wanted to sink. She didn't see herself that way, she didn't think she was, but she had just nearly erupted because of a general remark that didn't apply to her at all. At least not directly. She hadn't thought of herself as someone to see a slight in everything, but now she wondered. Worse, she knew from experience that a defensive person could be almost impossible to deal with.

It took her a moment to answer. "I never thought I was before." The ground under her feet seemed to be shifting. Could it be true?

"So it's just with me?"

That was nearly as unsettling as the idea that she might always be defensive. "I don't know. I'm sorry. I've always had a bit of a temper, but not over just anything."

"Temper is fine," he answered. "I have my share. What I was trying to get at was when I was in rehab, then later when I had my own place before everything went south, a number of women seemed interested in me. Crazy, considering I was a mess."

"I don't think that's crazy," she said quietly.

His gaze snapped to her face, but instead of responding to her comment, he continued. "Anyway, one of them, a volunteer at rehab, seemed to take a real shine to me. It was nice for a while. I was getting pretty good with the chair, so they started giving me passes, and we went out for lunch, occasionally for dinner. But after about two months, I discovered something, and there was no way I could argue myself out of it."

"What was that?" Her mouth was still dry from the horror and brief flare of anger, her heart still squeezed with pain—whether for him or herself. With one remark he'd caused her self-perception to teeter. She reached for the coffee mug to drink, to wet her mouth again. Man, this guy drew feelings out of her far too easily. Being around him seemed to put her on an emotional roller coaster.

"I discovered that I was the cross she wanted to nail herself to."

She stopped breathing. Shock froze her insides. Had he just said…? "How?" she whispered.

"I overheard her almost bragging to her friends about the sacrifices she made for me, about how glad she was to make them, and none of it was about me, but all of it was about her. Her self-created halo was almost blinding."

Ashley looked down. She couldn't even speak. It was awful, just awful, to consider how that must have affected him.

He astonished her, slamming his hand down on the table. "Sorry," he said when she jumped. "But I don't want to be an object of pity, and I don't want to be someone's path to sainthood. So I guess I'd better get it together."

She gathered herself, ignoring the ache he'd made her feel, the ache for all he was dealing with, the ache because there was really nothing she could do, short of finding a magic wand. In just a few minutes she'd ridden a whole host of strong reactions, and now her hands trembled a little, her fingers felt cold, her mouth as dry as sand. What was going on here? She felt out of her depth, as if she might drown at any moment. Matters were shifting rapidly, and she was no psychologist to offer help or even judge what was happening here.

Slowly, she raised her head. "When you got here, all you wanted was to be left alone."

"True," he acknowledged.

"What changed?"

"You think I'm blowing smoke?"

She shook her head quickly. She was certain he was telling the truth as he saw it right now. But it seemed so sudden! "Not at all. It's just such a big change in such a short time."

"It's the guy I used to be stepping forward again." He drummed his fingers briefly. "Enough of this crap. Feeling sorry for myself, hiding out, fearing another episode. I wasn't built to live in fear. I wasn't built to avoid challenges. I never used to. The only thing that's changed is inside me, and I don't like it."

That might be simplification, but she didn't want him to suspect she didn't believe what he was saying. It would be so easy to offer a casual response that might leave him wondering if she doubted him. *Careful choice of words*, she reminded herself. *Very careful.*

"Give yourself some slack," she said eventually. "Good heavens, Zane, you've been through a terrible amount of trauma. The war, your paralysis, your PTSD. How could you not want to hunker down for a while? How could you not *need* to? You're not Superman, and even he had his Fortress of Solitude. I think your reaction was probably very normal."

"Maybe." His gaze grew distant. Ashley immediately looked down at Nell, but she seemed calm and unworried. For a while, nobody spoke. Ashley felt as if an emotional whirlwind had just blown through her. The change in him seemed startling and sudden to her, but she had no idea how long he'd been approaching this moment.

Just because he'd claimed to want to be a hermit when he first arrived didn't mean he hadn't been thinking about all of this for a while. Not the man he used to be? Of course he wasn't. He'd been through hell. She suspected the can-do SEAL was rising in him, though.

He'd said this was like a mission. He'd never turned his back on a mission, and some of them must have been terribly difficult. If seeing it in that light helped, then he should go for it.

Maybe it *was* a mission. She put her chin in her hand and closed her eyes, considering it. He was still young, with a lot of years ahead of him. If seeing himself as soldiering through—as he had so often in the past— helped him, good for him. It might actually be the most positive way for him to deal with everything.

She had to give him points for determination. She'd been quite impressed with his attitude toward his paralysis, and now he was stretching that to cover the rest of his life. A challenge.

She opened her eyes and found that he didn't appear quite so far away. Okay, the guy had been a hero and had evidently become one the very hard way more than once. He had the grit and determination to pull this off, if anyone did.

"I like the way you think," she offered.

His eyes trailed back to her. "I was just remembering times when I did things that initially seemed more impossible than this. I mean, what's this except living?

Everyone has to do this, and for some it's harder. I'll see where it goes." Then he smiled faintly. "Does everyone in the world dump on you this way?"

"I don't feel dumped on. I feel honored." True, she did. He'd been incredibly frank, offering a trust that struck her as breathtaking. He'd practically opened his soul to her.

"Anyway," he said. "Pumpkin. Class to meet Nell. Cadell called this afternoon and asked if I could bring her out to his place for some additional work with Mikey's dog."

She almost gaped and felt a small bubble of laughter in the pit of her stomach. "You did get dragged into it."

"Into the world. I hope I didn't kick and scream too much." But he smiled faintly. "Anyway, want to come with me to see Mikey's dog tomorrow?"

She didn't hesitate. "Sure. I love Cadell's dogs. If he was just handing them out, I'd take one. Maybe his wife, Dory, will be there. She's new in town, too, but nobody sees much of her. She's a computer geek who works odd hours, I understand. I'm told she insisted on Cadell keeping the ostriches."

"You mentioned that." His brows lifted. "I still think it's weird that he has them."

"So does everyone else. Join the crowd. Pumpkin?"

He glanced at the digital clock on the microwave. "It's dinnertime. How about we take care of that then decide about pumpkins and candy tomorrow?"

Just like that, he'd cemented them together that evening and the next day. A long way from being a hermit. She wished she felt as confident in this extraordinary change.

* * *

Being a SEAL had made Zane hypersensitive to some things. The tone of a voice. The faint microexpressions that continually crossed a face. It had been necessary to his survival and worked often even when he couldn't understand the language. Reading his fellow SEALs had become second nature.

So he'd read Ashley and had no doubt that she was uneasy right then. She'd met a grumpy man who said he just wanted to be a hermit, and now here she was, a couple short weeks later, with a man who was busting out of his hermitage.

Of course she wondered if something was wrong with him, if the change was only temporary. Outwardly she'd handled it well, but inwardly she was struggling, probably wondering when he'd next withdraw or grouse at her over nothing.

But the truth was, the self-declared hermit had been the temporary him. A reaction to being evicted. A conscious decision to make sure something like that never happened again. He'd had enough. Life was difficult enough these days without accusatory neighbors. So he'd gone into an emotional crouch, and he rather despised himself for it.

No, he didn't want to be scaring people with his PTSD. Losing it wasn't good for anyone, himself included. But it happened, and it would continue to happen for the rest of his life, although with less frequency, he hoped.

When he looked at Ashley, he saw a woman who had accepted him as he was. She'd come over when Nell went to fetch her. She'd helped him get up off the floor and scolded him for refusing to ask for help. She'd had to guts to ask him to help with Mikey's dog, and then the guts to ask him to visit her classroom.

He was just glad she hadn't seen him in one of his total wipeouts, cussing and swearing and trying to dodge bullets that weren't there. He suspected she'd handle it as well as the rest, though. She'd certainly handled finding him lying on the floor because he'd been trying to dive for safety.

Remarkable woman. Sexy woman. Still, he was too messed up and didn't want to mess her up as well. Although she *had* invited herself over because she hadn't seen him all week. Worried about him. She didn't need that, either.

Dinner. He'd mentioned that, hadn't he? The question was what to do about it. He certainly didn't want her to think he expected her to cook for him. "You said there was a pizza place somewhere?"

She nodded. "Just east of the city limits. A popular teen hangout." She screwed up her face a little. "I may have taught most of those kids and I'm sure they wouldn't appreciate me showing up there. But the shop *does* deliver."

He liked that idea. He didn't want to disrupt enjoyment for a bunch of teens, either, and him showing up in a wheelchair might dampen their fun. "What do you like on your pizza?" he asked.

"Anything except pineapple and anchovies."

"Ah, no pineapple pizzas for you."

She laughed, and he was delighted to see it reached her eyes. "I might like it with another name," she admitted. "But that's not at all what I think of when I think of pizza."

"Me neither," he admitted. "Is this pizza good?"

"Good enough. It might disappoint someone from New York or Chicago, but at least the crust rises. None of that cracker-type crust."

"I suppose the pepperoni is good everywhere. What about veggies?"

Zane enjoyed chatting with her about something so innocuous. Comparing the relative merits of different vegetables on a pizza seemed like the safest and most comfortable place he'd been in a while. When they finally agreed on what they both wanted, she pulled out her cell phone.

"Observe," she said lightly. "I teach nutrition as part of my syllabus, and yet I have the pizza place on speed dial."

He laughed. "Pizza's probably not as bad for anyone as some other things."

"Like soda pop full of sugar," she answered drily.

"Or the candy we're about to hand out by the ton on Monday."

He watched her laugh, the sound easy and full. Dang, he liked everything about this woman. He liked the way temper sparked in her blue eyes when he annoyed her. He liked the way she kept acting as if he were perfectly normal even though he was quite sure he was not. And he liked the way she seemed to have completely moved past his disability.

He was paralyzed, obviously. He knew that it usually disturbed people, made them uncomfortable. But from the very start, she hadn't seemed at all uncomfortable. Just concerned. Her concern wasn't a terrible thing, certainly nothing he minded, especially since she didn't overdo it.

But she was drawing him out of his self-preoccupation,

too. Because of her he had other things to think about, even some things he could conceivably look forward to. He was nervous about meeting her class, because he didn't want to have an episode in front of them. They might be scared. But there was Nell, he reminded himself, kneading the dog's neck. She'd alert him before he completely slipped away. He'd probably have time to leave the classroom.

Of course, if he pulled himself out of his self-imposed pit, he'd have to figure how he could be productive for the rest of his days. He'd always been productive, at least until his wounding, and he couldn't stand the idea that he might spend the rest of his days in this wheelchair, in this house, and not do one useful thing for someone else.

Ashley finished ordering the pizza. He'd pushed his credit card over to her, but she'd ignored it and used her own. Man, he could probably afford this pizza better than she could on a teacher's salary.

"Got any super career ideas for a paralyzed vet?" The question popped out of him. He expected her to kind of shrug and say she'd have to think about it. She surprised him.

"Sure," she said. "A temporary one, anyway."

"What's that?"

"Let my friend's shop class come over and turn your kitchen into a project. They'd learn a lot, and you're not the only person in this county who could use the kind of modifications you'd need. You could even show them, so they wouldn't be guessing."

"Why would they want to do that? It's a big project."

"Alex—that's the teacher—has been bemoaning the fact he doesn't have any really big projects for them.

The auto shop? Sure, there's always a car that needs working on. But cabinetry and things like that? He says he's too limited, the things they can do are too small. And these are students who want a future working with things like this." She hesitated. "You'd probably have to pay for the materials, though."

"That wouldn't be a problem," he admitted. He'd saved most of his pay over the years and had a steady disability income, much of which he hadn't needed to spend during his time in the hospital and rehab.

"So, tell you what. I'll bring Alex over some time and you two can hash out the possibility."

Zane felt himself smiling faintly. This woman didn't let the moss grow. She moved immediately. He liked that. "Still, that's hardly a career," he reminded her.

"Stopgap," she admitted. "But I'm sure there are plenty of other things. Alex might have some ideas. You need to meet Jess McGregor. He was a medic in Afghanistan and lost his leg. Now he's a physician's assistant running the minor emergency clinic at the hospital. He'd probably have some good ideas, too."

His smile grew. "You're going to save me in spite of myself."

She flushed. "Sorry. You asked about careers, and my mind and mouth took off."

"It's okay." For some reason it was more than okay. She felt like an ally, which he liked, and not like a taskmaster pushing him, which he'd resent. "Maybe you just helped me get it all in focus when you asked me to help with Mikey's dog. I like you, Ashley. It's not just my dog that has a crush on you."

He watched her eyes widen, heard her indrawn

breath, and he enjoyed it. But the doorbell rang. "Pizza," he said, letting the sudden sexual tension slip away.

Best for both of them, because he might never be good for anyone. But for a few seconds there it had felt great.

Chapter Ten

The next morning Ashley awoke with an unusual sense of anticipation. Last night after they finished the pizza, they'd agreed to meet again this morning, first to go to see Cadell and the dogs, then to go to the market for candy, a pumpkin and whatever else they needed.

So a routine chore, grocery shopping, felt like a genuine outing to her, and she was definitely looking forward to seeing Mikey and the dogs. But mostly she was looking forward to the time with Zane. When he'd first arrived here, she'd never expected anything like this. Never thought he'd want to be out and about and certainly never dreamed that he'd want to spend time like this with her.

A niggle of concern troubled her as she showered, dried her hair and dressed. The man she had talked to might be ephemeral. She didn't know him well enough to know if he had major mood swings, ones that could change him suddenly. She wasn't worrying about his PTSD. That was something to be dealt with when it happened. No, she was wondering if he might be an emotional chameleon. The change still seemed fast to her.

But he'd said he'd been thinking about it for some time. Maybe getting out to Cadell's place and meeting Mikey had simply brought to fruition a change he'd been wanting to make for some time. Maybe it had finished the process of deciding he could still be a useful member of society.

Boy, feeling that he was useful had to have taken a ding, dealing with the problems he had. There must have been times when he'd felt caught in a nightmare, paralyzed, haunted by the war in ways he couldn't control.

But he'd said last night that the man he used to be was talking. That actually made sense to her. He'd taken some terrible blows, but he was still, somewhere deep inside, the guy who had been a determined athlete and an even more determined SEAL.

She decided that when she went over there, she would suggest he put his medals on display so he could remember the guy who'd done all those daring deeds. Maybe that would help him reclaim himself.

Then she stopped. No, she was not a psychologist. Those medals might cause him more pain. He'd already told her that he'd wanted to throw them away and had kept them only because an older vet had told him he might want them someday, and that they were the only reward he was going to get.

Which was pretty pathetic, when she thought about it. How could a box full of medals make up for losing your legs and part of your mind? Honestly, nothing could make up for that.

Glancing at her phone, she saw it was time to grab her parka and go to Zane's. Maybe it was time to keep her mouth shut and let him lead the way. He was the only one, after all, who had any idea where he wanted to go from here.

As she climbed the ramp, Zane's front door opened. She saw a happy Nell first, her tail wagging, then Zane as the door opened wider. He smiled, too.

Autumn had truly begun to move in, whispering of winter. The wind gusted just before she reached the front door, blowing fallen leaves around.

"Hurry in," Zane said. "Ice cube season is on the way."

"It feels like it," she agreed as she stepped into the warmth of his house. "I hope it doesn't snow and interfere with Halloween."

"Don't you keep up with the weather?"

"Only when I'm concerned." The door closed behind her, sealing her in warmth.

"I'm compulsive about it. Years of experience and training, I guess. So I can proudly tell you there's no snow in the forecast and we might see a slight warming on Monday. In the meantime, button up. Coffee?"

She hesitated. "Isn't Cadell expecting you?"

He shook his head. "Mikey has a cold. His mom's worried and doesn't want to bring him out, so no practice today for his dog. Add to that, Cadell said he'd been called in early to cover for another deputy, so there's no point in us going out there at all. I'm sure Nell would have loved running around in the paddock and I wouldn't mind a closer look at those ostriches."

She laughed, tossing back her hood and unzipping her parka. "Not too close."

"Well, I'm not sure I'd want those huge beaks too close," he agreed. "So, coffee? Did you have breakfast? I baked some cinnamon rolls from freezer dough."

"The roll sounds wonderful. I had an egg and toast, but I'm not too full to eat one of those."

"Then the store," he said as he wheeled into the kitchen. Today he wore loose jeans and a light gray sweatshirt. For the first time she wondered how he managed his clothes, but she didn't ask because it seemed intrusive.

She reminded herself of the jujitsu this man had performed to get himself up off the floor onto the couch and then into his chair. He probably had as many moves as a cat by now, or he simply wouldn't be able to live alone.

Once again he ferried the coffee to the table for them, remarking that caffeine was a good antidote to the cold. "I ought to know. I relied on it in quite a few cold places."

The rolls were already on a plate in the center of the table, and a moment later he set out two smaller plates. "Feel free to eat with your fingers. Do you like to butter yours?"

"I like them just as they are," she said, helping herself to one roll. At least they weren't gigantic. Sinful, but not gigantic.

Nell settled on the floor between them, gnawing contentedly on a rawhide bone.

"When does Carol come to clean for you?" she asked, to make conversation that would keep her from voicing errant thoughts, such as that he looked more delicious than the rolls. In fact, she wished she had the nerve to just sit on his lap and see what happened next.

Bad idea, she scolded herself. Entanglements too often produced pain. Besides, he'd already made it plain that he had good reason to doubt a woman's interest in him. It must have made him feel just awful that a woman he'd been dating had only wanted to offer herself as a sacrifice. Lord! He deserved so much more than that. For example, a woman who didn't think living with him was a painful or difficult task.

So far she herself hadn't seen a single reason to feel that way. He had some tough problems to deal with, all right, but they were tough for *him*. Someone who cared about him would share his pain, not seek praise for putting up with it.

She stifled a sigh, for fear he would question her about it. Simple truth was, she honestly liked this man a whole lot. She wanted to get to know him better. She wanted to spend more time with him. Then there was the sexual attraction that stayed with her even when she was elsewhere. Zane just kept popping into her head, occupying her thoughts and making unexpected appearances even when she was focused on something else, like teaching or grading or planning her lessons. If she wasn't careful, she was apt to let thinking about him take over her life.

Maybe, she thought as she licked her fingers delicately, she ought to just have sex with him and settle that issue. Maybe when the heated fog of desire wasn't winding its way around every cell in her body, she could break free of the fascination.

"You're smiling," he said.

"A silly thought, one I'd rather not share." She wiped

her fingers on a napkin and reached for her coffee. "What kind of shopping do you need to do today?"

"Only a little. Carol does that for me. You asked, so... She comes for the big cleaning on Mondays, then drops in a couple of mornings a week to take care of odds and ends and see if I need anything for the larder." He gestured to a magnetic pad on the refrigerator. "She saves me a lot of trouble, because unless I get a basket for my chair, I can't carry much, and even with a basket I wouldn't be able to carry much more. Sometimes I think I need a little wagon as a trailer."

The way he said it, the image it created, made her laugh. "That would be a sight. A little red wagon."

He smiled. "It would work, though. I've tried pushing a cart. I can, if I'm careful. But then there's the problem of putting items in it. Not everything can be tossed like a baseball."

That made her laugh again. "You're remarkable," she said honestly. "You really *do* take that chair as a challenge."

"No other way to look at it," he said firmly. "It's the rest of it that I've let overwhelm me. That has to stop."

She didn't know how he was going to stop it, but she figured he was probably determined enough to do just about anything he put his mind to.

A short while later they left for the store. He parked in a handicapped space near the front doors, one with the hash marks on the correct side of the van for his lift. She stood there waiting for him and Nell and looked at the car parked in the next slot. No handicapped plate. No handicapped hang tag.

She suddenly felt embarrassed that she'd never paid attention to that before, but at the same time realized she wanted to have some words with whoever was parked there. Really?

When Zane reached the ground and closed up his van, he wheeled toward her, Nell at his side. "What are you so fascinated by?"

She pointed. "Do you see a hang tag? Or a handicapped plate?"

He lifted a brow. "It's probably on the dash."

So she marched to the front of the car and looked. "Nope," she announced. "You go on inside. I want to talk to this person."

He tilted his head, studying her. "Ashley, you don't have to."

"No, maybe not. But there are plenty of people around here who need these spaces. I admit I never really paid attention before, except not to park in them. Now…well, I'm offended."

"Firebrand," he remarked. "Look, you don't know who it is. The person might give you trouble. It could be someone nasty."

"Oh, I'm sure it's someone nasty," she said, putting her hands on her hips and ignoring the way the chilly breeze nipped at her cheeks. "If they're not entitled to this parking space, they're nasty."

"Or just thoughtless, or in a hurry, or trying to avoid freezing. Let it go, Ash."

She faced him. "Why? What would you have done if you hadn't been able to find a space? Parked out at the end of the lot where you could get two spaces together? And what happens if you come back and someone's filled the space where you need to use your lift? You'd be stuck."

He seemed not to have an argument for that. She

felt a small bit of satisfaction that she'd made her point. "Look, I'm not out to embarrass this person if they just forgot to put up their tag, but if they couldn't park two slots farther away because they're lazy? Yeah, I want to embarrass them."

Then she saw that he was pressing his lips together while his eyes danced. "You think I'm funny?"

"I think you're an avenging angel."

She frowned. "I'm no angel. Like I said, this is something I'd never really thought about before. But now that I have…well, I'm going to do something. You and Nell go inside before you get cold."

"I'm not going anywhere without you," he retorted. "And I'm sure Nell feels the same. We'll turn into icicles together while we wait."

She huffed a bit, her annoyance refusing to abate. "Doesn't it ever make you mad when you see this? Doesn't it bother you?"

"It used to bother me a whole lot more. These days… well, I try not to think about it."

"But it's so wrong! Yeah, I'm angry."

"Righteous anger," he remarked, pivoting his chair and rolling toward the door of the store. "Let's go." Nell trotted at his side, leashed. Ashley realized that she didn't often see Nell on a leash. She was almost certain the dog didn't need it, either.

"Why did you want me to let it go?" she asked curiously as they hurried toward the store.

"Because you didn't have any idea what kind of person you'd be dealing with, which is dangerous, and because I learned a long time ago to pick my fights. Besides, it was probably just thoughtless. A lot of people don't get it. Then there's the possibility that it's some young mother with a small child, who saw two empty spaces were together and she thought it couldn't hurt to take one to avoid the cold. Or what about someone temporarily on crutches who wouldn't get a hang tag?"

Ashley flushed faintly. "So I overreacted?"

"I wouldn't say that. It's just that I've been dealing with this longer than you have. There were times when I was embarrassed when I gave someone a hard time over it. You could say I learned the hard way."

"I wasn't being very charitable," she admitted, a hot sliver of shame striking her. She always tried to be charitable, but there she'd been, criticizing someone she didn't know who might not deserve it. Who might have special circumstances of their own.

"You got angry on my behalf. Far be it from me to criticize you for it. It's just that I've been dealing with this a lot longer, and while some people are simply jerks, most people are innocent of any intention to create a problem. They're only going to be a minute, or it's raining cats and dogs, or…" He shrugged as the automated doors opened before them. "Lots of reasons it's hard to get really angry about."

She could see his point of view, of course. She'd never been an unreasonable person, but being out there with him, thinking of Mikey also facing such problems…well, it had frosted her, obviously.

Time to ease up and enjoy the company, and it wasn't difficult to do. Zane seemed in reasonably good spirits, as if announcing his intention to change his life around had made him feel good. Nell added to the enjoyment, drawing a lot of attention. She seemed to know it and was almost prancing beside Zane.

A number of people welcomed him home but didn't

try to delay him. A few kids wanted to rush Nell and had to be held back by their parents with the advice, "Never run up to a strange dog, and never bother a working dog."

Which led to some interesting conversations started by Zane. He *did* like children, it seemed, and he had no problem with halting and chatting, backing up their parents' warnings, explaining why service dogs shouldn't be distracted. "If she's paying attention to you, she's not taking care of me, and I could get sick."

That explanation worked like a charm with the kids, who immediately settled down. A couple of times, Zane called Nell to order, telling her to "sit and mind." If she'd been growing distracted, it ended there. Instantly her gaze fixed on him.

It wasn't a major shopping trip, which was good, because by the time he'd had a few conversations with the kids, Nell's attention to him was changing, and she butted his arm carefully.

"Time for me to go," he said.

Looking into his eyes, Ashley didn't question it. He had what she had heard called *the thousand-yard stare*. "Can you make it to the van?"

"Yeah. Yeah."

"Go. I'll check out. I won't be long."

She watched him start rolling toward the door, Nell at his side. The dog was no longer prancing proudly. Now she barely took her nose off his arm.

Time to hurry, Ashley thought. Not that there was much. Big bags of mixed candies to pass out, a jug of cider and pumpkin pie that Zane had wanted, and some Polish sausage that Ashley had wanted. The butcher here made his own, and it was mouthwatering. On impulse, she grabbed some hoagie buns deciding to make sausage dogs for dinner for both of them.

As long as Zane felt better.

Zane struggled to hang on to the present while the past kept trying to push its way out of the graveyard where it never seemed to stay buried for long. Nell helped, nudging him, whining at him, forcing him to focus on getting back into his van and closing the door. He didn't move to the driver's seat, though. Not yet. He had to be sure he wouldn't start the engine when Ashley climbed in the car and suddenly be driving down some mental road where every oncoming car posed the threat of a bomb or gunfire.

In his brain, images overlaid each other, not quite like double vision because the images were different, but more like two films one on top of the other. His ears seemed to be hearing sounds that didn't exist—explosions, gunfire, screaming.

Nell's whimpering and even a few barks reminded him of the world that was actually around him, keeping him from slipping completely over into the past.

Anxiety rode him like a devouring monster. He gripped the arms of his chair until his fingers ached.

Stop it, he yelled inwardly. *Stop it. That's gone. Done. No more.*

Then Nell jumped up into his lap and began to lick his face with her rough tongue. That reality began to trump the old ones that were trying to take over.

"God, girl, you're going to leave me raw!"

Nell woofed just as the passenger door opened and Ashley slid groceries onto her seat and looked in.

"How are you?" she asked, twisting to look at him.

"Coming back," he answered cautiously. He hadn't really slipped in time, but he'd come close, and he wasn't absolutely certain he was steady yet.

"Let me put these groceries in the back. We can sit here as long as you need."

It was a good thing that he couldn't feel Nell's weight on his lap. She was by no means a small dog, and it still amazed him that she could manage to balance this way on his thighs. Now she was sniffing him like an anxious mother dog, checking him out. She must be able to smell the changes in him. He could think of no other way she could be so on top of his moods.

Releasing the arms of his chair at last, he wrapped his arms around his dog, buried his face in her neck for a moment and gave thanks for Nell.

And for Ashley, who didn't hover over him, never once tried to deprive him of his own agency. He'd had people try to do everything for him, like a certain ex-girlfriend, and he'd hated the smothering. Ashley didn't offer to do a damn thing, not since the very beginning, but he also knew from experience that she would help when needed.

He hated needing help. Sometimes there was no escaping it. Trying to be independent could reach a level of foolishness if he wasn't careful. Like that rug in the living room. There was no way he could remove it himself; he'd have to get someone in to do it, so that if he ever tipped again for some reason he could slide across the floor. That rug was rough enough to make it difficult.

That was when he knew the difficulty had passed. Ashley was climbing in the front passenger seat. When he let go of Nell, she dropped to the floor of the van and didn't try to poke him or lick him again.

It was over. As his episodes went, it hadn't been that bad. He'd never completely lost touch. As for the trigger…maybe all the people in the store? Maybe he'd become stressed by the attention, by talking to the kids? If so, that was something else he needed to get over. He guessed he'd learn a lot about his limits when he spoke to Ashley's class.

He was able to drive them home. Ashley brought his groceries to him and placed them on his lap, except for the cider jug. "I should carry this in," she said. "If it slips Nell could cut her paws."

"Or try to drink it," he said lightly. "You going to stay for a while?"

"I still need to decorate my place. I've got my pumpkin hollowed out, but it needs a face."

He took that as a friendly farewell and figured he deserved it. "Let me know what I owe you for the groceries."

She waved her hand, dismissing it. Then she smiled, that beautiful smile that warmed his heart. "Do you like roasted pumpkin seeds?"

"Love 'em."

"Then I'll bring some over later if you want. I toasted them last night. And I have stuff to make us dinner if you like Polish sausage."

Inside, she put the jug of cider on his table, then took her own candy out of the bag and left with a friendly "See you later."

The house was once again empty of everything except him and Nell. For the first time since his injury, the solitude felt lonely.

He looked down at Nell. "She just left. How can I already miss her?"

Nell had no answer except a sweep of her tail.

A couple of hours later, Zane decided he couldn't stand it anymore. He needed activity, exercise. The trip to the store hadn't been enough. He needed a change of scenery, too.

The instant he started to pull on his jacket and gloves, Nell quivered with excitement, her tail waving so quickly it almost blurred.

"Yeah, you need it, too, don't you, girl?" Zane hardly needed her response.

As soon as they stepped out the front door and he closed it behind them, he received a surprise. Ashley was hanging a Halloween flag from a branch on the tree in his front yard, a black one with a grinning skeleton printed on it.

She heard them and peered over her shoulder. Since she was standing on a ladder, he called out, "Be careful!"

"I am," she answered. "I hope you don't mind, but I figured I didn't need it all in my yard."

He didn't mind. He was kind of pleased. "How much of that do you have?"

"Just a few more things. Want some cobwebs?"

"If it's not too much trouble."

"I'm going to hang them, anyway."

Zane looked down at Nell. "Amazingly enough, I'm looking forward to Halloween."

Apparently feeling his happiness, she swept her tail over the porch boards.

Once the flag was hanging and tossing in the chilly

breeze, Ashley climbed down and looked at it. "Good enough," she said, eyeing it. Then she turned toward Zane. "The skeleton glows in the dark. Much better at night. Be right back."

He watched her dash across to her house. Her own yard was evidently complete, with a ghost hanging from one of her trees and rippling very nicely. Cobwebs draped from her porch rails, not overdone, just a bit here and there. And her pumpkin, endowed with a smiling face, now sat on the top step, ready to be lit.

A few minutes later she came back carrying a clear plastic bag full of white stuff. "Where would you like it?"

"The same as what you did at your place. It looks good on the railing."

She smiled. "Also easier to clean up. Some of our neighbors here will put it everywhere, and I swear some of it winds up serving as snow at Christmas because it gets so tangled on things. Not that we need fake snow then. At least not usually."

She climbed the ramp, joining him and Nell on the porch, and studied the task before her.

"I can help," he said quietly.

Her head whipped around. "Of course you can! I'm just so used to doing this by myself."

She handed him the bag after pulling out a handful for herself. "I think it's got another year left in it. See what you think."

She went to the far end of the porch so he headed for the other. Of course he could do this. It might not look that good because he lacked practice, but he'd get it good enough.

When he pulled a ball of it out and tried to tug it

apart, it spread into a filmy netting. Not exactly spiderwebby. More like a cobweb, but clever. He hung it in patches over his end of the railing, and at the bottom of the bag found a huge rubbery spider. He held it up.

"Where's this live?" he called to Ashley.

"Anywhere you like, but not too close to your steps. Some little kids get really frightened."

So he tucked it into some of the webby stuff and wheeled back to take a look. "What do you think, Nell?"

Nell cocked her head, giving him that "Are you out of your mind?" look she sometimes achieved. He laughed.

Ashley joined them a minute later, scooping the remains into her plastic bag. "All done," she said brightly. "You must be getting cold. I'm feeling it myself."

"I was just getting ready to exercise with Nell. Around the block a few times, as fast as I can safely go."

She leaned back against the porch railing. "There's a special wheelchair for racing, right? It would let you go faster?"

"In the road, and yes, there are special chairs. For now I'm content with the sidewalks, although I've begun to wonder if I might be able to use the track at the high school or college."

"I have no doubt. But go for the college. They have that new material, whatever it is. The high school has cinders, remember. Give 'em a call. I'm sure they'll say yes. I see people out there jogging all the time, and they're not students. It's probably okay unless a team is training."

"Thanks." He began to roll toward the ramp. "Wanna come with?"

He was glad when she smiled and said yes. Maybe

too glad. He'd better watch himself with this woman. All he could do was blight her life.

Ashley enjoyed the brisk walk with Zane and Nell. Zane kept up a reasonably good speed, one that qualified as exercise for her. Cars drove past, people waved, but except for a few kids outside playing they didn't meet anyone on foot.

"I guess it's too cold," Ashley remarked.

"Doesn't it get a lot colder here? I seem to remember…"

"Then you probably remember how few people take a stroll come winter." She laughed. "Shoveling snow was it. Car the rest of the time."

He smiled as she jogged his memory. The track events he had participated in happened mostly in the spring and mud, but come late October even the football team was getting ready to wind down its season. Hot drinks, warming capes, helmets over knit caps, and some days even ski masks. Yeah, he remembered.

They crossed a few streets and rounded a different area of town before they turned to come back. It was definitely growing colder, and Zane noticed that Ashley coughed a few times.

"Are you okay?" he asked.

"Dry, cold air. No biggie. When I get back inside, my nose will start running. I hate that."

He laughed and pushed up the pace a little bit. Nell was enjoying every minute of being outside. She kept turning her head his way, as if checking that he was okay, then she'd continue prancing at his side, a brisk pace that she carried off with amazing grace. He wondered if even in his salad days he'd run as gracefully as the dog.

"So," he said to Ashley, "got any big dreams for your future?"

"Dreams?" It seemed to him that her step hitched just a bit. "Not really. I'm saving for a big vacation eventually, but mostly I'm pretty happy with my life. I'll probably be teaching fourth grade until they force me out the door."

He laughed quietly. "So nothing short-term?"

She didn't answer. But then, slowly, she turned her head and looked at him. Their eyes locked, and it was his turn to hitch as he rolled forward. Nell looked back, astonished at the sudden slowing.

But he couldn't help it. He'd been attracted to this woman since the instant he set eyes on her, and the attraction hadn't quieted one bit. Now, as their gazes met, he felt an electric zap that ran through every cell in his body, at least the ones that could still feel. He felt himself hardening in response and had a hazy thought that it was good his jacket covered the evidence.

But then he noticed that she had stopped as well and that her breathing had become more rapid. She felt it, too. Felt the electricity between them, the heightening desire, the need to venture into uncharted waters to find the waiting treasure.

Oh, God, he thought, dragging his gaze away. Trouble. Bad for both of them. What woman would want to take on his problems? And he wouldn't ever want to treat her in any but the most respectful and caring of ways. No one-night stands with this woman. His regard for her was too high. Plus, he had a little self-respect of his own.

They moved again toward his house and reached it with only a little more light conversation. But he still didn't want to say goodbye.

This woman had made it possible for him to connect again. Admittedly, it was only one connection, but it was a great experience in that it didn't involve another vet like himself. Those connections were easier to make, having a shared experience. Ashley was so very different, and her difference seemed to lighten him.

A regular woman liked him and treated him like he was capable. Worth a celebration, he thought. Plus he suddenly couldn't bear to see her walk away. "Come in for some cocoa?" he asked.

Chapter Eleven

"Sure," she said without hesitation. "Cocoa sounds great. Listen, I bought some Polish sausage and buns at the market. Want to join me for dinner?"

He paused as he let Nell push the door open for him. "I assume you mean here."

"Well, unless I could levitate one of your ramps over to my place, I guess so."

She said it lightly, as if the fact that he needed ramps, lifts and wheelchairs was a negligible matter.

He made instant cocoa from individual packets. As he boiled water in the microwave, then added a dollop of cream to each mug to make it richer, he thought about the thousands of times he'd cooked his meals over small cans that burned with a tiny flame, everything coming out of a packet, most of it needing only a little water. And the coffee crystals he seldom wasted the time to heat.

"Man," he said suddenly. "Too much time in the field. I need to remember how to cook normally again."

"I use this cocoa, too. No apology necessary."

She'd doffed her jacket by the time he turned his chair and brought her mug to the table. Then he got his own and joined her.

"So," she asked, "have you thought about modifying your kitchen? I mentioned it to Alex, and he was ready to jump on it. Great experience for his students."

He half smiled. "You know, when I first came here I'd made only the absolutely essential changes."

"Why?" Her brow creased.

"I thought I'd told you. Because I didn't know if I'd decide to stay. Bathroom, check. Bedroom, check. Front-loading washer, check. But kitchen? Big expense unless I was going to stay. Plus, doing it up for me would make the house unattractive if I decided to sell."

Her smile faded. "I didn't realize that, Zane. I'm sorry if I've been pushing you. I just assumed..." She trailed off and looked almost sad.

"You assumed I'd come home for good. Why wouldn't you? I never told you otherwise."

"I see." She averted her face and drew a long breath.

She felt bad, he realized with astonishment. She didn't want him to leave. Seriously? He cast his mind back, wondering what he might have done to make her give a damn what he did, whether he came or went. Little enough, he decided.

"I didn't say I'm leaving," he said. "I haven't thought much about it since I met you. I'm not thinking about it now. You did something special, Ashley."

She turned her head. "Me?"

"You. You made me feel like I really have come

home. I see that I haven't gotten out and made a whole lot of friends or anything, but…you've still made me feel like I'm home. And welcome. So…no, I'm not leaving."

Her expression lightened. "I'm glad to hear that. And you have reached out, you know. Look what you're doing for Mikey. You've decided to join the veterans' discussion group and come to my class and talk to students. Those are big steps for you, aren't they?"

He held out his hand, palm up, an invitation, and felt her smaller one as she laid it there almost trustingly. Her fingers felt a bit chilled as he squeezed them and let go. "Drink that cocoa and warm yourself up. And yeah, they're big steps, but it annoys me because they shouldn't be."

He liked the way her eyes softened. "Zane, I told you before, cut yourself some slack. You're doing all that now."

"Cutting myself slack was something I never did in the SEALs and I shouldn't do it now. I'm only thirty-seven. A lot of years ahead. I can't let them be pointless ones."

"But it takes time to set a whole new course in life."

He laughed without any mirth. "It didn't take much time to change my entire life."

She pressed her lips together and looked down at her mug. "You're right. It didn't. But maybe this is a little different."

"Only in that I have the luxury of picking and choosing and moving at a snail's pace if I choose. Look, Ashley, I didn't mean to sound like I was dismissing you. I've still got problems to deal with and I know it. Look at the way I had to leave the store this morning."

She lifted her head. "Was it too noisy?"

"That wasn't it. I was thinking about it before we took our walk. I think it was the chaos."

"Chaos?" She frowned.

This time his laugh was more genuine. "Chaos," he repeated. "I'm sure it doesn't look like that to you, but when I get into new situations I naturally grow more alert."

"I think most of us do."

He shook his head a bit. "But not high alert, life-threatening alert. That in itself isn't bad. It's a trained response—it's saved my life and the lives of others. But when I get in that mode, I'm trying to keep my eye on everything. Threat ready. No threats in that grocery store. Logically, I knew that. But being hyperalert and trying to keep my eye on all the moving people... I guess it started to overwhelm me."

He let her absorb that while he considered making more cocoa. Maybe coffee. Certainly something warm, because this house felt drafty today. Maybe he ought to check the heat, but just as he had the thought he heard the rumble of it turning on, then a little while later warm air blew through the vent. Okay, heat was fine.

And Ashley was still silent. He was beginning to worry that he'd said something wrong. Maybe told her too much. He shouldn't be talking to her about these things, anyway. She was a civilian. There was an un-spoken rule among vets that some things should never be discussed with those who had never walked in their shoes. The world's innocents would never understand some things.

Finally she looked up. "Thanks for the explanation, Zane. I think I understand better now. I couldn't imag-ine what had troubled you. Now I know."

"And next time there'll probably be a different explanation. You know, you'd think after all this time I'd know where my triggers are. Guess not."

"It doesn't matter, does it?"

Surprise rippled through him. "Of course it matters."

"Why? I mean, some obvious things can be important to avoid, but you've tried avoiding damn near everything, haven't you? How are you going to avoid the grocery? I just mean…" She trailed off, biting her lower lip. "Sorry, I'm talking out of turn."

But she wasn't. He reached out, seizing her hand this time and holding it tightly. She'd opened a new way of thinking about all of this, and he was turning it around, absorbing it, trying to decide exactly what it meant.

"You might be right," he said after a few minutes. "I'm going to think about it. For example, I had to leave the store, but Nell was enough to keep me grounded. Next time maybe my reaction won't be so strong."

She nodded, listening.

"I can't avoid everything…" But he trailed off. Her blue eyes met his again, and that electricity zapped between them once more. In that instant a switch flipped and he forgot nearly everything else. He wanted to resist, for her sake, but when he saw her chest rising and falling with quickened breaths, read his own hunger reflected in her face as if her whole being was leaning toward him… What if he was imagining it?

But the words slipped past his guard. "Ashley… I want you."

"I want you, too," she breathed. "So very much. I've been arguing with myself, but it won't go away."

He nodded, swallowing hard. "Are you sure you want

to deal with this?" He patted his useless leg. "There's nothing graceful, nothing…"

She squeezed his hand hard until he stopped speaking. "I'm sure if you could you'd want to just close the door behind us and leave everything to the imagination."

Surprised, he almost laughed.

"However," she went on, clearing her throat a little as her voice grew rusty, "I'd rather not close the door. I'm not asking for grace. I'm asking for you. Do you trust me enough?"

Nobody had ever put it to him that way before. Did *he* trust *her*? The tables were turned.

He knew how awkward this could be. With his saintly girlfriend, he'd had to go alone and get undressed and into bed before she wanted to have sex. She didn't want to see his disability laid out before her in all the complications it created with a simple thing like dressing or undressing.

For her he'd been fine in his wheelchair. Then she could smother him. But at points in between…

Hell, why was he thinking of that woman now when here was Ashley telling him she didn't care about all that? She wanted him the way he was. Well, he was damn well going to find out right now.

He backed out from the table and around to her side. "Sit on my lap?" he asked.

She didn't hesitate, rising from her chair and sliding into his embrace. Her arms wound around his neck.

"I can feel you," he murmured, closing his eyes, savoring the sensations, treasuring them. "In important places, I feel you."

"I feel you, too," she whispered. "I love it. I've been thinking about this for so long…"

It felt like forever, though it hadn't been. It was as if this moment was destined and he'd just been waiting. "Hang on," he said gruffly. Then he started rolling them toward his bedroom. That wasn't graceful, either. He hadn't widened halls or doors, but he'd gotten pretty good at three-point turns. As they bumped around, Ashley gave a little laugh but never loosened her hold on him.

"I like this," she said.

"Clumsy."

"No, more space needed, that's all." Then she set him afire with a kiss to his cheek that trailed to his lips. For a few moments the wheelchair stopped in the hallway, and as impatient as he was, he didn't care.

Her tongue sought his, tasting of chocolate, warm and enticing, promising greater wonders to come.

"Slow down," he said as he pulled his mouth away at last. "Or we'll be done before I get us to the bedroom."

"Then we'll just have to do it again," she answered. Her voice had grown husky with desire, a sound that pumped his passion even higher. *Do it again?* Oh, yeah.

The bedroom was a revelation to Ashley. A steel contraption rose from the floor and reached over the bed. Her first thought was *monkey bars*, but that wasn't it at all. As she surveyed it, she realized they were bars to help him get into and out of bed, to lift himself up and move around a little. Probably he used them to help him dress and undress.

Movement would be important, she thought. Until Mikey she'd never understood, but his mother had confided one of the reasons they wanted a better wheelchair was because of pressure sores. Mikey couldn't stay in one position too long.

It must be the same for Zane. He needed to get out of his chair, to get into a position that didn't put all his weight on his buttocks and legs. If he got a pressure sore, he'd probably never feel it. Later she'd ask him how often he needed to move.

"Ashley?"

She stopped staring at the apparatus and turned her head to kiss his cheek again. More important matters to think about right now, and desire that had quieted for a minute now began to hammer at her again. Screw the bars, screw everything—she wanted this man with every cell in her body.

"This will be awkward," he murmured.

"Stop worrying about it. Want help undressing? I wouldn't mind that at all." A quiet little giggle escaped her at her frankness.

He laughed briefly. "I like hearing that, but…" He paused. "If I'm going to dash cold water on this, I want to know now. So let me do it. You can see it all, the way it is for me now, okay?"

She understood his point. If she was going to have any problems with his reality, it was better not to even get started. She didn't think she would, but there was only one way to prove it.

So she slid off his lap. Her legs felt a little rubbery, and part of her just wanted to brazenly strip and fall into his arms. But he had to be ready, and he was determined to let her see it all for herself.

Her breaths became shallow as anticipation filled her.

She couldn't imagine that anything was going to make him less desirable to her. Not one thing.

He wheeled over until he was sideways beside the bed, then reached up to grab an overhead bar. Then, with powerful arms, he hand walked himself until he was fully on the bed.

"I couldn't do that in a million years," she remarked.

"I've always been able to do it. This is one of the few things I didn't have to learn. Upper-body strength was always part of my training."

But then he didn't seem to want to talk anymore, and she heartily agreed. Watching him held her attention, and watching him was making her entire body feel like warm syrup. She gripped a handy bar to steady herself.

He pulled his legs around, leaving them slightly splayed as if for balance. Then, sitting upright, he tugged his shirt over his head...and revealed the reason he could sit like that without propping himself: his abdominal muscles rippled and flexed, a perfect six-pack. She'd never seen one before in real life and felt her cheeks warming. Dang, he was gorgeous.

But then came the difficult part. He reached for the snap on his jeans then fell backward so he could unzip them. Man, she wanted to go help, to pull that packaging away and see the entire gift of him naked. But she stayed herself, licking her suddenly dry lips. Oh, man, had she ever felt a hunger this strong? What was it about this man?

"Now's the fun part," he muttered. He gripped the overhead bar with one hand and pulled himself up until his hips left the bed. Then with his free hand, he pulled his pants down below his hips on one side. Then he switched hands and repeated for the other side.

Ashley grew aware of only one thing. His erection was now fully revealed. Her heart hit top speed like a racehorse, and her knees nearly gave way. Her center began to throb in an ancient rhythm. She couldn't wait. But she had to. Must.

She closed her eyes briefly, then snapped them open, unwilling to miss even a second of filling her eyes, mind and heart with him.

He repeated the process several times until he'd pulled his jeans and shorts down below his knees. Then, in the most amazing way, he jackknifed his body until his hands reached his ankles, and tugged strongly until the last of his clothing came off.

"Told you it wasn't pretty," he said, looking at her at last, almost as if he expected to see rejection.

Ashley shook her head stiffly. "I've never seen anything more amazing in my life. I couldn't do that if I tried. I'm stunned that you don't just give up and wear loose jogging pants."

He smiled. "The more I give up, the more I lose. Come here."

That was easy enough to do. She was already weak with desire, and she fell onto the bed effortlessly. Maybe because she couldn't stand another moment. She kicked off her shoes before moving her legs to the bed.

Zane twisted, propping himself on his elbow, smiling down at her. "Now you," he said.

She reached for the hem of her sweatshirt, ready to pull it over her head, but he surprised her by helping. When he at last tossed it aside and looked at her, she felt the touch of his gaze like tongues of fire.

"Oh, Zane," she murmured, then gasped as he ran his palm down her side and across her midriff. He lowered his head, kissing her deeply, as if he wanted to reach her very soul. She felt herself beginning to float on the hot tide of passion, leaving the rest of the world behind.

Then his hand cupped her breast through her bra, and she arched into his touch, a small cry escaping. A spike of need drove through her.

He lifted his head at once. "You okay?"

"No," she said flatly. She pushed him a little so she could sit up, then she dispensed with her clothes swiftly. "You can advertise your disrobing skills some other time. I. Can't. Wait."

He laughed, but somehow it didn't dispel the rising heat that built between them, a blaze about to ignite into a firestorm. He tried to run his hand all over her, along her moist petals, but she hadn't been kidding about not being able to wait. Somehow he had brought her to the very peak of passion, and she didn't want to risk anything shattering the moment. She clung to his head as he sucked at her nipples, first one then the other, and soon she was out of her mind. She pushed him back while simultaneously gripping his shoulder.

"Now," she gasped. "Now."

As far as she was concerned, they could try the whole Kama Sutra. Later. Right now she wanted only to feel him deep inside her, answering the empty ache he had planted between her legs.

"I can't move my hips, so…" His voice was husky, rough. She didn't need him to finish.

Pushing him onto his back, she mounted him from above, her hair hanging around her face, her eyes feeling heavy. "Take me," she whispered.

Nothing in her life, no other lover, had ever made her feel the way Zane did. He reached down and he took her. Filling her with a satisfaction so deep it permeated her. She needed him deep inside. She ached for it.

His hands clamped on her hips, guiding her movements as she threw her head back and gave herself up to the miracle of being human.

He took her, all right. To the stars and back. She felt him jet hotly inside her, and then she shattered into a million glorious pieces.

Zane…

She lay curled against him, her head on his shoulder, his arm around her. The scents of lovemaking filled the room, but so did scents of Ashley. He fingered her beautiful hair gently and stared at the ceiling, giving thanks that war had seen fit not to take moments like these from him.

There'd been that girlfriend, the one who had been practicing for sainthood by smothering him, but sex with her hadn't struck him the same way sex with Ashley had affected him.

Maybe because it hadn't been just sex? He shied away from the thought, not wanting to head into those places. He looked at himself and often thought only a Mother Teresa wannabe could be happy with him.

But he'd escaped the one who had, and now he'd wound up holding a woman who didn't try to give him one ounce of help he didn't ask for. She made him feel competent, capable. She even made him think he could do useful things, like helping Mikey with a service dog, like talking to her class. Like looking into other things where his chair wouldn't be a problem.

Which left his PTSD. That worried him, because

he knew how bad it could get. Once it had gotten him evicted. What if he went over the edge like that again?

But Nell... Nell had so often called him back that he was beginning to wonder if she could prevent him from falling off the cliff. Even if he did...

Well, Ashley had so far not seemed disturbed when he went away, only concerned that he was all right. She'd sat through several episodes already, and said very little about it, leaving it to him to decide if he wanted to talk.

She was, in short, amazing. And she did it so easily. Maybe it came from dealing with kids for so long. Maybe she was used to seeing them struggle with something and used to not stepping in unless they absolutely couldn't get it.

She was certainly hands-off with him. She treated him as if he were just any other guy.

Which, he supposed, he was. Just any other guy. Sure, he couldn't walk. Sure, he had moments when he slipped in time, but everyone had problems, right?

He sighed quietly, wondering what he was trying to do here. Rationalize it all? Absolve himself in advance if he somehow hurt Ashley? Because it seemed to him that he was bound to do that. He didn't trust himself not to, not after all that had happened.

But in a very short time she had opened him up in ways he had thought he'd never feel again. He liked having her around, even though he'd decided he never wanted anyone around him again. He'd told her things that he'd never shared. He'd even told her how he felt about his medals, which except for one conversation was something he'd kept strictly to himself. In fact, she was the first person he'd ever shown them to.

And, in her wonderful way, she didn't try to argue him out of his feelings about them. She probably qualified as the most accepting person he'd ever met.

Sure, she'd ridden him about being able to call for help if he fell, but that wasn't out of bounds. She'd gently suggested he might be able to help Mikey if he got over himself a bit. She'd *asked* him if he wanted to participate in Halloween. And her suggestions about a kitchen remodel hadn't been pushy. She'd dropped it as soon as he said he might not be staying.

Then there was Nell. He suspected if he gave Nell free rein, she'd be knocking at Ashley's door all the time. The dog knew she wasn't supposed to leave him, but, well… Nell had a mind of her own. And sometimes she let him know what she thought of his isolation.

Nell, his personal live-in psychiatrist, apparently thought he needed his own pack. Heck, she'd probably like to see a few other dogs from time to time herself.

Maybe that was the key. Neither dog nor man was designed to live alone.

Ashley stirred. Her arm moved on his chest, rubbing gently. "You are the most beautiful man I've ever known."

"Beautiful?" The word stunned him. He saw himself as all busted up and broken in every way. Not beautiful.

"Beautiful," she repeated. "Physically beautiful, and mentally beautiful. Your heart is bigger than you give yourself credit for."

"Oh, really…" His mind began to rebel.

"Hush and just listen. You wanted to help Mikey. Much as you said you needed to avoid people, you helped that child. First with a big check to help get him the wheelchair he really needs, and then by going out to

Cadell's to help with the dog. You can try to convince the world, Zane, but you're no Scrooge. Not in any respect. You're innately generous. You've just been dealing with too much baggage to realize it."

"Ashley…" But he wasn't really protesting. She'd planted a kernel of warmth in his heart, a place that had felt cold and empty for too long.

"Anyway," she said, "you don't have to believe me. I'm cold and hungry, so can we make love again later, after we eat?"

That surprised a laugh out of him. "Absolutely."

"You don't need me to help you dress, right?"

"I do it every day." Even though he might have taken great delight in her assistance this once. Passion was renewing its flow through him. But still…

She kissed his shoulder. "I thought so." Then before he could stop her, she kissed his shoulder again and popped out of bed. As she pulled on her clothes, she said, "I'm going to run next door and get those sausages and buns. Make us some coffee when you get to it."

Then she darted out.

She left him smiling. He had his orders: get dressed and make coffee. Just like a normal guy. God, he loved the way she treated him.

Chapter Twelve

The entire weekend passed in a haze of lovemaking and mostly idle conversation. Ashley felt as if they were hunkered together in a private world, and she was perfectly willing to forget everything else. All of it.

Being with Zane was a constant delight and surprise. Occasionally they got serious, and she talked a bit about her past and her failed relationships.

"It was always easy to get a date," she admitted.

"I believe it," he answered, stroking her bare arm with his fingertips as they lay face-to-face in bed. "You're a stunner."

"Maybe. All I know is I never lacked for a date…if I wanted one. Which doesn't mean anything worked out. My mother once said dating is like trying on clothes. You look and say no, no, no until finally everything is right and you say yes. I came close to saying yes only once, and it wasn't the time I found out I was the other woman. That wouldn't have turned me off to relationships."

"What happened?"

She smiled faintly. "I woke up. I don't know how else to phrase it. It happened nearly overnight. I decided that I didn't really like the guy enough to spend the rest of my life with him. I'm sure he was okay and that he made someone else happy, but he wasn't for me. You know how you like your independence."

He spoke with a little humor. "I rather insist on it, don't I?"

"I do, too. His ideas about women...well, they clashed with mine. Not terribly, but enough to jar me. I like working. I love teaching. I wasn't going to give it up so he could be the breadwinner. I realize that was part of his self-image as a man, but as a woman..."

"What?" he prodded.

"I don't ever want to be economically dependent on a man. A million things could happen that would leave me needing to support myself and maybe a child or two. So, while he never made a big issue of it, never brought it to a head and a big fight, he was constantly nudging me into a more traditional role. I'm not built that way."

"No, you're not," he agreed.

"After that I pretty much stopped dating."

"Why? Just because of him?"

She shook her head. "No. Because I realized that had been the problem one way or another with every guy I dated. The one I hated most of all was the guy who insisted on ordering for me in restaurants. By the third date we were done."

He gave a short laugh. "I can sure as hell see why. Damn. Ordering for you? That's insulting."

"Maybe not in his world, but definitely in mine." She looked into his eyes. "So, Mr. Independent SEAL, I hear you guys are the ultimate in machismo. Do you want the little woman staying at home?"

He laughed, a full-throated sound of humor. "We're all about toughness. But I'll tell you something. Most of us, having to be away so much, vastly prefer to leave behind a woman who can take care of herself and everything else that comes up. Now, I'm not going to say we don't have any male chauvinists in the crowd, because I'm sure we do. But…many of us would rather not be worrying about the home front when we can't be there. We'd like to come home to a happy family, not a miserable one. Besides, as one of my buddies said, if you leave a woman at home alone with nothing to do but wait, she might find other ways to entertain herself. So…" He shrugged. "I can't speak for everyone, but I never had a thing for traditional roles."

She smiled. "Maybe because you were secure enough in your manhood you didn't have anything to prove."

He fell quiet, staring into space, but Nell, who'd taken up station behind him on the bed, didn't seem disturbed. "Funny you should say that," he replied presently. "My CO remarked on that once. He said you can tell the guys who've been on an active mission. They don't have anything to prove to anyone." Then he shook his head a bit. "But machismo? I don't like that word. It has so many negative connotations now. So I'll just leave it at toughness."

That was fine by her. She burrowed into his shoulder just as his hand found her breast and began teasing her toward the pinnacle of desire once again. She spared a moment to wonder wryly if she was going to be able to walk when she went back to work, then gave herself over to the wonder of Zane, the wonder of being free to touch him anywhere, everywhere, the freedom of enjoying his every caress anywhere on her body.

She felt as if she'd cast off shackles she hadn't even been aware were binding her. Fiery starbursts began to explode in her head and she straddled him once again, leaning forward so that her hands were on his shoulders, watching his face as she rode him, feeling him slipping in and out of her.

His eyes never closed. He stared right into hers even as his face began to relax, then to tense again as passion wound ever tighter in both of them.

Please, she thought as culmination overtook her at last in a blinding explosion, *don't ever let this end.*

Sunday night she had to go home to prepare for school the next day. She hated to do it but figured the space might be good for both of them.

She certainly knew she needed time to think. She knew she was growing deeply involved with Zane. She'd warned herself about her predilection to fall for guys when she made love with them, but she didn't think it was just that.

So she was worried. She'd given a lot to him, emotionally, and received a lot from him, and she didn't want it to end. But she also feared it would. He hadn't even really committed to staying in this town. What if he decided he needed a cabin on an isolated mountainside to be comfortable with himself? What if he just decided this little town was too small and any plans he had of making a future for himself would just wither and die here?

As she well knew, far too many young people left here as soon as they could, looking for brighter opportunities and brighter lights in general. It was a problem for all small rural towns, and she had no idea what could be done about it.

The community college had helped, but most of the students who went there left for four-year schools or jobs elsewhere. Before the semiconductor plant had closed, it had promised a future for young people, but it hadn't remained.

The proposed ski resort on the mountain, which somehow never seemed to come to pass, though attempts had been made repeatedly...well, what kind of jobs would it provide for the most part? Not that it mattered, since the landslide had put construction on hold indefinitely while more surveys were done. So far all Conard City had gotten from it were brick-paved sidewalks in the downtown, fancy new streetlights in the main areas around the town and some fresh paint in a few places.

So what the heck was a guy like Zane supposed to be able to do here? Bleak prospects indeed.

Her phone rang several times, disturbing her work. She'd turned off her cell as soon as things heated up with Zane, and now as her friends touched base she simply said she'd been visiting someone and refused to say any more. Each of them in turn giggled, suspecting something romantic, but she blessed them for not pressing.

She and Zane didn't need to be an item. They *weren't* an item. They'd had a weekend fling.

Like she believed that's all it was.

Shoving her disturbed thoughts aside, she bent her attention to her work. She couldn't afford to let that slip, not for any reason. Soul-searching would have to wait.

So would remembering the weekend. Her mind kept summoning memories that made her shiver with delight and longing. She never wanted to forget a single detail.

But math papers stared back at her, and she gave herself a hard mental shake. Later. She'd deal with everything else *after* she finished her work.

Just as she was sliding the papers and lesson book into her backpack, there was a rap at the front door. Glancing at the clock, she saw it was nearly eleven.

Good grief. She jumped up immediately and wasn't at all surprised to see Nell standing there with a bone in her mouth, her own self-improvised knocker.

"I'm coming," she said immediately and yanked her jacket off the hook. Her heart raced as worry and fear consumed her. What was wrong? Was Zane hurt?

She closed her own door, not worried about locking it, and raced after the dog. As she approached the ramp, she noticed the light from inside seemed dim. Flickering.

Flickering? Oh, God, fire?

Scared half to death, she raced up the ramp, patting her pocket for her phone, realizing she'd left it at home. Her stride broke just a little, but she decided it was more important to get inside and check on Zane. If she needed to call for help she could do it then.

Nell pushed the door open and Ashley raced inside.

And found herself standing in a candlelit wonderland.

Sitting in his wheelchair at the foot of stairs he would never climb, Zane watched Ashley with a faint smile as she froze just inside the door and looked around, her mouth dropping open. Candles flickered on every flat surface in the small foyer, in the living room and kitchen. He'd wanted to do his bedroom as well, but common sense took over. Candles posed a danger and he didn't want them burning where he couldn't keep an eye on them.

"Hi," he said, watching her look around.

"Zane… What…?"

"For you," he explained simply. "Beauty for you."

She looked at him, wonder on her face. "This is so special, but how…?" She just shook her head.

"Freitag's was open. I ventured out and bought every candle they had. Because…you."

Vaguely she heard Nell close the door behind her. Then her terror of just moments ago hit her hard. "Do you realize how scared I got? It looked like there was a fire in here, and Nell showing up so late…" She almost hated herself, given what he'd done for her, but the adrenaline hadn't settled yet.

His smile faded. "Damn. Didn't you see the note in her side pocket?"

She turned and looked at the dog. Indeed, the corner of a piece of paper stuck out from a slit in the dog's service vest. The last of the adrenaline began to seep away.

"I'm sorry," she said, turning to him again. "I jumped to a conclusion."

"Clearly."

Had she ruined this for him? For an instant she almost hated herself. "I'm sorry," she said again, beginning to feel miserable. "This is so beautiful! It's like a wonderland."

"I hoped you'd think so." It was his turn to pause.

"Will you ever be able to believe that Nell has come for you for some reason other than that I'm in trouble?"

The question hung on the air, seeming weighted with significance. Something important was happening here.

She struggled for the right way to answer, not wanting to give him the wrong impression. "Zane, when my phone rings at this time of night, I answer expecting bad news. Nobody makes a friendly call at that hour."

His face relaxed. "I didn't think of that. So Nell was like a too-late phone call?"

She nodded, saying not another word.

He swore quietly. "Not the effect I planned at all. The note asked if you could come over for a surprise."

"It's a fantastic surprise," she assured him, looking around again. "The instant I saw it, my first thought was that I'd stepped into wonderland."

His smile began to return. "That was what I wanted. I guess you were full of adrenaline when you got here."

She nodded. "I didn't mean to ruin it for you."

"You couldn't possibly ruin it for me." His face, which often looked hard when he was lost in thought, which spoke of a hard-lived life and past tragedies, was suddenly so gentle her throat tightened up in response.

"Could you come a little closer?" he asked.

She stepped toward him until she stood right in front of him. He patted his lap, so she shed her jacket, throwing it to the side. She hardly noticed that Nell grabbed it and dragged it out of the way as she settled onto Zane's lap.

Wrapping an arm around his shoulders, she kissed him warmly, then leaned back to look around at all the candles. They cast a dancing glow over everything that was almost otherworldly.

"I know it's late," he said. "I was sitting here after you left and realized I was missing the hell out of you. I knew you had to work, so I amped myself up to go out, and as I was driving by I saw that Freitag's was open."

"It's the time of year," she answered. "Usually the sidewalks are rolled up at around six or seven. Well, except for Maude's diner."

"I remember. Anyway, I was just killing time. They have a nice ramp in their doorway, so I went in to wander around. Very nice ladies in there. They even pushed a few tables of clothing to the side so I could navigate. I picked up a few items of cold-weather gear and then... then I saw the candles. I was surprised they had so many. Must be the approach of Christmas."

"Maybe," she said, watching his every expression, drinking him in as if the hours without him had parched her deep inside.

"Anyway, I saw those candles and thought of you." He gave a quiet laugh. "I bought so many those dear women had to help me carry them out. But they were laughing and teasing me, demanding to know if I was buying them for a special lady."

She felt her own smile grow and her heart swell. "Thank you, Zane. Nobody's ever done something so... so...amazing for me before. It's like the biggest-ever fiery bouquet."

"I hoped you'd like it." His arm closed around her waist and snuggled her even closer. "Ashley?"

"Hmm?" She rested her head on his shoulder, inhaling his wonderful scent: man, soap and now candle wax.

"You haven't known me very long. I mean, it's only been a few weeks."

"I know." She nearly sighed, trying to square this explosion of candles with the feeling that he was about to break off their relationship. He'd wanted to be a hermit, after all, and she'd kind of spoiled that. But she didn't want to give him up.

"But I don't think falling in love requires time."

Her heart stopped. She couldn't draw a breath. What was he saying? She managed to push out his name with the last air in her lungs. "Zane?"

"I'm probably crazy," he said. "In fact, I know I am. But I've never felt about anybody in my life the way I feel about you, Ashley. I'm mad about you. I don't want to be without you. I want a future with you."

At last she could draw a breath. She tilted her head, trying to see his face, feeling his other arm wrap around her in a bear hug.

"I won't blame you if you tell me no. I've got a lot of problems, and you might not want to deal with them. I'm not sure why anyone would. So I'm not asking for any kind of answer unless you want to walk away right now."

Finally some strength seemed to be returning to her. Her heart felt swollen with hope. She ached with it.

"It kinda just happened. I'm not going to ask you to marry me, even though I want to, but that wouldn't be fair. What I *am* going to ask is that you'll try life with me for six months or so. To see if you can stand it, if you want me and all my mess."

Six months? He wanted a six-month trial when she realized in an amazing blast of self-understanding that she wanted it all, and she wanted it all right now.

"Zane…"

He lifted one hand and put a finger to her lips. "I love you, Ashley. You eased your way into my heart before

I even knew it was happening. You warm me. You take away the chill. And you treat me like an ordinary man. I can't begin to tell you how much that all means. So if you'll give me six months to try to win you…"

Win her? She wiggled until he let go of her. She slid off his lap and faced him. Now he looked as if he expected bad news.

"I love you, too," she said baldly. "The whole time I was next door trying to work, it kept hammering at me. I love you. But I was afraid you didn't want me or anyone else… You wanted to be a *hermit*!"

His expression lightened. "Not anymore. And certainly not when it comes to you. So I get my six months?"

"Only if you insist. I'd marry you tomorrow."

His smile was so wide and bright that it was like dawn. "Six months," he repeated. "You deserve that. Then I'll ask you to marry me."

"Oh, ask me now, darn it." She dropped into his lap again. "Ask me now and I'll settle for a long engagement as long as I can move in with you."

He threw back his head and laughed, the freest, happiest sound she had ever heard from him. Then he turned his face to her as laughter died. "Marry me, Ashley."

"Absolutely," she answered as her heart began to sing. "But I don't want a wedding on Valentine's Day."

He blinked. "Why not?"

"So cliché. The day after. But not one day more."

Then she wrapped her own arms around him and twisted to kiss him until they were both breathless.

Behind her Nell gave a happy bark.

A while later, surrounded by the flickering candles

and the warm scent of wax, he said, "Thank you for coming over to welcome me home."

"I feel like I came home, too," she answered. A place she thought she'd already had until Zane. He'd given her a different kind of home, one she hadn't known she was missing. A home in his arms.

* * * * *

For more stories of healing and homecoming,
look for
A CONARD COUNTY COURTSHIP,
available October 2017 from Harlequin Special Edition!

And don't miss Rachel Lee's next story of
love and danger,
CORNERED IN CONARD COUNTY,
available August 2017 from Harlequin Intrigue!

#2557 THE MAVERICK FAKES A BRIDE!
Montana Mavericks: The Great Family Roundup
by Christine Rimmer
Travis Dalton needs a fake fiancée fast, or he'll be cut from the final cast of a cowboy reality show. Bold, adventurous Brenna O'Reilly is perfect for the role. Too bad pretending they're lovers for the cameras quickly has Travis and Brenna wishing this game of love would never have to end.

#2558 A SECOND CHANCE FOR THE SINGLE DAD
Matchmaking Mamas • by Marie Ferrarella
Dr. Luke Dolan is a recently widowed, floundering single dad who also happens to need a nurse for his new practice. Lucky for him, the Matchmaking Mamas know just who to call! Kayley Quartermain is a nurse looking for direction and perhaps a happy ending of her very own...

#2559 SAY YES TO THE COWBOY
Thunder Mountain Brotherhood • by Vicki Lewis Thompson
Tess Irwin is elated to find herself pregnant, though not so much about the fact that Zeke Rafferty is the father. But the former foster child can't turn his back on his child. Can they work out a visitation compromise without getting their hearts broken in the process?

#2560 A BRIDE, A BARN, AND A BABY
Celebration, TX • by Nancy Robards Thompson
Lucy Campbell is thrilled Zane Phillips finally sees her as more than his friend's little sister. Until she gets pregnant! Refusing to trap him into marriage, she rejects his proposal. But Zane is beginning to realize he just might want everything Lucy has to offer after all.

#2561 IT STARTED WITH A DIAMOND
Drake Diamonds • by Teri Wilson
When Diana Drake, a diamond heiress, and Franco Andrade, a disgraced polo player, pretend to be engaged for their own selfish reasons, their charade soon becomes more real than either of them intended.

#2562 HOME TO WICKHAM FALLS
Wickham Falls Weddings • by Rochelle Alers
Sawyer Middleton swore he would never return to his hometown, but when a family emergency forces his hand, he meets Jessica Calhoun, an intriguing teacher who has *forever* written all over her. Will this free-wheeling city boy give up his fast-paced life in the face of love?

HSECNM0617

My gaze fixed on the living, breathing sculpture.

My heartbeat quickened as I searched my memory for
where I knew him from. I was awestruck by this breathtaking
Adonis, who was reaching for a white shirt hanging on the
back of a chair. He was tall and devastatingly handsome
in a rugged kind of way. Thirty, maybe? Those short, dark
golden locks framing a gorgeous face, his three-day stubble
marking him with a tenacious edge and that thin wry smile
exuding a fierce confidence. His intense, steady glare stayed
on mine as he calmly pulled his arm through a sleeve and
covered that tattoo before I could make out more.

A gasp caught in my throat as it came to me that we'd
never actually met, probably because this was Tobias
William Wilder, a billionaire. He moved in the kind of
refined circles one would expect from a business magnate
and inventor who owned TechRule, one of the largest
software companies in the world.

And I'd given this playboy mogul his very own peep
show.

I'd read an article on him, featuring his Los Angeles–based art gallery, The Wilder. It was an acclaimed museum that was one of the most prestigious in the world.

Although I'd imagined one day I might bump into him with the art world being relatively small, never had I imagined a scenario as racy as this.

"I'm looking for the stairs," I managed.

"That way." His refined American accent felt like another blow to my reason.

That alpha-maleness made him look like he'd just returned from a dangerous adventure in the Himalayas or even the jungles of Peru…

A waft of expensive musky cologne reached me with its sensuous allure and did something crazy to my body.

"You might want to put some clothes on," I said firmly.

"Well, now I'm dressed."

Yes, he was, and this was a changing room, apparently, and I'd not exactly represented a pillar of virtue.

"Well that's good." I swallowed my pride. "Please keep it that way."

His gaze lowered to my feet.

And I remembered my strappy stilettos were flirtatiously dangling from my left hand, those spiked heels hinting at a sexy side I wished I had.

Intrigue marred his face, and then his expression softened again as his jade gaze returned to hold mine.

I left in a rush, shaken with just how this man had affected me merely with a smile.

I felt an inexplicable need to run back in and continue to bathe in the aura of the most enigmatic man I'd ever met.

Will Zara risk it all when she finds herself on a collision course with danger and desire?

Find out when THE CHASE by USA TODAY bestselling author Vanessa Fewings goes on sale in June 2017.

THE WORLD IS BETTER
WITH
Romance

Harlequin has everything from contemporary, passionate and heartwarming to suspenseful and inspirational stories.

Whatever your mood,
we have a romance just for you!

Connect with us to find your next great read, special offers and more.

f /HarlequinBooks

🐦 @HarlequinBooks

www.HarlequinBlog.com

www.Harlequin.com/Newsletters

ⓗ HARLEQUIN®

A *Romance* FOR EVERY MOOD™

www.Harlequin.com